# MANIPULATING LOVE... MY TURN

ISBN: 978-0-578-86315-3

Printed by Power Of Purpose Publishing
www.PopPublishing.com
Atlanta, Ga. 30326

*To my husband Kelvin and my children Kaelyn and Kelvin, Jr, thank you all for allowing me to steal moments to complete this book. You all are my motivation and support!*

*This book is dedicated to Shamia Marteen Johnson. I could go on forever about how much of an impact you have made in my life. But I hear your voice telling me to SHUT UP, Jocelyn! While smacking on some type of food. I love you and I miss you. Rest well Mama Mia!*

# MANIPULATING LOVE... MY TURN

JAE MOORE

# CHAPTER 1

As the alarm clock goes off for the third time this morning, Brianna knows that it is just best to get up and not hit the snooze button again.

"I need a vacation," she says aloud as she stretches and makes her way to the bathroom.

This routine has been engrained for years, a mindless task it has become. The only thing that varies much these days is the time she actually runs on the treadmill. Habitual snoozing or lack thereof dictates the workout. Today, about a good forty-five minutes is all that will be given to the old outdated machine.

"Champ! It's time to wake up," she whispers softly into Glenn's ear.

"But mom, I'm still sleepy," he whines.

"Me too! BUT, we have to get going or we're going to be late. What do you want for breakfast?" she asks in hopes that the conversation will get him going.

"I'm not hungry." He resists.

"Don't start this morning Junior. What do you want to eat?"

He rolls over and places the covers over his face.

"Guess what today is?" Brianna quizzes trying to find another way to get him going.

"Uhm," he peeks through a breathing hole that he's made himself. "I don't know."

"It's Friday!"

"It's Friday?" he asks excitedly as he jumps out of bed. "Is Dad coming to get me?"

"Look at you all bright eyed and bushy tailed now," she smiles. "No, I think Samantha, but you are going to Dad's today. So, what are you eating for breakfast?" Bree tries her final attempt to pry something out of him before she makes what she wants.

"Oatmeal. Where are my clothes?"

"And?" she pauses waiting for the remaining items on the menu.

"Mom, my clothes?"

"What else are you eating?"

"Just oatmeal."

"And fruit."

"And fruit," he sighs. "Where are my clothes?"

"And toast, over there," she points to the dresser. "Now hurry down because we are running late." Brianna says as she sprints into the bedroom to grab her phone.

"Hello," she says breathy as she heads downstairs to start on breakfast.

"Hey Remi," the familiar voice on the other end chimes. "Good morning. What you doing girl?"

"What do you want Nia?" Bree cuts the nice girl act short.

"No good morning."

"Huh no, because I know you calling with some mess this early. Why are you even up?"

"Can't even call my bestfriend to see how she is doing..."

"What do you want?" Brianna cuts her off again.

"Don't you remember that party that I invited you to last week?" she gets straight to the point.

"The one for Charles's job?"

"Yeah."

"Hum huh." Bree lets out an eye-roll with her, I knew you wanted something tone.

"Well Charles's co-worker was checking you out."

"Who?" Brees asks uninterested.

"Charles's co-worker." She repeats like that alone will jog Brianna's memory. "His name is Reggie. He was the tall milk chocolate brother with the goatee. You don't remember? We introduced y'all and I gave you the nudge and the wink."

"No and why are you telling me this?"

"He wants to take you out on a date tomorrow and I already told him yeah and gave him your number." She spits rapidly in hopes that it would lessen the burn.

2

"You. Did. WHAT!" Brianna yells as she picks up the spoon she dropped on the floor.

"I mean you're not doing anything. And Junior goes with Manny this week. And truth be told you need to get out around some actual adults and do things that adults do." Nia says as she sprinkles some encouragement on her excuses.

Brianna cannot argue with that. She does not get to spend much time out with the girls. And the time she does spend, she always seems to be the only one without a date. She has to stop the friends with benefits or more loosely, boy toy situationships.

"Profile?" she huffs giving in.

"Well his name is Reggie," she repeats. "He's a Communications Director, graduated from A & M, born and raised here in Houston, a brother and a sister, parents still together, never married, no kids and hell he's trying to date you." She runs down with a deep breath following.

"Well damn," Brianna laughs, "Inspector Gadget you are." She continues in her best Yoda voice. "Sounds too good to be true though."

"That's what I thought. As you can see I have been digging a damn grave site and no bones. He never even had a speeding ticket." She proudly makes it known as if that will be the determining factor to solidify Brianna's reason to date him.

"There has to be something. Spill it!" Brianna demands knowing her BFF too well.

"Okay," she sighs in forfeit, "He was engaged. It's been over for about eight months now, so that should not be a factor."

"Well…"

"That's not a factor, Brianna." Nia scolds.

"I don't know if I want to go."

"Too late, you're going. I'm not saying marry the damn man. I just want you to get out and have some fun."

"Alright girl, whatever. Let me go and get Junior off to school or I'm going to be late. I'll talk to you later."

"Later girl. Oh, and don't forget I gave him your number so if he calls or text don't be a bitch."

"I'll try not to." Brianna spits sarcastically.

"Bye."

"Bye."

# CHAPTER 2

"Why did I agree to this shit?" Brianna asks herself while touching up her make-up in the mirror. Although she doesn't really want to go, she is ensuring that she looks extra good. Just in case. She hasn't had a serious steady relationship since Ed in college. Needless to say, he has moved on, with a wife, three kids, a house, three cars, a dog and a white picket fence. But hey, who's keeping up with him? Meanwhile, Brianna has her pride and joy Glenn, Jr., a house, two cars, no pets and most importantly no man. Desperation is filling her heart as she yearns to settle down and have a wholesome family. Something she's always dreamed of. With her not having a cohesive unit in her childhood, she is very adamant to provide her offspring with something better, more loving if you will.

"Ok, wait a damn minute let me get this straight. Y'all stupid asses pick me up and y'all are going to leave me with a damn stranger in hopes that he brings me home?" Brianna asks confusingly as she pulls herself forward with the driver and passenger seat.

"He's not a stranger, I work with Reggie." Charles replies as he readjusts himself in his seat.

"He's a stranger to me AND I don't want him to know where I live."

"Listen, if you are not comfortable we are going to bring you home Rem. Damn we ain't gone do you like that." Nia offers her spill.

"Good." Brianna sits back into her seat. "Because y'all will be bringing me home," she announces.

"You'll like him Rem."

"You sound so sure."

"Yeah I do. He's such a nice guy. Down to earth and looking for the same things you are." Nia replies with sincerity in her voice.

Brianna sits back and lets Nia's words resonate within her. Could someone possibly be looking for love with the same or more dedication than she? It's rare these days to find a man that wants to settle down. The deal breaker will be Junior as always. She could never seem to find someone that she grew close enough to that makes her want to introduce her son to him. In addition, it's always fun and games until a child comes in the mix. The scheduling conflicts, the responsibilities of being a parent and not to mention her complex relationship with Manny, Junior's dad, always seems to drive men away. How much time is she willing to waste on another failed attempt?

As they walk into the restaurant, Brianna is hoping that she likes what she sees and the conversation will go smoothly. With Charles and Nia there it shouldn't be so bad. Reggie is already waiting, so they all walk right in to the table. Surprisingly, he's seated at a table for two. Once Brianna got her glimpse she was not mad at the set-up. Typically, Nia would get cursed out for pulling a move like this, but Reggie is a mixture of, "Damn Daddy how you doing?" and, "He can get it!" There is absolutely no mistaking  that he is Willy Wonka everlasting gum stopper eye candy. She wouldn't mind chewing on that forever. His smooth milk chocolate skin looks as if he will never age, his muscular tone looks as if he lives in the gym, and his smile is to die for which shows he knows his dentist very well.

An uncontrollable smile appears as Brianna goes in for her introduction. "Hi Reggie, I'm..."

"Ms. Brianna," he interrupts with a smile. "Thank you for joining me," he says as he pulls out her chair.

As they all exchange their hello's Nia finally says, "Well let us get out of y'all way."

Everyone silently agrees with the proposal as there were no objections. Charles and Nia made their way to their table and once they were out of ear shot Brianna decided to break the ice.

"Thank you for the invite. How was your day?"

"It's a pleasure. I was surprised when Nia said that you agreed to a date."

"Why?"

"Do you remember meeting me?"

After a slight pause she replies, "No," and gives a nervous chuckle while lowering her head.

"I don't know if that's a good or bad thing." He admits.

"Neutral. Was I mean or something?"

"Oh no! You were very polite."

"Just stand-offish?"

"That explains it."

"Can you tell I get that all the time?" Bree admits.

"Hi my name is Alicia, and I will be your server this evening can I start you with anything to drink and maybe an appetizer? This is our wine for tonight," she said nudging the merlot towards Brianna for her to get a look at the label.

"No thank you. May I start with water please?"

"And you Sir?" Alicia turns to Reggie

"A coke is fine."

"Any appetizers?"

Brianna looks at Reggie with an uninterested look.

"No thank you," he says, directing his attention towards Alicia.

"Do you drink?" Bree asks.

"Occasionally. When I'm watching a game, I may have a Heineken. Maybe a Henny on the rocks in social settings, you?" Reggie asks.

"Very seldom."

"Oh yeah, I forgot you're a nurse. Don't judge my reckless behaviors," he chuckles.

"That's not why I don't drink and I don't meddle in anyone's business who is trying to live their best life. You only live once right?"

"Right, so tell me about yourself Ms. Brianna."

"Well I was born and raised in OKC." She smiles. "I have a four year old son, he'll be five soon. I have one sister. She and my mom are still in Oklahoma with my two nieces and nephew. What do you want to know, because that's about all I have," She laughs. "Oh and I just turned 27, 30 is knocking and I don't like it."

"That explains the babyface. I thought you were closer to Nia's age."

"Is my age a problem? How old are you?"

"32. I'll be 33 in April."

"Aries?"

"Taurus. Is my age a problem?" he asks.

"Not for me. Is my child a deal breaker?"

"No. Drama is a deal breaker."

"Agreed. So how about yourself?"

"Born and raised here in Houston. Both my parents still live here. I have one brother and one sister. Went to A & M, heard you're a fellow Aggie," he nods. "I have lived in Texas all my life although I have lived outside of Houston before. No kids. Never married although I have been engaged." He gives his run down. All of which Bree has heard from Nia.

Alicia arrives with the drinks and is ready to take the order.

"Can we have a couple more minutes?" Brianna asks.

"Sure, just wave when you're ready." Alicia retreats.

"Have you been here before?" Bree speaks with her nose in the menu.

"One of my favorite spots," Reggie answers.

"I don't frequent, but I've been here a couple of times. What have you tried?"

"Steak."

"And?" she pries hoping to get a recommendation for an item to try.

"Steak." He repeats

"So, that's all you get, every time you come here?" She shifts her eyes from the menu to get a good look at him.

"Yes, I like it. The best in town."

"I like it too," Brianna agrees, "But I like to try new things," she confirms looking back at the menu. "I've tried the steak, the shrimp and grits and the blue crab mac and cheese. This time I think I'm going to try the red snapper."

"I'm going to have the Cowboy redeye," Reggie confirms, sticking to his usual.

They place their orders and silence fills the air for a moment.

"Good. You asked and I didn't answer, my day has been good. How about yours?"

"Well seeing as though I only get one Saturday to sleep in a month and today is that Saturday my day has been going great." Bree responds in an upbeat voice and a smile.

"How do you manage to sleep in with a four year old?"

"He's with his dad."

"Ah!" Reggie nods as it makes perfect sense now.

Silence rears its ugly head once again.

"This is weird. You know never officially meeting or having any type of conversation prior to this evening." Brianna makes known.

"Not too bad. Why did you become a nurse?"

"Happenstance. When plan A didn't work out, I had to find an alternate avenue."

"And what was plan A?"

"Sports medicine, occupational therapy, physical therapy, pretty much any route that would have allowed me to work in a sports atmosphere, or close to the athletes. I ran track and you know the chances are slim when it comes to being in the Olympics or hell even on the National team. Well that slim chance disappears when you grow up poor and without resources, so I figured a job in one of these fields or the like would have offered me the opportunity to still be around the sport that I love."

"Interesting. So did you run in college?"

"Nope! High school senior year is when my plan detonated."

"Injury?"

"No. Life! How about you?" She swiftly changed subjects. "Communications Director?"

"I know, I know most kids don't say I want to be a Communications Director when I grow up," he laughs. "I never knew what I wanted to be growing up honestly, however, when I was a freshman in College I took a business communications course and became intrigued. The more I researched the subject the more I fell in love with the idea of pursuing a communications degree. Communication is essential in life period."

"Very true. So where outside of Houston have you lived?"

"San Antonio. I lived there for almost 3 years."

"What made you come back this way?"

"Besides my dream job?" he says like that alone is enough to migrate while adding, "Life!" he spat mimicking Brianna's monotone when she bypassed a subject.

Brianna let the conversation go because she knows how bad she doesn't want to divulge in her past.

"As a basketball fanatic I have to ask Rockets or Spurs?" she asks knowing a Texan will stick with one of the home teams.

"You like basketball?" he asks surprisingly. "Rockets all day long."

"Boooooo," she chants with her thumbs down. "Thunder over this way." She says as she pulls her keys from her purse displaying her lanyard.

"Look at you," he laughs. "Football?"

"I watch, not too big of a fan. By default it's the Chargers. My son loves them."

"Pretty good team, I go for the Texans. Does he play?"

"No. He plays basketball and soccer. He hasn't expressed any interest in football just yet. He also likes art."

"Nothing wrong with that."

"Nope!"

"So, Brianna, Remi," he says waving his hands in an unbalanced motion. "How did that come about?"

"Remi was my alias on the dating scene years ago. Needless to say, Nia loves it. She's the only one who calls me that. To most I'm Bree. To Manny, my son's dad, I'm road runner."

"Track."

"Yup! Is Reggie short for Reginald?"

"Surprisingly no, just Reggie or Reg."

A waiter brings out the food and as they are inspecting it Alicia makes her way over to make sure everything is looking good. After a refill on drinks and a drop off of napkins, she disappears again.

"So what brought you to Texas?" Reggie asks, starting up another conversation.

"School." Bree offers the short easy answer.

"No interest in going back to OKC?"

"None whatsoever." She replies hesitantly as she reaches for her phone. "Excuse me," she looks at Reggie. He gives a nod of approval.

"Hello!"

"Hey Bree," she hears Manny's voice on the other end say nervously.

"What's wrong?" she asks sternly knowing that something is going on.

"Are you sitting down? Please tell me you won't get mad. No Junior doesn't have to come home. Yes, he's alright…"

"What is going on? I am not in a place to be dealing with your mess right now." She makes it known thinking it's one of his many pranks.

"Promise me you'll just listen until I'm done."

"I'm not promising you that."

"Just please don't get upset, just listen."

"I'm listening…"

"Junior broke his arm, he…"

"What, wait, how? Where are you? Where is he?" she asks in a panic.

"Calm down, he's okay" Manny reiterates.

"Is everything okay?" Reggie whispers.

Brianna just shakes her head no and closes her eyes. "I'm listening," she says on the phone.

"Well we've been riding four wheelers. I told him not to tell you because I know how you would get. He's been showing skills for the last couple of months, so earlier I decided to let him have a go. Only because he asked and Bree I really did feel comfortable, I would not have agreed if I thought he would hurt himself. He didn't even lose control or anything as far as user error, there was a dip in the ground and he went airborne. If he didn't try to break his fall, he probably wouldn't have broken his arm."

"Great!" she says in a sarcastic tone.

"Say something Bree. I know you're going to be mad at me but he's fine really. He'll heal in no time."

"I told you I'm not in a place to be fooling with you. Let me talk to him." she sighs a deep breath.

"Hey, Champ." Bree sings into the phone as if she didn't just hear the devastating news.

"Hi Mommy, did Dad tell you that I broke my arm and have a cast?" He asks excitedly.

"He did. What color is it?" she asks, matching his excitement.

"Blue and green the Doctor let me get two colors because I was being so brave."

"That's awesome. Well save me a place to sign. How are you feeling? Do you want to come home?"

"I'm fine. No, I don't want to come home. Mom don't be mad at Dad I begged him to ride the bike, it's all my fault."

"No, it's no one's fault. Accidents happen and I'm glad that you are doing well."

"What are you doing?" Junior asks.

"Having dinner. Did you eat?"

"No, Dad said we are going out to eat when we leave here. Ok, Love you Mom, here's Dad."

"Okay love you…"

"Hey," Manny says to the receiver.

"Dang, tell him I love him, why did he rush me off the phone?"

"The gang is here and he has to flaunt his battle scar."

"I see. Well have him call me later."

"Aiight. See ya!"

# CHAPTER 3

"So are you going to go and get him?" Reggie asks sensing the uneasiness in Brianna's demeanor.

"No, a red eye or a 22 hour drive is not in the cards tonight. His Dad lives in Los Angeles."

"Ah! Chargers!" he says, making the football connection. "Do you mind if I be nosey? I mean just so you can get it off your chest."

"He broke his arm riding a four wheeler. A four year old, riding a four wheeler. What sense does that make?"

"Well I'm not here to pass judgment or take sides." He is sure to make known.

"No, no don't backpedal now, you asked."

"He is a bit young. I'll give you that, but it's just what guys do. He's with his Dad spending time and as you said accidents happen. I think you handled that very well by the way." He smiles in hopes she backs up a bit. It works.

"Yeah, they do. I'm cool. I would prefer he comes home, but he looks forward to these ten days with anticipation. I can't take it from him."

The call is a major blow to the mood. The small talk is very small from that point as Reggie can tell that Brianna's mind is preoccupied with her thoughts.

"Dessert?" he asks as their plates are empty.

"No, I'm ready to go."

"So am I taking you home?" he asks shyly.

"If you don't mind, I'd like that." Bree expresses. While she isn't one hundred percent herself, she is enjoying his company.

As they pull up to the house, she isn't in a rush to get out of the car. Even though she knows that she isn't going to invite him in, she figures they can chill and talk for a minute. Besides she wants to get to the bottom of his engagement before the night is over in hopes to know if the ex is gone for good or for now. She reclines her seat a bit.

"Getting comfortable," he inquires.

"Yeah," she looks over to him. "Are you in a rush?"

"No," he replies, turning off the engine but leaving the radio playing for background noise. He cracks the windows and follows suit with the seat recline.

"I am enjoying your company, kind of prolonging the departure." She admits.

"Don't mind it at all."

Silence fills the air, but it's not an awkward silence. It's a peaceful, relaxing comfortable kind of silence; very refreshing. Brianna closes her eyes and just listens to nature and the neighborhood. The sounds of the wind rustling the leaves, the crickets chirping, the dogs barking, and cars rolling up and down the street is calming.

"You're beautiful. I don't know if I told you that or not."

"Thank you," she smiles as she looks at him. "Not too bad yourself." She nudges his arm.

"Not too bad, huh?" he repeats.

"You're very handsome." She clears to let him know that the physical attraction is there. "I just don't need you getting a big head and all," she laughs.

"Oh I have a big head," he chuckles.

"I'm sure I'll never find out." She says as she turns her head away from him and closes her eyes.

Silence again. The comment makes her want to take a glance in between his legs to try to confirm his statement but she has to be subtle about it.

"So, given all that we've talked about, if you had one question you could ask me that I have to answer wholly and honestly what would it be? Just Reggie." She throws her head to the left to get a good look at him.

"Ooooh let's see. This is good. I have so many questions. How can I ask just one?"

"Is that your question?" she teases.

"No that's not my question." He laughs. "Ok, since I cannot decide, why don't you pick something that you haven't told anyone else."

"I met you today and you want a secret already. Daaaammmmmmnnnn!"

"You started this." He reminds her

"Yeah, yeah, yeah. Ok, let's see. Something that I haven't told anyone else," she says sifting through her mind. "No judgment?" she confirms.

"No judgment." He agrees.

"Why am I nervous?" Bree asks rhetorically as she rubs her hands together. "Ok, uhm. How can I put this so it doesn't sound bad? Manny and I planned our Son."

"How is that bad?"

"Well considering that we are best friends, never loved each other romantically and never had a relationship one would think it's sort of silly to have a baby together."

"Wait, so the two of you never dated? So why did you have a baby?" he asks confusingly.

"My point exactly! As I said Manny is my best friend. We met when we were about 14 or so. There was a slight attraction there, but he isn't my type. We agreed to just be friends. Well Manny knew he was always going to be "someone". He came from a wholesome family, had money, resources and talent. So fast forward to college, as he is heading into his senior year, mind you I was a year behind because I took a gap year, we were getting a little tipsy and he asked me to have a baby for him. His case was that he didn't want another woman to have his baby and try to use the baby to extort money from him. He felt that with me, that our child would be safe, loved and I wouldn't dig into his pockets. So, I agreed. Yes, my immature frontal lobe did not account for my life, adulthood, nor did it process the fact that I would be doing this alone, mostly. And honestly, I agreed just to shut him up. He is a mess while drunk and I was kind of trying to end the night before it started. I thought the whole situation was water under the bridge until about a month later, after I broke up with the guy I was seeing, he asked about it. Yes, I agreed to have his baby while I was in a relationship with another guy. Don't judge me. And it further proves the point that I thought the request was empty." She glances his way for some type of redemption. "Anyway, he approached me about it and talked about it every day and how I gave my word, drunk or not. Mind you we shared an apartment, so this was daily. Yes, he was my roommate. Okay, let's just say a lot of things in my young adult days didn't make any sense. Don't judge me." She begs. She wants her actions to be stricken from her record on the fact that she was young and dumb. "Finally, I gave in and got pregnant. Whoo!" she finishes with a sigh of relief. While this is not technically the truth, it's the closest anyone has gotten to it.

"And no one knows this?"

"No, everyone thinks that we got drunk, had a one night stand and I ended up pregnant. Now I don't know how much of that anyone believed because when I came up pregnant it was like, 'We knew you guys were together all along.'" She mocks. "And we weren't, but I just left it alone. Hell us being together secretly was better than the truth." She says laughing.

"So how do you feel about it now?"

"Right now today, I feel great! I love my son, I love Manny and our unorthodox family works for us. If you would have asked me this when I was pregnant or in the first year after my son's birth, then you may have gotten a different answer."

"What would it have been?"

"That I should not have agreed to such an arrangement and actually did a full blown follow through. But in hindsight, I only felt that way because of how his mother treated me. She treated me like I was some whore trying to trap her son and take his wealth."

"She didn't like you?"

"Oh yes! She loved me like a daughter until I got pregnant."

"Damn. Well how is ya'll relationship now?"

"Cordial." She said leaving it at that. "Your turn and I want to ask about your broken engagement." She quickly shifts the spotlight.

"I knew that was coming." He looks at Bree. "Well Toya and I had been in a relationship for about two years before the question of marriage came up, and no it was not me popping the question it was her asking why haven't I yet. I wasn't ready at the time, so when she wanted to move to San Antonio to be closer to her family, I agreed just to get the whole marriage talk off the table for a while. Within like our first two months there her best friend had gotten engaged and here comes the pressure once again. So, I bought a ring and asked her and of course she said yes." He laughs as he finishes.

"So, you do not believe in the institution of marriage?" Bree asks in a serious tone bringing him down because this is not a laughing matter.

"I do. I just didn't see myself marrying her. She wasn't the type of woman I wanted to be with long term. Our relationship was fun and I loved her don't get me wrong, but I wasn't in it for the long haul in the beginning. But when you look up and years have flown by you sort of talk yourself into making some foolish decisions."

"What made you pop the question?" Bree starts because pressure isn't the reason and she knows it. "How did it end? And what is your current emotional state?"

"One question," he gives a glare but proceeds to give the follow-ups he asked. "My emotional state is intact, no worries there." He assures her. "As I've said, I wasn't 100% in it from the beginning. I have no lingering feelings for her and I'm sure she doesn't have any for me. Honestly, I cheated a couple of times. Not something that I am proud of and I'll offer no excuses. She always found out. I don't know if it was her detective skills or my careless actions, either way she always found out. Well this one particular time, she felt that this other woman was the one that would snatch me away. I wanted to move back here to Houston and she thought it was because of this other woman. It wasn't, I just didn't like San Antonio and didn't want to stay there. Besides the horrible job market in my field, I was reestablishing my whole life and I didn't want to make a life there. Well she said she was pregnant and I like a fool popped the question with no questions asked. Then she had a "miscarriage" and things went sour. I found out that she lied about all of it. With that, I packed up my stuff and came back to Houston."

"Oh wow. I'm sorry to hear that. I don't know why people play about bringing life into this world."

"It's cool. Deep down I didn't fully believe her, but I felt that by marrying her, I would be doing the right thing. No one liked her which should have been a clear sign. Not even my mother, and when I tell you she can find the good in anyone, she can, but she never liked Toya."

"That woman's intuition, can count on it every time."

"Well what does yours say about me?" he slips in to change the subject and get out of the hot seat.

"That you're trying to fuck." She says with no regard.

"True, true. I won't deny that." He confirms. "I definitely have a physical attraction towards you. It's what drew me to you." He speaks honestly. "But what does it say about me?"

Brianna leans up and rests her elbow on the console. She stares into his eyes for a moment to try to process the sea of emotions rushing inside of her. As a smile forms on his face, she can't help but to return the gesture. "Goodnight Reggie." She says as she hangs her head low to break the trance.

As she begins to get ready to exit the vehicle he grabs her arm, "Don't leave. Can we seal that moment with a kiss?"

Against all the bells and whistles sounding off in her head telling her to exit and let him hang on to it for awhile. Her gut told her sealing it with a kiss would make it all the more worthwhile. With that she leans in and kisses him so passionately. The chemistry is definitely there. She doesn't remember feeling anything like this in a long time. She has never met a man who has matched her in the kissing department. He is just as passionate with his lips, the soft moans are enjoyable and he's not jamming his tongue all up and through her mouth sloppily. Once she realizes that her panties are so wet it feels as if she has urinated on herself, she decides to bring it to an end before it goes too far. She takes his bottom lip in between her front teeth and bites it gently while letting out a sweet sound of pleasure. Then she takes his chin in her hand and gives his lips one last gentle touch. When their eyes finally open and lock, she says, "Goodnight Reggie!"

With that she leaves the vehicle and doesn't look back. But before she left, she made sure to look down and he does have a big head.

# CHAPTER 4

"Sooooooo," Nia sang on the phone as Brianna adjusted her eyes to see that the neon numbers on the clock read 8:25.

"Good morning to you too, Nia," Brianna half sighs and yawns in a sarcastic tone.

"Girl get up,"

"Just because you have to be up and deal with those bratty ass kids this morning doesn't mean that I join in," Bree interrupts.

"Stop talking about my babies. How did it go last night?"

"It went well."

"And?" she asks enthusiastically fishing for the details

"And that's it!"

"I mean will ya'll see each other again? Have you counted him out already? Is there hope for the future?" she interrogates.

"I mean he's cool. We haven't talked today, yet! If he asks, then I may go for a second date." Bree replies through a series of yawns.

"Damn girl did ya'll stay up all night or what?"

"NO! I'm tired. I've been working all week and I finally get a chance to sleep in and relax and you wake my ass up at 8 in the morning."

"8:30," Nia interrupts. "And I work too, shit!"

"Well it's not my fault you don't get a break. Let me get my rest and I'll talk to you later."

"Bye Bish!" And with that Nia hangs up the phone.

Now Brianna is wide awake with nothing to do and no place to go. As she lies in the bed her thoughts wander to Reggie. Not wanting to seem pressed she extinguishes the feeling of wanting to contact him and turn on the Sport Network to catch up on the games that will be played today. OKC is playing Washington so this game should be in the bag. She doesn't need to hear the commentators trying to persuade the public to side with either team by discussing benched players, injuries or stats. OKC is the better team period. Even on a bad day.

*Good morning, Beautiful?* She smiles as she reads the text that just came in from Reggie. She wonders if she should text back or make him wait it out. What she really needs to know is if she entered the rotation of morning rounds.

"OK, Brianna. This is no time for games. If you're going to go all in, then go all in. Make the decision or don't waste his time." She gives herself a pep talk. There's no reason that she shouldn't try to make something of all the potential that she has within her reach. So she decides to put all the game playing to the side and catapult into whatever this might be. If it blows up in her face, so be it. The only way she will find someone to build a life with, is to actually try to be serious for once. So she decides to call; just to make sure he can answer the phone.

"Good morning," Reggie says in his sexy morning voice

"Good morning, You. Trying to catch a worm?" she asks.

"Only if you are the worm," He says so smoothly that Bree feels a warm sensation slither through her body. "I feel that beautiful smile radiating through the phone." He states matter of fact.

"Are you finishing laying it down?"

"Only if you stop picking it up."

"I don't like you." She smiles.

"I know. It's cool. Liking me comes and goes. Love is constant."

"Love is a choice." She declares.

"Enlighten me."

"Constant means?" she quizzes.

"Continuous over time." He spat.

"Or?"

"Unchanging."

"Bingo! Life is ever changing and the depth of love depends on where someone is in his or her life. Therefore, love cannot be constant. One can vow to love in spite of; however, one saying that they love you and that will remain forever is not considering any outside factors."

"Interesting. I'm trying to see through your lens. Is love a feeling?"

"I don't think so, do you?"

"Yes."

"That's where the differences lie I guess." She says giving up on the conversation.

"But why isn't it a feeling? This is strictly on a relationship level." He clears his distinction while letting it be known that he's not done with the conversation. "When you meet someone and you feel all the warm and fuzzies, the relationship progresses and next thing you know you are expressing your love in more ways than one. Do you not have a feeling about that?"

"Yes, one does. I'm not denying the falling in love or the infatuation phase. I'm saying that those feelings do not last forever. Eventually, they fade. That's where the commitment to love in spite of those feelings not being felt at the present moment comes into play. And to me, a commitment is a choice not a feeling." She repeats. "You don't FEEL like going to work, but you go because you made a commitment. And why are we having this discussion?" Bree asks because she thinks it too damn early to be talking about love in a commitment or feeling sense. This is not the topic she wants to be having a second conversation in.

"Because of my big mouth, but I like it. And I see your point. I just never thought of it that way. Guess that's why many relationships fell to the wayside, because I was continuously searching for the feeling of love."

"Perhaps, but I couldn't confirm. This is just my theory."

"Have you ever been in love?"

"Yes."

"And?"

"And what? My ass is single." She laughs.

"How was it? In one word."

"Draining."

"Damn. I'd say deceiving."

"Hell that too, but you said one word."

"What are you doing?" he switches gears merging from the fast lane.

"Now you ask. Watching SportsCenter. OKC is going to crush Washington later on. I will be front in center on my couch for all the action."

"Want to watch the game together?"

"Where?" she asks with an attitude.

"Well damn, my place. I mean why did you have to ask like that?"

"Don't be trying to get all up in my panties Just Reggie. We can meet at a public spot. They're plenty of restaurants showing the games."

"Well Ms. Brianna, I am not trying to get in your panties, at least not today." He chuckles. "And I have some work to do, so I can kill two birds with one stone if you come over here."

"Uhm huh. Work? Two birds?" she laughs. "All jokes aside. That's cool. I have a couple errands to run this morning, but I'll be there before tipoff. Just send me your address."

# CHAPTER 5

Finding his place is harder than expected. Brianna didn't know that this type of luxury apartment living existed in Houston or the surrounding areas. She has never been on this side of town and rightfully so. It doesn't appear that she makes enough money to be invited let alone fill out an application. Once she finally pulls up to the amazing 50 story building that showcases only windows and balconies, she calls Reggie to let him know that she has arrived.

"There she is," Reggie greets Brianna at the door with open arms.

She continues to push past him dismissing the invite. "Here there, Just Reggie." She says letting her stomach guide her to the aroma coming from the kitchen. It is a must to see what is simmering that smells so good.

"No hug?"

"Nope, what this?" she questions as she begins to wash her hands before she removes the lid to the crockpot releasing the steam of the amazing smell.

"Comfy?" he asks as he stands back and watches her maneuver around the kitchen. "Chilli." He answers.

"The quickest way to my heart is my stomach," she smiles. "I love, love, love chilli." She soaks up the words with glee.

Reggie's face beams as he walks to retrieve a spoon to let Bree have a taste. The moment is perfect as she stands face to face with him looking into his eyes as he blows the steam. As he spoon feeds her she closes her eyes as the flavors tap dances on her tongue. The taste of black pepper, cumin and various chili's are bold, but she knows without a shadow of a doubt that this is Texas chili as no beans are present in the mix. This recipe with some beans would be to die for.

"O.M.G this is so good. I could kiss you." She teases.

"Kiss me then." He provokes.

"Nope," she said, pushing past him towards the couch but stopping short of sitting. Her eyes are glued to the TV as highlights of the previous games are being aired.

"He is a force to be reckoned with cannot deny that," she makes known as she watches King James dunk over his opponents. She turns around to make sure he heard what she said and catches him in a lustful gaze towards her.

"What?" she asks as if there is nothing to be gawking at. She made sure to put on her extra tight jeans that hug her bottom half perfectly as it showcases her fat ass. Her fitted OKC jersey highlights her slim waist and her size C cups that in proportion to her body give the look that she's busty.

"In those jeans...." He playfully begins to sing Ginuwine and he sways towards her.

"Oh, you're being foolish," she jokes as she plops down onto the couch to stop the madness although she enjoys it.

"Scoot over," he pushes her towards the other end to sit in the tiny space available between her and the arm of the couch. He cops his feel as he nudges her along.

"Just ask to touch it, don't be a creep."

"Well can I?"

"Can you what?" she looks at him.

"You know,"

"Know what?"

"You are a piece of work." He sighs. "Can I feel all up on your ass Ms. Briana?"

"No!" she said sternly.

Through his nervous laughter she can't tell if he took her seriously or knew that she was just pulling his leg, so she clears the air.

"I'm joking." She surrenders.

"Get over here," he says as he pulls her towards him and places a kiss on her lips as he runs his hands over her ass. He doesn't overdo it. Just enough contact to make each of their hearts race a little. Bree made sure to run her hands across what she now knows is a solid six pack and works her way up and around to his triceps. Her type of body, she was never sure if she got off more from a man's body or his actual performance in the bed room. Either way this is a win-win situation for her…nice body and big head.

"Call me crazy, but this is it!"

"Meaning?" she asks for clarification from him although she knows where this is leading. This would not be the first time that someone has proclaimed that she is the ONE. She's heard it countless times and still remains single. Manny told her a long time ago that she is no doubt wife material, and he couldn't understand why she is still single. Time after time, relationship after relationship, the end result is always the same. Everything seems like it's going good and then, slowly the drift happens. She has tried being freaky, agreeing to questionable behaviors. Overly engaged in their life which in turn made her lose herself and even tried to be exactly what they expressed they wanted her to be. All of this and more to no avail. This time she figures she would be herself and if that's not enough then so be it. She'd live the life of the happy and single.

"I can get used to your kisses." He tones down the conversation to avoid being too creepy. He knew Bree was the one when he first laid eyes on her. The way she moved through a crowd. How everyone seems to enjoy the energy that she radiates. Then when he talked to her last night, he felt so comfortable, so at ease. Something that he's never felt before with anyone. He felt he could be himself. There are not many women who made it to his home and definitely not on the second date. Like a magnet he's drawn to her and it may seem crazy to some, but he knows how he feels and it's indescribable. To try to explain it to her now might make her run, so for now he'll refrain until the time is right.

"Well don't, I'm not a kissing booth," she laughs.

"You always have something smart to say."

"So.." she cuts him off, "It's because I don't like you and you keep inching in like that will change."

"It will." He says confidently as he gets up to move out of her space as he sees he's wearing out his welcome. Even though he knows that the more she says she doesn't like him, the more she's falling for him.

He goes to set up his laptop on the TV table to begin some work as they wait for the ingredients to continue to marry in the pot.

"Can I count on you to root for OKC during this game or are you one of those people who only cheer for your own team?"

"I'm down to cheer them. Only for you though." He makes clear.

"Great, but I'm one of those people so I will not be rooting for the Rockets or any other team EVER." She smirks

"That's cool, I understand your team needs all the positive energy it can get to help them along. My team will be fine without your screams."

"Fucker!"

"That's my pet name?" he looks up, teasing with her.

"Maybe."

"It'll grow on me."

"You're such a loser, you know that?"

"The first I've heard, but coming from you it must be true." He says with a wink.

Bree can't help but smile at him as she retreats onto the couch. There is no winning with him and she cannot tell if she likes it or not. She has to see how long it takes for him to cave and let her get her way. That will be the determining factor in seeing whether his smart ass mouth is cute or not. But one thing she can't deny is that it is a turn on. She wants to go jump on him and kiss him until he gives her the last word and stop with his smart remarks.

"So you don't want to sit next to me?" she asks after about five minutes has passed and she realizes that he's settled over on the other chair typing away.

"You kicked me off the couch." He says without missing a letter or looking up from his screen.

"No, I didn't."

"Well it kinda felt like you did."

"Here you go with these feelings. When are you going to let them be?" she asks, wanting to know why he leads with that, when he could just ask for clarification. So much for being a great communicator.

"My bad," is all he offers, still not making eye contact.

Bree gets up to go to him since it seems he's not budging. Not wanting to sit on the arm of the chair and seeing that there is nowhere else to sit, she moves the TV stand back a tad and sits on his lap.

"What are you doing?" she asks looking at a screen full of words and no clues hanging about.

"Nothing now that you're in the way," he says as he grabs her waist and directs her to sit on the arm of the chair.

"I don't want to ruin your furniture, I prefer to sit here." She repositions herself back on his lap. This time instead of sitting directly on his manhood she shifts to sit on his right thigh to give him some space.

"Fine." He gives in and helps her settle into a place where he's comfortable and can concentrate. "I'm editing an article we go to print this week and when someone drops the ball I have to pick it up."

"So you work from home often."

"Sadly, yes. With frequent meetings and managing staff it's difficult to get work done in the office. I don't mind working at home though, I am able to zone out and work uninterrupted."

"Is that my cue for me to go back to my spot and shut up?" Bree asks while laughing.

"Is that how you took it?"

"Yeah."

"Guess it didn't work because you're still here."

"Nope! Because you invited me here, now keep me company," she whines.

"Don't do that." He says referencing the whining. "I invited you because I wanted to be in your presence. I told you I had work to do, which meant I am not in a position to entertain. I thought that is what the game is for." He says matter of fact as he begins to attempt to make her rise off of his lap.

Bree sits stunned for a moment. She has never been in a predicament where a man held his ground especially before getting in the panties. Usually, it's whatever you want until they get what they want. This is different and she's not sure how to take it. So she makes one more attempt to win him over. She lays on him in a fetal position and buries her face into his neck. His cologne is not a fragrance she's familiar with but it's mesmerizing. After she gently kisses his neck, she whispers, "hold me."

After a long sigh, he wraps his arms around her and kisses her forehead. "I didn't take you for the spoiled baby type, yet here we are." He speaks softly.

"Well typically I'm not. I don't know what it is with you." She speaks honestly as she continues to melt his embrace. "I swear I don't like you." She lets him follow as she begins to try to convince herself not to fall into the open trap door that she sees so clearly with neon flashing signs.

"Look at me," he says as he raises her chin to face him. He places a soft peck on her lips then he says, "Give me about an hour to finish this up and then I'm all yours." He smiles.

"Can you switch that around," she asks playfully.

"What?" he asks confusingly.

"Tell me you're all mines first." She demands.

"Unbelievable," he laughs out loud. "Ok, ok, I'm all yours now get up and give me an hour." He pushes her playfully.

"Not convincing but given the circumstances I'll take it." She gets up and walks back to her spot across the room.

As he watches her walk back across the room, Reggie thinks of how life would be with Bree. While he is holding back from fully caving in, the way she makes him feel is something like he's never felt, he acknowledges to himself again. Had another woman attempted what she just did he would have flipped out and he has. With Bree, there's just something that makes him rethink his actions before he flies off the handle. The softness about her makes him want to deal with her delicately. While he's never really labeled women or cared to know about their feelings, with Bree the **Handle with Care** label is clearly displayed and he plans to do just that. Whatever will form from their interaction will allow him to reestablish the man that he always wanted to be but have a difficult time being. He returns back to his work to get done and give her his full attention as he promised.

"Bullshit" Bree jumps up off of the couch and screams at the TV.

Reggie was startled as he was in the groove of editing and hadn't realized that about 30 minutes had passed.

"I'm sorry, about this foolishness," Bree turns to him and apologizes for her outburst. "Can you just take a minute and look at this. This is not a flagrant, that's bullshit," she reiterates.

Reggie locks his eyes on the TV screen without a word to watch the replay. "Uhm, that's kind of a close, hard call to make." He replies uninterested.

"Close is not good enough, he didn't do that intentionally, nor with any malice, he's trying to get the ball. Great defense is not a foul." Bree continues to make her case.

"Perhaps," he agrees and continues back at his work.

The referee made the decision to not call a flagrant and Bree joyfully applauses.

"See I told you," she directs towards Reggie although he already checked back out. "Stop being crybabies and play ball," she yells at the TV.

"Ok, you're much more invested in the sport than I," he made known without looking up.

Bree shrugs as she sits back down to get back into the game. OKC is up and this is the way she hopes they keep it. As Reggie's presence has been brought back to her attention, Bree is getting restless. If she was going to watch the game alone she could do it in the comfort of her own home. No expectations were set with coming over Reggie's to hang out, but this is not what she thought it would be. As soon as she was about to announce her departure, she received a text from Aaron. Aaron is the boy toy as of late. It's about time for him to make contact, as it's about time for her to get her back blown out. It's understood, their sexual relationship, even though they do manage to get in a date or two from time to time. He knows Junior is gone for the week, so now is the time for him to show up and get all the goodies he can get before Junior comes back. There were never any objections to the set up and Bree is not sure if she would object now. No doubt that there is chemistry with Reggie, but she would be fooling herself if she said she doesn't want Aaron. As she opens the text message the dick pic puts an instant smile on her face and solidifies that Aaron will be at the house tonight.

*Just what I need in my life,* she replies. *Sliding through around midnight?* she asks. Making sure to leave her enough time to get home and talk to Reggie before announcing she's going to bed.

*I was hoping to cum earlier than that* Aaron replies.

Bree chuckles at the play on words as she replies, *Well you can handle that now, so I will have more time to handle you later.*

"Who's stealing my smiles?" Reggie asks confidently.

"I thought you were working and I'm to not bother you." Bree makes her case.

"Sounds kind of harsh when you say it like that."

"Is kind of harsh as I sit here waiting on you."

"You never answered me."

"Don't think you deserve an answer."

"Wow! Okay, well tell HIM that this is my time,"

"Which you're not taking advantage of," Bree interrupts, confirming his accusation.

"This is my time," he continues, "and you can talk to him later. Maybe." He says looking at Bree.

"IF you're done, then maybe I can cut this conversation short." Bree pushes the envelope to see what Reggie will do.

He stands up and walks towards her. Bree feels intimated, so she stands to try to gain leverage in the conversation.

"If you wanted him for more than a fuck," Reggie starts, "let me rephrase that. If he wanted you for more than a fuck, then you would be with him and not here with me. No man in his right mind would let his woman be alone with another man in his home. Now, I'm not saying that you and I need to get between the sheets, all I'm asking is that you stop that bullshit ya'll have going on. Give me a fair chance without him pulling your emotional strings in the opposite direction." He suggests. His request isn't unreasonable. Reggie notices that he was about to get demanding and had to stop himself short of going there.

"That's a fair request," Bree says giving in. And that it is. If she allows Aaron to continue to pop in and go as he pleases, then Reggie will never have a fair shot at a relationship or whatever it is that this may become.

"Tell him you have to go. Let's eat." He says as he turns and heads toward the kitchen.

Bree hesitates before she replies trying to determine which route she will take.

"Think long, think wrong." Reggie yells from the kitchen.

With that Bree cancels the night and tells Aaron she'll hit him up later in the week.

# CHAPTER 6

There is silence at the table as they wait for their chili to cool. Not a comfortable silence, a which person is going to say the first word to see where this will go type of silence.

"Did I fuck up your plans for tonight?" Reggie asks, being the first to speak and getting straight to the point.

"What plans?" Bree asks in ignorance.

"Ah don't play me for a fool Bree. Your son is gone and you're free to do whatever. He's calling to get his piece before your son comes back to disturb the peace."

Damn. Did he read her mind or the text messages from across the room she wonders?

"While yes I tend to be a little loose when my son is away, that's not what was going on here."

"Lies, don't lie to me and don't play me for stupid. Just put him in his place and we'll be cool."

"I'm trying to figure out who said I wanted to be with you?"

"You did tell me to tell you I'm yours."

"Naw buddy, you said that shit on your own, I just asked that you rearrange the order in which you let the words flow from your mouth." She clears the misunderstanding.

"Touche" he pauses. "Carry on."

"I don't need your permission." Bree makes it known.

"Agreed."

Silence fills the air again. This time it's an awkward *get me out of here* silence. Bree loses herself in the food wondering what in the world did she get herself into. There's no doubt that Reggie is cool and there is chemistry there, but for him to want her to drop her toys after two days is a bit much for her.

"I apologize," he offers as he breaks the silence again. "It's just that you can't kiss me like you did last night and not expect for me not to be jealous at the thought of you possibly kissing someone else. Do you kiss everyone that way?" he asks genuinely.

"No. I don't. And I didn't or don't plan on kissing anyone else. It's just that regardless of how comfortable each of us feels and the powerful chemistry between the two of us, I just met you yesterday."

"Weird I know. Definitely seems like it's been longer."

"It does seem longer and that's scary. But it doesn't change the fact that we just met. I don't appreciate you trying to discard people out of my life."

"Not people, the dude that you're fucking. What's wrong with that?"

"Nothing if we were together. A lot since I just met you yesterday."

"So you're telling me that there is no potential? That the way you passionately kissed me means nothing? The way you buried yourself in my lap and yearned for my attention is not real?"

"That's not what I said. What I said is that this is scary because we don't really know each other."

"Don't twist words to fit your narrative, answer the questions. Do I need to repeat them?"

"No you don't." Bree says as she gathers herself. "Yes, there's potential. Yes, the kiss means something and yes, I yearned for your attention. Still doesn't negate the fact that this is scary and I don't know you."

"How can you get to know me if you're  fucking and sucking someone else?"

"Damn," she says, taken aback by him being so forward and vulgar. "I'm not and if I was, I'm sure I can handle it."

"Bullshit!" he laughs. "Ok, you got it Brianna." He surrenders.

Silence rears its ugly head again and her mind is telling her to just leave, yet her heart is telling her to comfort him and reassure him that he has a fair chance at whatever this might be.

"Listen, I get it. I understand your case and agree that it would be difficult for me to totally invest in you or us, if someone else is allowed to steal my energy and time. However, what we are not going to do is pretend that you didn't ignore a couple of texts and silence a couple of calls since I've been here. It's been two damn days at maximum and as I don't expect you not to have people that you need to get rid of, IF this turns into something, then you should know that I have to do the same. Do I have to be intimate with him? No! Am I going to get rid of him right now? No, not until I'm ready. So, you can take your jealous feelings far the fuck away from me and deal with your own insecurities." Bree lashes out.

"Agreed." Reggie calmly offers and that's all he offered. He decides that he is not about to let his insecurities control this relationship. He is going to try to be reasonable and take things slow for once. Although he doesn't know how long he will be able to hold on from going off the ledge if she continues to think she will have conversations in front of his face.

"Are you about to leave?" he asks, giving her the out that he feels she wants.

"Thinking about it because I have to work in the morning, so..." she let drift off.

"Can you at least stay and let me make up some ground. I want to at least have some hope that you'll call me." He rises to walk next to Bree. He grabs her chin as he often does to get her full attention. "Please?" he asks looking into her eyes.

"Fucker!"

"Yes," he rejoices knowing that he nudged her right back into his sweet spot.

# CHAPTER 7

"Girl, ya boi is crazy as shit." Bree tells Nia on the phone as she is eating her lunch.

"What happened?"

Bree goes into the story about what happened yesterday at Reggie's apartment and didn't hold anything back.

"Well damn you receiving dick pics and entertaining the shit and you expect him not to be mad."

"Okay, he could feel a way, BUT for him to make demands like a jealous lunatic and like we're together is a bit much."

"True that. Well you have to take into consideration that although you just meet him Saturday, that he has been digging you for longer than that, and I have been playing you up for weeks, so he does have kind of a one up on you in that regard."

"I guess."

"Outside of that, do you like him? I mean what's the deal?"

"Well I haven't talked to him since I left his place. He sent a good morning text and I replied, but a closed reply. He hasn't tried to make contact again and neither have I. I do like him and there is chemistry there. I think I'm just scared. I haven't felt this way in a while. It seems like we've known each other forever. That's how comfortable it is around him. I don't know Nia." Bree sighs.

"Well take your time no rush. But he is a good guy and he really likes you that I know. And what dude wouldn't be jealous if the person he likes is entertaining someone else. Someone else that doesn't even want them at that," Nia offers. "Does Aaron want to be with you?"

"I don't know. I've never asked. I know that I don't want to be with him because Junior is a problem for him. Well not so much Junior but my relationship with Manny. Aaron is not mature enough to handle that we still talk and actually are friends."

"Well there you go. Why waste your time on something that will never be?"

"Because the sex is good," Bree laughs.

"Well before you settle because of that, make sure that Reggie's isn't better." Nia laughs.

"True, true. I'm going to call him."

"Don't let him wait too long. He might just walk away."

"Then it wasn't meant to be."

"If that's your gauge then have at it. I'll talk to you later."

"Aiight girl. Bye."

"Bye."

Bree sits under the nice warm breeze thinking about Reggie and how she is going to play this hand that she's dealt. Should she be scared of his jealous tendencies or should she accept them out of love. She has never had anyone upset that she was entertaining someone else before not even Eddie. When dudes around campus tried to talk to Bree, Eddie would play it off and say, "No one is better than me. He can't take you. You'll be back." And that alone made Bree not want to move one. She thought it was pointless and that no other relationship would work out because Eddie the Man had said so. It's difficult to navigate romantic relationships when Bree rarely had any and the ones she had fell way short of conventional. Her trust meter is in the negative, so Reggie will have a lot of ground to make-up and it's not even his fault. She decides

All she can do is try not to make him pay for the mistakes of her past and love honestly. That's all she has and that's all she can do. However, she is still going to make him sweat to see where his head is at. So, maybe she'll give him a call Friday or Saturday.

"Hey Beautiful Brianna, I thought I wouldn't run into you again." Bree hears the familiar voice coming up behind her.

"Hey Dr. Simms. How are you?"

"Damn, I don't get a Boo?"

"Hell to the naw!" Bree scolds.

"Just threw me to the curb just like that huh?"

"Not the way I recall it, but sure if that's what you want to go with then let's roll with it."

"How are you liking the Maternity Ward?"

"Love it. Did you think you were ruining my life by sending me off?" She asks sincerely with a warming smile.

Jason was a boy toy with much potential that was ruined by another woman and his bright idea to do some sly shit behind her back. When things started to get a bit shaky between them, he took it upon himself to transfer Bree from his department. However, Bree still has a soft spot for him. She really thought something would evolve from their nightly love affair.

"I need you on top, but we'll save that conversation for another time."

"I thought we were past that?"

"You said you're past it. I, on the other hand, don't know why you stopped talking to me."

"Really?" she makes a face of astonishment. "I find out that you're fucking someone else and instead of you admitting to your shit, I find out from a coworker that I have been "selected" to go to day shift."

"There was nothing to address with the sleeping around mess. I told you I wasn't. In regards to the day shift, I thought I would get a thank you. You did need to be on dayshift to spend more time with your son? The late nights and frantic work schedule was cutting into your family time right?" he asks knowing that it's true.

"Yes, but that was not your initial reasoning for sending me packing. You fucked up. Just admit that for me please."

"I did. I wanted the smoke to settle for us to try to take a stab at it again, but you left without a word."

"I did. Serves you right." She nips the conversation in the bud. Now is not the time to try to revisit what they had. "Is there anything of substance you want to discuss?"

"Guess not. Hopefully, you'll come around and we catch up soon. The gang misses you. We should do lunch sometime." He says as he walks away.

Brianna does miss her old squad. Melissa, Rodney, Cheyanne, Kayleigh and Dr. Simms, the ultimate ER night crew, the fun times they had will always be remembered. She misses them too; however, moving on was the right thing to do. Fraternization is strongly discouraged for this very reason. Dr. Simms and Brianna dated off the record for almost a year and as soon as she was becoming comfortable enough to introduce him to Manny it all blew up in her face. Her feelings were extremely hurt and it took awhile for her to move on from it. And in the midst of her trying to tend to her wombs he hit her with a wrecking ball and sent her to day shift. She doesn't want anyone who would treat her in such a way. He disposed of her without an inkling of guilt.

Love is a stranger to Bree. At her rate she doesn't even know if love is welcomed. For the sake of Reggie's feelings hopefully she can dish it out, better yet receive it.

# CHAPTER 8

It's Thursday and Bree has managed to make it through most of the week without actually talking to Reggie. Afew texts here and there were all she offered to him. She could sense that he was becoming restless, so when he asked to drop by after work today it didn't come as a surprise to her. She was shocked it took this long and can't dismiss the fact that she is excited to see him. It has been torture for her to ignore him and play like she doesn't want to talk to him. She missed him like crazy and wanted to feel his lips on hers since the day she left his apartment. Even though she said she wasn't going to play any games, she had to let him play out his jealous ways really did take her back just a little.

"Mr. Jealous," she says sarcastically as she opens the door to let him in.

"Still stuck on that I see. How are you today Ms. Brianna?"

"Great, and you?"

"Let's see," he extends his arms for a hug. Bree walks into the embrace she's been longing for without hesitation. "Great! My day is going great!" he says as he hugs her tightly.

Bree let the moment take her in and do something to her. His embrace is so loving and safe, she feels as if she could live here forever.

"I've missed you." He tells her.

"I've missed you too," she replies. "Crazy ass," she adds as she turns to walk away from him.

"Just couldn't leave it at that huh? Smells good," he says as he follows behind her. "Am I invited to dinner?"

"Nope! You called and said that you wanted to see me. You see me right? Even got a hug and an, *I miss you* to boot." She delivers her sly remarks over her shoulder.

"Stop playing Bree."

She pauses and looks at him once she makes it into the kitchen. The way he looks at her makes her want him even more. No one has ever looked at her so lovingly. He walks over to her and traps her between himself and the counter.

Looking into her eyes he says, "Say something Baby."

Bree feels her whole body melt to the floor and slide away. She is immobile and speechless. She wraps her arms around his waist and pulls him near. After a moment she looks up at him and finally breaks her silence, "You can stay for dinner."

"Thank you." He says appreciatively and walks to go and sit down. Mission accomplished. "What are we having?"

"Gosh, I don't like you. I think it's slowly turning into hate." She warns with laughter.

"Well if the warmth of that beautiful smile, the kindness of those kisses and the tender of those touches are hate, I'm in for a spectacular reward when love rears its head." He shoots back.

"Close your eyes while I poison your food, you're sickened."

"And you love it," he spat.

Bree leaves well enough alone and decides to move on with the conversation. "Well seeing it's the salmon I'm sure you smell, that's what we're having. I have a weird cold salad on the side that I'm sure you don't want. Do you like mushrooms and spinach?" she asks, already reaching in the fridge to sauté him something to go with his salmon.

"What's the weird salad?" he asks intrigued like he's willing to give it a try.

"Well it's like a mango type of salsa, I say type of because I add a bunch of other things I like and it's over rice."

"Cold rice?" He says making a face.

"Yes, cold rice." Bree confirms.

"Mushrooms and spinach for me."

"Starch?"

"No need. I'm sure I'll be hungry later."

"Great! Then you can eat when you get home." Bree insinuates letting him know that spending the night is not in the cards tonight. Not that she doesn't want him to, it's just that Aaron may be paying her a visit, if she confirms.

"Well damn, I feel so welcomed. How was your day or should I say week?"

"Jokes huh Mr. Jealous? It was good. Caught up on some much needed things that I was prolonging. And yourself?"

"Could have been better had you not been playing me in circles. But I can't complain now. And for how long do I have to endure this Mr. Jealous bit?"

"For as long as you act crazy." Bree says throwing the veggies in the pan. Then proceeds to lean on the counter and adds, "You decide."

Before he can respond with his snide remark Bree phone rings.

"Hey, what's up?" she asks nonchalantly into the receiver.

"Save me Bree." Manny pleads.

"From what?" she asks even though she really doesn't want to because Manny is always with the shits, so she's sure that this is no exception.

"Sam took Junior out. I decided not to go and now I'm regretting my decision because I'm getting all these texts that are calling my name." he begins to laugh at himself because he started off serious before he let his humor take over.

"I see," She says, waiting for him to finish up with his shenanigans.

"Where's the bathroom?" Reggie interrupts.

"Down the hall to the right." Bree points but decides to walk over and turn on the light for him to follow the directions.

"Who's that?" Manny inquires

"So, I guess this is a step in the right direction for you. I'm taking you haven't contacted anyone?" she continues dismissing his question.

"Let's not change the subject. Who are you talking to fast ass?"

"Does it matter given the fact that I'm single and so is he?"

"The burn." He laughs. "I'm sort of, kind of single in my own way."

"You have a whole live in girlfriend for almost five years and you're single. OooooKay!"

Bree rolls her eyes. "Well giving the fact that you are trying to make progress I can say that I'm proud."

"Still on the phone?" Reggie asks as he returns in an uneasy tone.

Manny picks up on it and taunts, "Ooooh, somebody's in trouble."

"Mind your damn business. Mr. Jealous is just trying to make his presence known. I'm sure he thinks you're someone else." Bree shrugs as she looks at Reggie.

"Does Mr. Jealous have a name?"

"Reggie. Reggie, Manny, Manny, Reggie." Bree announces like she is introducing them in person.

"What's up?" Manny is the first to respond.

"He says what's up." Bree relays.

"Sup?" Reggie responds and returns to his seat.

"Told you he thought you were someone else. He's bummed out now." Bree laughs. "Well as I was saying I'm proud of you. I hope you can be strong and find something to do with your time right now. We're about to eat dinner, so I gotta go."

"Okay," he sighs. Usually, Bree is the go to. She and Manny can talk for hours about nothing. Their friendship is still strong and nothing has changed in that she likes to keep him out of trouble when she can. "I'll talk to you later."

"Have Junior call me when they get back."

"Will do. And be prepared to tell me all about Mr. Reggie."

"Bye."

*Click.*

"Don't do that." He scolds as soon as Bree puts the phone down.

"Do what?"

"Mr. Jealous," he looks like that alone should allow Bree to fill in the blanks.

"Again, that's what you're acting like." Bree stands her ground. "Besides, it's just Manny. It was not out of disrespect."

"Felt a bit disrespectful."

"Noted."

"That's it!"

"Yeah. I note the fact that you can't take a fucking joke. That your ego is so fragile that I have to ensure that my words are as sweet as a pecan pie."

"No apology?" he continues to move on to his point dismissing Bree's malice.

"I'm sorry you're so sensitive."

"Fair enough." He let it go.

Reggie doesn't feel like getting into why those types of games between them are cool but off limits with others. Maybe that's Bree's immaturity rearing its nasty head. Not a flaw that he thinks he's capable of dealing with. With his temper and her whimsical nature, it could definitely be a disaster.

Bree senses his uneasiness as she places their plates on the table. He walks over from the island to take his position still not uttering a word or glancing her way.

"Have a taste." Bree puts the fork close to his mouth for him to taste the rice and salsa concoction. This is her move to attempt to break the ice although she knows that she needs to offer up some type of apology.

Reggie leans in to clean the fork and after he swallows the contents utters, "Surprisingly, good. Not what I expected at all. I mean. I don't want any" he made sure to clear up, "but I could eat it on a warm summer day."

"Yes, typically my summer salad, but I have a taste for it every now and then." Bree hesitates because she knows she has to say something of substance. "Look, I get it. I'm sorry. I know that I can be a bit immature in the humor department and that was out of line. It's just that Manny is my friend and that is how we talk to each other. He wasn't bothered by it and didn't take it to heart. I can assure you that. And he doesn't think of you as less of a man or anything. I know it's hard for you to grasp that because you don't know him. However, I will refrain from saying such comments like that to him or anyone else for that matter."

"Thank you." He says and offers nothing more. He's not into beating a dead horse. She said it won't happen again and he's going to hold her to her word.

Bree moves around the table to sit next to him and tries to butter him up. She starts by unloosening his tie, "Get comfy and stay a little while. You look nice by the way. You're dressed to the 9's for work. Who are you trying to impress?" she teases.

He grabs her hand and stops her in her tracks. Bree is caught off guard by the firmness of his grip. She looks directly into his eyes knowing that he is still in his feelings. The tension is so thick that she feels like she can't breathe and wants to turn away but she can't. Their gaze is locked. The longer she looks at him the more she feels his tension easing. She decides to play on the little tenderness he's displaying. She drops her eyes and murmurs, "Too soon. I'm sorry. I just thought we passed it," while simultaneously lowering her hand from his tie. She repositions her chair to continue to eat her food.

He turns his chair around to face her and then proceeds to turn her chair to face him. "Gosh!" he smiles. "You have done a number on me." He admits. "Go on, take it off." He says as he leans in on her thighs for her to loosen his tie enough for it to fit above his head.

# CHAPTER 9

The playful dinner continues without a hitch and they were back in each other's good graces.

"Thank you for the bird meal, it was quite tasty."

"You're welcome," Bree says as she clears the table and loads the dishwasher.

Upon sitting back down she throws both of her legs in his lap. He gently caresses her soft freshly shaven legs.

"So, Just Reggie," Bree takes the opportunity to continue to get to know the man that she is falling for. "If I interviewed your mother, your best friend and your ex-fiance', what would they each have said about you?"

"Damn. You have these interview questions on tap don't you," he spits. "Well seeing as though I'm the baby boy my mother would boost quite heavily. While she would make mention that I was the most hard-headed of the bunch with a fly off the handle attitude, she would smooth it over with my intellect, my humor and my accomplishments. Let's see my best friend. He would talk about our many drunken nights and the chaos we've caused, my less than forgiving attitude when it comes to things of importance and my spontaneous nature. In addition, he would rave about my braveness, my loyalty and my career driven attitude. At last, the one you really want to know about," he gives a nervous chuckle. "My ex would probably say that I'm a lying ass cheating, manipulating hot head. I can give accuracy because she actually said that," he admits. "But honestly she would have nothing but negative things to say at this point. I don't think she could find a nice word to muster from within. Had you caught her when there was still love present, she would probably have said, despite my flaws, that I'm a genuine, charming, loving and thoughtful person."

"Interesting," Bree gives off an intriguing glare. What all three have in common is what she noticed when she met him, that he has a temper.

"And you?"

"Well, my mother would not have a nice thing to say about me honestly. Only because she doesn't know the new me. What she will disclose is Brianna in her adolescent and teen years. The Brianna that wore a chip on her shoulder, had, well I still do have a foul mouth. The disrespectful Brianna that thought it was her against the world. My best friend," Bree paused, "If she was still alive today she would say that my tough exterior is only present to guard the mushiness inside. That I'm sarcastic and funny as hell, loyal to a fault and have absolutely no problem knocking anyone out. Since I've never been engaged, I'll go with Manny. He would probably say that I'm the hardest working person he knows. That despite what I've been through, I've never let it defeat me. He'd mention that I have a difficult time asking anyone for help and he would also add that I'm funny, loyal and I keep my word."

Reggie knew that his **handle with care** label was right on point after hearing this. "If you don't mind," he proceeds with caution. "Your best friend?" He makes his implication. "I mean you don't have to."

"Bullets in the hood have no names. She was killed going into my Senior year in college. Have you ever heard that when there is a death, then there will be a birth announcement?" she asks sincerely.

"No, haven't heard of that."

"Well that's what my grandmother used to always say. I guess I believe it for comfort. When I learned of Coco's death, I immediately rushed home. After staying there for about a week helping her mom with the arrangements and ensuring that she was okay as she was going to be, I went back to school. And you know what," she asks as her face brightens. "I found out I was pregnant."

"Well then it must be true." He offers his kind words and gives her leg a gentle squeeze.

After a brief moment of silence he continues, "So, you and your mom's relationship."

"Damn dude, I didn't ask you any follow up questions," Bree objects.

"Well you could have your bad."

"It sucks; it always has and probably always will."

"Ok, ok, I get it. You don't want to talk about it."

"Thank you," she let out a sigh of relief. "Let's go see who is playing. It's not OKC I know that for sure."

Reggie gets up to follow Bree into the family room. As she grabs the remote he lets out, "Damn, I'm tired," through a stretch and a yawn.

"Long day?" Bree asks as she turns back around to meet him face to face.

"Yes, finally sent that journal to print so I can breathe a little lighter with my fingers crossed. Hopefully they don't call me this weekend."

Bree starts to unbutton his shirt. He stands and watches her wondering what is going on. He let her take the lead and made sure not to interrupt this time. Once his undershirt is showing, she removes his cufflinks and sits them on the end table. Slowly she removes his shirt and hangs it on the closet door handle carefully to ensure no wrinkles can be made. "Come," she grabs his hand and leads him to the sofa. She directs him to the end chair and reclines it back as far as it can go. She removes his shoes and grabs the throw blanket and tosses it over him. She then grabs the remote before sitting next to him and nestling under his arm. When she turns on the TV she sees the Celtics playing. "I'm good. Do you want to watch this?"

"Nope!" Reggie replies as he is soaking up this royal treatment. He hasn't had a woman that catered to him like this. He doesn't know if he didn't allow it or if it was just the type of women he dealt with. It really doesn't matter; he can get used to this.

As Bree is surfing the guide to find something to watch, she notices heavy breathing coming from Reggie. "Didn't take long for him to go to sleep," she says aloud.

She lies there watching the news, just to pass time. Not wanting to move from her comforting spot, but not wanting to lay here neither. She doesn't want to go to sleep. Taking a nap this late in the evening will have her up all night. Something she could not afford. After chilling for about 30 minutes she decides to go and shower and then bake the most wanted cake from her co-workers

\*\*\*

Bree turns around as she hears Reggie making his way towards the kitchen. "He is alive!" she says stretching her hands to the ceiling.

"Something smells good in here."

"There are toothbrushes and rags in the linen closet. If you hang a left instead of a right down the hall, it's in the guest room bathroom."

"Damn, can you smell my breath from here?" He asks laughing because he's at least 15 feet away.

"No, but I'm sure morning breath was kicking in. That wasn't a damn nap. It's 9:45 you were asleep." Bree makes it known that he has been M.I.A for the last 3 hours or so.

"My bad," he says as he makes his way down the hall.

"So what've you got?" he questions after he returns and lingers over Bree's shoulder.

"An iced lemon pound cake. Since I was in here bored out of my mind, I figured I could surprise Latrice, it's her favorite. She's been bugging me for weeks. Want some?"

"Yes," he replies like she knew better than to ask such a thing. "Sweets are my vice."

"How do you stay toned?"

"Work out like it's a drug and I'm addicted. If I ever stop, then I don't know what I will look like," he admits.

Bree cuts a piece of the cake. She made sure to slop it in her homemade icing. The fact that it's still warm will make it even better. She feeds Reggie. His eyes are closed and he's chewing in slow motion like he's in heaven. Bree begins to laugh at the dramatization.

"Tell Patrice,"

"Latrice," Bree interrupts.

"Patrice, Katrice, Latrice, whomever, that she has to wait for the next one. This one is mine."

"You can have a couple slices but you don't need the whole damn cake."

"And why not?"

"That's entirely too much sugar."

"Ok sugar police, read me my rights."

"You have the right to leave empty handed, keep playing with me."

"Damn officer who stole your donuts and coffee."

"Two slices, you can eat one now and one tomorrow."

"So I assume I'm coming back over to get it because it would be hard for you to monitor when I eat it if I take it home." He teases.

"Well first off, if you tell me you will save it, then you should keep your word. Second, since you want to be a smart ass, just take this and wait for the next one." She shovels a piece of cake into his chest.

"Damn, you are tough." He makes it known while taking the cake from her.

"I have a soon to be five year old, cute faces and butter me ups only go so far." She said firmly.

"Duly noted. I think I should give you this 'D' that'll teach ya." He winks.

"It might, no promises."

"You're naughty Ms. Brianna."

"You brought it up, and I'm naughty one."

There soon to be frisky conversation that may lead to what Bree wants is rudely interrupted by Reggie's ringing phone.

"Don, talk to me." Reggie bellows.

As he engages in his phone call, Bree takes the opportunity to clean up her mess and individually pack the slices of cake for her co-workers. Against her earlier statement, she is setting aside another piece of cake for Reggie.

"Bree are you going to the party Saturday night?" he startles her out of her mechanic routine.

"Didn't plan on it." She replies.

"Why?" he asks intruding in her personal space. She hadn't realized that he ended his call.

"Nia, told me about it but I have to work this weekend."

"I thought you don't work on weekends." He offers a confusing look.

"I work one weekend out of the month and THIS is THAT weekend."

"Where will your son be?"

"With his Dad."

"I thought he would come home this weekend."

"Yes, Sunday evening. He comes home after I get off work." She says annoyingly. She can't believe he actually remembers all of that information.

"Oh." He says like any of the information means anything to him. "Why don't you come with me?"

"Are you asking me out on a date?"

"I guess I am. Ms. Briana, would you like to hit the town with me Saturday night?"

"I can come out for a bit. I'll just meet you there because I'm sure I'm going to leave early."

"Now, what type of date would that be if you escort yourself."

"An, I'm going to meet you there, date."

"I don't do those."

"Ok, Mr. Escort. I just ask that I'm home no later than 11:30, I have issues going to sleep. I have to ensure I employ my winding down routine."

"Oh I can put you to sleep." He jokes.

"I'm sure you can," she brushes off.

"You suffer from insomnia?" he asks more seriously.

"Nope, I suffer from graveshiftomnia. I have been on the 11 pm to 7 am shift so long my body is taking a long time to get used to this day schedule. If I'm not sleep by 1 in the morning, my overdrive kicks in and I cannot go to sleep at all. Then I go to work the next morning feeling like I'm pulling a double."

"That's not good. I will have you home. Just want to show my face. Chop it up with some of my crew."

"I'm in. I'm sure Nia will be excited. She stays trying to get me out and in the crowd. She is such a social butterfly."

"That she is. I was thinking that you were the same way."

"Disappointed?"

"Nope!" he makes known. He is actually happy that Bree pretty much stays to herself, makes for less drama. "How did you and Nia meet anyway?" he pries.

Bree lets out a slight chuckle, "At a bachelorette party of a person that I don't like and she didn't know."

"Oh gosh, I hate to ask but am too intrigued not to. How did that come about?"

"Lisa, the bride, married a friend of mine Slim. Of course, I can't hang with him and his buddies to celebrate, so I was doing the girl thing with Lisa to show my support. Nia and Lisa share a mutual friend, Ty'shelle. Ty'shelle dragged Nia to the party. It seems that both Nia and I were there for the drinks and entertainment. Long story short is, Nia introduced herself to me since she noticed I was playing the background. Once the entertainment showed up neither of us were impressed. We wanted to end the night. Nia rode to the party with

Ty'shelle, so I offered to take her home because I was leaving. And the rest is history, I guess."

"Pretty cool. At least the time wasn't wasted. A great friendship developed."

"True. We still talk and laugh about it to this day." Bree smiles.

As Bree finishes tidying up the kitchen, Reggie re-enters into her personal space. "I don't recall getting a kiss today." He mentions.

"I don't recall you asking for one."

"Now I have to ask? Usually, you are very inviting."

Bree locks her hands behind his neck and goes in for what she's been waiting all evening for. There were plenty of opportunities for her to make her move. None seemed like the right time. The timing now is perfect. She has on her silk pajamas, no bra, no panties, freshly showered smelling of floral fragrances. Maybe she can get him in the bed tonight. As she begins to kiss him passionately, he rubs her body softly. Light moans can be heard from the both of them. As they release their lips, Bree begins to kiss gently on his neck. He picks her up and places her on the countertop. Quickly taking the lead, he kisses her neck making his way down to her breast. As he's kissing all of her exposed skin, he stops short of taking off her shirt.

"You almost had me. I'm not that easy." He teases.

"What?" she asks in outrage. Now is not the time for games.

"I think I'm going to go."

"And leave me like this."

"Yup! I'm the mouse. You left me hanging the other night. I'm returning the favor."

"So we're keeping score," she laughs realizing how ridiculous this all sounds. She may have left him stiff when she left his apartment, but that was for a reason.

"Not keeping score, keeping this fire burning. I don't know about you but I kind of like it."

Bree doesn't want to admit that she likes it as well. Not having what she wants is making the anticipation build. She just hopes that it's all worth it in the end.

"Come here," she grabs his shirt and pulls him towards her. She wraps her arms around him tightly. "Look at me," she demands. "If I find out you fucking someone, then it's going to be me and you." She informs him, shaking her head.

Reggie burst out laughing.

"I'm Mr. Jealous, yet you're threatening me," he says through laughter.

"So what? I'm a horny piece of shit right now and you're playing around."

"Feisty!"

"Leave me alone," she whines.

"I am getting a kick out this; I hope you know that."

"You're such a fucking loser."

"You told me." He chuckles.

"Goodnight Reggie," she says, pushing him to the side and jumping off the countertop.

"Are you mad at me?" he asks, walking behind her as she gathers up his things.

"No, I'm not."

"I'm not sure if I believe that," he discloses with uncertainty.

Bree stops in her tracks and goes over to him, "I'm not upset, just horny. I'm good. I mean, you're playing me, but it's cool." She wraps her arms around his waist and looks him in the eyes. "Kiss me again at least."

After what seems like an hour long passionate kiss, Reggie breaks the silence, "Go to bed."

"What's that supposed to mean?"

"Don't call anybody to do what I'm leaving unfinished."

"Well finish," she demands.

"Brianna, don't play with me."

"But you can play games though?"

He pauses to let her know that he is serious about this matter. "Promise me."

"Promise you what?"

"That you won't call him. You said you're a woman of your word."

"I am."

"Then tell me you won't. Better yet, do you like me enough not to?" he plays on her emotions.

"I'm not." She caves in without hesitation to let him know that she likes him more than enough.

"You're the best," he says as he seals it with a kiss.

"Am I now?"

"Want to talk on the phone until I get home?"

"Nope! Just call me when you're settled."

# CHAPTER 10

Bree made the mistakes of not only taking a nap when she came home from work but washing her hair when she was in the shower. She has no time or energy to blow dry, braid down and fix this lace front on top of her head. "Wash and go it is," she says to herself looking disappointed in the mirror. She retrieves her favorite curling gel from the cabinet along with the diffuser. As soon as she finishes diffusing her hair she hears Reggie's car pull into the driveway. Quickly she throws on her dress and tries to find the accessories that she's going to wear.

"Hey, you look nice," she says in a rush tone as she gives Reggie the glance over.

He has on a leisure blazer with a button down underneath, some nice shoes that she doesn't recognize, which probably mean they're out of her budget, and some relaxed fitted jeans, that with his muscle mass looks similar to a straight leg. He has a fresh line around his hair line and goatee.

"Damn," she says as she stops in her tracks. She knows the smell of Creed anywhere. The one cologne that she always loved but never had anyone worth buying it for. "That smell is alluring."

"So it works," he smiles. "Slow down." He grabs her into his embrace.

"I'm ready, I'm ready," she says as she begins to go upstairs.

"You're not," his voice trails as she continues on her journey.

"Five minutes," she yells.

Reggie knows all too well that five minutes is at the very least twenty and more realistically thirty. He sits down in the chair debating whether or not to turn on the TV. This is the first time he is really getting a glance at her place. In that, he realizes that there are no pictures, no personal touches or feel to the room. It reminds him of a showroom in a furniture store. It seems as if she walked in and said, give me everything, even the coasters. He hears Bree fumbling upstairs and then immediately hears her thumping down the steps.

"I said five minutes," she smiles.

"You did and you look gorgeous Baby." He says as he gives his first once over. Her curly hair is so beautiful. It falls just below her shoulders and frames her face perfectly. The bodycon dress is hugging her curves as if it's part of her skin. The gold shimmery color complements her caramel complexion and her heels have her standing almost eye to eye with him.

"Thank you," she expresses while giving a blushing smile.

"How did you get your hair like this? I mean the other day it looks as if it was bone straight." He asks, going into touch her curls.

She quickly slapped his hand. "Huh, don't touch my hair. I'm not a pet. Well this is my hair, the straight shit is a wig." She says unbothered.

"Damn, I'm sorry." He offers for invading her personal space. "If your hair is this beautiful why do you wear a wig."

"It's easier to manage." She gives the easy answer.

"Well for the record, I like this better. Shall we go?"

"We shall," she turns and walks towards the door.

There's not much conversation heading to the venue, Bree is praying that she doesn't see anyone that she currently or use to talk to. It seems that she always picks the guys that have no problem causing a scene in random places. Cory approached Aaron at the movie theater as if he had grounds to do so. Bree is not or never been in a relationship with either one of them. Yet, there they were going back and forth trying to force her to choose. Needless to say, she chose Aaron. Not because he was the better guy, but that was the guy who she was on a date with. Cory's crazy ass is always in the know around town. Hopefully, he stayed his ass home tonight. Now that Bree thinks about it, she always finds the crazy ass dudes. She's hoping that Reggie will be an exception.

As soon as they walk in, who is the first person they see?

"Charles, what's going on?" Reggie asks, going in with a handshake.

"Damn, Son, you got Bree out the house on a Saturday night? This is cause for a celebration, shots all around." Charles screams. He always makes every little thing into a celebration so he can drink.

"No, no, I don't want a drink. And I do come out. Just not often." Bree reminds him, going in for a hug. "Where's Nia?"

"Around here somewhere. Go find her before she finds some trouble."

"I'll be back," Bree tells Reggie.

He places his hand on the small of her back and whispers, "I'll be waiting," and seals it with a kiss on her cheek.

"God damn, what the fuck ya'll two got going on. Acting like ya'll in a relationship and shit."

Bree continues to walk away to allow Reggie to tell him whatever he wants to tell him about what the two of them have going on.

"Niaaaaaa," Bree sang when she finally found her friend.

"Oh shit, what are you doing out of the house. Got your hair all curly, smiling and shit. What the fuck is going on?"

"Don't do me like that."

"I'm just saying it's like pulling teeth. Want something to drink?"

"Naw, I'm good. I'm not going to be here long. I have to work in the morning."

"Eleven o'clock curfew." She sighs

"You know it." Bree responds proudly.

"I guess something is better than nothing." Nia gives in. "Well look who's here talking to Charles, let's go and say hi." Nia starts to walk towards the door as she spots Reggie.

"I know we came together, but sure you can go and say hi." Bree nonchalantly replies.

"Say what," Nia says as she takes a b-line while grabbing Bree's wrist. "Ya'll been kicking it and you haven't told me. You're fired." She says trying to brush Bree and the news off. "Spill it." She eagerly insists moments later.

"Well this is date number two I guess. Nothing to spill. Talked through text all week leading up until today. I had shit to do and he had a publication to get out or something." Bree says trying to make the lie believable while brushing it off.

"So what do you think of him."

"I mean he's cool. Treading lightly. Nice convo."

"Alright, alright." Nia says as if she's accessing the situation. "Well let's go mingle before you have to go."

As Bree and Nia are making their way across the room, Bree spots a woman in the corner sipping her drink. Bree stomach churns at her sight but she doesn't understand why. As soon as she follows the path to where her eyes are gazed. She see's Reggie in her line of vision. Now that Bree's antennas are up she watches the two of them closely. Reggie seems as if he acknowledges her presence but doesn't want to be bothered with her. Meanwhile, Sis is determined to make her presence known. Bree knows her wheels are turning because she can see it in her eyes. Before ole girl can muster up the courage to walk towards him, Bree goes and blocks her view.

"Hey there," Bree says a friendly tone while tapping Reggie's arm.

"There you are, mingling away aren't you."

"Yeah, haven't seen some of my peeps in a minute. Must admit it feels good to get out. Thanks for the nudge."

"My pleasure, wouldn't want to be here with anyone else, or alone for that matter."

"Is that so,"

"What's wrong?" he asks, sensing the uneasiness in her voice.

"Six o'clock. Who is she?"

Reggie gives the nervous laugh that she's heard before.

"A girlfriend, an ex, a fuck? What?" Bree continues

"Does it matter?"

"Kind of does. She's been eyeing you since we got here. I'm sure she's going to make her way over here and I need to know how to play this."

"Just be yourself"

"Just tell me. Dude, we're not together if she's a fuck say it. You know about mine."

"Yeah she is...and don't lead with Dude." He cautions. He let it slide before but he doesn't like it.

Bree rolls her eyes at the request. "Cool," she says in a calm voice. "Got it!"

"Hey Reg," a voice from behind him blurts out.

"Don", Reggie greets, going in with a handshake. "This is Brianna. Bree this is my homie Don."

"Nice to meet you," Bree smiles but is unenthused by the lackluster introduction.

"How is the man treating you, good guy you have right here." Don vouches for Reggie while patting his back.

"He's alright," Bree gives a playful side-eye. "I'll be back," Bree looks to Reggie and grabs his belt buckle. "Kiss," she leans in. Reggie complies and gives Bree a quick peck on the lips.

As she proceeds to walk away, Reggie grabs her waist and whispers in her ear, "No need to mark your territory."

Bree continues with her brisk pace walking away from him heading straight to the bathroom. She needs to go and take a breather not knowing what's in store. She's uncertain about his remark, while she wants to accept it as reassuring banter, his tone did not put her at ease. There is most certainly a need to mark territory. They are here together on a date and his side piece that is about to get a rude awakening is in the building. That kiss should put her in her place or expedite the statement that she needs to hear. Either will work for Bree, she just wants fuck buddy out of their space. If things take a turn for the worse, then Bree knows her plan. She just hopes that he plays into it.

Lo and behold when she finally makes it back in the mix, she sees Fuck Buddy all up in his face. They are standing at the bar heavily engaged in a conversation. It looks as if Reggie is not making a statement he is more or so making excuses. She watches for a moment before she makes her move to find Nia. She doesn't have to go far because Nia is looking for her.

"Who is that bitch all up in Reggie's face?" she asks immediately.

"One of his friends or some shit. It's cool." Bree says trying to act unbothered.

"It's not cool. She is flirting big time I can see that shit clear across the room. Go and nip that shit in the bud, NOW!" she demands.

That is just the push Bree needs to do what she already wants to do. With that, she heads over their way to extinguish the flames. Or at the very least try to. She's not up for acting a fool in public and besides she and Reggie aren't together, so she figures she'd keep it short and sweet.

"Hey," she says looking directly at Reggie while ignoring the girl and interrupting their conversation. Before she gives him a chance to fumble over himself she says, "I'm going to make my rounds and then I'll be heading up out of here." With that she takes the drink from his hand and places it on the bar. "Designated driver," she mumbles as she runs her index finger across his chin.

"Cool," Is all he manages to get out as his eyes follow her behind her departure when Bree calmly walks away.

Nia is on her heels, "What. The. Hell. Was. That? He is supposed to leave with you."

"Nia I can't make that man do anything he doesn't want to do. I told you she's a friend and I'm cool."

"Want me to go and say something."

"NO! Let's get this last dance in because he's about to take to me home."

Nia gives her the eye that means she knows Bree is lying. But to avoid going back and forth she agrees to the last dance and doesn't utter another word about Reggie.

Once the song is over Bree goes to make her rounds getting ready to head out. Reggie isn't coming to look for her, and she doesn't have to go far to look for him. He is in the same spot talking and drinking. So Bree requests a Lyft to lift her the hell up out of there.

# CHAPTER 11

The car ride gives Bree time to think things over and put everything into perspective. She and Reggie aren't dating. Aren't fucking for that matter, this is probably the reason why they aren't. She tries to check her feelings and find a lane to put herself into no avail. The whole scene was hurtful and could have very much been avoided had she just stayed home. She wonders how long will it take for him to come and chase after her, if he cares enough to chase.

Once in the house she pins her hair up to try to preserve her curls for tomorrow and takes a nice long hot shower. As much as she tries to get her mind off of Reggie she can't. She wants to call and curse him out. She wants to scream, she wants answers, but why? That's the question she can't answer. There is nothing to her and Reggie but clouds of magnetic emotions hovering over a non-existent relationship.

Her nightly routine goes off without a hiccup. She thought for sure, she'd be interrupted by a call, a text or something. She goes downstairs to drink her tea to calm her nerves and her mind in hopes that she will be able to get to sleep tonight. As soon as she makes it to the kitchen a text comes through:

*Where are you?*

*Home!* Her reply and she leaves it at that. Pedal to the metal is an understatement for how fast Reggie had to be flying to make it to her house within twenty minutes. Just as Bree is about to take her cup upstairs the doorbell rings.

"Why did you leave?" he asks, pushing past her inviting himself in. "Didn't I tell you I was bringing you home? If I take you somewhere, then you don't leave without me." He keeps on with his rant.

Bree turns and starts walking towards the kitchen without a word. She is not going to engage in a shouting match, especially not over this. Clearly, he's wrong.

"Don't walk away from me." He continues with his demands.

"I can hear that shit your yelling in the kitchen because you're loud as fuck," she says.

The nonchalant tone is making him more upset as Bree continues on her path to the kitchen.

He follows behind her and sits on the barstool next to her. Bree is facing the refrigerator, but she can feel him staring at her face.

"I've been looking for you for over thirty minutes. Why did you just up and leave?" he asks in a more mild tone. Not completely controlled but not raging.

Bree is sipping on her tea unbothered by his fiasco. When he doesn't say anything else she turns and gives him her undivided attention.

"Say something." He encourages in hopes to get some answers.

"I'm not talking to you like this. You're loud and I have neighbors." She says peacefully. "And I'm surely not talking to you with that," she points.

"What?"

"I'm about to touch you," she announces as not to startle him. "That," she says as she quickly touches the vein that is bulging from his neck. "Come here," she grabs his hand and walks him to the mirror in the hall. She flicks on the light and places him in front of the mirror. "See that?" she asks. "That's the crazy vein. Get rid of it." And she steps to the side for him to stare at his reflection.

Reggie stands in the mirror looking at himself like he's never seen this before and he hasn't. No one has ever talked to him calmly when he was having one of his moments. Bree walks him back to the kitchen but this time she sits him on a chair at the kitchen table. She mounts him so they are chest to chest and she begins to breathe slowly. When Reggie catches on to what she wants him to do, he matches her breathing. Bree then starts caressing his body trying to get him to relax. As she feels the tension leaving his body she grabs his face and kisses him as passionately as she always does. She places her forehead and his and waits. After about three minutes has passed she gets up, grabs her tea and sits next to him at the kitchen table.

"What time is it?" she asks him breaking the silence and forcing him to open his eyes.

"Huh?"

"The time, what time is it?" she asks again.

"12:45" he answers slowly while looking at his watch. He is unsure of where this is going.

"Ok, so you come in here an hour and fifteen minutes after the time I tell you I wanted to be home beating on your chest like a maniac asking me questions regarding my whereabouts. When clearly I told you that I wanted to be home by 11:30, anytime after that time should tell you that I would be home."

"Brianna that's not the point, the point is that I told you I was bringing you home and you left without a word."

"I do recall telling you that I was making my rounds and then I was heading out. Remember?"

"Yeah, but I thought that you were going to come back and get me."

"Why would I? That wasn't my responsibility. Does your boss wake you up every morning or are you responsible to show up to work on time?" she asks in a condescending manner. "Furthermore, I took your drink from you because you were to drive me home. I look back at and you're sipping away. Gamble with your own life." She looks at him with a serious face. Yeah he may not have been drunk and yes he made it there safely, but that's not the point. Bree rationalizes in her head. "Look I'm not fucking you tonight, so I wasn't going to mess up your possibility of getting some. Guess you were right," she agrees "Marking my territory didn't matter." She huffs

"So, that's the issue that I was talking to her about ?"

"No, you missed the point. Better yet, if you want to think so, then go ahead. Remember you are the man that was mad that I was texting another man, but proceeds to talk to another woman in my face." She says dismissively. "Know what? I need to get to sleep so we can talk about this in the morning or not, doesn't matter."

"I'm trying to figure out the problem. Why couldn't you just come and get me and all of this could have been avoided."

"All of this could have been avoided a number of ways. First, I didn't even want to go. Second, I offered to take my own vehicle. Lastly, even though I didn't have to, I told you I was making my rounds giving you a heads up on the time." She pauses to see if that makes an impact. When there is still silence she continues to try to make herself clear, "Once you asked me to come and not to bring my own vehicle I became your responsibility. I told you I wanted to be home by 11:30 and you said that you could do that. Then when I told you I was making my rounds, instead of ending your conversation and coming with me, you stayed and showed what is more important. You should have set a reminder, checked your watch every two minutes. I don't know. What I do know is we showed up at that party around 9, we only had two hours to play with at best. But no, you lost track of time and now you're blaming all this on me. Even after I disclosed how I need to wind down to go to sleep. So miss me with the bullshit. And if the situation isn't already fucked up, I told you I need to be to sleep by 1 and here you are showing up to my house at 12:45. No regards whatsoever." She dismisses him again. "Then you don't even lead with an apology, you come at me in an accusatory manner." She says in a disappointing voice. She is not about to sit here and let him place the blame on her.

"You're right. I apologize. I lost track of time and it was my responsibility to get you home. I don't know what to say."

"You didn't have to say anything. You could have apologized and took your ass home. I'm a big girl and I can handle myself. Am I upset I had to pay someone to bring me home when I have the means to? Yes, am I going to lose sleep over it, no! Are you staying or going because I'm going to bed." She rises to make known that the conversation is over.

"I'll stay." Is all he manages to get out.

"Good night, I'm leaving around 6:15 in the morning."

"Ok. Good night."

With that, Bree put her cup in the dishwasher, set her house alarm and headed upstairs.

# CHAPTER 12

Both Bree and Reggie tossed and turned throughout the night contemplating whether either of them would make the first move to cuddle together. Neither of them made the move which made the night last that much longer. When Bree finally gets out of the bed around 4:30 she realizes that she may have had more sleep than Reggie. She wakes to a text message from him that was sent at 3:47 it reads:

*I feel so small right now. I am embarrassed and ashamed that I let myself neglect my responsibilities, renege on my word and showed up at your home acting an ass. For that, I sincerely apologize. It would be a disservice to skim over the fact that you've held your composure. Your patience was and is appreciated. You could have handled this situation in various ways, yet you displayed maturity and tact as I was being juvenile. Thank you. I hope that you can forgive me.*

Bree throws her phone onto the bed and begins to prep as she is going to commit to her daily routine. Had he led with an apology all of this could have gone more smoothly. While she's sure she can hold her own, his attitude does cause her a little concern. She's not for the arguing and fussing at all, and especially not if her son will be in the house. As many thoughts run through her mind she goes downstairs to outrun them on the treadmill. About fifteen minutes into her run she hears Reggie moving about in the guest room. Moments later he peeks his head into the den to see what woke him from his slumber. Bree makes brief eye contact and redirects her attention back to the monitor resting on the treadmill. With earbuds in, she'd figured that he would retreat and leave her alone. He did just that. There is no sound travelling to her ears. She is reading subtitles to the motivational speech that she is watching. After last night Bree needs to find a way to recharge and get her head back in the game.

"Good morning," she says as she taps on the door making her way into the room to face Reggie.

She stands in the door frame not wanting to go completely into the room. Besides the fact that she has sweat dripping and she most likely looks a mess, she wants to head to the kitchen to get a drink of water.

"Good morning," he replies. "How did you sleep?"

"Restlessly." Is the quick short answer she gives. "I unset the alarm, so feel free whenever you're ready." She makes the implication emotionlessly.

"Come here." He says as he sits on the edge of the bed.

Against how she said she would handle this interaction, she hesitantly walks towards him. She stops just short of an arm's length distance. Reggie leans forward and grabs her arm to pull her closer.

"I'm sweaty" she makes known as if it's not obvious or better yet as if that's the reason that she is being distant.

"I'm sorry."

"I've read." She snaps back.

"Are you still upset? We can talk about it."

"No, I'm over it."

"No you're not." He challenges knowing that she's lying

"I'm at a loss. What do you want me to say? That I forgive you?"

"That would be nice, but more importantly what's on your mind."

"It's like beating a dead horse. I've said all I had to say last night. If you lack the comprehension skills to sift through what I said and make something of it, then that's not my problem."

He takes a deep breath along with the jab. Something that he's not used to doing.

"What do I have to do?" he asks, giving in and not wanting to get into another argument.

"Start with basic care and respect. That'll get you far." she pauses. "Look, I'm not a party girl never have been." She begins to explain. "I go out every once in a while. And I'm not saying this so you have to cater to me and stay at home. Quite the opposite, I'm disclosing this because I need you to know that there will be times that I don't want to go anywhere and if I do, I may stay for an hour or two like last night. If you want to stay and mingle, then be my guest. However, respect my decision not to. Maybe we need to engage in meet up dates if you are going to continue to lose track of time. Because one thing is for sure, that when I'm ready to leave; I am going to leave. But what pissed me off is the fact that you knew the reason I was leaving. It isn't a bitchy empty request, like I am trying to control you or end your night of having a good time. It is a legitimate reason and still that meant nothing. That was like a slap in the face honestly."

"I get that and Brianna I apologize. I should have been more mindful. You told me the deal and I agreed and didn't follow through. I don't want you to think that I don't care or respect you though. That's a bit on the deep end. It was an honest mistake that I will ensure does not happen again. I just don't want this to be a reason for you to kind of push me to the side and not trust me."

"The whole situation wasn't okay, but I'm okay."

"Are you sure?"

"Yes," she assures him.

He grabs her and begins to hug her damp body. "Ewww, stop. I'm sweaty."

"So," he says as he places a soft kiss on her lips. "I care for you," he whispers as he continues to hold her in his embrace.

This is hard for Bree to believe. They just met and he hasn't even gotten her into the bed yet. But he cares for her. She has to take things slow with him, because it seems that he's blowing smoke.

"Want some breakfast?" is Bree's response to the comment. She'd rather eat real food and not his tasteless confessions.

"Sure, do you mind if I shower?"

"You have clean clothes?"

"In my car."

"So you knew you were staying the night" Bree asks, giving him the side-eye.

"No, but I keep a gym bag in my car, just in case I have to burn steam after work."

"Uhm, huh. Ok. I don't mind."

\*\*\*

"Your hair looks cute, beautiful," Reggie compliments as he walks into the kitchen.

"This is the result of my hair not looking like it did last night." Bree points to the messy bun on top of head. "But thank you," she smiles. "Now do you see why I wear wigs?" she asks looking for some approval for her investments.

"No"

"Well," she continues as she reaches for the bowl. "This is not a traditional breakfast. I am making shrimp for my lunch salad and decided to be lazy," she says as she sits the bowl of piping hot shrimp and grits in front of him.

"I'm not complaining," he says.

"Excuse me," she says as she grabs her phone. "Good morning,"

"Bree Boogie, good morning, good morning. What are you doing? Have you talked to your moms?" Manny asks with excitement in his voice like he has been up for hours and it's about 4 in the morning in California. She can bet he's on his way to the gym.

"I'm getting ready for work and what type of question is that this time of morning or more realistically, ever?" Bree asks because Manny knows she doesn't talk to her mother like that. "I'm going to go out on a limb here and guess that you've talked to her and you want to share what ya'll talked about," she continues sarcastically.

"Yeah, your sister got evicted and had to move in with her. Bottom line money troubles."

"Bottom line you gave it to her?" Bree says unmoved. Manny always gives in to her mother.

"Coffee, OJ, water..." Bree let her voice trail off as she's looking at Reggie.

"OJ please."

"Whoa wait a minute. Is Mr. Reggie there eating breakfast? Somebody's downplaying something and I won't say who and what."

"Mind yo damn business." Bree chuckles.

"Do I need to meet Mr. Reggie?" he asks playfully.

"Nope. Not there yet. But huh did you tell me all you had to tell me? Or is there more?"

"You can get back to your Boo, Junior and Sam lands around 7, be there or be square."

"I'll be there. Have him call me when he wakes up."

"Will do! Bye fast ass."

"Bye!"

"Let me clear the air." Bree says wanting to nip her and Manny's friendship in the bud, as it has been the cause of her relationship downfalls. "Manny's and I relationship is different in that,"

"You guys are friends," he interrupts with a mouth full of food.

"Yeah, you're good?"

"Yes, you told me the story. There was no romance between the two of you. I'm assuming that he killed your previous relationships?"

"Yes," Bree let out a sigh of relief, she's happy that he's understanding about it all.

"I can see how. Calling you whenever just to chat, not really talking about ya'll son and the conversation flows." He makes known. "If I didn't know the history, then I would probably have a problem too." He admits

"I'm trying to take a different approach with you. I've been told that I was guarded and secretive when it comes to him. And I'm not denying that I did have my ways. I didn't talk to him in front of people I've dated, he didn't know their name and a select few knew him, so it looked suspicious. I'm trying to be open and transparent with you. If ever you feel uncomfortable, then please let me know."

"Will do." He confirms. "Gosh! That was delicious." he changes subjects

Bree is not sure how to take his demeanor. Is he really that easy going about this or is he hiding his feelings to bring it up in a later conversation. Only time will tell.

"Why thank you," she bows. "Well, it's about that time that I head up out of here and watch lives enter the world," she smiles at the thoughts of the many births she's seen in such a short time. No matter what, it never gets old as it's always a unique, joyous and refreshing occasion.

"What time does your son come in?"

"They land around 7, why? What's up?"

"Can you come and see me after work? I'm not sure of the next time I will see you again."

"I can do that," Bree smiles as she walks over towards him.

After a passionate kiss he looks at her, "You are like no woman I've ever met before."

"And you sir are a loser," she tries to say in a genuine tone but snickers follows.

"A pretty lady told me that once," he grabs her face and laughs.

# CHAPTER 13

The ride to Reggie's house seems like a road trip across the country. Bree is so tired that she is barely alert on the road. If only she didn't tell him she was coming, then she could have already been in her bed snoring right now. Unlike her last visit, she does not need to call and announce her arrival. She knows exactly what to do to make it to his front door.

After a soft tap, Reggie opens the door with no shirt and no words. He immediately grabs Bree and closes the door. From the kisses that she's receiving she knows that he is hungry and she's on the menu. He unbuttons her shirt while trying to lead her to the bedroom. Bree tiredness exits her body as fast as arousal enters. Not knowing how fast he is working, Bree is in a bra and panties before leaving the kitchen, the bedroom is just too far away at this point. Reggie puts her on the sofa. Bree is trying to insist to be the one in charge trying to make him sit, he makes it known that he is to be the headliner right now. She senses the urgency radiating from his body, but he is taking his time. He's kissing every part of her body as he inspects it with lustful eyes. With every kiss, Bree's body is sinking further into ecstasy. Her breathing is slow and sultry. Soft moans are offered to let him know that she is enjoying the treatment she is receiving. As every second goes by, she is craving for him to be inside her, yet he insists on letting her silently cry for his manhood. He finally reaches the lips that he's been waiting to kiss since laying eyes on her, the lips that no one gets to see and after this no one else will be able to touch. Bree lays in total satisfaction as her body hasn't been touched like this before. The passion between the two of them is something she's never felt and the chemistry they share is as if they've known each other forever. He knows exactly how to touch her. He's navigating her body as if he studied a map and memorized it for this very moment. He stops short of her climaxing to keep the anticipation going. He comes eye to eye with her and begins to kiss her as he thrusts his manhood deeply inside of her. They both let out a sigh of satisfaction as if this is the moment they each have been waiting for their whole life; and it was worth the wait. As he strokes, Bree is trying to take it in stride, but he is bigger than she's had. She grabs his back and buries her face in his neck to try to ease the tension. "Relax, I got you," he whispers in her ear and he changes his stroke. The more Bree allows herself to relax, the better it's beginning to feel. Every inch of him is massaging her insides gently. When her back arches he knows he found her spot and he teases her until she can't take it anymore. "Don't stop," is all she repeats as he keeps moving about. The sound of her sexual cries is turning him on more and more. Knowing that he wants to release he follows her advice and lets her cum. The throbbing of her walls pulsating on his manhood is a new exciting feeling for him. He knows that when he reaches his climax he is going to go as deep as he can to release, with that he kisses Bree to take her mind off of the pleasurable pain she's about to endure. "Ahhhhh!" she let out a gratifying cry.

Hot, sweaty with their hearts racing they lay on the couch caressing each other with their eyes closed. "Let's go to bed," Bree insists as the sleep monster has returned, throwing sand in her eyes. She doesn't like couch sleep especially after a long day of work.

Reggie doesn't utter a word but begins moving in agreement. He picks up as many items as he can and carries them into his room. Bree is already snuggled under the covers. He slips in and wraps her in his arms. Bree doesn't remember him climbing in bed or falling to sleep, but she wakes up to the sound of someone knocking on the door.

"Hey," she nudges, "Reggie, someone is at the door."

Reggie reluctantly gets up and heads to answer the door. As much as Bree wants to be nosey, she drifts back off to sleep, because her body has shut down.

The commotion in the front room has awakened her out of her sleep again, and Bree knows that she definitely hears a woman's voice. She sits up completely to ensure that she doesn't doze back off. All she hears is, "I have to pop up to get a response from you? I called and text you all fucking night. Just tell me where you were last night." After a moment of silence, the voice continues, "You know what it's cool. I have always been down for you and you continuously treat me like shit. You blew me off for Toya, then this Shannon shows up and now you're out and about with another chick. I told you I'm tired of this back and forth. I want a commitment Reggie!"

"Just go," is all Reggie offers after her whole spill.

Bree has begun to put her clothes on because she's leaving and she wants to make her exit so that she can see the person in the other room. She runs through her mind all the names and faces she knows thus far. Toya, ex-fiance, Shannon, unknown, but could very well be fuck buddy because she doesn't know her name. And now this woman. What has she gotten herself into?

As she exits the room, who does she see? Fuck buddy! That threw a monkey wrench into her whole vibe. Reggie is such a liar. No wonder why he couldn't pull away from her last night.

Reggie's face looks like here we go and Bree is unsure if it's on her part or this other woman.

"I can't sleep with this commotion, I'm going home." Bree announces, but directs her comment towards Reggie.

"That bitch, I thought you didn't fuck with her Reggie," the woman yells. Her anger level is rising.

"Whoa," Reggie begins, but Bree cuts him off.

"Wait a minute," Bree says, taking a break from putting on her other shoe. "Don't you ever disrespect me again or I will clean this floor with your face. I'm not sure why I'm the topic of ya'll discussions but my name is Brianna if you need to use it."

"Is she threatening me?" the woman looks to Reggie and asks in an appalling manner.

"I was being considerate and extending your ass a warning, but if you take it as a threat so be it!" Bree states.

With that she grabs her keys and walks through the space between them. Reggie grabs her arm to attempt to stop her but it doesn't even slow her down.

"Clean up your shit, Just Reggie," Bree demands as she leaves out of the door. As soon as she hears the door click behind her she lets out an exhausting sigh. She cannot believe that after all the people that she could have given a chance to, she gave a chance to the not so eligible bachelor of Houston. If she could beat her own ass, then she would.

Transparency gets you looking like a fool. Now she'll have to hear Manny's mouth about this for at least a month inquiring about Reggie.

Once she makes it into the house, she is not mad that she's here. She can shower and get herself together before heading to the airport. The only thing that worries her is Reggie showing up to her door bellowing his less than valid concerns. She doesn't want Junior to witness that.

Bree scrubs her body because she wants to scrub his alluring scent from her skin. She wants no traces of him on her, that's the least that can happen since the thoughts are taking over her mind. The more she scrubs the more she realizes that it seems the scent is affixed to her nose hairs, she can't get rid of it. As she hears cars pass up and down the street her hearts racing wondering if it's Reggie. Her heart hopes it's him, but her mind can do without seeing his face ever again. Her heart wants to hear the plea for forgiveness, the promise it will never happen again and the assurance that the other woman is out of the picture. Her mind destroys the wishful thinking, acknowledging that if that does happen, his ass is lying. Her heart skips a beat as she hears what she thinks is a car pulling into her driveway. After a moment, her hopes are snatched from her

because no one is at her door. She stands and let the water runoff her body and down the drain hoping it takes her feelings with it. What's the avenue of her approach? When the conversation is had today, or someday in the near future, what will she say? What will she allow herself to believe? Does she even want to waste any more time on this courtship that failed to launch? And this here is why Bree stood clear of relationships. The mental gymnastics is not worth it. After about five minutes has passed she hears a car door close. Not wanting to get her hopes up again she ignores it, but moments later her doorbell rings. She relaxes herself and begins to make her exit from the shower. The doorbell rings again, accompanied by her phone ringing. She dries off enough not to drip water all through the house and wraps her towel around her. Making her way downstairs her heart is softening with every beat. When she opens the door she wants to jump in his arms, she wants him to caress her body like he did hours ago. She wants to forget all that has happened and smile. Instead she says, "Come, I need to get dressed," in a cheerful manner as if she doesn't have a care in the world.

Reggie follows behind Bree as he's going upstairs for the first time. He doesn't utter a word because he doesn't know what to say or where to begin. He sits on the bedroom bench and throws his phone onto the bed. Bree drops the towel and finds some undergarments to cover herself with. The silence is excruciating but she doesn't want to be the one to utter the first word.

"I apologize," Reggie leads with an apology first this time. "It was not intended for you to go through that."

"I understand. You can't control people. She came under her own will." Bree says. He clearly didn't know she was coming. Bree's trying to be cordial about this but realizes that she just threw him some ammo in this battle.

"And then calling you out your name," he continues.

"Took care of that," Bree reminds him.

"You could have stayed."

"Why do you insist I stay in situations where I'm unwanted? Stay for what? For her to have uttered some more disrespectful shit and I have to punch her in the face. Sorry, that's not me anymore. I have a child and I'd be no good for him in jail."

"No! I wouldn't allow that to happen. And stay to stand your ground. You were invited there."

"Stand what ground? You said you don't fuck with me, so had I stayed my words held no weight."

"That's not what I said," he defends.

"But you didn't refute it when it came from her, so let's just go with you did say it. And it's cool. Because technically we're not together, so no you don't fuck with me, you just wanted to fuck me."

"Is that what you think? That all I wanted to do was sleep with you? Brianna if I wanted you for just a fuck, then I would have fucked you the first night." He spits in a cocky demeanor. "And why do you always have to make known that we're not together. No we haven't officially made any commitments, but Bree you know you would be lying if you said that moving towards a relationship isn't implied."

"Yet you're entertaining her and who knows who else."

"Nobody," he begins.

"Shannon," she refreshes his memory with the name that has been thrown into thin air.

"I don't talk to her anymore." He says with disgust like she left a bad taste in his mouth. "Shannon is long gone. She is the woman that Toya thought I was leaving her for."

"Ok," Bree says leaving it alone.

"Anything else you need to know?"

"Why are you here?"

"Brianna stop playing. You know I'm here because I want things to be right with us. Again, I thought we were moving forward in making what we have a solid relationship."

"Why can't I fit any of my jeans!?!?!?" Bree cries out to the ceiling as she's attempting to pull the jeans around her ass while also letting him know that she doesn't want to hear his shit. "I'm going to live life in sweat and yoga pants." She gives in, throwing the jeans in the corner and retrieving some yoga pants from her drawer. "Things are good between us," she says after she gets her pants on. She makes her way to sit on the bed to put her socks on. Normally, she would sit on the bedroom bench but she doesn't want to sit next to him.

"Well I was coming to apologize and ensure that they are."

Reggie's phone gets Bree's attention as it lights up across the bed. A text message notification comes across the screen:

CeeCee: FIRST OF ALL MUTHA...

Is all that Bree is able to view because six messages come in back to back. This girl is reading him for filth, Bree is sure of it. Her petty meter is to the max wanting to get some popcorn and watch this go down like a highlighted scene in a reality TV show. Instead she chooses to live in her reality and address the matter.

"How did the conversation end?" Bree pries to see if he would tell the truth.

"I told her not to call me anymore."

"BULLSHIT!" she says as she stands up from the bed.

"I did," he defends.

"Well why is she texting you?"

Reggie looks at his phone on the bed and takes a deep breath. He reaches for the phone and key in his password. He begins reading the lengthy message without a word. He looks to Bree knowing he needs to do something to make this right. He clicks the phone icon at the top of the message screen and hits the speaker.

"That's what I have to do to get you to call me. You are a piece of work Reggie." CeeCee yells.

"Didn't I ask you not to call me anymore?"

"You don't mean that shit, I don't know why I keep going in these circles with you. One minute, you all up my ass then the next I catch you with other chicks. What's it going to be?"

"Didn't I ask you not to call me anymore?" he asks again in a trying tone wanting to keep his composure for more reasons than one.

"So the fuck what!" she continues to yell.

"Didn't I ask you not to call me anymore?" he asks, yet again.

Bree is beginning to think that this is all he is going to say. Yes he may have said it, but he sure isn't enforcing it at the moment.

"Well I didn't call you, you called me. I texted you."

"Well don't fucking text him either damn," Bree finally opens her mouth. "Do you really need it spelled out for you? Don't. Contact. Him. Anymore."

"You got me on speaker phone?" CeeCee asks in shock. "Fuck you, Reggie."

"I'm handling that too," Bree says sarcastically.

*Click.*

"Thank you," Reggie lets out a sigh of relief as if Bree intervening meant she was on his side.

"That wasn't for you," Bree makes known. "Her voice is fucking annoying."

She brushes past him and goes to the dresser to put on her accessories.

"How are we in such a mess? It feels like we've known each other forever."

"It's been a week," she reminds him in a short snippy voice.

"I know what it's been, but it feels longer."

Bree can't deny that. They hit it off right away, they are able to talk about anything and the inside jokes are plentiful. They do mesh really well and it seems as if they've known each other forever. Reality is though it's only been a week.

"Yeah, but it's only been a week," she says again. "And we're in a mess because apparently your life is a mess." She offers an explanation.

Reggie takes the jab and gets up and walks behind Bree. "Here," he reaches his phone to her.

She looks at his reflection in the mirror and mumble between her lips as she's holding her earring post there, "What do you want me to do with that?"

"Scrub it!"

"I don't want to do your dirty work." She says clearly as she has removed the post from her lips.

"Fair enough. I would do a factory reset, but I don't know anyone's phone number," he lets off a light chuckle.

Something Bree could agree with. She only knows about three people's number by heart and that's because they have the same number from back when you had to memorize numbers to make calls. She doesn't extend the olive branch though and continues to look at him. He wraps her in his embrace.

"Do you care about me,"

"Maybe,"

He looks at her reflection in the mirror because he wants a serious answer.

"Yes," she assures him knowing he's waiting for it.

"How much?" he asks as he spins her around to face him.

"Enough that you're here after what happened last night and today."

He grabs her arms from her side and wraps them around his neck. He encourages her to stand on her tiptoes and he leans in for a kiss.

"I love all of this," he says as he is caressing her thighs and ass. "Especially this," he smacks and grabs her ass cheeks in his hands.

Giving the looks of CeeCee, Bree knows he's been missing some ass in his world. CeeCee is slim and has a nice shape, she just can't fill in any jeans or have defining curves to make a dress pop.

"Keep it all right here." He says as if he read Bree mind that she needs to shed the pounds she's gained over the summer. "Sign me up as a financial contributor of the new jeans fund."

"Well you're about to be missing all of this if you don't get your shit together." Bree threatens.

"I know and I don't want to have to think about it because you're mine." He says as he picks her up. "Come take a ride." He says seductively.

"As bad as I want to," Bree admits. "I need a rain check. I have to go."

He turns and looks at the clock. "You have time, they have to wait for bags...."

"There are no bags, he lives here and there. I have to go. I'm sorry." She says sincerely as she jumps down out of his arms.

"When will I see you again?"

"I can call the sitter and see if she's available this week and we can go out. What days are you available?"

"Whenever you are free."

"Don't start that." She warns. "That's a dangerous play."

"Touche'" he agrees. "Thursday or Friday"

"Cool, I'll let you know."

# CHAPTER 14

"Good morning, Lady bug." Latrice says to Bree as she walks onto the floor. Latrice is in her early forties and has been doing labor and delivery for years. She probably should retire and become a school or at home nurse but she loves her job too much to part with it. She's one of the first nurses to befriend Bree when she came to day shift about three months ago. She has a sisterly yet motherly vibe to her.

"Goooooood morning," Bree sings with the brightest smile on her face.

"Uh oh, new comer alert that smile is too bright for anything else." Latrice says tapping John.

"Ooh yes, gawd. Someone should be a noodle because her back should be blown all the way out." He agrees in his sassiest voice.

"Whatever, let's have some couth about us shall we," Bree rolls her eyes to fix her attention to the white board. "What's going on today?"

"Couth activated until noon. Couth squad unite!" John says extending his fist for Latrice to bump; and she did just that.

"Well we have two for sure that will be coming before three. One scheduled for labor induction and McKinney, room five, came last night, but she is ready to pop I tell ya." Latrice addresses the nature of their business.

"So when are we going to get the dets?" John asks with his fist props up on the desk.

"Well we all can't go to lunch together, so never is the only option." Bree teases.

"No, no, no, you are not getting away that easy, when Crazy Craig was in the mix ya'll were pressuring me every day for updates like I was on a VH1 show. You are going to spill these beans, sweep them up, heat them up and serve those babies." Latrice laughs. "Dust bunnies and all."

Bree knew that she wouldn't get away that easy as discussing everyone's romantic rendezvous is always the highlight of the shift. Actually helps them get through it faster.

"Well he damn sure ain't no Crazy Craig," Bree laughs.

"That you know of chile, because Crazy Craig was just Craig at first too," John warns, rolling his eyes to look at Latrice.

"Amen!" Latrice agrees.

"Well I have referenced him as a crazy ass, but he's not Craig crazy, I'll tell ya that." Bree makes known. Damn if Latrice didn't have to get the law involved on their relationship. Craig is currently on probation and served with a protection order that doesn't expire for a year.

"He's an amazing piece of work." she smiles getting back to Reggie's personality. One thing she is not about to do is disclose the less than smooth sailing weekend they had. She'd much rather focus on his good attributes and the sex. "He's about 6"2, dark chocolate, secured job, own place, own vehicle, no kids, never married, and hit all the right places; a dream come true." She loses herself in her words.

John is staring off into space as well as if he's trying to picture his Prince Charming. "Girl if he's not for you, then I can turn that man into my man."

"You think you have the golden rod that will turn any straight man crooked," Latrice swiftly pops his bubble. "I've seen that little raw pecker of yours and ain't nobody checking for that," she laughs.

"You know what," he looks and Latrice and gathers his things. "I know plenty who like it. I'm doing my rounds." He says as he walks away.

"That was cold Trice," Bree laughs. "You know he's sensitive about his peen."

"Girl he's always going after someone's man, it's sickening."

"He's just joking, Trice."

"Well dammit, then so was I."

With that they both split to do some work. Bree knows why this is such a delicate situation for Trice. The guy who she thought was her best friend used her to get next to her brother. And if that wasn't bad enough, the best friend didn't even want her brother, he wanted to out him; he did so by releasing a sex tape for the whole world to see. Talking about a Jerry Springer episode.

All day as Bree moves about she can't get Reggie off of her mind. She wants to see him tonight but knows that is out of the question. Between Junior's basketball practice which she is still planning on taking him to although he can't play, and getting him to bed Bree knows that she will be knocked out right behind him. They have such a routine. It's a gift and a curse. Bree mind is racing trying to find ways for her and Reggie to spend time the three weeks that Junior is home. The easy answer would be just introduce him to Manny and forget prolonging the inevitable. But the scary thing is she doesn't know if this will last and she doesn't want to expose her son to random dudes every couple of months. Dating with kids is such a difficult task and Bree chose to avoid it since Junior was born. However, she can't continue to live her life like this. One day Junior is going to be an adult out of the house and she refuses to be alone and lonely. If she doesn't start investing into her love life now, she'll be alone forever. Manny is very open to the idea of Junior meeting men that Bree dates. His take on it; Junior is not looking for a father figure or "Dad" he has one. And that my friends, is the end of that! He believes it's as simple as that. Like there will not be attachments or feelings. If only it were easy, then all of these blended families would go off without a hitch. Bree talks herself into trying to keep Reggie at bay at least until Junior leaves next month. Manny will have him extra days giving his doctor's appointment is in the middle of the week, so they will be able to make up for all the time they're losing. Her only concern is how long will Reggie wait before he calls one of his follow-ups.

# CHAPTER 15

Bree and Latrice are sitting in the employee's lounge waiting to get started on their shift. John comes busting through the door with a brisk walk, his hand at the ready, his lips perched and his eyes read guess the fuck what.

"It's too early for you to be bringing a damn bone." Bree dismisses shaking her head. Not at six thirty in the morning.

"Don't nobody want to talk to you anyway, Ms. I don't gossip. I'm sure you already know because you know everything, you just don't tell." He scolds.

"Those that bring bones, take bones." Bree replies letting him know why she doesn't run her mouth.

"Well, Latrice," he says rolling his neck and enunciating her name. "Girl, Bree's friend is pregnant."

"Who?" Bree chimes in because she hasn't received any announcements.

"Mind your business," he says looking at Bree. "Cheyanne," he says to Latrice.

"For once, you are carrying some positive news. That's awesome! I have to tell her congrats."

"Wait! You didn't know?" he looked at Bree surprisingly. "Well that's not the good shit anyway. Do you know who her Baby Daddy is? That's the real question?"

"If I didn't know she is pregnant, then why would I know that bit of information?" Bree quizzes.

"Dr. Simms," he says proudly as he has been waiting to say that since he entered the room.

"Shut up!" Latrice finally opens her mouth.

"Now, John. Don't do that," Bree says in a serious tone. "This gossip is damaging. They both have professional careers that need to be protected."

"Well Ms. I want to look out for everyone and protect their shit, it's not gossip it's true."

"And how do you know? It doesn't matter." She quickly follows her question, throwing up her hands. "I'm getting out of here. I want no parts of this conversation. See you guys on the floor." Bree dismisses herself from the conversation and exits the room.

Bree can bet that John and Latrice think she left because she doesn't like to gossip and they would be partly correct. John's words brought a thick cloud of air that Bree couldn't inhale. Was Jason fucking Cheyanne when he and Bree were sneaking around? Did he have Bree moved to get her out of their way? Was he playing her all along when she thought they had something special? Bree thought she took her heart back from Jason, but it seems that he is still within reach to scorch it. As bad as she wants answers to these questions she decides to leave it alone. Her mother always told her, it's best to leave some questions unanswered. This is one of those times where she feels that the advice fits perfectly. Jason answering any of these questions will not change their status, add or take away from their life. She is going to let him deal with his shit and she's going to keep moving along.

*We need to talk.* Is the text that Bree just receives from Jason on her way home. How ironic that when she hears this undesirable news he shows up in her inbox. Bree ignores the message and continues on with her routine. She is going to stop by the grocery store, pick Junior up and count down the moments until she and Reggie have their nighttime chat.

"Mom,"

"Yes, son."

"When am I getting this cast off? It itches in there. Can you scratch it?"

"Hopefully, next time you're with Dad if you healed well. It's not best to scratch it Junior you can tear your skin and risk infection. If it's moist under there, then I can blow some cool air down there with my blow dryer."

"Will it help?"

"It should, do you want to give it a try?"

"Yes."

Bree goes to retrieve the blow dryer and notices the flashing light on her phone.

*We need to talk, NOW!* Jason sends message number two.

Bree ignores him once again and attempts to help Junior relieve his itching feeling before she puts him to sleep.

"Hey there, how was your day," Reggie answers his phone.

"Long, I miss you."

"Is that right? Junior sleep?"

"I don't know if he's asleep just yet, but he's in his room."

"I am in bed comfortable," he throws out there.

"I wasn't hinting on you coming over here. I can't disclose that I miss you without wanting something."

"You can."

"Well act like it."

*STOP IGNORING ME! NOW IS NOT THE TIME!*

Bree reads Jason's message. Finally she decides to reply.

*Bree: What the fuck do you want?*

*Jason: We need to talk*

*Jason: face to face*

"What are you doing?" Reggie asks.

"Texting," Bree answers.

"Well call me back."

*Bree: Why*

*Jason: I'll tell you when I see you*

*Bree: Tomorrow*

*Jason: I'm on my way*

"I'm done damn." She snaps at Reggie and for no reason at all. She's upset that Jason is making his way over. This is why she hates when men know where she lives. They feel they have an open invitation to drop by when it's convenient for them.

"Who were you talking to?"

"Nobody."

"Okay nobody."

"Why are you in bed so early? You didn't wait for me." She switches topics.

"I didn't know that I was supposed to."

"You are," Bree let it be known.

"Next time. Send me a picture."

"No!"

"Why not? You mad?"

"Duh!" she sings. Usually their nightly routine consists of videos or pictures as they change for bed.

"It'll make you feel better," he pressures.

"It'll make you feel better, not me," she laughs at his attempt. "Planning to be here tomorrow night?" she asks. "You must be resting up for something."

"I can. I'm tired. Had a long week, I don't know how you hang. You have a child to take care of as well and I have less energy than you."

"I can't afford to be tired. Trust me… if I…. was in your shoes with….. no responsibility other than….. myself and work, I would be taking breaks too." Bree says in a choppy manner as she gets up to look out of the window because she hears a car pulling in the driveway. She looks out of the blinds and Jason is pulling up. He must have already been on his way. There is no way he made it from his house that fast. Bree is relieved that Reggie isn't here. She is also in panic mode because she thought she had enough time to get him off the phone.

"What's wrong?"

"Nothing, let me call you right back."

"Bree…"

*Click.* She hangs up and rushes downstairs before Jason knocks or rings the bell.

"That was quick," she says letting him in.

"Yeah, I was trying to get this done earlier had you not been ignoring me." Jason says as he walks in and heads to sit on the couch.

Bree phone rings. She doesn't answer. She ignores the call and text asking Reggie to give her a minute.

"What's up?" she asks, wanting to get this conversation over and him out of her house.

"I'm not sure if you heard the buzz around the hospital, but I'm in some shit."

"No I haven't" she lies. "You know I stand clear of the gossip."

"Let me start off by saying that I apologize. I was not trying to lead you on. We had something special, but I wasn't honest with you. I got myself in some shit," he says again without telling Bree what the shit is. "I know it seems like I threw you to the wolves, but Bree I was protecting you. I knew this day was coming months ago. The hammer is coming down and I didn't want you to get smashed in the process."

"Can you just tell me," she rushes him along because she doesn't want to go back to their dark space.

"I'm going to lose my job, possibly my license, ugh," he says rubbing his face. "Because you worked under me, they are going to bring you in for an interview." He reveals continuing to bypass his shit. "They're going to ask a shit load of questions regarding my professionalism, character, work ethic, everything. I'm not asking you to lie about me. However, they do not know about you and me and our personal relationship. I need you to deny any sexual contact or inappropriate behavior between the two of us. Do you understand?"

"Yes, but..."

"Bree I'm telling you. Don't let them scare you, they know nothing. Deny it. You can say anything else you want to say outside of that." He reiterates. "You don't deserve to go down in this sinking ship."

Reggie texts back that Bree's minute is up. Then he calls. She ignores it and gets back to Jason.

"What the fuck is going on," she asks in disbelief. While she has some information about his dilemma it seems she's missing more than half of the pieces to this puzzle.

"Don't worry about it. Just do what I told you to do. Got it!"

"Yeah,"

"Alright, maybe I'll see you around." He says getting up to leave.

"That's it!"

"That's it!"

Bree walks him to the door and locks it behind him. She doesn't know what's going on but she's going to do as she's told and hope this blows over for her.

Bree picks up her phone to call Reggie and he doesn't answer. She goes upstairs to wait for him to return her call. Her thoughts are running a mile a minute. It has to be more to this baby situation but how can she find out. She is going to have to step outside of her comfort zone and put her ears to the street intentionally for once. She's scared to go to work now. When will they come for her to have this interview? How much information are they trying to get out of her? Is she going to be able to deny their secret relationship if they have proof?

Bree is making herself nauseated with her thoughts. She picks up her phone to call Reggie again.

"Open the door," he says right before hanging up.

Bree goes to the window but his car isn't outside. She guesses that is her cue to let her know that he is on his way and to have the door ready for him. Following their booty call ritual, Bree unsets the alarm, unlocks the door and goes to wait for Reggie in the guest room.

"What is your problem?" he walks into the room furious. It takes Bree completely by surprise.

"Huh?" she asks with a look of confusion.

"You think it's okay to play me to the side to talk to someone else? Did someone come over here?"

"Hi Reggie, how are you?" Bree says dismissing his outburst. How dare he come over here like he owns the place?

"Bree I don't have time for your bullshit right now."

"I'm not fine, thanks for asking." She continues.

"You think this is a joke?" he asks.

"No. I don't understand why you are here. Last you told me you were comfy in bed."

There is silence as Reggie paces the floor.

"You have to check this attitude. I am not engaging in this back and forth with you because my son is upstairs sleeping and I need it to stay that way." She advises.

"I'm pissed the fuck off!"

"Clearly," Bree cosigns. "You left your house, drove over 20 mins and you're still at 100. At no point on your way over here did you even try to calm yourself down just a little. You said that drama is a deal breaker for you, well this here," she looks around as if he can see the tension, "Is a deal breaker for me. You have got to learn to control your anger."

"I," he begins

"No, no, get yourself together before you speak. When you're at a level where I feel I want to talk to you, then I may answer some of your questions."

Reggie looks at Bree with an unsettling look. However, he takes her advice and calms himself down.

Moments later he asks, "Who were you texting?"

"Hi Reggie how are you? I wish I would have known you were coming over." She ignores his question to get him to greet her.

He takes a deep breath. "Hi Brianna, who were you texting on the phone?"

"Jason,"

"Did he come over here?"

"Yes,"

"Are you not all in with us let me know, because it's inappropriate to not only talk to another man while you're on the phone with me, but hang up with me as he comes to your home."

"I'm all in," she responds

"Then why was he here."

"To give me some advice."

"About what?"

"Work."

"Have ya'll ever had a sexual relationship?"

"Yes,"

"And you expect me to believe that he came over here to talk about work?"

"It's the truth. Believe what you want."

"Why are you playing this game?"

"What game?" she interrupts. "I am answering your questions. It's not my fault you don't like my replies."

"Forget it!" he says, walking to the door to leave.

"Forget what? Are you implying that you want to let our relationship go?" she asks for clarification. She's unsure if she's to forget just this conversation or him all together.

"Do you think your actions were okay?" he comes back because when letting go the relationship flies from her mouth he realizes that it's not what he wants.

"No, my actions were all types of suspicious." She admits.

"You know why I'm upset?"

"Yes, I do."

"Why do you act like my anger isn't justified?"

"Didn't say it wasn't, I just need you to handle shit differently. Stop showing up to my house yelling at me trying to intimidate me. It's not going to work. I am not going to respond to your outburst nor am I going to rise to your level of anger. I would like if you come to me like a mature adult and get your questions answered, concerns addressed, ego stroked, insecurities boosted, or whatever the fuck it is that you need. I told you I am not fine and your selfish ass still doesn't care.

Let's not worry about me possibly losing my job when I have a child to take care of, let's talk about your concerns about this rocky relationship."

"Lose your job?" he halts his feelings in an instant. He now knows she has way bigger issues than him right now.

"Yeah, but tell me why you're mad."

"Why didn't you tell me?"

"Well I just found out and you didn't give me a chance to?"

He redirects his emotions and turns to Bree with concern. He hopes that she knows he's sincere.

"We can discuss my feelings later, what is going on with you?"

"I told you. I could possibly lose my job."

"I want to know why?"

"Being young and stupid," she sighs. "If it's my consequence, then it's cool."

"Don't beat around the bush, what happened?"

"Jason is a doctor, my former supervisor and my former sexual partner." Bree begins and feels ashamed to have to tell him this. "Apparently, some shit went down with him and another employee, I don't know all the details, he left shit very vague. But his main point to drive home is I am to deny, deny, deny everything that has happened between us."

"Do you think that's good advice?"

"I don't know. I trust him. I don't think he would do me dirty. He actually looked out for me when I thought he was being shady, so I'm going to roll with and see how it goes."

"When was the last time you two had physical contact?"

Bree knows that while he's trying to be concerned he's going to fish for as many details as possible.

"Damn, two. Maybe three months ago, I'm not keeping a record." She answers honestly.

"How are you feeling?"

"Honestly, I don't know. You killed my vibe."

"I'm sorry about that,"

"Are you?" Bree turns to look at him. "You have to talk to me, not at me. I have nothing to hide. I don't mind disclosing information if it'll make you feel better, but you have to control your temper."

"I understand. And yes, I am truly sorry. It would have been nice if you would have been honest with me on the phone though."

"It would have been nice but I didn't even know what he wanted and was pissed that he showed up to my door without sufficient notice. What did you want me to say to you?"

"That he was here,"

"And how would that have worked out for me? I didn't know what he wanted, you would not have believed a word I said and we would still be in this same situation. It's not the problems, It's how you handle them."

"I hear you. I get it."

He gets up to start taking off his clothes because he doesn't plan on going back home at this hour. Bree stays put on the edge of the bed. She is unsure if she's going to head back to her room or not. Losing her job is not the worst situation for her; however, she would prefer to stay employed.

"Are you okay?" he asks again standing in front of her.

"Yes,"

"Are you sure,"

"I'm sure." She confirms.

"You're not going to lose your job. Everything is going to be okay."

"Thanks," she says as she gets up and heads to her room.

# CHAPTER 16

Despite their run in, Bree and Reggie have managed to get by on late night calls, sexting and texting and a few fly by night fucks. It feels like a high school relationship, in that, they are sneaking to talk to each other. It's rather exciting. Anticipating the texts, missing each other's presence, and longing for each other's touch, is keeping them both heavily engaged. When they are unable to talk to one another, the sheer thoughts of their next encounter keeps them occupied until the next phone contact. Manny is picking up Junior this week and it seems that they can no longer hold on the closer it gets. They are making plans as if they don't have a life or jobs for that matter and they are going to spend every waking moment together.

*One day and a wake up!* Bree texts Reggie with emojis to express her happiness.

It takes several hours for him to reply and when he does she can sense his less than enthused tone via the text.

*Can't wait.*

It is short and dry and Bree doesn't know if it is something she'd done to make him change his tune.

*Are you okay?* She asks, putting a spoke in his wheel. She's been waiting for three weeks and now that it's finally here, he's acting funny.

*It's work.*

*Want to talk about it?*

*No!*

And with that Bree leaves it alone. She knows how work issues can have someone in their head. She was elated when she escaped the consequences of her immature actions with Jason. All she needed to know at this moment is that it isn't her causing Reggie's attitude. It isn't anything she can do about it. He doesn't want to talk and she has to respect that. It doesn't change the fact that it killed her whole vibe. As she works she thinks of how she can make things better for him. She wants nothing more than for him to be happy. She decides that she will pay him a visit before she goes to pick up Junior.

*Hey, I know you're not yourself at the moment. I was wondering if you wanted me to come by your job and see you real quick?* She texts

*That would have been nice. However, I'm at the store. I'm heading home. I couldn't stay at that place any longer.* He replies.

Bree doesn't know if that meant he left for the day or if he quit his job. Either way she isn't about to ask. She decides that she is going to make a bold move and meet him at his house. She packs up and heads out on time in case she has to fight traffic.

"Not wasting anytime." John says as he sees Bree clocking out. The clock just turned three when she made it there.

"Nope, I have an appointment. Good night. Tell Trice I'll see her tomorrow."

Bree drives all the way across town and pulls up in front of Reggie's building. She scans the parking lot and his spot is empty. She immediately feels stupid. "Why did I come here?" she asks to herself. He probably lied to get rid of her because he's doing something else. After about ten minutes passed she decided to call him. If the store was just a pit stop, then he should have been here by now.

"Hey Baby," he says into the receiver happy that Bree has called him.

She is relieved because not only did he answer but he called her Baby.

"Hey You. Have you made it home? Are you okay?"

"I'm about to pull up and yeah I'm good. Just one of those days I guess. They happen every once in a while."

As he's talking Bree sees his car pull up and he whips into his reserved spot.

"Gets to be a bit overwhelming at times if I'm being honest, that's why I had to cut up out of there and clear my head. Gosh! I wish you were here."

"Well get out your car," Bree says smiling.

He exits his car and his attention is drawn directly to her. She walks over to him and gives him a hug.

"I can't stay long," she announces. "I just wanted to come and see you because you said you were having a bad day."

"I really appreciate it. You don't know how much this means to me."

He grabs the bags and they walk into the building. Bree feels so good right now. This could have gone many ways, yet, it's going the way she wants it to. She shows up unannounced, he's not upset, he's welcoming as if he has nothing to hide.

"I'm sorry for just popping up on you like this. Last minute decisions call for last minute actions."

"I understand. Like I said, I'm glad that you're here. Seeing you has made my day that much brighter."

"And if I'm going to be honest, then I have to say I was scared." She admits. "Didn't know how this would play out. Trust me when I said I've tried to run through all the possible scenarios."

"I bet," he says walking over to her. "Don't overwork your brain on such nonsense. I'm with you," he says so smoothly as if that line is well rehearsed. Yet, Bree still couldn't help but eat it up.

"Come," she grabs his hand and leads him to the sofa. She sits down and has him lay with his head rested on her lap. "Talk to me." She says rubbing his goatee opening the lines of communication.

"Just one of those days dealing with unreasonable people," he shrugs. "I was tasked with a project. Nothing I'm not used to, so I was up for it. It was a bit challenging and required more than my normal dedication, but again I was up for it. I finished ahead of schedule and did a damn good job might I add; then the lead decides he wants to change direction and go with something else. Everyone didn't understand. It wasn't like he was asking me to tweak certain things, no he is scrapping the whole presentation and going in a completely different direction. It's just frustrating because I know he's doing it because he doesn't like me. It's taxing. I'm tired of trying to prove myself and overworking myself for essentially nothing."

Bree sits there rubbing his hair listening intently.

"And if that isn't enough he tried to take me off the project all together. However, the President

stepped in and said he wants me on the team. He enjoyed what I presented and doesn't understand why the direction is changing. He trusts Ron so much that he goes along with whatever he proposes." He continues.

Bree is still listening soaking in his dilemma and can completely understand how things can be when you are clearly talented or good at your job and others try to dim your light.

There is a moment of silence as Reggie is replaying the day in his mind.

"Say something," he encourages.

"Oh, I'm sorry. I thought I was just a listening ear." She speaks honestly. "Did you say anything?"

"Yeah I said something to Ron before I left and of course I look like the crazy one. He doesn't understand why I'm not being a team player." He shakes his head.

"I can't say that I've been in this particular situation because I haven't worked many places. Being a nurse we follow more than just company guidelines, so there is not much room for someone to have a personal agenda about how work should be performed. However, I have been in situations where someone makes my job difficult for me out of jealousy. Not completing their work to make me late on mine or intentionally changing things I've done so that I had to do them again. And I know that it is a very tough situation to be in. You said that you want to start your own business, right?" she asks the rhetorical question. "Well I'm not sure of what that will be as you've never disclosed what it is you do exactly; however, if your business is doing any remotely close to what you are doing now, then use this to your advantage. Stop looking at your job as a safety net where there is this harmonious structure of "team work" although you and I both know that it should be. Instead look at yourself as your own entity. You have your own business and your job is your client. If you change your outlook, then it wouldn't be so bad. Embrace these curveballs and learn from them as you will have to deal with clients exactly like your co-worker." Bree says hoping that's enough to help him because she's really at a loss. She's jealous that he actually gets to voice his opinion, had she opened her mouth about anything she felt slighted about in the office she would have been labeled the angry black female.

"You're right!" he smiles. "And if this serves as anything it will be the fire under my ass to get my shit started sooner than later." He says as he sits up. "Thank you!"

"You're welcome, glad my inexperienced self could help. Well as you know I have to go," she says sadly getting up to head out the door.

"Don't remind me," he sighs, "It's only 4:30 he can stay at the center until 6:30 right?" he asks looking at his watch.

"Yeah he can but he has basketball practice and although he can't play he needs to show up and support his team. And practice is in an hour."

"Awe Baby," he says, wrapping her in his arms. "I know you have to go. I wish you could stay though."

"Would you feel like driving to me later?"

"Why would you ask that? I would drive across the country for you." He pulls her back to look at her.

Bree feels so good in this moment. She can tell his words are genuine and it feels good to have someone to want her. If she was ready to say 'I love you' this would have been a moment to let it be known. She just thinks it will be best if he utters the words first. She doesn't want to rush things.

"Well practice is only an hour. We'll get home, hang out a little, eat dinner and he'll be in the bed by 8:30. If you want, then you can come after 9? I know this is not ideal but I'm trying to work something out. I don't want you in the bed alone after today. You may decide to call your little girlfriend," she chuckles, lightening the mood.

"Yeah, yeah, you know that you are my one and only, so don't go there. And I'll be there tonight. Now I have to figure out what the fuck I'm going to do for the next couple hours."

"Brainstorm your business ideas," she says walking towards the door.

"True," he says walking behind her, "Where's my kiss?"

"They're not yours," she says playfully poking him in the stomach, "they're mine. I just let you have some."

He grabs her face, "Wrong! They're mine, I let you walk around with them." And with that he kisses her like he wants her to drop her clothes right there and if she didn't have anywhere to be, she would have.

# CHAPTER 17

Bree has been anticipating Reggie's 'On the way text' for the remainder of the day, since 8:30 came Bree has been looking at her phone like any moment now. Moments came and went for the next thirty minutes. At 9 he texts that he will be there soon, with that,Bree told him the door was unlocked and to set the alarm when he got in. She had something in store for him and it required him to walk into the setting. She pops in some smooth jazz on low volume, lit some candles and changed into the sexy silk pink lingerie that she purchased just for him. The light from the bathroom illuminates the room just enough and with the candles flickering the ambience gives off a sexy vibe.

"Wow, waiting for me?" he asks as he begins to unbutton his shirt.

"Took you long enough," Bree says coming to her knees on the bed. "Come, I'll get that, you just lock the door."

Reggie walks over to her and lets her undress him. As she is taking off his clothes she is ensuring that she is letting her lips land on every part of his chocolate skin. Her licks and soft nibbles are getting the panting responses that she hoped they would. Reggie has been the driver of the sex train since the beginning and now it's time for her to take the reigns. She pushes him back on the bed and grabs his dick in her hands. "Oh, I've missed you," she says before she begins to kiss it seductively. She grabs the flavored lube that she purposely sat on the side of the bed to help her

tackle his massive manhood for the first time. She squirts some on her tongue. As soon as she wraps her lips around his head, he releases a sensual noise. It turns her on in an instant. She forgets about the size and her reservations and becomes completely engulfed in pleasuring him. The thought of him enjoying it is making her want him more. Her sounds of satisfaction from pleasing him has made Reggie want to fuck her as hard has he could. He picks her up, lay her on the bed and mount her ready to enter.

"Wait," she whispers. "You sit back," she encourages as she maneuvers to switch positions.

"I want you," he objects.

"I want you too. I want all of you." She says.

He complies and puts his back on the headboard awaiting her next move. Bree slowly begins to undress as she straddles him mid-thigh. She touches herself gently as she removes the articles of clothing. As she squeeze her breast she rolls her head biting her bottom lip, letting out a cry of yearning.

"Get over here," he demands.

She slowly makes her way over and begins to kiss him. He's trying to enter her but she refuses his advances because she wants more than just a sexual experience right now. She wants him to give himself to her in the way she has been longing for and in the way he hasn't.

Looking him directly in the eyes she says, "I want you here with me."

"I'm here," he tries to assure her.

She disregards his declaration and starts to gently caress his body as she lets her lips graze his neck. Every so often she places a kiss leading with her tongue. "I want you," she moans.

"I'm all yours," he says without hesitation.

Bree knows that he's not fully committed yet. She can feel the distance that she wants to disappear. She looks him in the eyes again, "Give yourself to me. Stop holding back."

She resumes trying to open him up through soft kisses, caressing and professions of wanting him. Reggie throws his head back, closes his eyes and concentrates on being present with her. His breathing slows. His heart softens. And every place Bree touches the feeling is intensified. Sensing he has finally gotten on one accord with her, Bree slowly sits on his manhood. When he let his fingers slide down her back the feeling was electrifying. As she throws her head back he licks her cleavage and sends her into a heightened state of ecstasy. Looking directly into each other's eyes sends a powerful message that neither of them has ever felt before. When their lips touch it's a feeling they've never felt. The kiss of passion that they use to share is long gone compared to the hot sultry kiss they are experiencing right now. The thought of reaching a climax is long gone. This moment brings forth the epitome of sexual gratification. Their movements are in sequence. There is no rushing. This is a space where they could both stay forever and they are enjoying every minute of it. Bree has finally found the depths and angle that hits her spot. As she massages it for maximum pleasure her heart begins to race and her breathing changes pace.

"This feels so good," she cries out.

He grabs her ass to assist her as she is about to be caught up in her moment. Burying his head in her neck he whispers, "I love you," as he wraps her up in his arms.

He didn't know that he was going to cum at the moment, it took him by surprise. He bites her shoulder as he releases what feels like a sea of emotions inside of her. Bree releases a lustful sound of pleasure, "I love you too" she says as she collapses into his embrace.

Reggie is unsure what all just happened. Never has he experienced love making. And that's what he thinks just occurred. The bond that he now feels for Bree is tenfold. While he has wanted to tell her that he loves her, he is ashamed that it came out during a sexual encounter. How inconsiderate. He is wondering if he should clarify to her that it just isn't sex talk and that he is in fact in love with her. He battles with the thoughts for about 10 minutes and decides he'd wait until they are fully clothed and out of this blissful space. He kisses her forehead and repositions their bodies so that they could go to sleep comfortably.

# CHAPTER 18

"Hello" Bree speaks groggily into the receiver.

"Hey are you okay? Are you sick?" Manny asks in a concerning manner. Bree is never in bed when he calls in the morning.

"Yeah, no, I'm sleep."

"Bree, it's almost six o'clock" he informs her.

"What!"

"What's wrong?" Reggie jumps up to inquire what she is screaming about.

"It's almost six o'clock." She delivers the news to Reggie.

"Oh shit," he says, mimicking her same shocking tone.

"Somebody being nasty and it caused her to be late..." Manny sings to Bree.

"Ah shut the hell up, we'll call you when we get into the car." She says short of hanging up the phone.

"Are you going to shower or are you getting up out of here now?" she looks to Reggie

"I'm going to shower." He replies.

"You want breakfast?"

"Do you have time for that?"

"I am going to make time because Junior needs to eat. I'll be flying in on two wheels but I'll make it on time. I just won't have time to pack lunch though."

"Yes, I'll take breakfast to go. Good morning by the way, beautiful."

"Good morning, Baby," she kisses him on the lips.

With that Bree takes to the kitchen to make omelets and sausage. Not only is it Junior's favorite, it is also a quick easy meal. About fifteen minutes later Reggie emerges with a t-shirt, shorts on and bag in hand. Bree packs up his breakfast and kisses him like she won't see him again.

"Damn, you're trying to start something this morning."

"No, no, I'm going to miss you that's all. In my mind, this morning was supposed to go completely differently."

"Tell me about it."

"I'll show you about it another time," she smiles as she wraps her arms around his waist.

"Promising me a good time?" he teases.

"A great time."

"Can't wait! What time are you going to lunch?"

"Around eleven thirty as usual."

"I'll bring you a bite to eat."

"Are you sure, I know..."

"I know what I have to do and I said that I will bring it to you."

"Alright, alright," Bree backs off. She has a habit of being more conscious of other people's time and commitments when they are not concerned about it themselves. "Thank you!"

"You're welcome." He says walking towards the door. "I'll see you later."

Bree rushes upstairs to get Junior out of bed and downstairs to eat as she showers and gets dressed. Luckily for her, he is being very cooperative this morning. They were in the car by 6:35, five minutes before Bree scheduled.

"Hey, hey, hey." Manny answers his ringing phone.

"Hey Dad," Junior sings excitedly

"Good morning Champ, how are you doing? Are you ready for school?"

"Good morning. Yes. Is Mom-mantha coming to get me today?"

"No, tomorrow."

"Awe man," he sighs

"Why are you in such a rush?"

"I want to see if I can get my cast off because Mario's birthday party is coming up at Disneyland."

"Oh yeah, I forgot about that. We have to get him a gift."

"I got one with Mom already."

"Yeah, he is uber excited." Bree chimes in.

"I see. Did you eat breakfast?"

"Yeah he ate breakfast. You messy," Bree laughs.

"I ate an omelet and sausage." Junior confirms

"How many omelets did Mom make?" he laughs.

"You know what! I made one, and we have to go. We'll call you later."

"Bye Dad."

"Ya'll have a good day."

"We will," Junior confirms as he unbuckles his seat belt.

***

Bree clocks in at 6:58. "Two minutes to spare" she says as she sticks her tongue out at John as he was yapping his gums about her rushed arrival.

"And why are you late Ms. Smiles?"

"I'm not late."

"Now you know you get here no later than 6:30," Trice chimes in, "cook them beans girl" she laughs knowing that it has something to do with Reggie.

"I woke up late that's all," Bree announces modestly.

"Well how late did ya stay up? Was Mr. Reggie was tending to some ground work," he nudges Trice as they laugh.

"Whatever. You guys really need to grow up, like yesterday." She says taking her charts to make her rounds.

As she is making her rounds she finds that it's difficult to stay focused because all she can think about is last night and the fact that they both expressed their love verbally. She wonders if it was just sex talk for him. She knows that she meant it. Their love making session was out of this world. She has never opened up completely to anyone and she's never been able to have someone open up to her. This lets Bree know how much Reggie trusts her. She is unsure if she would be able to get him out of the macho man persona. He carries this arrogance about him that's subtle but packs a punch. Contemplating whether or not to bring up the topic at lunch Bree is completely zoned out. She doesn't want to pull the trigger for it only to backfire, but she doesn't know how long she will allow their professions to float in the universe unattached.

"Earth to Bree," Trice snaps her out of her trance.

""Hey what's up?"

"What are you daydreaming about Missy,"

"Nothing, what's going on?"

"Uhm huh, well Felicia said that you, me and John can take lunch together. Her, Monica and Pam got it. No action happening."

"Ok cool, but Reggie is meeting me for lunch, so I have to catch up with ya'll later."

"John," Trice looks around for her partner in crime to show his face.

"Hay Gurl," he says looking like he's about to get some gossip.

"This girl is ditching us for Reggie already, he's coming to meet her for lunch," she mocks.

"Can we join…"

"NO!" Bree quickly interrupts.

"Well damn, guess we are now second class citizens." He looks to Trice after rolling his eyes at Bree.

"It's not like that, I just want some time with him today. We have some things to discuss."

"Do tell girlfriend," John says, redirecting his attention back to Bree like he's her best friend now.

"Let's just wait until after lunch."

"Don't tell me you're breaking up with Prince Charming already? Damn you move fast."

"No, I'm not. We'll talk about it later." She reiterates. "Y'all can head out. I'm going to wait for him to call me to tell me he's here before I head down."

"Ready John?' Trice asks, "Guess we're two peas in a pod since we lost a musketeer."

# CHAPTER 19

As Bree approaches the picnic table she feels a ball of confusion inside. The emotions of apprehension, anxiousness, excitement and elation are tangled into a knot inside of her stomach. She doesn't know how to feel, but without notice an immediate espresso boost of confidence changes Bree's demeanor. Her posture is more secure, her chin held a tad bit higher and it seems as if she is walking on clouds as her stride takes on a different beat. She feels as high as a hippie on 4/20.

"There's my baby," Reggie smiles, sealing his greeting with a kiss.

"Hey Handsome, thank you for bringing me lunch."

"You're more than welcome."

"Ooh, streets tacos my fav."

"Everything is your fav," he chuckles. "How is your day going?"

"Good," she pauses to chew. "How about yours?"

"Every day with you is great," he smiles.

"Cheesy fucker. Are you eating?"

"No, I didn't eat my breakfast until about ten, so I'm not hungry." After a moment of silence, "Bree about last night..." he decides to jump right in.

"Huh oh,"

"No, no it was amazing." He insists. "Sadly, I think that's the first time I've ever made love to anyone. And while it was fitting for me to confess my love for you in that moment, it is not intended to be taken lightly. I love you, Brianna."

Bree's heart flutters at the sound of his confession. This is just what she needs to hear.

"I love you too, Baby." She says while looking him in the eye and touching his legs.

Immediately she is overwhelmed with loving feelings. The apprehension and anxiousness is at bay. While him telling her is a great feeling within itself, when she utters the words she knows that they are truly genuine as her heart melted with every syllable. She leans into his chest to be covered by his embrace as she feels the world is watching and can sense her vulnerability. In this moment, she knows that the dunce cap of love has been affixed to her head. The love blinds has officially closed, covering her eyes. She is now in the realm of love.

He wraps her in his arms and confesses, "You have taught me the difference between sex, love and intimacy. The way I feel about you is indescribable. I cannot even articulate how comfortable I am around you and how I feel free to be completely me without judgment. I'm telling you now, that you're going to be my wife."

Bree soaks in his words as they flow from his mouth. The way she feels matches his feelings like a reflection in a mirror. Although she wants this moment to last forever, she decides to break it up. She doesn't want to float away too easily into his ecstasy. While she knows the emotions of her heart knocked out the logic of her brain, she cannot afford to let logic lose the round. She has to shake off the blow and proceed with caution.

"Just when I thought you couldn't get any worse; you go from loser to total loser," she smiles as she pushes herself away from him and directs her attention back to her food.

"An upgrade, I'll take it." He celebrates.

"Just so we're clear you can't stay the night tonight. This morning was a complete mess. I hate to rush."

"I don't understand how we both missed the alarm," he laughs. "But huh, I can sense this getting old very quickly or more realistically us getting caught before it even gets old."

"I agree."

"So?" he looks for a solution to the problem.

"So what?"

"What's the plan?"

Bree sighs and after a bit of a hesitation she states, "I don't know if I'm ready to let you meet Junior. I'm too afraid. However, I don't mind you meeting Manny and when I'm ready we can just jump right in and not have to wait on him."

"I don't agree with your stance but I understand. Bree I'm not out to hurt you or your son. I'm trying to step into your life. I feel like I don't completely have you. These last three weeks were torture. How are you so close, yet so far away? I don't like it. But at this point I'm willing to take whatever, so you can plan for Manny and I to meet."

Bree really isn't ready for him to meet Manny either, but figures that she needs to begin to make some type of forward progress since they professed their love.

"You don't have children so I don't expect you to understand how I feel. It is my responsibility to protect my son emotionally, mentally and physically, a failed relationship is a potential threat to his well-being. I know some things are beyond my control and this is one of those situations, I'm just not ready to let go yet."

"Brianna I get it. Look at me," he insists. "You are going to be my wife. I am not going anywhere. This is it! I am claiming it. I want to live a happy fulfilling life with you and your son while possibly growing our family. Now I can't promise that it's going to peaches and cream, because we are going to run into our fair share of issues. That's just life. However, I can promise you that no pain will ever be intentionally inflicted."

Bree sits there with her head hanging to the side trying to pick up what he is laying down but it's difficult to fully trust anyone. The only person who has not turned their back on her is Manny and they were never in a romantic relationship, so this is really a first for her.

"I got you," he says, lifting her chin so they can look eye to eye.

"Hay Gurl," Bree hears John yell from across the lawn.

"Oh brother, here we go." She looks at Reggie.

"Are you going to introduce us," Latrice asks while they are still approaching but are within earshot distance of each other.

"Damn, can ya'll get over here first? Baby, this is Latrice and John. Ya'll this is Reggie," Bree introduces in an unenthused manner.

"Nice to meet you Mr. Reggie," John cheerfully shakes his hand. "Whatever you are doing, keep doing it because Bree is full of smiles; glowing and shit."

"Will do," he confirms.

As Latrice extends her hand she says, "Reggie?" looking for a last name.

"Clarkson." He answers knowing exactly what she wants to know.

"Don't give them any ammo."

"What do you mean?" he looks at Bree with a puzzling look.

"We gone call her ass Mrs. Clarkson," they both said in unison and high fived.

"See what I mean? They are so childish."

"Why we gotta be childish?" John cut his eyes at Bree.

"No worries. You guys are faring better than I. When I told her she is going to be my wife she called me a total loser." Reggie shrugs

"I'm ready to head back to work." Bree announces, embarrassed that he would even bring that up with them.

"Latrice, your cake almost didn't make it to you. Bree put me on a one slice restriction, so you're lucky." Reggie jokes while he rubs his stomach.

"Who can just eat one slice? Well you get her in that kitchen baking, take your slice and send the rest to me." She laughs.

"I got you." He smiles. "Nice meeting you guys. Talk to you later Baby," he says to Bree as he grabs the small of her back and places a kiss on her lips. "I love you."

"I love you, too." She smiles.

As Reggie walks away John and Latrice are looking as if they have just witnessed a romantic scene in a movie.

"I felt that," John said clutching his imaginary pearls.

"Me too," Trice confirms.

"Can we go now," Bree interrupts their fairytale thoughts.

"You can hand his ass right on over when you're done, my spidey senses are going off." He says with a shake.

"Your little balls tingle around anything with a dick," Trice cuts him where it hurts again.

"Damn, who is that?" John asks, looking at the fine physique that is walking about a hundred feet in front of them.

"See what I mean, he lost his train of thought already." Latrice solidifies her case.

# CHAPTER 20

It's going to be a long night Bree thinks to herself. She misses Reggie like crazy and having to wait another day to see him it's agonizing. She's keeping herself busy by cleaning and washing clothes. The gesture doesn't hurt as she wants some fresh sheets on the bed for when he comes over tomorrow. Bree slowly makes her way over to her ringing phone. She would bet it's Manny. She and Reggie don't usually talk until after 9. To her surprise it's Reggie.

"Hey Baby," she sings cheerfully. "I miss you," she gets right to it.

"I miss you too. Since I can't see that beautiful face, your voice will have to suffice for now. What are you doing?" he asks

"Laundry and cleaning."

"Where's Junior?"

"In the tub probably making a mess. What are you doing?"

"Trying to occupy my time with work and it's not helping."

"Well we will have ten whole days together after tomorrow."

"I'm trying to wait patiently."

"Hold on, let me find my earpiece."

"MOOOOOOOMMMMMMM!!!!!" Junior yells from the bathroom.

After Bree has secured the earpiece and put her phone in her pocket she goes to see what the yelling is about.

"Yes," she says resting on the door with her hand on the knob. "Why do you have all those bubbles?"

"Oops!" he covers his mouth. "The cap came off. Can you count how long I can hold my breath?" Junior continues with the reason he has called her.

"Where are your goggles? I would hate for you to accidentally open your eyes with all that soap."

"In my room can you get them please?"

"This room is a mess." She says to Reggie even though she doesn't know if he's listening. "Where are they?" she yells.

"I don't know. Maybe my dresser."

Junior eagerly reaches for the eyewear as she enters the bathroom.

"Hold up, Son. Let me fix the straps. How do you want me to count? Fast like 1,2,3 or slow like 1 Mississippi, 2 Mississippi, 3 Mississippi?"

"Uhm, slow."

"Okay go," Bree begins to count and becomes impressed as his head is still submerged and she's midway into the teens. "22 seconds. WOW! You've been practicing."

"That's pretty good. How old is he again?" Reggie asks.

"How old are you?" Bree quizzes.

"Mom you know how old I am," he laughs.

"I'm just saying that's great for a four year old."

"But I'm about to turn five."

"Well played," Reggie commends.

"Yes you are. Four more months."

"Mom can I ask you a question?"

"Anytime, what's up?" she asks as she sits on the toilet wondering where this is going.

"What does dating someone mean?" he asks innocently while playing with the bubbles.

Bree is taken back by the question wanting to know what he's heard.

"Dating is when two people hang out to get to know each other. Sometimes dating leads to a relationship like Dad and Samantha then to marriage like Papa George and Grandma Lillian."

"Oh ok. Are you going to date when I leave to go with Dad tomorrow?"

"Where did you get that from?"

"Well I heard Dad tell Mom-mantha that you are dating someone."

"Did you talk to Dad about it or did you just overhear him saying it?"

"I just heard him say it."

"Uh oh!" Reggie chimes in.

"How would you feel if I am dating someone?" Bree inquires.

"Sad."

"Why? You're not sad that Dad is dating Samantha."

"No not sad that you're dating, just sad that you didn't tell me."

"Oh Wow!" Reggie chimes in again.

"Junior look at me," she requests. "I am dating someone and I'm sorry if you're sad that you didn't hear it from me. But Mommy has to protect you. I had to make sure that Mr. Reggie is serious and will not hurt you or me. It's sort of like when you want to taste spicy food and I always try it first. Then only after I try it, I tell you if I think you should eat it. Sometimes I say, no Junior that is going to be too spicy right?"

"Yes."

"And you don't try it because you believe me and trust me. The same with Mr. Reggie I had to see if we should give him a try. I think we should."

"Really," he brightens up. "Tell me about him."

"I didn't take you to be this excited." She admits. "What do you want to know?"

"What does he look like?"

"He's very tall."

"Taller than Dad?"

"Taller than Dad," she confirms. "His complexion; his skin color is like PaPa George. He's very smart. He's nice. He's funny."

"Does he play basketball?"

"He doesn't play on a team, but he does play with his friends."

"So will he come to my games and stuff?"

"Say yes," Reggie coaches Bree.

"If he has the time, then maybe he can come to a couple."

"Does he have any kids?"

"No,"

"Awe man, I thought I would have someone to play with," he expresses sadly. "Does he want any kids? Dad said he's happy I can stop bugging him and Mom-mantha for a baby."

"Tell him I have a nephew that is six and a niece that's four." Reggie requests.

"He does want kids. And guess what?"

"What?"

"He has a nephew that is six and a niece that's four. I'm sure they'll love to play with you."

"Cool," he says with excitement. "Can I meet them when I come home?"

"Oops," Reggie says with a chuckle.

"We'll have to see. Dad has to meet Mr. Reggie first; then we'll go from there?"

"When will Dad meet him?"

"I don't know. I have to talk to him and ask him when he is free."

"Mom," he lowers his eyes and asks in a voice of uncertainty. "Do you think, what's his name again?"

"Mr. Reggie?"

"Yeah, Mr. Reggie would like to hang out with me with Kevin and his Dad?"

"Say yes," Reggie coaches again.

"If he has the time, then I don't see why not?"

"Okay," he says half heartedly.

"Get washed so you can get in the bed."

With that Bree walks out of the bathroom and sighs in her mind. She had to get out of the hot seat.

"Why did you do that?" Reggie asks in a short snippy tone.

"Do what?"

"You presented me with shaky credibility."

"How so?" Bree asks confusingly.

"Bree when he asked if I would be present for him your only response should have been yes."

"I did say yeah. If you have time, then yeah."

"But you should have just said yes. He's old enough to understand that things come up and I won't be at everything, but he needs to know that my initial response is always yes. You don't make everything due to work or random things that come up and he understands. Don't give me shaky credibility. Let him form his own opinion of me is all I ask."

"I'm sorry I didn't look at it like that. I just don't want him to get his hopes up and…"

"Bree where am I going? I told you that I'm here and I'm not going anywhere. He can get his hopes up because I'm going to be here for him. I understand that he has his Dad; however, I also understand that when he is with us that I'm the father figure in those moments. I accepted that when you told me you had a son. I know what it means. Don't sell me short."

"Ok, ok," Bree gives in. "I'm just a nervous wreck. This is all new for me and I'm just scared of the unknown. Just bare with me."

"Do you trust me?"

"Of course, I do."

"Then just let it flow."

"Easier said than done, but I'll try."

"Trying is doing." He encourages. "So," he goes in to change the subject. "Guess this meeting is going to be closer than either of us expected."

"Guess so, this is going to be interesting," she chuckles.

"MOOOOOOOOOM!!!" Junior yells from his bedroom.

"Gosh! Why do you have to call me like that all the time," she asks while tickling him. "Your TV is going to go off in thirty minutes."

"Ok," he yawns as he is about to be out in the next five. "Mom, do you think Mr. Reggie will go on the Dad/Son camping trip with me? I know it's a long time away, but if we ask him now then he can plan right?"

"I'm in," Reggie says, "I love camping."

"He would love too, camping is one of his favorite things to do."

"So he knows how to pitch a tent and make fire?" he asks excitedly.

"Yup," Reggie says proudly.

"Yes, he does," Bree confirms.

"Awesome! This is going to be so cool," he hugs Bree. "Now I have Dad and Mom-mantha at his house and I will have you and Mr. Reggie here." He smiles and in that moment Bree feels horrible. She had no idea he was missing such bonding moments.

"You will." She confirms. "Goodnight Champ. I love you."

"Goodnight Mommy, I love you too!"

***

"I had no idea he felt this way," Bree confesses to Reggie once she leaves the room. "You know what, now that I think about it all the little boys he hangs with have active Father's in their life. He's been silently crying out and I didn't notice." She says softly, continuing to beat herself up about it.

"Don't worry about it Baby, all we can do is move forward from now and give him the best we can." Reggie speaks inclusively to help ease her anxiety.

"I agree. I'm still bummed out though," she tries to laugh through her pain. "He's so excited. He's probably planning all the shit ya'll are going to do without me."

"I'm sure because girls have cooties and we don't want to hang with ya'll or we might catch it," he laughs.

"I have a lot of things for you to catch and cooties isn't one of them, Sir."

"You're nasty Ms. Brianna."

"You love it Just Reggie."

"I do and I love you."

"I love you too," she says looking at her phone. "Dammit, let me have Manny tell him goodnight and I'll call you back in a few."

"I'll be waiting."

"Called just in time. He's about to go to sleep," Bree announces before saying hello.

"Well hello to you too,"

"Hey," she says unbothered. "Well damn, he's out. I just kissed him less than five minutes ago."

"Guess he had a long day. What's been going on?" Manny asks, making usual casual conversation.

"Glad you asked," Bree says excitedly ready to get this conversation going. "I need you to stop talking about me and spreading my business."

"What are you talking about?" he gets defensive.

"You did tell Samantha that I'm dating didn't you?"

"Well yeah, it's just Samantha," he says like that's a given. And typically it is.

"It's just Samantha with your son ear hustling from God knows where."

"Oh shit, he heard me? He asked you about it?"

"Yeah. I talked to him about Reggie because he made me feel bad. I told you to watch what you say when he's around. He's always listening."

"Damn, my bad. Are you cool now?" is all he offers knowing that the damage is already done.

"Yeah, you left me explaining dating."

"How did it go?"

"Good I guess," Bree says as she tells him the analogy she used.

"Bree you compared your relationship to spicy food," he laughs like it's the funniest thing he's ever heard.

"Well shit that's all I could think of that he would understand. It worked. Now Junior's dying to meet him. I had no idea that he was missing that male interaction while with me. He's already inviting Reggie to shit and he hasn't even met him yet."

"What did he say?"

"What do you mean?" she asks

"How do you know that?"

"Oh because he was like now I have Dad and Mom-mantha at his house and I will have you and Mr. Reggie here. He asked if Reggie would come to his games, hang out with his friends and attend the father/son camping trip."

"Wow! That stings."

"Tell me about it. Reggie was like, ``That's to be expected he wants to do guy stuff, blah, blah, blah." Bree rambles.

"So how does he feel about stepping in, is it something he's ready for? Bree if this dude hurt my son you know I'm going to go crazy right."

"I know, I know. I feel the same way. But he was like I know he has a Dad and is not looking for one, that he understands that he's standing in that role while Junior will be with us and he's up for it. I found out he actually likes camping."

"Well good, because I'm not with that shit." Manny lets out a light laugh. "Well if he's going to do the right thing you know I support you and your relationship."

"Thank you," Bree smiles.

"Bree you are an awesome friend, extraordinary mom and will make a wonderful partner. He's lucky to have you and I'm sure you'll push him to be a better man, than he already seems to be."

"That's so sweet. Thank you, Manny."

"If I didn't have so much shit with me, then you could have been mine."

"Whoa, whoa, wait a minute. Let's not go down this road because that is not true."

"Bree if I wanted you I could have cuffed you a looooonnnng time ago."

"Glenn you're delusional,"

"So now I'm Glenn?"

"Apparently, because you're talking out the side of your neck."

"Oh really?" he questions. "So when we were making Junior you didn't say something of the sorts."

"Ok, where is Samantha with you talking like this? Jealousy doesn't look good on you Manny. Stop with the bullshit. This conversation is dead. Let's talk about what we need to be focused on. When are you coming to meet Reggie?"

"You of all people know why Samantha is here."

"I said the conversation is dead."

He laughs for a while before he proceeds, "Alright, let me stop tripping. If I can't bring him home, then I'll arrange for a day trip soon. I have to look at my schedule."

"Cool. I appreciate it. Goodnight, Glenn."

"Goodnight, Brianna."

# CHAPTER 21

Junior is gone and Bree has made herself comfortable in Reggie's place. She showered, washed her hair, cleaned up a little and is now preparing dinner before he gets home. Per her ritual, she has her glass of wine with her music blasting celebrating her freedom for the next ten days. Usually, this is done home alone, but this time around she can celebrate with Reggie.

Reggie walks into his place and he is pleasantly pleased. The aroma from the kitchen, Bree in boy shorts and a tank, and the place looking spotless is something he can definitely get used to.

"Even though I wanna see…how you put that thang on me, I can't …let you… get the best of me." Bree sang with glass in her hand dancing over to Reggie.

She continues to rub on his body and dance on him as he stands there taking it all in. He came in on the best part of the song when Jay-Z raps his verse. As she grinds on him, he begins to get aroused, she turns and backs away from him, "That's high school making me chase you 'round for months, have an affair, act like an adult for once." They sing in unison.

Reggie walks up to her and places a kiss on her lips, "What's a little me on top gone hurt? Maybe a little," he continues with the lyrics.

"Maybe a lot," Bree makes known.

Reggie ignores her remark because he knows last night was not the best for her. He has to be mindful when he throws her about. Her small frame can't handle what he has to offer.

"What's this?" he points to the bonnet on her head.

"I'm deep conditioning my hair because I'm wigging for the next couple of days."

"Oh gosh!" he rolls his head. "What's for dinner?"

"Steak, baked potato and asparagus. You have about thirty minutes or so if you want to shower or get comfortable" she let her suggestions trail off as she takes a sip.

"I'll take you up on that. You're just in here having a little party by yourself huh?"

"I'm where the party is," she says while still dancing. "I celebrate when Junior leaves I'm free," she waves her hands in the air.

"Yeah, yeah, in two days you're going to be crying talking about how you miss him." He brushes her off.

"And? Let me have my moment please."

With that Reggie leaves to go and wind down. Bree gets back to her music and dinner. In about twenty minutes Reggie appears in his pajamas. He figures since she's cooking and conditioning her hair that going out tonight is out of the question.

"Sexy can I?" Bree sings as she acknowledges his presence.

"You can sex me anytime." He teases. "And weren't you in a crib when these songs were heavy in rotation."

"Don't come at my age like that Just Reggie. I was young but I was with it." She confirms continuing to dance. "Ready for dinner?"

"Yes," he says, pulling her close. "You are wonderful." He smiles and goes to take his seat.

Bree makes the plates and heads over to the table where Reggie is waiting.

"I mean, it's not your favorite rib eye but it should be quite tasty," she says referring to the steak. "How was your day."

"It was good. How was yours?"

"Fun! You know it's joke time with me and my crew. Speaking of joking you know I wasn't joking about what I said right?"

"About what?"

"If you want kids sometime in the future, then you cannot try to demolish my damn reproductive organs." She makes it known. After Junior left last night she made a booty call to Reggie's and he wore her all the way out.

"My apologies, I have to be mindful. You ask for it though."

"I do, because I be wanting it until I remember what you're going to hit me with and then I'm screaming abort mission in my head," she laughs. "I'm trying to run with you, but apparently I can't run or walk. I think I'm in the crawling phase." She continues.

"I got you Baby. The last thing I want to do is hurt you or damage your internal organs," he laughs. "I'll be mindful. So does that mean that I'm not getting any tonight?"

"Probably not. I look like I'm chilling but everything is sore thanks to you."

"I'll kiss it for you then," he winks.

He gets up to answer his ringing phone. Bree is kicking herself for even letting him know that he's wearing her out. Men tend to get big heads when they know they are up on their game. But she knows she can't take the beating for the next ten days.

"Eating dinner with Brianna," he says coming back to the table.

"Tell her I said hello. When am I going to meet her?" His mother asks.

"My mom says hi and asks when is she going to meet you?"

Bree sinks in her chair and hides her face, "Hi!" she says shyly.

"She's over here trying to act shy. I'll bring her through soon enough."

"Well I can wait to meet the woman that has you head over heels. What is she doing on Thanksgiving? Maybe she can come to dinner"

"That's a great question. Baby what are you doing for Thanksgiving?" he looks at her for an answer.

"Working," she smiles thinking she got out of whatever they're trying to plan.

"You work on Thanksgiving?" he asks with a puzzled look.

"Hospitals don't close," his mom informs him

"If you have the power to stop births, deaths, illnesses and injuries, then by all means activate." Bree adds not knowing that it has already been addressed.

"But you still get off at three right?"

"Yes,"

"Then you can come over around four right?"

"More like five, but yes, that's not a problem," Bree gives in although she would rather not. "Do I need to bring anything?"

"Noooo! Tell her we'll have everything."

"My mom says she's good. Wait Mom, Bree makes a mean cheesecake and it's your favorite. I think you should get one."

"Really, well in that case, I'll take it. But you know your father is going to be mad with us because he has to watch his sugar intake."

"Has the results come back?"

"Not yet, but he was told to cut the sugar out."

"Yeah you know his sweet tooth will be going crazy. Mom let me get back to dinner and I'll talk to you later. Tell Dad that I'll be over there in the morning to help him with the shed."

"She wants a cheesecake?" Bree asks with a skeptic look on her face.

"Yup!"

"Fucker! I know it's for you."

"No it's not. It really is her favorite dessert. My Dad is having labs done. They think he has diabetes, so he's going to have to sit this out. He loves sweets, so we may have to sneak it in the house."

"Oh yeah, that's nothing to play with. He has to take care of himself."

Bree falls silent and begins to eat her food. She hopes that all goes well with meeting his family. She tends to avoid situations like this.

"Are you okay?" Reggie asks sensing her distance.

"You said your mom's house is the hot spot for holiday's right?"

"Typically yes, she loves to entertain. However, this year given my Dad's situation he didn't want her to host this year. And he didn't feel like the five hour drive to my Aunt's house. It will be just me, my parents, my siblings and their kids."

"Whoo, I was about to have a nervous breakdown," Bree sighs.

"Why?"

"Just not my thing."

"Now we do have a lot of family and friends in the area, so I must warn you that people will pop in and out, but no one is staying all day long. You'll be okay, they'll love you."

"Considering I'm 0 for 2 with Mother's I disagree."

"Since your mom is off limits," Reggie says slowly as he looks for an indication that she may want to open up. When he sees she's not budging he asks, "How did you meet Manny's mom?"

"Well.." Bree begins as this is a much easier topic to tackle.

"Before you start, this steak is so good. I don't even need any steak sauce."

"Thank you," Bree smiles. "Well," she begins again. "There was no build up or planned meeting for us. I met his parents at the athletic camp that Manny and I met. We had competitions during our couple weeks stay and parents were allowed to be spectators. Given that he lived so close, his parents attended everything that they were invited to. Well on the last day when I was hauling my stuff to the bus, his parents stopped me and congratulated me on winning first place in my heat. Manny came walking towards us and I thought that he thought that they were my parents and he was coming to start shit. When he joined us his Dad was like have you met my son? And of course, Manny was like yeah. Like who doesn't know me. He swears he's God's gift to the world. But anyway, I told them that he was nice enough to come out with me in the morning while I ran and that he was a nice guy. His Dad gave the eye with the head nod type of deal like get on that, but his mom was not having it. So I just reassured her that he was not my type. I was like he's cool, but I'm not a part of the fan club and told them they needed to worry about the girls that were following behind him. So his mom and I joked about how thirsty the girls were and then we left."

"So you've never dated anyone that wanted to introduce you to their family?"

"I mean I have, but it's just not my thing. Manny's mom was mad cool until…then she flipped the switch. It's hard for me to trust people I guess. And the fact that you were engaged doesn't help our situation."

"My family wasn't really feeling Toya."

"Perhaps, but they didn't start off not liking her."

"True. When she began to show her true colors and the person I had become while with her made them not like her. It was gradual. But it didn't take long."

"So how were you?"

"Completely off my block. I've done things, said things, and engaged in things that I typically wouldn't. She brought out the worst part of me and I hate that I let it get that far."

"Example?" Bree inquires  because she knows his anger is a contributing factor.

"I can admit that I had become verbally abusive, she was too. It was just a toxic situation. My anger is not the best," he finally admits, "And she didn't help the cause. I think that's why I love you so much, you are the first person that has helped me manage my anger. That night when you calmed me down, I was appreciative and impressed. I think you put a spell on me," he smiles to lighten the mood.

"I wish I did know a damn spell, maybe I could have concocted a potion and made some changes in my life. But honestly, I have had major anger issues, so I recognize the signs. I'm not into that anymore it leads to nothing but drama coupled with trauma. That's why I walk away from you because I know how I can get and it will be ugly. I appreciate you being aware of your problem and making the effort to control yourself. Just know that we can talk about anything and I mean anything. I don't want to go down that road."

"Neither do I. As long as we are honest, loving and open, we'll be good."

"Agreed," Bree concurs.

"Baby I know that you rather not talk about your upbringing or more notably your mother, but it kills me to know how did ya'll relationship become so estranged."

Bree takes a deep breath knowing that he is not going to let it go and the sooner she lets it out, she can let it go. "I'm not going to tell you everything I've experienced in my childhood because we'll be here for days and besides I have my therapist for that. I will tell you the last incident that tore us apart, well not the last because we had another run in, but the incident that got me locked up, kicked out my home and ruined my dreams all in one swipe when I was 16."

Bree goes back to the warm spring day when her decision to not go to track practice caused her life to go into a downward spiral. Getting off the bus and walking home was a normal routine as was seeing her mother's boyfriend Pauly.

"Bree, tell your sister to come here," he says in a demanding voice.

Bree ignores him as usual. She didn't talk to him and preferred he not talk to her.

"Bree," he yells. She turns around to look at him. "I said tell your sister to come here."

"I heard you motherfucker," she says rolling her eyes.

As Bree walked into the house there was an eerie silence. She didn't call her sister. Instead she went upstairs to find her. She opened her room door and without looking said, "That motherfucker said come here."

Camille jumped at the sound of Bree's voice. When Bree finally looks at her, she sees her sister wrapped in sheets crying.

"What's wrong?" Bree walks over to her. "Mill, what's wrong? Did that motherfucker touch you?"

"Please Bree don't say anything he'll be mad at me."

Bree walked around with a pocket knife on her at all times. As much fighting as she got into she needed the protection. She doesn't remember running down all the steps in the house, in fact she likes to think that she jumped down in one leap. Bree runs out the door full speed and grabs her pocket knife as she runs. Pauly knew she was coming for him but couldn't move quickly enough. Bree stabbed him right in the chest trying to get his heart. He was strong enough to throw her to the ground before he'd collapsed and more importantly before Bree drew her hand back and stabbed him again.

"You raped my sister you sick piece of shit," Bree screams. "Fuck you, let me go," she says to the man that grabbed her, "I'm going to kill him."

By that time all the people who were in their homes came out to see what the commotion is about. Bree continues to kick and scream and hits anyone who came close to her. When her mother pulls up, Bree finally calms down hoping that she will be justified in her action. But she was wrong.

"So you go locked up? How? Why? There was no investigation?" Reggie asks, confused by the whole ordeal.

"When the police came to get a statement my mother already coached my sister on what to say. Now I was a bad kid, terrible. I had an attitude problem, I was mad disrespectful, I was not a good person at all. I admit that, but one thing I am not is a liar. You may not like how I say something or my angle of approach, but I speak the truth. So, the cops are trying to get statements and put the pieces of the puzzle together. By this time Pauly is heading to the hospital. So it's my sister's word against mine and whatever Pauly told them before he left."

Reggie looks at Bree and he can tell that she's in another place, her eyes become glossed over as she's staring at him; however, he gets the feeling that she's looking through him.

"When my sister goes to give her statement, she said that I was a liar. That none of that ever happened. She looked them dead in the eyes and said she wasn't even in her room when I came in. My heart was so hurt. But in that moment, I knew that this situation was bigger than me and I couldn't beat myself up for the outcome. Then my mother goes off on a tangent about my behavior and how she can't take me anymore. That I hated Pauly, which I did because it was something about him I didn't like, and I was right. She told them she didn't want to deal with me anymore and to take me out of there and do whatever. They asked if Pauly was pressing charges and my mom said yes."

"WOW! I'm so sorry Brianna." Reggie slips in.

"Then when I came home, or what I thought was home after Manny's parents pulled a damn rabbit trick out of thin air and got me community service and anger management classes, I was told that I could no longer live there. 16 and nowhere to go and no one to help me. Sure my grandmother was willing to take me in but her house was the neighborhood trap house. My uncles had traffic all up and through there on a daily. So my best friend Coco's mom took me in. She told me that she wanted me to graduate so she was offering me a place to stay, I was to not cause any shit at her house and when I crossed the stage I was pretty much homeless because I had to go. With that I quit track and worked after school. I had to save as much money as I could so I could afford a place when I graduated."

Reggie went over to offer a hug. He takes Bree's hand for her to stand up and places her in his lap and cuddles her.

"I'm sorry I have no words."

"You don't have to say anything," she murmurs.

"Baby," he grabs her chin in Reggie's fashion. "Has anyone ever touched you?"

"No," she affirms looking into his eyes.

"Thank you for sharing, I know this was probably difficult for you. But it's given me so much clarity and understanding into who you are and why you act the way you do. Especially when it comes to Junior, I can see how it's difficult for you to allow someone to get close to him."

"I will start WWIII if someone fuck with my baby."

"I know Baby. But I'm here for you and with you. Let me protect you. I don't want you to walk around like this. You deserve much better. I am going to give you much better."

Bree doesn't answer, but she tucks herself under his chin and rests. She hopes that he lives up to his words because she's tired of walking around fighting the world. She wants to put down the weapons, hang up the armor and enjoy life. And if Reggie is going to take the role, she is gladly going to give it to him.

"I love you," he whispers as he kisses her head.

# CHAPTER 22

"These jeans are cute," Bree says holding up a pair of dark washed jeans with a rustic look.

Given that she will be meeting his parents for Thanksgiving she decides to take him up on his monetary offer to buy her some new jeans.

"Let me see how that ass looks in them though," Reggie whispers in her ear. "You need jeans that are not going to have me trying to jump on you every five minutes."

"Control yourself Just Reggie. Ooh wait! These will match my jersey perfectly. Ok let me try these on." She quickly dismisses him getting back to the task at hand.

Every pair of jeans that Bree walks out of the dressing room in, they receive the same "Nope!" from Reggie. Against his judgment he purchased all eight pair.

"You're manipulating you know that?"

"How so?"

"You know you are," he smiles. "Want to grab a bite to eat?"

Arriving at the food court they decide to sit down and sort out what they want to do versus standing in everyone's way. As they are getting lost in the conversation, Bree feels someone watching her. As she is trying to remain comfortable and engaged she senses that the person watching is not letting up.

"Hey, what do you want so we can be eating and talking at the same time?" she asks, wanting to move from the spot that they are in.

"Pizza,"

"Meh, I'm going to go to the bathroom and then grab a sandwich, meet you at a table in a few."

Bree gets up and walks to the bathroom. The last time a woman was staring at her in such a way, she was confronted and told that the person whom she was with was engaged. She is praying that this is not the case with Reggie but knows that the look means trouble. As she walks out of the stall the woman is waiting. Not for an open stall, but waiting to talk to Bree.

"Hey," she approaches slowly. "Are you dating Reggie?" she asks forward in her approach.

"No, we're just shopping together." Bree replies in a sarcastic tone.

"Well if you would like to know about the man you're dating, then I can be of some assistance."

"No thank you," Bree politely declines.

"Well giving that I'm his ex-fiance I may have some valuable information. I'm just trying to help a sister out." She says in a conniving tone.

"Toya?"

"He's told you about me?"

"Briefly." Bree shrugs

"I bet it wasn't the truth," she laughs. "Well like I said if you want to know about the man you're dating, then call me," she says handing Bree a piece of paper with her number on it. And with that she departs and leaves Bree standing looking at herself in the mirror. While she wants to throw the number out wrapped in the damp paper towel that is in her hand, she slides the number in her purse and proceeds to continue on with her day.

As she walks towards the table where Reggie is sitting she wonders if Toya made her presence known to him.

"Are you okay?" he asks between chews as he looks up at her.

"Yeah, I'm good. Bummed I have to go to work tomorrow," she expresses sadly.

"I'm not. I have work to do and with you not being home I won't feel bad about it."

Silence fills the air as Bree is contemplating on what she is going to do with this number. A part of her really wants to know what she is getting herself into because she's still a little uncomfortable with his temper. While he is managing to keep it at bay, Bree needs to know what will push him over the edge. The other part of her wants to leave well enough alone because she knows firsthand that certain characteristics in people can bring out the best or worst in others. As bad as anyone says her attitude is or was she has never had a falling out with Manny and that's because Manny doesn't treat her the way others have treated her. With that, she doesn't want to place Reggie in a box knowing that Toya has to take some of the blame for both of their actions.

"Are you okay?" Reggie asks again confusingly. "You look like you're in deep thought over there."

"I am. Yeah I'm good." Bree shakes it off.

"Are you still thinking about Thanksgiving?"

"A little."

"Bree let it go you'll be fine."

# CHAPTER 23

After a night of tossing and turning Bree made the decision that she is going to talk to Toya. She doesn't want to talk over the phone, so she arranged a meet-up for Toya to come to her job when she goes to lunch. Toya happily agreed and Bree has been on edge all morning. She's rehearsing

different scenarios in her mind trying to find the words she's going to say; trying to find the demeanor she's going to have. Never has she willingly engaged in any dialog with an ex of the man she is dating. But somehow she keeps feeding herself excuses as to why she is doing this. At the end of the day, she just hopes that it doesn't change the way she looks at Reggie. And every time she has that thought, she doesn't know what this meeting is supposed to accomplish if not exactly that.

Bree walks outside on this cool fall day to meet up with the woman that can essentially break her existing relationship.

"Here we go," Bree says as she spots Toya standing and waiting for her by the bench. "Hey Toya, thank you again for meeting up with me, I know it's the holiday's and I don't want to steal too much of your time. But do you mind if we sit in my car? I don't want to speak out in the open."

"You're welcome. That's cool." Toya says, as cool as a cucumber.

Brianna doesn't really like the vibe she is getting and is starting to think that maybe she made a mistake.

"So, what do you think I should know?" Bree gets straight to the point while turning on the radio for some background noise.

"Before I get started, what did he say about me?"

"That the two of you were engaged and that ya'll called it off." Bree brushes pass the subject because that is not why they are here.

"Haha," she gives a factious laugh, "So I'm guessing he told you I lied about my pregnancy?"

"You lied?" Bree tries to act surprised. "No, he said you had a miscarriage."

There is silence. Bree is sure that Toya wants to dog him about that topic and she wasn't about to let her. "So what should I know?" Bree asks again.

"Well Reggie is going to seem like the perfect gentleman, charming, loving, thoughtful, but all of that will go out the window once he gets comfortable. He's very controlling, jealous, and manipulative. Oh and he's a damn cheater." She discloses getting straight to the point.

"He told me he cheated on you." Brianna makes it known. "Made a joke of it actually. Not laughing that he cheated," she reassured Toya. "Laughing because he always got caught. Said something about he didn't know if he was sloppy or you were a good detective."

"Well did he tell you he was abusive?" she says with slight anger in her tone.

Bree knows that this conversation is not going the way Toya thought it would go. Especially given that Reggie has offered up so much information about their relationship.

"Abusive?" Bree questions? "Are you talking emotional, fist to face, verbal..." she let it linger for Toya to pick it up.

"While he's never hit me closed hand, he did slap me once. But his go to is choking and pushing. You know the shit that really can't leave visible scars but will scare you enough to straighten up? However, he pushed me so hard one time I fell to the ground and almost fractured my wrist, trying to break my fall. But mainly it was verbal to answer your question."

"He's admitted to verbal, said it was a two way street but nothing other than that." Bree admits as she thinks back to how Reggie said that Toya had him off his block. Maybe this is what he meant when he made that statement. If Reggie thought that she was about to become some sort of object for him to abuse when he goes in his manic rants, then he definitely has the wrong one.

When Bree's phone rings she answers it via Bluetooth as she can't find her phone in her junky purse.

"Hey Baby," Reggie's voice echoes throughout the car.

"Hey you."

"What's wrong?" Reggie immediately picks up on Bree's distant response.

"Nothing, I'm trying to look for my phone, I'm about to get out of the car. What's up?"

"I didn't want anything. Just checking up on you letting you know I'm about to go out and shoot some hoops for a few. What did you need from the store? I can pick it up on the way home so you don't have to stop."

"Oh just a few odds and ends, when I find my phone I'll text you the list."

"Okay, I should be home before you. If not, then I'll be right behind you. I love you."

"Okay Baby, I love you too." With that Bree quickly pressed the phone button on the steering wheel to get him off the line. She didn't want Toya to say anything to out her distrustful tactics.

"WOW!" Toya says in amazement. "WOW! Damn, he was never that tuned in. And to tell you where he's going. WOOOOOW!"

Bree doesn't say anything; she lets Toya talk to herself and process whatever she needs to process so that she could move on.

"Look," Toya finally addresses Bree again. "I'm not going to front; when I stepped to you in the bathroom it was on some jealous shit. I saw the way he looks at you and in the moment I was upset that he's never looked at me that way before. And now to hear the way he speaks to you. Honestly, I don't know if this is the Reggie I know." She pauses briefly. "I'm going to act my age and not my shoe size. Maybe Reggie and I were just toxic for each other. But please don't discredit anything that I have said to you though, as I have not lied." She looks to Bree. "I'm just going to say this, if the Reggie I know rears his ugly head, then trust that it's not going to get better. You can't fix him. Don't try to stay and wait it out. With that, I wish you nothing but the best in your relationship."

"Thank you and I appreciate you being real with me. I heard what you said and if nothing else I will keep that bit of advice."

Then Toya exited the vehicle and left Bree in the car with her thoughts and music.

# CHAPTER 24

"Thank you for picking me up, Just Reggie. I could have met you there though."

"For us to have to drive back in two separate cars? I'll pass. Are you nervous?" he asks, touching Bree's knee.

"A tad," she turns her head to look at him. "Sorry I didn't get dressed. I just don't have it in me today." She makes known.

Bree would have at least attempted to look like something meeting Reggie's parents, but today it's a jeans, running shoes and jersey kind of day.

"You're good. I told you it's just us and no one is dressed up for the occasion." He reassures her.

Bree drifts off into her thoughts as she often did ever since the conversation with Toya. She has been skimming through memories of her and Reggie trying to find some inkling of his abusive ways. It's not surprising that she's found plenty. There was the time she felt intimated in his apartment and stood to face him, the time when he grabbed her hand when she was trying to take off his tie and let's not forget the blow up after she had left the party. In these instances and many more she could think of, one thing remained; he caught himself and held his composure. Daily she battles with the thoughts of her being the one to offer him the chance to change. And while her heart always answers yes, her mind is thinking at what expense?

"We're here," Reggie announces, putting the car in park. He let Bree live in her thoughts on the car ride. He thought she needed to build herself up for this moment. "Just be yourself," he encourages.

Reggie slips her hand in his as they walk through the door. It's nothing short of chaos inside. Bree immediately feels comfortable as this is just your average family at an average family gathering. The kid's toys are everywhere as they run around the house. The TV is on blast in the family room while music is playing from the kitchen. The aroma of good food is flowing throughout the house. There is more than one conversation floating about and everyone is trying to engage in all of them at once. It feels like home. The only thing Bree had to compare it to is Manny's parents and their house which is so spick and span that you feel the need to sterilize yourself and your clothes before entering; and upon entering you don't feel welcomed to sit or touch anything. This is a breath of fresh air and Bree instantly relaxes.

"You must be Brianna," his mom says as she makes her way around the island to greet Bree.

"Yes ma'am," Bree replies as she opens up for the hug his mother is giving.

"Oh, call me Lynn," she insists.

"Baby this is my sister Tasha and Brandon," he introduces.

"Nice to finally meet you," Tasha says while standing for a hug.

"My big bro Clint," Reggie moves along, "And his fiancée Zoe."

Bree moves right along with Reggie meeting the adults in the room. She guesses she'll meet the kids when they slow down and pay her some attention. She could picture Junior in here running around having the time of his life with the kids.

"Now who let a Charger's jersey inside my Texan home?" his dad bellows coming out of the garage with sodas in hand.

Bree threw her hands up surrendering, "Hey I'm fluid when it comes to football, now if you want to talk basketball there's no budging."

"I know it's OKC or bust, Brianna," he makes known as he comes in for a hug like he's known her all her life.

"Yes Sir,"

"Call me Harold." He says looking at her. "Wait a minute, first I have to deal with you being an OKC fan, then I have to deal with you coming in my home with a Chargers jersey on, now I have to deal with you bringing sweets that I can't eat?" He looks at the cake Lynn is taking out of the bag. "You're wearing out your welcome Brianna, I'll tell ya that." He smiles.

"Well you can just give back the sugar free chocolate chip cookies that I made you for your dietary restrictions, Mr. Harold." She smiles.

"Sugar free and cookies don't even belong in the same sentence," he jokes, "but where are they at?"

Everyone couldn't help but laugh at how quickly his tone changed in that one sentence.

"Sugar free," he continues to talk smack as he opens the container. "How in the hell can a cookie be a cookie without sugar? Isn't that a cracker? It looks legit," he says inspecting the cookie as if he can tell by the naked eye that it's sugar free.

"Just eat the damn cookie Harold, you're going to eat them all anyway because you're greedy," Lynn laughs.

"These are actually tasty, maybe it's because I haven't had sugar in a while," he tries to offer a reason.

"No, they're just good. In another life, I may have been a pastry chef," Bree boasts.

"Alright, I take a strike back but don't come in here talking that nurse mess trying to get on me about what I eat, that'll earn your strike back quickly." He warns.

"That's exactly what you need." Lynn chimes in.

"I wouldn't do that. I'm not going to bust your chops because you are grown and you already know what you should and shouldn't be eating," Bree turns the onus on him. "However, I will encourage and offer healthy alternatives."

"You messed up and found a slick one to join their crew," he directs his attention to Reggie. "Let me take my cookies and get out of here."

Reggie and Clint follow him into the family room and turn their attention towards the game. Bree takes a seat on a stool next to Tasha.

"Thank you for desserts Brianna. And if you don't mind, may I have the recipe for those cookies?" Lynn asks.

"You're welcome and of course."

"I wish we could stay and mingle with you guys but I have to head over to my parents for a few," Zoe says as she gets up from her seat. "We have to have a girl's night Brianna so we can talk. It was great to put a face with

the name." she smiles.

"That would be nice," Tasha agrees.

"It was nice to meet you, Zoe. Yes, we have to get together." Bree agrees.

"See ya Zo," Tasha says as Zoe is giving Brandon a kiss.

As Lynn walks Zoe to the door to see her out, Tasha takes advantage of the time to get to know the woman that now has her brother's attention.

"Brianna, I thought you had a son?" she jumps right in.

"Yes I do, he's with his dad until Sunday. And you can call me Bree."

"Oh the kids were looking forward to meeting him."

"Awe...trust he's ready to meet them as well. He will have a field day being around kids his age. Most of his friends are via school and sports, so he doesn't interact with them at home. My friend's kids are either younger or older than he is. May I?" Bree extends her arms towards Brandon, he has been squirming like a worm trying to get to Bree.

"Girl you can take him with ya'll. He is a handful. My other two were not like this."

"Hey cutie pie," Bree smiles at Brandon. "Whoa he's healthy. How old is he?" she continues as he begins bouncing on her legs.

"He's fat, four months," Tasha laughs.

"Are you hungry?" Reggie asks Bree as he walks up.

"Not right now. You?" she looks up at him.

"I can wait for you. Get off my woman," he scolds Brandon. Brandon immediately puts his face on Bree's chest.

"Don't do that to him," she says as she consoles him.

"He's always treating him like that," Tasha makes known. "Leave my son alone."

"He's alright. Toughen up squirt." Reggie smashes his face.

"Stop," Bree pushes Reggie away. "Be nice," she continues as she puts her back to Reggie and shields Brandon. "Go away," she dismisses Reggie.

"She only knew that boy for five minutes and she already threw you to the curb." His dad instigates.

"Reggie are you messing with my grandson?" his mom asks as she makes it back to the kitchen.

"Put that boy on the floor and let him toughen up, ya'll babying him." Harold instructs.

"He is a baby," all three women say in unison.

"Let me get out of here," Reggie retreats to the family room knowing that he won't win against this force.

"Let me mind my business," Harold turns back around.

"Where's your son Brianna?" Lynn asks.

"With his Dad for the holiday's, since this will be my first year with Christmas." Bree expresses excitedly.

"So is Reggie imposing on ya'll arrangements?" Lynn asks.

Bree senses where she's going and plans on clearing up any questions she may have about the situation.

"No. Manny lives in California. Junior goes with him 9-10 days a month. Nothing will change."

"How does he feel about you dating?" Tasha asks.

"He's cool with it. He's been in a relationship for years. He's pretty excited actually. He wants my son to stop bugging them for a baby." Bree chuckles.

"You know Frankie wants to introduce me to his little girlfriend." Tasha says turning the conversation to her.

"Tell Frankie to sign the papers before he starts to move on," Lynn says clearly annoyed.

"Mom the custody situation is taking care of," Tasha sighs and redirects her attention to Bree. "How did you deal with meeting his girlfriend?"

"Well..." Bree says knowing her situation is completely different from Tasha's. "Manny and I have known each other since we were 14 and our friendship produced a baby. In college, a drunken night turned into something else and I ended up pregnant. With that said, we always knew we would co-parent. He moved to California when I was pregnant and met Samantha soon after his arrival. They've been together ever since. I don't mind it because she loves my son and my son loves her, that's all I can ask for."

"Does he call her mom? I don't think I can deal with that."

"He calls her Mom-mantha. And I'm cool with that. It shows me that he loves and respects her. I always joke with Manny that if he and Samantha ever break up, then he'll have to share his days with Sam because Junior is not going to give her up."

"Whoo girl, I'm not there yet."

"Oh I get it. If there were feelings involved, then I would probably be handling this situation differently. However, Manny and I are friends and we are not out to make each other's life difficult or our son's for that matter."

"Brianna are you ready to eat?" Lynn asks.

"Sure," Bree replies while bouncing Brandon on the stool. "Baby, I'm about to eat." She tells Reggie hoping that bringing him over will change the conversation.

"Beautiful," Reggie says, placing a kiss on Bree's cheek. "Give knucklehead back to his mom."

"No, he's my friend aren't you B," Bree says to Brandon as he smiles. "You're so cute."

"Huh oh, somebody is going to have baby fever." Harold warns.

"I work in the maternity ward, I get my fix daily. Reggie on the other hand just might," Bree shares. "Here," she passes Brandon to Tasha.

"Oh I'm going to knock you up soon, don't you worry." He whispers in her ear and pats her ass.

"Get-a-room!" Tasha puffs at his gesture.

"Shut up!" Reggie says as he takes a seat and pulls Bree closer.

"Uncle Reggie who is this," the little girl that looks as if she has been rough housing for hours has finally decided to take in her surroundings.

"Princess Tabby, this is Ms. Brianna." Reggie introduces.

"Is this your girlfriend?" she asks innocently.

"What do you know about girlfriends," Reggie asks playfully while tickling her.

"Nothing, but that's what Frankie said," she gives up the informant.

"Frankie," Reggie yells, "get your little butt in here."

Frankie walks in like he has not one care in the world fumbling with the toy in his hand.

"Give me that," Reggie snatches the toy. "What you know about girlfriends?"

"I don't know," he shrugs.

"So why are you talking about things you don't know about?"

"I don't know," he gives the same reply with the same demeanor.

"Do you want to meet Ms. Brianna?"

"Is that your girlfriend?" he chuckles.

"Boy," Reggie pushes his head, "Yes, sheesh! Why is that so important?"

"Because you said she had a son and I thought you were bringing him over to play." He says like Reggie knew better than to ask such a thing.

"He's going to come next time. He had to spend time with his Dad today." Bree offers

"Ms. Brianna when you pick him up can he come over and play with us?" Frankie asks

"He won't be home for a couple of days, but I can arrange something with your mom when he gets home, okay?" Bree asks politely although she knows that dumping Junior in this environment was not what she had on the agenda, at least not so soon.

"Okay," he says sadly like that is what he's been waiting on all day.

"You know what?" Bree squats down to get eye level with him, "I know ya'll will have fun because he has those same toys at home. Raving racer is his favorite he has the whole collection of cars."

"For real? I do too! When you bring him over tell him to bring his cars please." He says excitedly.

"Will do." Bree confirms directing her attention back to her food.

"Can you play the dance game with us?" Tabby asks.

"After I finish my food, I'll play with ya'll." Bree agrees.

"Yeaaaaaaa," Tabitha runs to tell Harold that he has to give up the TV in a few.

"Girl good luck! They are going to dance you under the table," Tasha warns.

"I'm up for the challenge."

# CHAPTER 25

The evening is going well. Brianna fit right in with his family and their shenanigans. It feels good for her to feel welcomed. Nothing about the evening feels fake with his family. The conversations are genuine. Not to mention every time Reggie touches her he sends chills up and down her spine. There's no denying that she has definitely fallen. She doesn't know what to do with these feelings or how she should act. The newness of this level of love is scary. She's unsure of how to handle this, contemplating the day that this explodes in her face. What will be the story? Cheating? Beating? She can't help but to sporadically replay the conversation she had with Toya from time to time. Why can't I just enjoy the moments, she questions herself as she breaks her tragic daydream.

"Ms. Brianna, are you ready?" Tabby came back once she realized that way more time has passed than it should have.

"Ready," Bree confirms patting Reggie's leg as she gets up.

"Look at you," Lynn breaks Reggie's gaze at Bree. "You are in love," she smiles.

"Isn't he though?" Tasha agrees. "I'm going to need someone to look at me like that," she giggles.

"She surely is different from Toya," Lynn shutters.

"Polar opposite," Reggie concurs.

"She's in town you know? I saw her the other day when I was at the grocery store. She spoke." Tasha shrugs.

"Didn't know and I don't care. I hope I don't bump into her," Reggie expresses.

"Get it Bree," Tasha encourages.

"Girl these kids got these routines down pat, I can't keep up." Bree says out of breath from her mini workout.

"Doing great Baby," Reggie cheers her on. "Your phone," he holds up her phone in case she doesn't hear his words, "It's Manny."

"Can you get it?" Bree asks.

Reggie doesn't know if that is such a great idea, especially giving the environment. He's not sure of how this would go. However, he did as he was asked and answered.

"Hello," Reggie attempts to sound confident while answering, not knowing what's on the other end.

"Hey, is this Reggie?" Manny asks.

"Yeah, Bree is playing a game."

"Oh geez, she's so competitive. Can you ask her what Junior's favorite ice cream is please?"

"Don't tell him mom," Reggie hears Junior yelling in the background.

"I'm using my life line, be quiet," Manny laughs. "Can you ask her?" he asks Reggie again.

"Well he wants to know Juniors favorite ice cream, but I should add that Junior is screaming don't tell him," he smiles as he relaxes feeling welcomed into their circle.

"He knows that," Bree dismisses while continuing to display her moves.

"I said strawberry," Manny replies.

"He said he said strawberry," Reggie relays.

"Oh shoot he changed like two weeks ago. Ask if I can give him a hint."

"Can I at least get a hint?" Manny asks Junior.

"No hints," he screams.

"Nope!" Reggie laughs.

"Oh well, he better run through all the flavors," Bree laughs.

"Do you have a minute while I have you?" Manny asks Reggie in a serious tone.

"Sure,"

"Will you be available Sunday evening? I will be bringing Junior home and figured it would be a great chance for us to meet."

"Yeah that's cool." Reggie says hesitantly as there is a beep in his ear. He looks at the phone and sees the bubble of the message notification that reads:

*Derrick: I miss you too. Lunch tomorrow? We need to talk…*

"I appreciate you coming this way." Reggie says in a much smoother tone as he put the phone back to his ear.

"No problem. My son is dying to meet you. And Bree is happy to have you. It's only right. Well tell Bree we'll holla at her later. Let me go and try to guess an ice cream flavor,"

"Will do."

Reggie puts her phone back on the counter but can't help to think about the message she just received. He never heard of Derrick as far as family or friends and for him to say that he "misses her too" implies that she offered the sentiments first. He doesn't know his next step or how he is going to approach the situation. He hopes he isn't getting played for a fool.

"Whoo! I can't hang with them. No one warned me." Bree came back over out of breath.

"I said good luck, that was my warning," Tasha laughs. "I told you that they were going to dance you under the table." She continues letting Bree know that the warning was there.

"What?" Bree says looking at Reggie. She thought it was something Manny said, so she asked, "What did he say?"

"He's bringing Junior home Sunday," he responds in a monotone.

Bree just replies with a deep breath. She is unsure if she's ready for this meeting.

"Hey, hey, hey, my peeps," a female voice from the door interrupts.

Bree turns around to match the familiar voice with the face.

"Hey Best Fren, that's my Best Fren," Tasha sings as she walks over to CeeCee and gives her a hug.

Bree looks at Reggie in shock. He was fucking his sister's best friend? Isn't this quite the surprise? Bree nudges Reggie trying to give him a look and he can't bring himself to look at her. So she just snickers and squeezes his hand. She is about to have some fun with this one.

"Hey Mama Lynn," CeeCee continues to make her rounds.

"Brianna, this is my best friend Crystal," Tasha introduces. "This is Reggie's girlfriend."

"Hi Crystal, nice to meet you," Bree says extending her hand. The animosity is left in Reggie's apartment; she wouldn't dare bring it to his parent's home.

Crystal keeps her composure and extends her hand and graces.

"Hey Reg," she pushes his shoulder a little.

"Hey Cee," Reggie replies and gives her the side church hug with the pat on the back.

"Girl them love birds will make you sick, stand clear." Tasha warns.

"Where's my little man?" Crystal asks.

As they begin to engage in their conversation Bree decides to turn her attention to Reggie to clown him about this and to see why he was so uptight a few minutes ago.

"Is everything okay, sister friend fucker?" she asks softly.

"Not here." He says sternly.

"What's wrong?" she looks wanting to get to the bottom of his demeanor. If nothing else she doesn't want Crystal to see them in a moment so she began retreating.

"Nothing."

"Well how about you fix yourself up until we get home." Bree suggests.

"Do you love me?" he asks sincerely.

"Of course I do," Bree replies unsure of where this is coming from. She grabs his face and says, "I love you." And seals her words with a kiss. She hopes that he's not thinking that she is going to start some drama at his parent's house. She said all that she wanted to say to Crystal and she figured her cordial gesture would put his mind at ease.

"Ah, here they go," Tasha grunts.

"We're about to leave," Bree turns around playfully giving Tasha the eye.

"We were enjoying your company," Lynn says.

"Same here, but I have to work in the morning. I have been summoned for a return by the kids," she reminds them.

"This cheesecake is the bomb Mama Lynn,"

"It is. And I can't take credit for it. Bree made it," She informs Crystal.

"Oh, it's really good," she directs her comment to Bree without saying her name.

"Thank you. Are you ready?" Bree looks to Reggie.

"Let me go find my Dad first," Reggie says getting up.

"I'll make ya'll some plates to go," Lynn scurries into the kitchen.

Bree picks up her purse and her phone and sees the blue LED light flashing. Once she turns on her phone she sees the message from

Derrick. So now she knows why Reggie has an attitude. Instead of addressing the issue and clearing her name, she decides that she is going to wait to see how Reggie is going to handle this. There is no reason why he can't come to her for an adult conversation and get his questions answered. If Reggie doesn't address this going home in the car, then Bree is going to play it her way.

Once in the car Bree makes the final attempt to see if Reggie will address the issue.

"What's wrong Baby?" she asks again

"Nothing, just a little tired. It's been a long day."

"That it has been. So, how are you feeling about Sunday?"

"I'm good. I don't see why it wouldn't go well."

"I agree." Bree pauses, "So, felt a little awkward in there for a moment," she chuckles. "Banging the Bestie how original," she continues.

"Poor decisions," he says indifferently.

Bree decides to let this conversation fall by the wayside and employ her trap. With that, she replies to Derrick.

*Of course, always up for a chat.*

*At the bench? He* questions.

*Yup, the usual.*

*I'll be there. Good night!*

*Goodnight!*

Now she will lay her phone down for Reggie to read the text and see how tomorrow goes.

# CHAPTER 26

Last night went as planned. Bree hopped in the shower and left her phone on the bed and as expected Reggie rummaged through her personal conversations. Once she got out of the shower he pretended to be asleep, so Bree turned in for the night then got up with her usual morning routine. Only difference is this morning she left her lunch in the fridge.

Reggie hasn't made any type of contact and Bree is hoping that her master plan she set in motion is in fact moving forward. She resists the urge to make conversation with him and try to enjoy her morning waiting to see what the lunch hour brings.

Reggie sits in his car waiting on Bree to emerge from the building. He already sees the man in which he takes it upon himself to name him Derrick waiting on the bench in the distance. He showed up before Reggie even pulled up. Talk about wanting to be prompt. As Reggie watches Bree walk from the building Derrick immediately stands with a smile on his face and open arms. There is no hesitation for Bree to walk into the familiar embrace. He extends his arms to get a good look at her like he hasn't seen her in awhile. Reggie sees Bree smile from a distance, she's eating whatever he is saying and inviting him to sit.

"So, what's going on stranger, long time no hear, there must be trouble," Bree dives right in to get "the talk" going.

"Yeah it's been awhile and things are not looking so good."

"Well what's going on?" Bree asks again.

Derrick looks up as the tall unfamiliar face approaches where he and Bree are sitting. Bree turns to see Reggie coming and right on time. She immediately stands up to greet him.

"Hey Baby," she says leaning in for a quick kiss.

"Hey, you forgot your lunch. I was heading across town and decided to drop it off."

"You're so thoughtful," she smiles. "Well come," she invites him into their space.

Derrick stands knowing exactly who is facing, "You must be Reggie," he gleams swinging his arm back to get a good shake in there. "I've heard so much about you. I'm Slim."

"Derrick," Bree makes clear.

"That's what the papers say," he confirms.

Reggie feels microscopic right now. He has heard of Slim as Bree has talked about him on a few occasions.

"Baby, I don't mean to throw you to the curb, but Slim needs to talk and I'm unsure if it's personal?" Bree says cautiously.

"Ah naw, he's fam now, it's cool." Slim assures Bree.

They all take a seat and Bree is waiting for whatever this news is that she needs to hear and why he needs to talk to her about it.

"Well," he says nervously twisting his wedding band. "Lisa and I are getting a divorce."

"Wait! What? Why?" Bree asks quickly and confusingly. "I'm so sorry Slim," she says as she scoots towards him and grabs his hand.

He slowly turns to Bree, "Bullshit, you know you don't like Lisa," he says sadly.

"Now I can admit that we don't see eye to eye…"

"That's an understatement," he interrupts.

"We're not on the best of terms, but I would never wish this on you Slim." She says sincerely.

There is a moment of silence. Reggie is just a spectator. Bree is trying to find the right words to say giving her and Lisa's terrible relationship. Slim is trying to find out how he is going to ask Bree the magic question.

"Why didn't you tell me she fucked Manny, Bree?" he spat out not knowing how to phrase it.

"Because I didn't know." She answers.

"Lisa said you knew."

"I promise you I didn't know. Now I'm not going to say that I didn't know some things went down, but them fucking is new to me."

"Bree, you know everything about Manny. How could you let me look crazy like this? I thought we were cool."

"Given her track record and what I do know, I don't put it past them. BUT Derrick I swear I didn't know. Are we talking recently?"

"No. I don't know. I don't think so. Maybe college?" He says unsure of his words. "But that doesn't matter. You were supposed to have my back. How could you not tell me whatever it is you know? You always talking that shit about how you're trying to keep your hands clean but you always come up in everything. This is fucked up."

Bree feels Reggie hesitating. She's sure he's not feeling the way Slim is talking to her right now.

She turns to Reggie and rubs his leg, "It's cool," she lets him know.

"Well are you going to say something?" Slims asks.

"Are you finished?" Bree pauses. "Slim look," she continues because he doesn't say anything. "I know you're hurting right now and you need someone to blame for your life being tossed up in this hell storm. If you want to blame me and beat me up about it, then go ahead and jab away. I can take it." Bree offers. Whatever issues he and Lisa are having has absolutely nothing to do with her or the dirt she knows about Lisa. She knows that Slim is redirecting his pain and as a friend she'll share the burden.

"That's not what I'm trying to do," he says after a couple of minutes of silence. "I just want to find out the truth."

"When I first got wind of you and Lisa I told you to smash and dash, but by that time you were already too far in. It's not my place to be the hoefax reporter and tell you how many miles that girl has on her pussy, the holes that's been plugged or the damage to her frame. But I did warn you that she was loose, did I not?"

"You did."

"And you said that was her past and asked that I move on from it as you have. I have been nothing but the friend you asked me to be. I speak to her, went to that dumb ass bridal shower and brought a great gift might I add. I attended that stupid ass bachelorette party. I participated in the wedding. I was there for your kid's baby showers, birthdays and anything you have asked. And now you want to tell me that I don't have your back."

"You're right. You have been there for us. But I'm asking you as a friend to just tell me what you know."

"You of all people know that I can't stand that girl, and you of all people know that I don't tell people's business. I don't like her but I'm not going to talk about her."

He closes his eyes and taps his forehead with his fist. "Bree it's over, she's pregnant and the baby may not be mine. Just. Please." He begs.

Bree is trying to figure out how Manny's name came up in this conversation of her being pregnant by someone else. She wants to get to the bottom of this ASAP because if Manny has been smashing that shit, there will be hell to pay.

"I cannot tell you that girl's business. I'll call Manny if you want and have him tell you. Do you want that?"

"I don't care." Slim caves in and goes with her suggestion.

Bree is happy with his compliance as she wants to hear what Manny has to say.

"Manny are you busy?" Bree asks.

"Depends."

"Well I'm on some dumb shit, so if you're doing something, then by all means continue."

"Naw what's up?"

"I have you on speaker and I'm here with Derrick, Slim." She clarifies

"OK." He says unconcerned. Manny and Derrick are not friends. They never were.

"Have you talked to Lisa recently."

"Hell no, I haven't talked to her ass since college."

"Did you fuck Lisa back in the day?"

"Naw, she wanted to smash though," he chuckles.

"When I walked in on you and her, what was she doing?"

"Sucking my dick," he says proudly as if he's receiving an award.

Bree knows he's enjoying this a little too much and now wants to get him off the line.

"And I didn't smash because I don't sleep with the enemy." He said taking his jab at Slim. He always warned Bree that Slim was not her friend because he married that girl. "I know you don't like her. I thought if you walked in on her while she was on her knees you would use it for ammo, and you didn't. You're so damn ungrateful." He says with disappointment in his voice.

"Get off my line. Bye." Bree hangs up. Once Manny gets started it's no stopping him and the fact that he doesn't care for Slim doesn't help this situation at all.

"See that's what I walked in on, and like I said I would not have put it passed them, but I didn't think he smashed." Bree clears her name with Slim.

"So why would she say that?" Slim asks confused.

"Because she's so fucking vindictive," Bree answers. "She's trying her best to do and say anything that she knows will hurt you. Because she knows that she fucked up." Bree lists reasons.

Silence fills the air again.

"You know what?" Bree breaks the silence. "You spared her. I wanted to reconstruct her face with the bottom of my boots and I couldn't do it because she was your girl. But I thank you now because the universe got her ass back for me without me having to do a thing. That boomerang she threw at me five years ago has finally returned." Bree confesses.

"What are you talking about?" Slim asks.

"You know she was the one who fueled the rumor and told Mrs. Lillian when I got pregnant that I wasn't pregnant by Manny? She confronted Eddie and told him that Junior was probably his and when he showed back up in the picture it didn't help the already fucked up relationship that me and Mrs. Lillian were having. I know who my son's father is and looks at her in limbo."

"I didn't know that. Why did you tell me?"

"Slim you were so far up that girl's ass nothing was getting through to you. But I didn't tell you because that was the least of my concerns at the time."

"So you're happy I'm in this situation?"

"Not at all. Am I happy I can witness her karma, yes. Not happy that it's at your expense. This situation is sad and unfortunate. You have been nothing but an amazing husband, father and friend. You have had her back when no one else has. And besides your personal life suffering, you guys have a business together. I know that this is a lot on your plate and you don't know what to do right now, but I'm telling you from the bottom of my heart that I support whatever decision you make. I know you don't want to leave her. Don't think about what anyone has to say because only you have to deal with your decision. Now, I still don't like the girl," she laughs to lighten the mood.

Slim let out a slight chuckle. And this is why he wanted to talk to Bree because he knew that she would encourage him to do exactly what he wanted to do which is stay.

"I know you will never like her, but I hear you. Thank you for listening and I apologize for coming at you like that."

"That's what friends are for," Bree says.

"Well let me get out of ya'll hair," Slim says while standing. "I apologize for my drama," he directs towards Reggie, "hopefully we can get together soon under better circumstances." He offers.

"No problem. Will do." Reggie confirms.

"Damn. I would lose my mind if my wife told me she is pregnant and isn't sure if it's mine." Reggie says once Slim is out of earshot.

"Well YOU don't have to ever have to worry about that AND his problems left with him." Bree says because she doesn't discuss other people's business. "Do you owe me an apology?" she brings Reggie back to their life and the reason he's here.

"For what?"

"Why are you here?"

"Alright, you got me." He confesses. "I apologize for going through your phone and not trusting you."

"I appreciate your honesty. But I must say that I'm disappointed. Was our conversation about being open and honest just for shits and giggles? You do know that you can talk to me about anything for the millionth time."

"I know, I know. I didn't know what to do."

"Talk to me."

"Sounds so easy."

"It is very easy. Bree, who is Derrick? Would have started it off quite nicely. You cannot boil your own blood and then come to throw the hot contents on me. That's exactly what you did and was about to do when you showed up."

"You're right." Reggie agrees. He was ready to go off when he showed up. He has to get used to honesty and transparency as Bree is very comfortable with both.

"And I would appreciate it if you refrain from rummaging through my personal belongings. If you feel that uneasy about anything, then ask and receive permission first. I have no problem with helping you erase your concerns, but you have to afford me the opportunity to do that."

"I apologize Brianna. I don't want my immature actions and insecurities to damage the trust in our relationship. I was way out of line for going through your phone and it won't happen again."

"We've had this conversation about our anger and I'm trying to keep it together, but to be honest you are testing my patience. I cannot be the only one working to ensure that we stay in a safe place."

"I understand and I agree."

"Do you?" she asks because this is not a place that she wants to revisit again. She doesn't know how much longer she can hold on before the real Brianna shows up.

"Yes. We won't be back here again." He assures her.

Bree isn't sure how much she believes the declaration but she doesn't feel like washing mud pies, so she decides to move along.

"I left my lunch on purpose, so you didn't come up here looking crazy," she reveals while laughing.

"Good call. Thank you," he laughs. "You are amazing, you know that? You're a wonderful friend."

"Thank you. Let me get to work." Bree cut it short. While she is smoothly taking all that had happened in stride, she's not fond of him not trusting her.

# CHAPTER 27

The highly anticipated day has arrived and for Bree to say that she is nervous would be an understatement. There's so much at stake. She hopes that she has done a good enough job showing who she truly is and how this blended situation can work.

"MOOOOOOM!!!" she hears Junior yells in his something maybe terribly wrong but it's really not voice.

Bree comes from the kitchen, "Hey Champ, I've missed you so much." She says as she picks him up for a hug.

"Beautiful Bree," Manny opens his arms, "Oops am I allowed to say that?" he teases.

"Whatever," Bree gives him a hug and a kiss on the cheek.

Reggie makes his way down the stairs and is in shock.

"You must be Reggie," Manny extends his hand.

"Glenn Hicks?" Reggie questions as he extends his hand with a puzzling look.

"Manny," he confirms unbothered. Manny is an A list celebrity actor known as the sexy boyfriend in romantic movies. He has recently been exploring action films and they all have done very well.

"And this is Junior," Bree interrupts.

"Hi Mr. Reggie," Junior says shyly.

"Nice to finally meet you," Reggie smiles.

"Well we are going to go and get ice cream for dessert while Dad and Mr. Reggie talk," Bree says to Junior.

"Yay! Ice cream, see you later Dad," He runs towards the garage.

Both Reggie and Manny's hands go into their pockets. "Sorry," Manny nods to retreats.

"I can buy ice cream," Bree assures the both of them. "I'll be back," she kisses Reggie on the lips.

"Take my car, I'm blocking you in," Manny hands Bree the keys.

"C'mon you," she says to Junior leading him to the front door.

"I've heard so much about you." Manny dives in. "But from the looks of your face Bree has left something's out about me." Manny addresses Reggie's shock to see who he is.

He makes his way to the couch to get comfortable and finish his conversation.

"I trust Bree and in the end that's all the matters. The fact that I am meeting you speaks volumes about how she feels about you and your intentions, so I won't question that. I just need you to tell me if I am overstepping my boundaries when it comes to y'all's relationship. Bree and I talk a lot. She's my best friend, but I don't want that to interfere with your relationship. So please call me out." He lays on the table again. "I treat Bree a certain way for our son, which is why my hand also went into my pocket for the ice cream." He pauses to let Reggie take that in. "I treat Bree this way to show my son how to treat a woman and I know that his first line of an example is the way I treat his mother. Bree doesn't carry bags, open car doors, go into her purse, amongst other things, but I will make the conscious effort to stand down and let you take that role. As far as Junior, I'm sure Bree will fill you in on our parenting. As of right now, we don't spank him, but that is an option if needed and I feel it coming soon," he admits. "There's a little testosterone developing in those testicles. I hear how he tests Bree sometimes when we're on the phone. Disrespect towards her will not be tolerated. She only needs to make her request one time. He doesn't get to give her lip service. Having you around will hopefully get him to straighten up. Let's see... there's not anything else I'm really concerned about. Like I said, I trust Bree's judgment. Do you have anything for me?"

"First off are we going to sit around and act like you're not Glenn Hicks?" Reggie asks as he is a little star struck.

"Yes, because Bree doesn't care," he laughs. While she supports him, his stardom means nothing to her. "Besides this is one of the few places that I get to come to and leave the light off. More importantly, Bree prefers not to live in my shadow and I respect that."

"I get it. And to answer your question, you've pretty much summed up my concerns. Bree has been very open about the dynamics of your co-parenting and friendship, so I'm good. I'll definitely keep my ears open for any disrespect. I haven't heard any when Bree and I are talking, but then again it is always bedtime."

"Are you up for stepping into this parenting gig? I mean I think good years are gone. The older they get the more difficult it becomes." Manny warns of his unknown dangers.

"Yes, I am ready. Bree made sure of it," he chuckles. "And considering I was my mother's pain in the ass, I know the best is yet to come."

"Excuse me for a minute," Manny says, raising his ringing phone towards Reggie.

Reggie nods and heads to the kitchen to give him some privacy, but also to start the garlic bread so that dinner can start when Bree gets home. He's trying not to let his thoughts run ramped; yet, it's difficult not to compare himself to the man that has been voted the sexiest man of the year two years in a row. He can't imagine why Bree wouldn't just live the life with Manny and be a family. It's hard to fathom when someone opts out the easy road for something more challenging. Not that Bree's life is troublesome, but why not just sit back and enjoy the perks? It makes Reggie think that maybe their relationship or lack thereof is not what Bree makes it to be.

"Hey Baby," Bree walks up behind Reggie, breaking his daydream while placing a kiss on his neck.

"Hey, I didn't even hear you guys come in," he admits.

"I can tell. Thank you," she nods towards the oven. "We brought you some dessert," she smiles, waving the candy bar knowing Reggie isn't a huge fan of ice cream.

Since Bree knows that diabetes runs in his family she monitors his diet now, more importantly his sugar intake. Eating a pack of candy bars a day is not what she will sit by and watch him do.

"Damn I'm so deprived, because I am so excited right now," he laughs. "That's a damn shame you know that? I'm a grown ass man." He announces as if Bree doesn't know.

"I'm looking out for you though, that should be appreciated I would think."

"Doesn't change the fact that I'm deprived," he says grabbing the candy from her hand.

"After dinner," she makes known as she grabs it back. "What?" Bree asks thinking he is about to go off on a sugar addiction tangent because of his facial expression.

"Glenn Hicks," he leaves in the air for her to catch it.

"So," she brushes it off as if that is not semi-important information.

"Why didn't you tell me?"

She grabs him by the waist and looks into his eyes, "Because he's a nobody." She jokes. When she realizes that he's serious she asks, "Would it have impacted the way you feel about me?"

"No!"

"Well that's why. It doesn't matter."

"Still matters."

"We'll talk about it later," she seals with a quick kiss on his lips.

"Are you guys making a baby?" Juniors asks as he walks in to witness the affection.

"No," Bree says, squatting to his level. "Kissing someone does not make a baby. Go tell Dad we're about to eat."

# CHAPTER 28

"Mr. Reggie, when will I be able to meet your kids?" Junior starts the conversation as they sit at the dinner table.

"Well, I don't have any kids, but I have two nephews and a niece."

"Oh yeah, I forgot. When can I meet them?"

"We will have to arrange something. Maybe this weekend?" he glances at Bree.

"We'll see. Frankie is dying to meet you. He wants you to bring all your Raving Racers." Bree says trying to sound excited.

"He likes Raving Racer? Cool!"

"I have an announcement." Manny interjects, breaking up their excitement. He figures he should catch Junior on a high note, so he doesn't sink so low. "I have to go to Canada for a few months."

"Why dad?" Junior whines. "I don't want you to go." He continues. One would think that he wouldn't care if Manny is in California or Canada, but it matters to Junior. He is much better when he knows Manny is home. It gives him comfort knowing that he will visit soon.

"It's for work and I will be back before you know it. You aren't coming to visit me next month anyway remember? You are spending Christmas with Mom."

"I know but I thought you were coming here."

"I never said that." Manny clears the misunderstanding.

"We're going on a vacation," Bree expresses excitedly to save Manny from the brutal beating that he's about to get.

"When? Where?" Reggie asks as this is the first he heard of a vacation.

"During the week of Christmas, I took off because he'll be with me. I'm not sure of where we're going yet. Somewhere with sun and a beach," she discloses.

"Jamaica, Junior loves it!" Manny suggests.

"Yeah, I love it there. I can catch the fish with my hands," he says excitedly, confirming his dad's statement.

"That could work. I have to get on it and get the ball rolling. I have less than a month."

"Kim can handle it. Call her and tell her when you want to go." Manny says nonchalantly offering his assistants services.

"Thank you. But I'm capable of taking our son on a vacation." Bree says in a short tone. She hates the fact that Manny doesn't let her do much for him monetarily.

"That's fine Brianna." He offers the same tone. "I'm just saying that her services are available to you."

"I know," Bree confirms. Just like she also knows that if she calls Kim that he would foot the bill. "When does your flight leave?" she asks before stuffing her mouth. If one thing can make them go at it, it's him shoving unwanted money at her.

"Tomorrow, I'm heading to my parents house for the night."

"You're still welcomed to stay here," Reggie intervenes. Bree has told him how Manny would sometimes stay there with Junior if he had a next day flight.

"Thanks, but I have to spend some time with the old man." Manny declines. "Hi Mom," Manny says into his phone.

Bree rolls her eyes at Manny but they both know that it's directed to his mother. Bree doesn't feel like being the bigger person today. It's so easy to tell someone to turn the other cheek. Turning the other cheek takes a lot of energy sometimes. Especially, if the other person's energy bank is already in the negative; Mrs. Lillian offers no help in assisting that their interactions run smoothly. Bree removes herself from the table by starting to clean.

"Want your ice cream now Champ?" Bree asks Junior.

"Yes, please."

Reggie follows suit and helps Bree clear the table. Once they are out of ear shot he asks, "Are you okay?"

"Yeah I'm good," Bree replies, not looking at him.

"Are you sure?" he repeats knowing she is lying.

"Just watch," she sighs.

As they both go to sit back at the table, Reggie takes her advice and sits back to observe. Manny is still on the phone. He is trying to explain to his mother that bringing Junior was not part of the plan.

"I understand that, but Bree hasn't seen him in over a week and I didn't ask ahead of time." He continues. "Sure you can talk to him."

"Mom can I go?" Junior asks right before Manny gives him the phone.

"Sure you can go. You haven't seen them in a long time." Bree manages to say nicely.

"Grandma, my mom says I can come to your house." He shouts without a hello. "I'm going to pack my bag." He hands Manny back the phone.

"We'll see you in a few." Manny ends the conversation. "Thank you," he looks at Bree with a face of exhaustion.

"Did you see that reaction?" She implies her reasoning.

"You would think she would see him more than me. They're less than thirty minutes away."

Bree is silent. She agrees that Junior could and should see them more. She would also embrace it. Besides the fact that her family is so far away, mending a relationship with Manny's mother would be easier than her own mother at this point.

"Why can't ya'll just make amends already?" he asks Bree. Manny never wanted to get in between the two of them because he doesn't want to have to take sides. While if it was his mother against Bree, of course, his mother would win hands down. However, right now it's his mother against his son, and in this battle she loses. She wouldn't see it as Manny choosing his son; she would view it as him choosing Bree. And that is the situation he's hoping to avoid.

"I don't have a problem with your mother." Bree expresses. "You can thank my therapist for that. You know the whole forgive the other person even if they don't apologize because forgiveness is for yourself, bit. Yeah that works!" she continues sarcastically. "Your mom has a problem. She doesn't talk to me or call her grandson. Hell we haven't even been in the same room without you being present."

Manny takes in her words and tries to shift through his memory to find a time where his mother and Bree had an interaction in his absence.

"I'll give you time," Bree offers. "You won't find one though." She says as she knows exactly what he is trying to remember. "The last time your mother and I talked alone was when I gave her the results of the DNA test." Bree offers him a timeline which would put Junior at two months old.

"Okay and I thought that moment cleared everything up and things would be fine. I thought apologies were offered. On both ends," he clarifies.

"No apologies at all." Bree confirms. "Like I said, your mother has the problem. I let Junior call them on birthdays and holidays. He calls on their anniversary. Send them cards for Christmas. I mail school and sports pictures. And they are even included in the mass emails of his game schedule. I don't know what else to do." She pauses. "I mean what else do I need to do? I hope she doesn't think I am supposed to apologize first?" Bree questions Manny.

"I agree that she should start. She was out of line often. I cannot believe she never apologized to you though," he says reaching for his phone.

"What are you doing?" Bree asks as she gets up and snatches it from his hands. "I don't want a forced apology."

"Well she at least needs to call you directly and ask if Junior can come over." He says trying to push dialogue between the two.

""Why? And if she doesn't, then what? He doesn't go? And how is that fair to him as he is packing a bag? Teach her a lesson another day." Bree demands. "And don't go over there beating on your chest with this BS. I don't want her to think I put you up to this. It's been almost five years. The apology train is long gone. You can encourage her to be more active in his life though."

"MOOOOOOMMMMM!!!! I can't find my blue shirt," Junior yells.

"Don't bring what's buried back to the surface. We can all just move on and be there for Junior. I don't need a relationship with her." Bree says looking Manny in the eyes before she disappears to go and help Junior.

# CHAPTER 29

When they retreat into the bedroom for the night, Reggie decides that he would keep his promise of an open dialogue and address the concerns of Bree hiding Manny's identity.

"Hold me, my love," Bree says as she climbs onto the bed into Reggie's arms.

Reggie holds her for about 10 minutes before he breaks the silence. "Baby, can we talk?"

"Sure," she gets up to look him in the face. "About what?"

"Manny."

"What about him?" Bree doesn't know if he is uncomfortable with their interaction at the table. She can admit that once she and Manny got on the topic about his mother that Reggie's presence disappeared.

"Why didn't you tell me?"

"I don't know." She answers realizing he's back on this subject again. "It's a difficult subject I guess. I don't claim any affiliation to his celebrity status. I keep that part separate. He's just Manny to me."

"Although, I do understand your position; I can't quite explain how I feel. But if I had to use a word it would probably be uncomfortable."

"About what? Do you think that we are seeing each other or we are still engaged in sexual activity?" Bree asks knowing that this would be the case as always. Dammit! Can she not have a healthy relationship?

"I don't know."

"You've have got to be kidding me?"

"No Baby, I don't think that. I am saying I don't know because I don't know how to describe how I feel."

"Are you jealous?" she offers to help him out with the word he's avoiding.

"If I'm being honest, then yes a little. He was voted the sexiest man of the year two years in a row. My mother, sister, female coworkers, hell just about all the women I know gawk over him."

"I don't"

"You don't," he says with his lips twisted to the side in doubt.

"No. I don't. And I don't know how you feel but if I could guess, you feel like he's the man of the house away from home. I can see why, but I can also assure you that any financial assistance Manny gives me is for our son. No he didn't purchase or assist me in purchasing my home. I worked my ass off for this. He brought the Benz in the garage and as you notice, I only drive that car when I have Junior because that's his car. Any other time, I drive my Mustang. I don't ask him for anything and he doesn't offer anything if it doesn't concern Junior. Now I'm not going to pretend like I don't benefit from his financial help with our son because I do. I don't have to pay for Junior's education, childcare expenses, healthcare or damn near any other expense for Junior. And I realize that it has given me a one up on my peers to purchase my own home as quickly as I did. I was able to pay off my student loans and have the opportunity to be debt free. But I still worked to get here. And I will continue to work to take care of myself. If this is your concern, then you don't have to worry about that. I will not undermine you in financial situations. Or run to Manny to provide something that you wish to. That's not me. If I was going to use Manny for his money, then I would damn sure have a bigger house than this," she smiles to get him to ease up. "I'm happy with my life and what I have."

Reggie doesn't speak for a moment. He soaks up Bree words like water in a sponge. "You hit the nail on the head with this. That's it! The financial aspect about our life together is in question. I need to know that I'm the man of our home and the sole provider for our family. I know that Manny will take care of his son, but I'm speaking on us and if we decide to extend our family."

"You are my Man and The Man. I'm all yours Baby. You are the driver of our home now and always. Got it!" she asks as she straddles him to look him in his eyes.

Reggie has never felt so powerful. Bree's words have planted a seed of fiery passion that he plans to water so that he can grow into the leader that she's counting on him to be. "I got us." He assures her.

# CHAPTER 30

As Reggie is spending the majority of his time at Bree's house he is trying to find his way into their daily routine. Bree machine is well oiled with the only hiccup being Junior dragging his feet every now and then. Even that sometimes doesn't cause much of stir as Bree has managed to factor that in as well. They are heading to the Warriors last game of the season but Reggie's first game as a spectator. He is unsure how he will fit in with the crowd. Upon their arrival, he is meeting many of those people in Bree's circle that aren't seen as much.

"Glad this is over," an average height brown skinned male says as he plops next to Bree.

"Hey Khy, bitter and sweet. I'm sure Junior will be bugging me about another activity shortly. Khy this is my love, Reggie. Baby, this is Khyree is Kevin's dad."

"Nice you meet you," Reggie extends his hand as his memory jogs back to the question of them hanging out from Junior.

"Same here, so you're the person I'm exchanging numbers with so we can get together?" he chuckles.

"In the flesh," Reggie smiles.

"Well let's do that now so I don't forget because I will never hear the end of it." Khy says, pulling out his phone.

They exchange numbers and start a casual conversation as the teams are huddled planning their course of action.

"Baby, let's switch," Bree suggests as she moves to scoot on the other side of Reggie so they can talk and not over her.

The game is underway and Junior is ensuring that their eyes are on him. After a quick wave he turns his eyes to his teammates to contribute his fair share of athleticism to the sport.

"He's pretty good considering," Reggie nudges Bree. "If he can get a better handle on the ball and a follow through he would surpass his peers by a long shot."

"I agree. He'll get there."

"Oops," Bree turns around to see the little nugget pulling her hair. "Layla, Layla, come here baby girl." She says as she swings the tiny toddler into her lap. "Hey Meghan, how have you been?" she asks Layla's mom before she completely dismisses her and turns her attention to Layla.

"I'm good, glad this mess is over." She mimics Khy's sentiments.

Layla looks at Reggie and smiles. "Give him a hi five," Bree encourages and she complies. "How have you been Lay? Do you see your brother? Where's MarMar?"

"MarMar," Layla points to the floor at her brother with excitement.

Then just like that she wiggles her way back to her mother and greets the next parent in the stands.

As Bree is bringing her attention back to the game, she feels Reggie's phone vibrating as it is shaking against the bench. Knowing that Bree is aware Reggie pulls his phone from his pocket. Bree tries to keep her head straight ahead but her eyes drift to the screen causing it to move slightly. Tracey is showing under incoming call. Bree has never heard of Tracey and giving the name is unisex she doesn't want to jump to conclusion. He ignores the call. Rightfully so, with the noise level it would be pointless to attempt a conversation in here. He puts his phone back in his pocket, places his hand on Bree's knee and redirects his attention back to the game. Bree gives Reggie a brief glance to let him know that she saw what he did and put her sights back on her son.

After the game, the mingling of the parents and the playing of the kids commence. Junior's team lost ending the season 8-2. Not too bad considering that this is the Coach's first year. After Bree finishes with her normal crew she looks around to gather the boys and head out. Junior is running the floor with Kevin and Reggie has found a circle and he is enjoying the conversation that they are in. Bottom line, neither of them looks like they are ready to leave and it's already 7:45.

Junior needs dinner and a bath. His 8:30 bedtime will be missed tonight.

"Ready?" Bree walks over and taps Reggie on the arm.

Reggie turns to her and nods in agreement, but turns back around to continue to talk. After what seems like forever for Bree which was probably only about two minutes he says, "Hey I'm going to head out. Khyree hit me up."

"Will do, can I pass your number along?"

"Sure. We'll all get together soon."

"Junior," Bree calls, "It's time to go. Goodnight Kevin." She quickly says before they can whine and ask for five more minutes.

"Way to go, Champ!" Bree praises Junior as soon as he's within arm's reach so she can extend a high-five.

"Thanks Mom."

"Great job! You look pretty good out there," Reggie says as he rubs Junior's head.

"Did you see me make a shot?"

"Yup. Now I'm going to teach you to follow through so you can make more shots." He promises.

They had their own little conversation excluding Bree the entire way home until they walked through the door and asked what's for dinner. She was tempted to tell them to figure it out, but can't deny that she enjoys seeing Junior actively engaging with Reggie.

"Pulled chicken sandwiches, corn on the cob, beans and if you take your bath now then I can make you some fries."

"And can you make some of the little sausages too?" Junior asks excitedly. This is one of his favorite meals.

"If we have some, then yes. I have to check though."

Junior runs off to go and take his bath.

"Don't put too much water in that tub," Bree yells.

"Okay!"

"I really enjoyed myself today," Reggie tells Bree as he follows her into the kitchen.

"I'm glad you did. Junior is so happy that you came. Thank you."

"I'm sad that it's over. What's the next sport?" he asks eagerly.

"You'd have to ask him. I typically go with the flow. I don't plan these things out. He hasn't expressed any interest in anything, so I'm laying low for the winter." She says uninterested.

"Well I'm here to take him."

"Again take that up with him. If ya'll find something, then sign him up! But know that it's a commitment."

"I know, I said I could do it," he interrupts.

"Not my point."

"Enlighten me."

"Nevermind." Bree huffs and continues making dinner.

At that moment Reggie knew this had nothing to do with Junior and everything to do with Tracey. Bree is retreating back into her comfort zone, which is a fortress of brick walls that shut out emotions.

"Come out of hiding brown recluse and talk to me." Reggie offers. The name is very fitting as the brown recluse unintentionally attacks and when Bree retreats in her dark corner she's liable to do just that out of fear.

"Is Tracey a man?" she asks, swinging her head around to catch his reaction.

"No," he answers swiftly knowing this is the conversation she wants to have.

"Well who is she?"

"Tracey is a college friend. Yes, we've been in a relationship before while in college. Very short lived. We've discovered that we are better off as friends so we always kept in touch. We have lunch dates when possible. She no longer lives in Texas but her business travels bring her this way every now and then." He gives Bree to the run down to give her the comfort she most desperately needs.

"Do you plan on calling her back?"

"I do. Not tonight, but I will if it will make you feel better."

"No, it's cool. I just asked."

"So, what will make you feel better?"

"Me building a bridge." She says sarcastically.

"I can help with that." He assures her.

Bree isn't trying to hear it although she can admit she's being a bit unreasonable giving his offer. She's just not feeling it right now.

"I don't know. I trust you and I believe you. It's just you were acting real funny in the gym and that doesn't sit well with me. And that's why I say that I have to get over it myself."

"I can understand how it looked suspicious because I was a tad bit nervous." He admits. "Given I've never talked about her and here she is calling and at that moment I had no choice but to decline. The series of unfortunate factors formed into this cloud of doubt that you're in. But

I'm here to blow it away by telling you that there is absolutely nothing going on between me and Tracey and again will offer to call her to ease your mind."

"No baby, you're fine. I'm good." She expresses still with a bit of uncertainty.

"Are you sure," he asks as he comes chest to chest with her.

"Yes, I'm sure," she says and offers a kiss of peace.

# CHAPTER 31

"Hey girl," Bree says as she takes her seat in the booth across from Nia. "Thanks for coming out for lunch night owl or should I say vampire," Bree teases.

"You're welcome. I haven't seen you in a minute and if being in the sun is the price I have to pay then so be it," she chuckles. "So how's everything going? It seems you and Reggie has hit it off quite nicely. Is this lunch on you since I'm the matchmaker and all?"

"Always trying to get a free meal, I guess Cupid. What have you been up to these days?"

"Let's not shine the light on me. You know I'm here to find out about Mr. Reggie. I mean damn has he moved in already?"

"He has been staying there, but he still has his place." Bree answers in the mind your business tone.

"Don't come at me. Hell you allowed this setup," Nia laughs at Bree's demeanor. "It's not my fault you're dickmatized!" she continues through laughter.

"Honestly Nia, that's not it." Bree gets serious. It's really not about their sexual relationship and more about how she feels when she's around him and how much she's changed for the better.

"This is definitely a new level of love for me. I don't know if it's his age or the fact that I'm maturing, but the timing was right. Now, he has his fair share of shit with him. Girl," she lets out a sigh as she thinks back to the little hiccups they've been through; hiccups that she plans on keeping to herself. Especially the conversation she had with Toya. "He can be a piece of work, but we worked through it you know. And that's the positive out of it."

"Remi, what are you holding in?" Nia asks after her heartfelt confession of love. She knows Brianna better than that. "Don't get me wrong I am very happy for you and I knew that ya'll would hit it off, but I know that voice." Nia continues.

Brianna lets out an exhausting sigh. While she knows that Nia isn't referring to their hiccups, she would be lying to herself if she says that something isn't bothering her. "From the beginning I have been on the transparency and trust kick. And I have been holding up my end of the bargain until I went and got me some birth control." She confesses.

"What's wrong with that?" Nia asks.

"You're right there's nothing wrong with taking birth control," Bree starts, but Nia interrupts.

"No, no, no…I'm not siding with you. I'm trying to figure out why you feel guilty about it."

"It's ultimately my decision," Bree dismisses her interruption and continues on with where she was going.

"Why do you feel guilty?" Nia stresses her question again. "If you felt in your heart that you made the correct ultimate decision, then you would not have brought it up." Nia ignores her remarks and turns the knob to increase the temperature.

"He continuously talks about marriage and kids," Bree discloses.

"And what's wrong with that?"

"Nia it's been two months. It's all happening too fast."

"I get that and that's why I asked what's wrong with taking birth control. He should understand if this is how you feel."

"I don't know how he feels about it."

"So you haven't told him?"

"No!"

"Now I see your dilemma. Why not? This is not a big deal Bree, just tell him."

"I don't know how."

"How long has it been?"

"I started as soon as we made us official."

"Just tell him that you've always been taking them." Nia offers her backhanded remedy.

"That's the thing. We had a conversation about it and he knows that I wasn't. On top of that, I happily engage in the marriage and growing family talks. I want that Nia really I do. But just not right now." Bree pleads as if Nia is the one that needs convincing.

"Sooner is better than later Bree." Nia offers her caution. She's at a loss on how Bree should handle the situation other than getting it over with.

"I know, I know. I'm going to do it. You know he met Manny right?"

"Oh yeah, you never told me how that went though."

"Surprisingly good. Too good." Bree states.

"That's great! Ya'll are just moving right along." Nia smiles.

"He was a bit taken back when he realized who Manny is," Bree discloses.

"You never told him Bree? What the hell, that is not something you spring on someone."

"He told me," Bree laughs. "It all worked out though. I had to do a little reassurance, but we're good."

"I bet with Manny's sexy ass. Reggie has a right to be jealous." She says taking up for him.

"I don't want Manny."

"Doesn't change the fact that he's fine and paid." Nia shrugs.

"Okay, I'm done. What about you?" Bree restarts the conversation after the waitress leaves.

"Same 'ol shit different day over here. I thought hooking you up with Reggie would aid in us getting together more, but I was wrong." Nia admits.

"We get out." Bree defends.

"Not as much as I thought. You got him tied down in the house talking about marriage and shit."

"Well ya'll both have a long time to wait for that," Bree says. She wants marriage and kids but again not right now.

"Okay Ms. Let's Wait Until Later. If he proposes soon, then the answer from you would be no?"

"I don't want to think about it," Bree answers honestly.

"Why not? You talk about it."

"I don't think I would say no, because I want to but I would feel kind of pressured if I'm being honest."

"Fair enough. I would too I suppose. Hell Charles and I dated for about four years before he even wanted to talk about marriage. I just think that Reggie is serious. He's older and ready to settle down and he found the woman for him. As my Grandmother always said, a man knows if a woman is marriage material when he first meets her. That's why she has never really caped for Charles because in her opinion he took too long." She rolls her eyes at her Grandmother's sentiments.

"I agree with that. I know he's the one for me. But it's one of those things like it's within reach staring you in the face, what do you do?" Bree speaks gazing at the ceiling. "And how did we get back on me again," she snaps her head to look at Nia.

"Well shit!" Nia starts. "I was living vicariously through you and your little boy toys, now your ass is about to join the club. Guess we have to hang up our good years." She says dreadfully.

"Nia, we're not dying damn," Bree laughs. "Just shifting focus. I'm sure this new chapter will bring on a whole different set of things to talk about." She reassures her.

"I guess, girl. We're getting old."

"No," Bree interjects. "You're getting old. I'm only 27," she laughs.

# CHAPTER 32

Florida in December is the ultimate Christmas vacation! Junior has been to Disneyland but never Disney World. Bree has been to neither so she is exciting enough for the both of them. Even though Bree is on the losing end of the spectrum with this vacation she still plans on enjoying it.

After going back and forth with Reggie for days about how she wanted to take Junior alone, Junior literally cried for Reggie to join them. Then after declining all Manny's advances to fund the trip, since Reggie came along he ended up footing the bill. Bree has to realize that she just won't win. She ended up with two men in her life that loves to protect and provide.

Prepaying for most of their tickets offered them some sort of rough itinerary; however, landing mid-day left them in limbo as their festivities doesn't officially begin until tomorrow.

"Do you guys want to tour the resort and then hit the pool to pass time?" Bree asks as they enter their room.

"Sounds good to me," Reggie answers first.

"Can we go to the arcade?" Junior pleads.

"We can stop in once we find it." Bree says, "First let try to unpack a little and put on our swimwear."

"Alright Disney, show me that you're worth it," Reggie says as he peruse the room and makes his way to the window to check out the view.

Against Bree's objection, he opted for the suite to offer more space. For the price Bree said she would go outside if she needed some space. And from the looks of things the standard room would have sufficed.

It's very nice and spacious, but Bree doesn't see them utilizing all the amenities this room has to offer.

"Thank you," she says as she hugs Reggie from behind and peeks at the view. It's beautiful and she can't wait to take the pirate adventure on the boat she sees sailing on the water. The people look like they are having a blast.

"You're welcome Baby. I'm glad I was able to come along. I love you," he raises her hand to place a kiss on it.

"I love you too. Junior come and see." She calls him to let him take a glance at the boat. "That's the pirate adventure boat." She points

"Cool. Are we going today?"

"No, I think Tuesday, I have to check, but it does look like fun. I see you're all changed. Let us get ready and we'll head out."

Bree goes to dig into the suitcase and unpack a few items as she looks for her bathing suit. When she grabs her toiletries bag a weird thought crosses her mind. Did she pack her birth control? After checking the bag and not finding them, she checks her purse. Not in there. She pauses for a minute trying to gather her thoughts and retrace her steps starting with waking up. She remembers reminding herself to get them out of her brown purse, but cannot recall actually taking that action.

"Everything okay?" Reggie asks as he comes out of the bathroom.

"I think I left my pills."

"What pills? Are you sick?"

"No my birth control pills." She says dismissing him as she's still sifting through her memory bank.

"You take birth control," he asks shockingly.

"Yes,"

"Why?"

"To control birth. It's literally in the name," she says in a condescending manner. Misfiring her anger because she's really mad at herself.

"I know that, but you told me you didn't take them."

"Well at the time I wasn't. Once we got hot and heavy I thought I needed to start."

"Without talking to me about it?"

"Mom are you ready," Junior shows his face at the door interrupting their rising conversation.

"Almost!" She turns to Junior with a smile holding up her bathing suit. "Yes without talking to you because I control my body." She put her sights back on Reggie. "And I prefer to drop this conversation until we get home. I want to enjoy this vacation, if you don't mind," she says looking Reggie in the eyes.

"It can wait, but it will be had."

Once dressed, Bree and Reggie grab much needed items and head out to explore the wonderful world of Disney with Junior.

***

Animal Kingdom, Epcot, Pirate Adventure, SeaWorld and Universal Studios have worn all three of them out. Bree is kicking herself in the butt for not allowing a day of rest before she heads back to work. The ringing alarm is making her angrier with every ding. She shuts it off and slowly gets up to go get this shift started. Reggie was smart enough to take the extra day and has agreed to let Junior hang with him. Because of that, Bree was able to sleep in until six o'clock this morning. But the extra hours don't seem to be helping at all.

"Tired Baby?" Reggie rolls over and asks as Bree sits on the edge of the bed.

"Yes, but I'm getting up." She sighs

"You'll be home before you know it. Do you want us to drive you in?"

"No, let Junior sleep. His little body needs the rest."

"Did you find your pills," he asks.

"It doesn't matter, I can no longer take them. I missed too many days." She informs him. "And please not right now."

"I don't know how any of that works. I thought I was helping by reminding you. But I'll go back to sleep and stay out of your way." He retreats.

"Thank you," Bree says as she gets up.

Bree knows that she is misdirecting her anger as it should be at herself for forgetting her pills and not telling Reggie that she was starting to take them. While Bree wasn't planning on her and Reggie having sex in Florida the fact that she didn't have her pills made it that they couldn't get a quickie in if they wanted to. Now that they are home she knows that Reggie is going to want her as she wants him, but he is not going to like the idea of them having to use a condom. Bree is unsure how this conversation is going to go but she hopes it doesn't escalate into something terrible while Junior is here.

# CHAPTER 33

After dinner, Bree did her routine with Junior to get him in the bed so that she and Reggie can get this conversation over with. It's already been a week with this topic on the back burner and it's causing a strain that they both can feel even though they're trying to act like everything is okay.

"Are you ready to talk," Bree asks as soon as she enters the room and closes the door.

"I've been ready."

"I apologize for not telling you. I was wrong for that. But I honestly think that it's ultimately my decision. Had I discussed it with you it would have been more informational than asking for input."

"I just wish I would have known. I feel a little deceived. I understand that I cannot tell you what to do with your body, but I would appreciate it if I was in the know on the decisions you decide to make. I was under the impression that you weren't taking birth control and you are. Where's the transparency?"

"So all this time you were trying to get me pregnant?"

"No that's not what I said,"

"But that's how you're making it seem," she interrupts. "Like I somehow crushed your dream or something, it's just birth control."

After a long silent pause, Reggie speaks, "Let's reel this back in," he suggests taking a deep breath. "I'm upset because the last you told me, you weren't taking birth control. Now you are and you never said anything to me. It feels like you went behind my back. You could have come to me and we could have talked about this. Yes, I probably would have tried to discourage you because I want a family with you. But at least I would have known what was going on."

"I don't want you to think that I'm doing this because I don't want to have a baby with you. I just don't want to have a baby right now. I know that being married is not a guarantee to a successful family but I would at least like to start things off right this time. And I told you that from the beginning. I never knew how much last names meant to me until I had Junior. I want to have the same name as our child. I want our names to all be the same on the birth certificate. Ridiculous request, maybe, but it's what I want. And I want you to respect that."

"I understand. I didn't know that it meant that much to you. I apologize for making this about me and not considering your feelings. Just know that I want a family. With you," he adds.

"I do too, just not right now." She reiterates.

"And I would appreciate it if you talk to me about decisions that affect the both of us."

"Got it!"

"So where do we go from here? You said you can't take the pills."

"We have to use condoms as a back method. I have to wait until my menses come on next month to start taking them again."

"I can just pull out."

"Pulling out is not an effective method when a woman is ovulating, it only takes one sperm out of hundreds to get the ball rolling, pre-ejaculation included."

"I'll be back."

"Where are you going?"

"To go and get condoms." He says, like that's the only answer.

Reggie leaves to go to the store and leaves Bree with her thoughts. She feels unsure about his attitude about this. She is trying to dismiss the notion that maybe Reggie is trying to trap her into something that she doesn't want right now and she doesn't know how to deal with this. On one hand, she understands his position and how it may have felt a little deceiving. On the other hand, she doesn't know why he feels that way if he wasn't trying to get her pregnant. She's going to leave it alone and keep a lookout. One thing is for sure, if he doesn't put on a condom, then she is not having sex with him. She prays that they never have to cross that bridge. She prays that Reggie will abide by this and not have to be told to use a condom.

# CHAPTER 34

"So what do you think?" she asks Manny. Bree explained to him about the birth control situation to see if she's being paranoid.

"This is tough. I can see both sides. It was foul to go behind his back, but like you said if he wasn't trying to get you pregnant then what does it matter? And in that instance it shouldn't matter. But maybe he wasn't trying to get you pregnant per se, he just knew that by not using protection it was a possibility. And you said he wants a baby so he was open to the idea if it just happened."

"Wishing on a star?"

"Yup!"

"So basically a nice way of saying trying to get me pregnant?"

Manny pauses for a minute, "Well yeah," he laughs. "I was trying to help him out. I'm just saying I don't think it's a trap situation like you're making it seem. It's not that deep. I don't think." He restates in hopes that Bree lets it go.

"True. He was so crushed though. I just hope he understands that I want to be married before I venture down this road again you know? I'll admit that I'm a bit in fairy land with this but our situation with Junior is so unorthodox, I just want something a little more conventional."

"I get it. I know our situation isn't the best, but we make it work and I appreciate you for all that you've done for and with me."

"Same here. Teamwork makes the dreamwork."

"Are you good? Can I get a turn?"

"Oh geez what's up?"

"Sam and I are going to take a little break."

"What happened?"

"I guess she's just getting tired of the set-up. It's understandable. I'm not able to give her all that she wants. She wants a baby and I don't think I want to give her that. She's amazing with Junior but she has no independence about her. I want her to strive for a goal, get a hobby other than shopping, with my money, hell even volunteer her time to a special cause. She's rode the wave for too long. I'm ready to bring it into shore and chill out for a while."

"Who's the newbie?"

"Damn Road Runner, can I get a little credit? A little, just this one time?" he pauses waiting for an answer because he's legitimately asking for her to give him the benefit of the doubt. "There is no one else right now. I just want to chill."

"You are in Canada chilling right now, with whom?"

"I'll let you know if it turns into something."

"You haven't changed,"

"I'm good just the way I am," he chuckles. "What time are you picking Junior up?"

"No longer my thing, Reggie scoops him on his way home."

"He moved in?" he asks in an unbelievable tone.

"Nope!"

"When is the last time he's been to his place?"

"I don't know,"

"So he lives there," he interrupts.

"If he does?"

"I'm just asking."

"He still has his place. The only thing he has here are clothes."

"Ya'll haven't talked about it?"

"Nope!"

"Are you ready for it?"

"Honestly? I don't know. Some days I feel like I am. Other days I let my fear take over and I want to run." She admits.

"How are things going outside of this little hiccup?"

"Great! I'm happy. He's definitely moved the bar if this doesn't work out."

"That's awesome, I guess there will be wedding bells in the near future."

"Not too soon." She says hopefully.

"He wants a baby. It'll be soon."

"Yeah, yeah, yeah, you my friend have worn out your welcome. I'll have Junior call you when he gets in."

"Because you know I'm right. We need to start planning his party. Has he mentioned anything?"

"No, but I'll try to pull something out of him. See ya Junior's Dad."

"Talk to you later Junior's Mom."

Bree thinks about what Manny has said. It is just like Reggie to propose to get what he wants. She does love Reggie and could see herself spending the rest of her life with him, she still doesn't want a baby right now. How would she begin to explain still wanting to wait after getting married? She knows that Reggie is in a rush because he's pushing thirty-five. But Bree isn't even thirty, she has time. Besides, she is scared. Her whole pregnancy to include labor is a fuzzy period in her mind. She barely remembers anything and what she does remembers she tries to forget. The countless fights with Mrs. Lillian took a toll on her and robbed her of what was supposed to be a joyous occasion. Bree can't help but to feel like if she gets pregnant there will be a repeat of the horrible episode of family drama. She doesn't want to deal with that.

"Hey Nia," Bree answers her ringing phone while plopping on the couch.

"Hey Remi, we need to talk."

"Uh oh, what's up?"

"Charles is cheating on me." She blurts out

"WHAT!" Bree screams. Not Charles, he is one of the good guys. "Awe Nia, I'm so sorry. Are you okay?"

"No Bree, I'm not. This girl is saying that she's pregnant. I don't know what to do."

"What did he say?"

"What do you think? He denies it."

"Denies everything?"

"No not the cheating, the baby."

"This is a tough situation. Charles is your husband and you can't just dismiss him without a process. How do you feel?"

"Numb, I try not to even think about it. He walks around here like nothing is wrong. I'm keeping it together for the kids but I'm about to crack."

"When did you find out?"

"A week ago."

"You've been dealing with this alone for a week. Let's go get drinks and talk. You need to get out of the house. I'll come and pick you up."

"Thanks Bree, I need it."

"Hey Baby," Reggie answers the phone.

"Do you mind taking Junior to dinner and ya'll hang out tonight? I need to go and talk to Nia right quick." Bree gets to the point

"I don't mind. Is everything okay?"

"Yeah, she just needs a girl chat."

"Okay. I got him. Do you want me to pick you up something too?"

"No, I'll grab a bite while I'm out. I love you."

"Love you too!"

# CHAPTER 35

The ride to the restaurant is silent. Once inside Bree and Nia take their seats in the booth and Bree continues to remain silent to let Nia start the conversation.

"I want to believe my husband Bree, really I do, but even if the baby isn't his he still cheated."

"Is this the first time?"

"Sadly, no. He cheated a couple years back when I was pregnant with Charisma. We went to counseling, got ourselves back into a happy medium, forgave and moved on. Never in a million years did I think I would have to deal with this again. And a baby on top of it! I don't know if I want to stay. I don't know if I can stay."

"I can't tell you what to do Nia. I don't know how you feel, but I'm here to support whatever decision you make. I will not judge you for your choices. You have to do what you think is best for you and your children."

"I appreciate that." She pauses. "It will be extremely hard to get past this if this is his baby. Hell it's already difficult after seeing the images. She sent me pictures of him Bree. He's such an idiot."

"WOW! Yeah that's a tough pill to swallow. How do you feel about separation? I mean just to clear your head."

"I've thought about it. But I don't want to shake the kids up too much. If I'm going to leave, then I should just leave."

"Understandable. Have you talked to anyone else about this?"

"My mom but you know she's team Charles and in her words men will be men. She feels as long as he's taking care of home I shouldn't sweat the small stuff. You know that old wives mentality. And honestly

I probably would subscribe to it if a baby wasn't involved. How the hell is he smashing raw and want me sucking him down."

"Yeah, that's a no. That's the bullshit right there."

"And he didn't even do it out of town. Do you know he met the girl at the party."

"What party?"

"The one you and Reggie came to. She was there."

"Are you serious? So she has affiliation in the circle? Who does she know?"

"I don't know. I'm still trying to figure it out."

"Do you remember seeing her?"

"She didn't have her face in any of the pictures she sent me. I guess it was just for confirmation because Charles was in her bed."

"Well the girl that Reggie was there talking to turns out to be his sister's best friend."

"Well she was flirting big time if I can remember correctly."

"Well he's smashed a time or two. I said that to say that maybe I can keep my ears open when I'm around his sister to see if she's a part of that clique."

"I'd appreciate it. Charles is not trying to give up any information other than he's innocent."

"That's that suspicious shit right there. He should be laying it all on the table to save his family."

"You're preaching to the choir because I said exactly that. Enough about this," she shakes off the topic, "I need some drinks to clear my mind. How was ya'll vacation?"

"It was great other than the fact that Reggie found out I'm taking birth control."

"Rem I thought you were going to tell him."

"I was. Just didn't get around to it. So, it looks like I was being sneaky. And I wasn't. I don't understand the big deal anyway if we aren't trying to get pregnant."

"You know that shit was sneaky. We already had this conversation. You should have told him. Well what did he say?"

"Expressed his disappointment and we moved on from the matter."

"Well shit that was easy."

"Too easy."

"Well at least you know it's you he wants to get pregnant."

"Blah, blah, blah, I thought we were moving one from your woes."

"I know but it consumes all my thoughts."

"I get it. Go to individual counseling just for you to deal with your issues behind it while you think about what you want to do."

"That's an idea. I'll try. It beats doing nothing." She pauses to think. "I should have just slept with Tyree."

"Whoa! Wait. A. Minute. When did you see or even talk to Tyree?" Bree asks. Tyree was supposed to have moved to another state years ago.

"We've kept in touch."

"Has Charles ever found out?" Bree interrupts.

"Nope, maybe because he's too busy doing his thing. Well when he came to town I went to visit him at the Sheraton. I couldn't bring myself to do it, but I should have. Maybe I'd feel better right now."

"I'm sure that wouldn't assist with helping you feel better." Bree makes known. "And I'm mad you didn't tell me," she scolds.

"I didn't tell a soul. I had to keep that to myself."

"I guess."

"Charles will flip his lid if I go back to Tyree."

"Hell yeah, I'd see his mug shot on the news because he would off the both of ya'll" Bree expresses.

"Yes he would," Nia laughs.

It feels good to see Nia laugh because she is not used to Nia having a dark cloud over her head.

"Don't do it." Bree expresses

"I'm not, I'm not."

"Don't even tell him about this because he's going to see it as his green light."

"Too late."

"No Nia, please tell me you didn't tell him."

"I did Bree. I had no one else to talk to."

"Me, you could have called me."

"Well he's the only person I wanted to talk to."

"Speak the truth." Bree encourages.

"He's not doing or saying what you think he is,"

"For now."

"For now. Okay I may have told him for him to make me feel better. And it worked in the beginning but it isn't helping now. I love Charles too much. This shit hurts Bree."

"I'm sorry Nia, I know it does. But revenge isn't going to help it no matter how much you think it will."

"I'm starting to see that now."

"So are you going to continue to talk to Tyree?"

"I'm trying to wean myself now. It's difficult, but I'm going to do it."

"Just do it before Charles finds out. You don't want him to flip the script."

"That's what I don't want. Thanks for the talk."

"Anytime."

# CHAPTER 36

"We're taking you out for dinner tonight, be ready when we get home." Reggie tells Bree as she's preparing to leave for work.

"Attire?"

"Sexy," he smirks. "Hugging a little ass, showing a little breast along with easy access." He teases.

"With Junior in tow?"

"Mom it up a little," he advises with a pat on the ass.

"I'll see what I can do," she says before giving him a kiss and heading out the door.

For the past month or so they have both managed to stay out the middle of Charles and Nia's situation. Bree knows he talks to Charles about it because they are on the phone constantly. She keeps the talks with her and Nia private and never mentions anything about it. Not even after she came home from their girl chat. She swept it under the rug.

Bree is starting to get used to not having to deal with Junior in the morning and afternoon. He gets to sleep in a little later thanks to Reggie. Reggie drops him off and picks him up now. At first Bree was a little apprehensive with the set-up but figured why not get a break, even if it is only short lived. Reggie hasn't been to his apartment since he met Manny. She can tell that Reggie is getting close to asking about the living arrangements. He's already hinted around the notion of finding a bigger place. And he's picking up more responsibilities that can potentially have him around for the long term. Even though he still has his place, he's paid a couple of bills as they came through and took Bree's car for service on top of being of help Junior. She's not sure if she should be grateful or scared. In fact, she's both. This feels so right, but it's moving so fast in such a short time. Five months to be exact. When she arrived at work she decided to take the afternoon off. If they are taking her out, then she could at least pamper herself before. Facial, manicure, massage, and pedicure are on the agenda for the afternoon. She is pretty excited as they have been in such a routine lately that comfort is setting in. Good thing Reggie notices and wants to get things back on track.

"MOOOOOOMMM!" Junior yells as usual when entering the house. "We're ready."

"I'm ready too," Bree says walking down the stairs.

"You look amazing, I knew you would pull something off," Reggie compliments as he gives Bree a hug.

Bree looks at them and concludes that they must have taken a half a day as well. Junior has on a button down shirt with a little bow tie with some jeans. Reggie is business casual, but too dressed down for work.

"Thank you. You guys look handsome." Bree smiles.

"C'mon mom we have a surprise." Junior says with excitement.

"Well thank you very much Mr. Big Mouth," Reggie gives him the side-eye.

"I didn't tell her what it is," he says.

"But she didn't even know there is a surprise," Reggie continues.

"Oh a surprise, I'm excited!" Bree says grabbing Reggie's arm to get his attention. She can tell that he's a little bothered by Junior spoiling his plans. "Well I kind of figured that something special was going on anyways," she taps Reggie's ass as she heads towards the door.

The pull up at Vic's and Anthony Steakhouse and Bree is getting nervous. She's unsure what to make of this special night. It's not an anniversary. Too soon for a proposal and she's not prepared to take any news about a bigger place right now. Reggie isn't up for a promotion, he hasn't been looking for a better job, Bree is at a loss for the occasion. Even Valentine's day is a week away. They head in and get settled at their table.

"This is beautiful, thank you Baby," she says to Reggie. "Thanks Champ, I love it!" She gives Junior some recognition.

"Do they have ice cream here?" Junior asks, ignoring Bree as he scans the menu.

"I'll get you some ice cream don't worry," Reggie assures him. "So how was your day?" he begins to make small talk with Bree.

"It was good. Must admit I left early to get pampered."

"You deserve it." Reggie approves.

"How about you? What is going on with you?" she asks nervously

"Same. I cut out of there early. I grabbed Junior to get him dressed."

"And what's the occasion? Why are we here?"

"I need a reason to take you out? We haven't been out in a while and when we do go out, we leave Junior with Brittany. I figured he should start to come along."

"I agree, but I still want some solo dates."

"I'm not saying all the time. We just don't need to leave him as much."

"Agreed. So what are you getting? Steak?" she asks but answers herself as she begins to scan the menu.

"Yes, what are you having?"

"I'll get the lump crab cake, Junior will have the lamb chop with broccoli and mac and cheese."

The waiter came over to take the order and Reggie took care of it while Bree occupied Junior with a game of tic tac toe.

"Don't cheat," she laughs.

"I'm not cheating, I didn't mean to put it there, I want it here," he says scribbling out his X in the corner and putting it in the middle.

"I think you may have some type of strategy." Bree states skeptically

"I don't"

"Well next game no changing." Bree sets the rules. She is for sure he is about to win this game.

"Junior are you ready?" Reggie asks.

"I'm ready, Mom, close your eyes," Junior excitedly instructs. Then he walks behind Bree and puts his tiny hands over her eyes just to make sure they are closed.

Bree feels Reggie hand on her knee. Her heart reaches a rapid pace.

"Ok Junior, let her see,"

When Bree opens her eyes, Reggie is on bending knee with a 3 carat cushion cut diamond engagement ring. Bree is speechless.

"Brianna Monique Jones, I have loved you since I first laid eyes on you. When I think of my future, I picture you being a part of it. I cannot imagine spending any of the rest of my life without you. You encourage me to be a better friend, man, partner and overall person. I appreciate the love you breathe in my life and I need that like I need air to survive. Please do me the honors of being my wife. Will you marry me?"

The tears begin streaming down Brees face from his first word. As he spoke she kept their eyes locked accepting every word that was being said to her. His loving gaze, the sincerity in his voice and the tremble in his hands collectively made Bree's heart melt.

"YES!" she says softly for the two of them to hear. "I love you." She reaches in for a hug. Reggie insisted on putting the ring on first.

"Yay!" Junior jumps up and down. "I told you she was going to say yes." He tells Reggie as if he had his doubts.

For the remainder of the evening the smile couldn't be wiped off of Bree's face. It was difficult to enjoy dinner as strangers kept stopping by the table on their way out congratulating them on their pending nuptials. Bree is in Heaven.

# CHAPTER 37

Bree went to celebrate Junior's birthday at his home away from home. Junior insisted on having a Disneyland party like Mario's because he had so much fun. Since Reggie didn't come to partake in the festivities Bree figured that she would throw a little something at her house with Reggie and his family. She wanted to invite Charles and Nia, but they're still on a rocky road. Besides, Charles doesn't know Manny as Bree tries to keep him as incognito as possible. However, she knows it will be difficult to hide his identity from Reggie's family any longer. Now that the wedding plans are underway she needs to let them in.

"Hey Tasha. Frankie. Little Tabby." Bree acknowledges as she opens the door. "Let me get my little man. Hey B," she grabs Brandon and proceeds to head into the family room.

"Hey Bree, thanks for the invite. I know he doesn't need anything else but I had to bring him something." Tasha says as she places the gift bag on the table.

"Frankieeee," Junior yells as he's running down the steps. "Come on," he invites him to come upstairs to play.

"You can go too, Tabby." Bree encourages. When Junior and Frankie get together they tend to forget to include her.

"Where's Reggie?" Tasha asks.

"He went to go and pick up your parents. I guess they didn't feel like driving. It's just us," Bree makes known. "Since it's his actual birthday, I wanted him to have a cake. That's why I said that you didn't need to bring a gift. He had his real party already."

"How was Disneyland? I'm sure there were so many people. Did he at least get to enjoy himself?"

Bree didn't want to disclose that Manny shut down the park for his party, so Junior had a blast!

"Yeah, they were pretty accommodating for the birthday boy." She decides to say and leaves it at that.

"Junior leaves today right?"

"Yeah. Manny is coming in today. I think their flight leaves tomorrow though. He should get here before you all leave, so you'll meet him."

"Oh gosh! Frankie will be disappointed. He was trying to hang with him for the weekend." Tasha says rolling her eyes like she doesn't want to deal with the wrath.

"Tell him he can come and hang when Junior comes home. I need my time. I really do." Bree discloses.

"Girl you get a break every month,"

"And I'm used to it." Bree interrupts. "Come in the kitchen Tasha. I need to frost these cupcakes."

"Mom, Frankie hit me," Tabby comes into the kitchen pouting.

"Don't start that mess or we can go home." Tasha snaps.

"Hey Tabby, do you know how to frost cupcakes?" Bree intervenes.

"No," she replies sadly.

"Well if you're up for learning, then I can teach you. Let the boys play and we can play a game once I'm done."

"Okay," she reluctantly obliges.

"Well the good thing about frosting cupcakes, is that you can make your very own design. So why don't you make yours and Brandon's. What color frosting do you want?"

"Can I have pink and purple please," she begins to brighten up.

"Sure!" Bree says as she begins to explain how to color the frosting.

Tasha leaves to go and reprimand Frankie and leaves Bree and Tabby to their decorating.

"Hey Baby," Reggie greets and gives Bree a kiss.

"Hey Mi Amor,"

"Uncle Reggie, do you want me to decorate your cupcake? What colors do you want?" Tabby asks without receiving her first answer.

"Sure. Uhm, orange and yellow."

"Watch this," she says to him as she grabs the yellow food coloring to mix into the frosting.

"Auntie Bree has you in here learning how to bake Tabby?" Mr. Harold asks as he and Mrs. Lynn enter the kitchen.

"Hello," Bree offers a warm welcome to the both of them. "Yes, I have to pass these secrets to somebody," she jokes.

"I'm all for it," Mr. Harold approves as he gives Tabby a kiss.

"Do you want me to decorate yours too, Papa?"

"Of course I do."

Bree walks over to the sink to get a rag to attempt to clean up some of the mess Tabby is making.

Reggie meets her there and whispers, "Manny isn't here yet?"

"No. Why?"

"Because I still haven't told them and I need to do it before he comes because he's my mom's crush." He says with disgust.

"Oh, so you're pulling a me? It's more difficult than it seems."

"I see that now."

Tasha walks into the kitchen to inspect Tabby's work.

"Here's your chance," Bree says as they make their way back over to the table.

"Tabby go and wash your hand," Reggie demands

"Ok. No one touches the cupcakes until we sing happy birthday," she replies, setting her own demands.

As soon as she is out of ear shot, Reggie begins to try to hurry and get it over with. "Well, you guys know that you will meet Manny today and we have to be honest about something so it's not too much of a shock when he comes over." Reggie pauses.

"Is this a good or bad thing?" Mr. Harold slides his question in as Reggie gathers his thoughts.

"Oh no, it's not a thing bad." Reggie clears the air in case his Dad is thinking the worst. "He's just...Glenn Hicks." He blurts out.

"WHAT!?!?!?!" Tasha is the first to respond. "Are you serious?"

"He's just Manny," Bree says calmly as she decides that she should jump in. "I know it may be difficult for you to digest. And I'm sorry that we put this on you in such short notice. It was intended for you to know sooner. I'm very secretive about the matter."

"It's understandable." Ms. Lynn says.

"Well I guess, I'm about to be single. Lynn is going to shoot her shot," Mr. Harold jokes.

Everyone enjoys a nice laugh and Bree is happy that he lightens the mood.

"I'd just appreciate it if you all respect the privacy that I am trying to keep." Bree brings everyone back into the serious topic. She doesn't know what she would do if she'd had to deal with tabloids, paparazzi or reporters. "He doesn't deny our son. I just prefer that he doesn't speak on him. Junior can make the decision when he's older if he wants to live in his father's shadow." She continues sincerely.

"Well you are doing an awesome job," Tasha commends Bree. "I thought I knew everything about my Husband," she smiles. "But seriously, no worries over here. We have your back Bree. And now that you mention it, I can see the resemblance."

"Thank you." Bree sighs. "I really do appreciate it. Well we can eat now if you all are hungry. We don't have to wait."

They call the boys down and crack open the pizza to get the night going. Bree is still a bit apprehensive about his meetup. She has never let any outsiders in. Nia is the only exception. That meeting happened on a whim. Nia has kept the news locked away as Bree had asked. And if the news would have gotten out then Bree would have known that Nia spread it. Now there are too many people in the mix to point fingers.

"Mom is Dad coming today?" Junior asks to confirm.

"Yes, and Aunt Tasha and I have already discussed that Frankie can stay over when you come home."

"See I told you," Junior says to Frankie.

"Can I stay too Aunt Bree?"

"Noooooo," the boys sang in unison.

"That's not fair," she pouts

"Stay home with Mom all you're going to do is cry," Frankie offers his reasoning

"Moooom," Tabby whines looking to Tasha

"You can stay home with me. We'll find something to do." Tasha cosigns

"How come Frankie gets to stay?" she keeps pressing.

"He's not staying tonight," Tasha reassures her.

"Hey, hey, hey," Manny comes strolling into the kitchen.

"Dad!" Junior jumps up for this greeting.

"Hey Champ! Happy official Birthday," he shouts.

"Bree," Manny comes and places a kiss on her cheek. Then he heads to greet Reggie.

"Manny these are my parents Harold and Lynn. My sister Tasha and her kids, Frankie, Tabby and Brandon." Reggie introduces.

"Nice to meet you all."

"Don't bring your sexy ass in here trying to take my wife." Mr. Harold says playfully.

"Not Manny," he says smiling. "Now Glenn Hicks might go for a cougar," he winks at Lynn. Her blushing smile didn't go unnoticed. "Did you save me any pizza?" He asks working towards the stove comfortably.

"Dad, are we leaving now? Me and Frankie aren't finish playing"

"No, you have time. But we're not staying too long." Manny starts and before he could finish they run out of the kitchen with Tabby following closely behind.

Bree spins around in her chair to face him, "Where are ya'll going? Your flight leaves tomorrow right?"

"Yeah, my parents want to see him."

"Oh," she spins back around. And just in time to see Reggie answer his ringing phone. He gives her the eye to dismiss himself and exits the room to have his conversation.

"Well let me put this out on the table," Mr. Harold fills the silence while looking at Manny as he's heading to the table. "I am a fan of your work."

"Thank you so much!" Manny replies. "It has been a long time coming but I think I've finally found my stride. How is the wedding planning going Bree?" he changes the subject.

"I don't know, ask Tasha."

"It's going. I have taken on the role as the liaison to the wedding planner. Bree is all over the place needless to say." Tasha chimes in.

"I just wish someone could go into my head, get my ideas and bring them to fruition. I'm no good at this stuff. It's like I know what I want, but I don't know how to relay it. We still don't even have a date." She says rolling her eyes.

"But you know it's going to be in the winter?" he asks.

"Yes, a wonderful winter wonderland wedding." She says gleefully.

"If you said those words to a wedding planner, then I'm sure they could bring that to life. Sounds like such a fairytale. Where did you find this planner?" Manny digs for information.

"My coworker..." Bree starts.

"Fire her," he says firmly. "She's not doing a very good job. I know..."

"Next subject," Bree interrupts and dismisses his comment.

He abides by her request and moves on. "Mr. Harold, Mrs. Lynn, Tasha," He says, looking at each of them. "I appreciate you all taking my son in and loving him like your own. He always raves about you all when he's with me. And I am so thankful that Reggie has found Bree. He's an awesome addition to our family."

"You're very welcome." Mrs. Lynn speaks. "Junior is such a sweet little boy. Such a joy to have around. You both are doing a fine job."

"Can we eat the cupcakes now," Tabby interrupts to ask Bree.

"Yes. Go get the boys so we can sing happy birthday."

# CHAPTER 38

"Breeeee," Manny yells as he enters the house. She sees where Junior gets it.

"I'm in the kitchen," Bree yells back.

Manny has been on travel duty since he pushed Samantha to the side. Pick up and drops off are all done by him.

"Smells good, what are you cooking?" he asks, giving Bree a kiss on her cheek.

"Food," she says with an attitude because she senses his entitlement.

"I need a snack, I'm hungry," Manny says as he takes a seat on the barstool propping his arms up on the island like a kid.

"You know where the snacks are."

"C'mon Bree, please I'm tired. It seems like I was just here yesterday."

"So now you know how Samantha felt," Bree laughs. "Those flights take a toll. I don't know how Junior hangs."

"He's young." Manny offers his explanation.

Bree gets various snacks out of the pantry and lays them on the countertop for him to choose.

Manny grabs the honey bun and proceeds to open it.

"Are you staying for dinner?" she asks

"I'll check with Junior. Our flight isn't until tomorrow. We're heading to my parents house tonight."

"Have fun!" Bree says in a nonchalant tone. A resolution between her and his mother is still pending.

"Bree,"

"What," she says, turning to grab the cheese from the fridge.

"Look at me."

"What?" she stops and looks at him as asked.

"Are you pregnant?"

"Huh," she utters and proceeds to grab the cheese.

"If you can huh, you can hear. Are you pregnant?" he asks again.

"Mind your business Glenn."

"You are!" he yells.

"How do you even know?"

Manny stands up and grabs his crotch. "I'm horny." He sits back down. "I don't know what type of hormones you put off while pregnant but it gets me going." He admits as he tries to adjust himself back on the barstool. "I can't believe Reggie hasn't noticed."

It must be true. Manny told Bree she was pregnant with Junior off of the same indication. Bree remains silent. She hasn't told anyone. Not even Nia.

"I take it no one knows."

"OMG get out of my head. I can't stand you. We've known each other for too long." She rationalizes

"When are you planning to tell him," he laughs and continues to try to fish for information.

"I don't know. Not with Junior here. I don't want him to know just yet. It's still early and anything can happen."

"I understand my lips are sealed." He pledges. "Gave up on birth control after you got the ring!?" he isn't really asking just thinking out loud.

"You know I have been planning our wedding for months now. Don't play me sideways. No, I did not abandon the birth control." She begins to offer the explanation that he doesn't really need. "I lost them. I don't know how. I switch purses too much." She gives a reason. "Well by the time I found them it was too late to take them. We weren't as careful as last time with the backup plan." She says as she lowers her head. "Manny, I don't know what to do. I don't want to be a pregnant bride."

"How far along are you?"

"I'm guessing two months or so. I don't know. What I do know is my winter wedding is ruined. I'm not doing it. I will be big as a house by December."

"Postpone it."

"You make it sound so easy."

"It is easy. People cancel weddings all the time. And you know good and well that Reggie is going to do whatever you want to do. Just tell him next year. I bet he agrees and waits." He says, popping the last of the honey bun into his mouth.

"You're right." Bree says to get off this topic for conversation. Manny doesn't know how she feels about this and she's not about to explain it to him. She'll save it for Reggie.

"Junior will be happy."

"He and Reggie are going to have a party," she says rolling her eyes.

"Are you happy Bree?" he asks sincerely.

"Yes, I am. It's just the timing that's all."

"Well take a little more excitement with you when you tell him because you look like you just lost your best friend."

"Thanks for the heads up." She gives a quick fake smile.

He gets up and walks towards her to give her a hug. She walks into his embrace because she needs some consoling right now. She feels like her life is taking a turn that she's just not ready for. He wraps his arms around her and gives her a gentle squeeze. Then his hands move down to her butt and he grips a cheek in each hand. He proceeds to place a kiss on her neck. "Uhm," he moans. "Gosh I want you."

"That's enough," she squirms. "That was your freebie. Don't let it happen again."

"I know I know. Okay," he says, backing away. He doesn't even look at Bree when they unlock their embrace. "We're not staying for dinner. I won't make it!" he yells and slams the door to the guest room.

Bree stands there wondering what the hell just happened. She supposes she does give off some type of mating call via her hormones because she has been being hit on left and right. And Reggie can't keep his hands off of her. Every little thing she does turns him on. Bree takes her attention back to her dinner. At dinner she doesn't know if she will be able to stomach once it's done. Her morning sickness is getting more difficult to hide. She craves, she eats, then she vomits. It wasn't like this with Junior. Or at least she doesn't remember it being like this.

"Hi Mom," Junior says walking into the kitchen. This being five years old has made him mature instantly. There are a plethora of things that's beneath him since he's five and screaming for his Mom is one of them.

"Hey Champ how was your day?"

"It was good, I got two red stars."

"Did you? Congratulations Big Boy." Bree celebrates by giving him a hug.

"Hey Baby," Reggie walks in and places a kiss on Bree's lips.

"My love," she grabs his tie and brings him closer.

"I'm going to wear that ass out tonight, be prepared," he warns. When Junior leaves it's an all out love fest.

"Don't start," she cautions and pushes him away. She wanted to be close to him, giving her a moment with Manny, but it didn't seem right.

"Smells good. What are you cooking? And where's Manny? Isn't that a rental outside?"

"Yes, he's in the guest room. I think he might be asleep. Those flights are getting to him. Ribs, baked mac and cheese, greens, stuffing, honey cornbread and yams."

"Damn, are you about to feed a village?"

"I wanted something good."

"Hey Champ, how was school?" Manny says as he emerges from his slumber.

"Dad," Junior runs to give him a hug. Guess he's never too old to show his dad affection.

"What's up Reggie," he gives Reggie a shake. "Are you ready," he looks to Junior.

"Ya'll not staying for dinner? Bree's cooking a feast." Reggie inquires.

"No, we're having dinner with my parents. Had I known Bree was throwing down I wouldn't have made plans."

"I'm not mad. More for me," Bree says. "Come give me a hug," she directs her attention to Junior. "Be good. I love you and I'm going to miss you."

"Love you too mom,"

"Bye Daddy," he says to Reggie.

"See ya Squirt." Reggie gives him a hug.

"We'll call you later." Manny let the words hang as he headed towards the door. Reggie walks behind them to walk them out.

"Dinner is done," she says to Reggie when he returns. "Are you ready to eat or do you want to wait?"

"I can wait a few if you can."

"I'm a little hungry."

"Well then let's eat!"

Bree makes the plates and sits at the table. Her stomach feels queasy and she hasn't even taken a bite yet. "Man," she grumbles.

"What's wrong?"

"I don't know, maybe I've been smelling the food too long. I don't even want to eat it."

"You are crazy, these ribs are so tender. And I'm the one who said I wasn't hungry."

"How was your day?"

"Great! I may have some travel coming up so be prepared to handle Junior for a couple days."

"NOOOO!" She makes fun.

"You've been getting over like a fat rat. Don't think I haven't noticed."

"True, but you can't say ya'll want for anything."

"We don't"

"Can you grab this?" she says looking at the kitchen. She did most of the work with packing the food in containers, loading the dishwasher and washing the pots and pans. Bree likes to clean as she goes along, but there are still a couple of things to tidy up.

"Sure, you're not going to eat?"

"I may come back down, you can leave my plate. I need to go and change. I had these clothes on all day."

Bree couldn't get upstairs fast enough. What little is left in her stomach from lunch is now in the toilet. She figures she'll take a test then go have the conversation with Reggie so she could go downstairs and eat then vomit in peace.

# CHAPTER 39

Bree slowly walks out of the bathroom holding her towel above her breast with her right hand and the pregnancy test in the left. Reggie is sitting on the edge of the bed scrolling through his phone.

"I thought you were coming to change not shower." he sits his phone down and gives Bree his attention while he returns to taking off his shoes.

"Just thought I'd get it out the way," she says.

"Are you okay? Why do you look like that?"

"Can we talk?"

"Anytime. What's on your mind?" He says so smoothly as if he has nothing to hide.

"This happened," she says as she extends her hand with the pregnancy test. She doesn't know how else to say it.

Reggie grabs the test from Bree and looks at it. She made sure to get the test that reads 'pregnant' just so he doesn't get confused by the lines.

"Are you serious," he questions as he jumps up off the bed. "Please tell me you're serious."

"We're having a baby," she confirms hesitantly.

Reggie picks Bree up and hugs her tightly. Then he puts her down, strips the towel from her and immediately kisses all over her stomach.

"Thank you," he says as he finally stands. "I love you so much."

"I love you too, Baby." She pauses. "I had to wait until Junior left because I don't want him to know right now. It's still early in the pregnancy and anything can happen."

"What do you mean?"

"In the first trimester there is a risk of miscarriage. I don't want to get his hopes up and have to explain it if something happens."

"Well in that case you should have waited to tell me,"

"Impossible," Bree interrupts. "I can't hide this morning sickness any longer. I'm tired beyond belief. I really just need to sit down somewhere. I can't pretend I'm one hundred percent anymore. It's taking a toll on me."

"Awe baby, come here," he walks her to the bed. "Let me," he grabs the lotion and begins to rub her down.

"Did you forget that we have a wedding in five months?" she refreshes his memory

"No."

"I don't want to be pregnant in my wedding dress. If my timing is right, I'll be seven months come our wedding day."

"That's great. We'll be married before you have the baby. You'll have time to change your name."

"Did you hear me?" she asks sitting up. "I don't want to be pregnant at our wedding."

"What do you suggest we do Bree, get married now?"

"No. I was thinking about postponing it."

"But why would we postpone? Were you lying when you said that last names meant something to you?" he questions feeling himself getting angry.

"It does. I'm confused Reggie. I don't know what to do. Instead of trying to make me feel bad, offer some suggestions."

"I asked if you want to get married now," he reminds her.

"I want a winter wedding."

"Well write down all your wants and figure it out," he says with a snappy attitude. He's at a loss.

Bree gets up. She walks to the dresser to get some clothes. She's hungry and tired and more importantly doesn't feel like the back and forth.

"Bree come here," Reggie says in a sincere tone. "Next year December fourteenth is on a Saturday. This year on December fourteenth is on Friday." He shows his phone with the calendar. "You and I will go to the courthouse and get married this year and we'll plan to have our wedding next December on the fourteenth. How does that sound?"

"No one will know?" she questions

"Just me, you and the one officiating. That way you have the documents to change your name. All our names will be the same on the birth certificate. December fourteenth will still be our anniversary, we'll just know we're celebrating one year during our wedding."

"I can live with that."

"You can live with that," he repeats as he smiles.

"Yes, thank you. I knew you would figure it out."

"You're welcome. Are you going to eat?"

"I want to but I don't want to vomit again."

"That's why you came up here?"

"Yup. The smell of the food turned my stomach that quick."

"Is that good? You need to be able to keep food down."

"Right now I'm taking my prenatal vitamins so I am okay. But if I'm still not keeping anything down in a couple months and not gaining weight. That'll be cause for concern. But I'm sure I'll be good in a couple of weeks. Are you ready for this?"

"I've been ready."

"Are you going to move in already? We could be saving that money."

"I still have two months left on my lease. I can start consolidating and moving in the meantime. And this cannot be our final destination, you know that right?"

"I know, but with the baby and the wedding we don't need to add the expenses of moving right now. There's no rush."

"There is."

"But we have a room for the nursery."

"That room looks like an extra large walk-in closet. We need something bigger than that."

"But all the baby needs is a crib, changing table and maybe a rocking chair."

"Where are all the toys going to go?"

"What toys," she chuckles. "The baby doesn't need to play with any toys. Well at least not for the first couple of months," she clarifies.

"Juniors toys, there are entirely too many toys to fit in his room. He can keep that as his playroom. Well move out this furniture and put the crib there." He points to the seating area in Bree's room.

"Oh no!" she objects.

"Oh yes, if you're uncomfortable then we'll move sooner than later. Now get up and go eat," he says as he taps her ass to make her rise up off of him.

# CHAPTER 40

It's moving so fast and Bree is unsure how she feels about any of this. Sadly, she cannot distinguish if it's the hormones talking or if her feelings are really unsure. All she can think about is if she and Reggie don't work out, then she will have two kids by two different fathers. Not quite how she planned her life out.

"Hey Remi, come in so I can see that damn rock!" Nia says retreating back into the house.

"Hey girl, what have you been up to? Where are the kids?"

"Damn, Reggie did the damn thang. That's nice," she applauds. "Congratulations! Where's my damn finders fee?" She jokes. "The kids are at the center. Pick-up time is six o'clock. I'll be there by five fifty-nine." She smiles

"Thank you and for how long am I indebted to you? I thought I brought you lunch already."

"I'll let you know when you're clear," she snickers. "So how is the wedding planning going?"

Bree is so tired of talking about planning this damn wedding. She just wants a day to talk about nothing. Gossip even at this point. "I have to halt those for now."

"What? What happened? Did Reggie cheat on you?"

"No, no. I'm pregnant."

"Oh my goodness. What the hell is going on? I thought you were on birth control."

"I was. I misplaced them one day and it all went downhill from there. I don't want to be a pregnant bride, so we're postponing until next year." Bree sighs.

"Are you okay Bree?"

"Yeah, it's just all going so fast and I'm feeling a bit uneasy."

"That's the hormones talking," Nia confirms. "You are Reggie are meant to be. You guys act like ya'll be together forever." She chuckles.

"Yeah," Bree smiles, taking in her confirmation. "We are definitely something together. It's wonderfully scary."

"I take it Reggie knows. Have you told Manny?"

"Yeah."

"And?"

"And what?"

"How did he take it?"

"What do you mean? He's fine."

"I know he's fine and sexy as hell. But how did he take the news?" Nia pries.

"Good. Am I missing something? Is there supposed to be bad blood or something?"

"I mean. I don't know. As you said this is all moving fast and I'm surprised he's taking it well." Nia stirs the pot between Bree and Manny.

"I didn't foresee him taking it any other way. So, if he has a problem, then he's doing right by keeping it to himself."

"Don't get me wrong, I love you and Reggie together. I do. I just knew for sure one day you would tell me that you were moving to Cali to be with Manny. And I would be with the kids in tow telling you to hook me up with one of his friends." She laughs through the pain that Bree can clearly see.

"I got you now. You want him to be mad at me for you," Bree laughs. "How are you and Charles doing Nia?" She deflates the balloon and checks on her friend.

"Ok for the most part. I'm guarding my feelings. I know I am. Forget going the extra mile, he's running a decathlon. He's pulling out all the tricks to get me back into our marriage. And if I wasn't making a conscious effort to stay in this place of pain, then it would work." She admits.

"I'm not understanding," Bree begins yet Nia interrupts.

"Bree, we are playing the waiting game with this DNA test and I refuse to get back into a happy place only to find out it's his baby. I don't think I can handle that."

"I wasn't even thinking about the baby."

"Neither is he honestly. He is positive that it's not his. But I don't know." She says shaking her head.

"Now I'm not condoning the cheating," Bree places her disclaimer before she continues. "But typically men know. If he says it's not his, then it's probably not."

"How can he be so sure Bree?"

"I mean yes, if he slept with her, then there is a possibility. But you don't want to hear anything right now. What if they used protection? What if fucked her in the ass? What if she just sucked his dick? Her job is to sabotage the marriage at any cost. Therefore, she is going to let you think what you want. Even if it's a lie."

"I hear you, I don't even know what they did because I don't want to know."

"I wouldn't want to know either. We're grown. We know how sex works. We also know how side chicks work. If nothing else, then give him the benefit of the doubt on this. Yes, he cheated and it was wrong, but do you think he wanted a baby? I'm sure he'd tried to prevent that."

"Bree he deserves no passes."

Bree holds her arms up to surrender. She can't argue with how Nia feels. She's just happy that she got to plant the seed to give Nia something to think about.

"Anyway, I need to borrow Charisma. What is she doing this weekend? Frankie is coming over and I'm sure that Tabby is going to want to come and the boy's treats her like shit. So at least Charisma can be her company."

"That's right on time. You can take her. How long?"

"Probably just Saturday night. I'll let you know. What are you getting into?"

"Hanging over here, hanging over there," she smirks

"I hope I don't get into trouble."

"Naw, no trouble. Just trying to make this process less painful."

"Less painful with who?" Bree asks to make sure Tyree isn't in the mix.

"Ty'shell and I are hanging. I told you that other thing is dead." Nia tries to assure Bree.

"How is Ty'shell doing?"

"She's good. Oh, have you talked to ya boi lately because there is trouble in paradise. Lisa is pregnant girl,"

"What's wrong with a wife getting pregnant by her husband?" Bree casually dismisses the gossiping tone. Besides this news is super late, Lisa should be about due.

"That's the thing, it may not be his baby," Nia sings childishly.

Bree can bet that this makes Nia feel much better about her situation not realizing that Slim is the one in her shoes. "Well damn. My child's father is Reggie," she laughs hoping that Nia gets the hint that she doesn't want to talk about it.

"You're such a sour puss. I'm going to tell you about it anyways," Nia counters her dismissal knowing Bree doesn't like to talk about people. "Well it appears Lisa is sneaking around with a mystery man that no one knows. And now she's pregnant. At first she was telling Slim it was his and he was cool until someone spilled her tea."

"Sad situation," Bree decides to cut her off. "What do you know, I have a friend that I actually care about who is in a similar situation." Bree says as she looks Nia directly in the eye. And in that moment, the unthinkable thought entered her mind. She made her statement to bring Nia back to focus on something of relevance, it wasn't meant to stir the pot.

"Are you thinking what I'm thinking?" Nia asks slowly.

"Depends,"

"I know you are. I swear it better not be her," Nia shakes her head.

"Was she at the party? Doesn't she know that you and Charles are married?"

"She knows and I don't know if she was there. I swear Brianna, I will kill her, him and Ty'shell." She speaks in a voice of frustration.

"Just Charles, he's the responsible party to you," Bree clears the air. "And why Ty'shell?"

"Because I'm sure she knows."

"You cannot be so sure about that. You said so yourself it's a mystery man." Bree pauses to bring some sort of calm to the discussion. "Look, do not question Ty'shell's loyalty and trust on an unconfirmed theory. Don't ruin your friendship over it. Confront Charles with the name, the least he can do is confirm or deny whether it's her. If not, then your friendship with Ty'shell is still intact and no one has to know your business. If so, then you have some confronting to do, but still not with Ty'shell. What if she really doesn't know?"

"She better not know because this will be grounds to whoop her ass."

"Oh I'm with you on that!" Bree confirms. "Just take it up with Charles. Promise me that." Bree says in a serious tone because she knows how Nia can blow up.

"Promise."

# CHAPTER 41

"Bree it's me," Manny says through the crack in the bathroom door. He doesn't want her to be startled by his presence when she comes out of the shower.

"Okay," she yells as she turns her attention back to the soothing water beating onto her body.

She looks down at her growing belly and cannot believe that she is going through this process again. One thing is for sure, this pregnancy is much better than her first. She's not working as hard, she's able to enjoy the little moments, and most importantly she has Reggie to share it with. Just a week until they find out the sex and Bree couldn't be more excited. A part of her wants Junior to have a brother. He and Frankie have such a wonderful bond. It would be nice if he actually had a brother to navigate through life with. However, Bree would be lying to herself if she said that she doesn't want a little girl of her own. Besides the fun things they will be able to do together, Bree doesn't think she will ever do this again. Having a boy and a girl would curb the temptation to try again for a specific sex.

When Bree makes it into her bedroom she immediately looks at the clock. Two-twenty? She knew it was too early for Manny to be here.

"Where are you coming from?" she questions Manny as she comes down the steps.

"Minding my business and leaving yours alone," he replies without even turning her direction.

"Being a man whore I see. The flights from your end don't land here this early."

"Look at this," Manny says disregarding her remarks and extending his arms to touch her protruding belly.

"It's getting out there right?" Bree says looking down as he rubs her belly gently.

"Too cute," he states.

Bree sits down next to him and grabs the remote. The guide is still displaying on the TV as Manny hasn't selected a show to watch. "How are you?" Bree asks as she thumbs through the menu.

"Good," Manny leans over and kisses her on the cheek. "How about yourself? Why are you home this time of day?"

"I'm good. I have some time to burn at work, so I worked half a day today." She says then finally turns to look at him after she chose the SportsNetwork.

"Come here," he demands as he pulls her to snuggle up against his chest. Without hesitation Bree slides into his embrace. He rests his head on hers and begins to rub her belly. Bree sits immobile. She is not uncomfortable. She doesn't understand why. So she sits silently and keeps her eyes glued to the TV.

"Was that a kick?" He breaks the silence about five minutes later.

"I'm not sure if it was a kick but she's moving."

"She?"

"No confirmation yet, I'm just hoping." Bree clears up.

"Oh okay. This is pretty amazing. I've missed out on so much." Manny reflects aloud.

"You did. But you wanted to move to California and left me with my experiences alone." Bree throws out there. Not being malicious. More like a gentle reminder of how things went down in case he forgot.

"Nice tone." Manny acknowledges the change in her voice. "I offered to stay."

"I wasn't going to allow you to give up chasing your dreams. I told you that."

"I offered for you to come."

"I didn't want to chase your dreams. I told you that."

"You did. And I made my decision."

"I know."

"Are you mad at me?"

"No."

"Sounds like it."

"I'm not," Bree confirms, wiping her eye.

Manny sits up, "Brianna, are you crying? What's wrong?"

"Nothing. I'm okay," she speaks through a smile. She has been misty eyed lately over the minutest of things.

"Talk to me."

"It's nothing really."

"It's something. Do you feel like I abandoned you?"

"No. It was a contractual agreement. I agreed to it."

"Hey, hey, hey," Manny speaks as he turns to face her eye to eye. "Let's not pretend that we didn't make that contractual agreement to have a significant tie to each other. I'm choosing my words wisely, but I think you know what I mean."

"You're right!" Bree let flow from her mouth. She doesn't want to have this conversation.

"It's not about being right or wrong. It's facts! How are you feeling? Where and why was this buried?" he asks sincerely.

"I just felt lonely at times. But I knew what the deal was. And with that, I couldn't make a big fuss out of it. It's not your job to worry about how I feel. Well felt."

"I'm so sorry if you felt alone during a time that was supposed to be special. You were dealing with a mountain of issues and I was not present to help you by being there for you physically. I was immature to think that financial security was all that you needed. But we have been partners in this thing called life for so long. I don't ever want you to think that your feelings are not my concern because they are. I wish you would have told me this."

"It's okay," she states yet again.

"But you're crying."

"I am. And that's the feelings leaving my body. I have to admit I have harbored that for quite some time. Don't know why it came out today." She confesses. "Maybe it's this experience that I'm having now. I don't know. But don't beat yourself up about it. I'm good. I promise."

"Promise me that you'll always address any issues you have with me. We are better than this."

"I agree. I promise. We're good." She says through a deep breath to pull herself together. "And thank you."

"For?"

"Being a great friend," she smiles.

"No problem," he says, grabbing her head then he places a kiss on her forehead. No hesitation was made for them to retreat back into their comfortable position.

"You know this is wrong, right?" Bree questions. However, in her mind it seems more like a reminder for herself.

"Shhhhh," Manny mutes her by putting his finger over her mouth. She attempts to get up but he casually stops her progress and repositions himself.

"Manny..."

"Shhhhh, let me have this." He pleads.

Bree falls back into his cuddle and rests. Moments later she finds herself caressing his leg as they silently bask in the opportunity.

"Double R,"

"Hum,"

"I know that I am no longer the preferred safe space, but I will always be a safe space for you."

"I know," Bree lets roll off of her tongue in a cocky manner.

"Oh do you?" he shifts his body to get a look at her.

"I do."

"We're not getting married," he laughs.

"You're right!" she says, ending their familiar atmosphere. "I need to get dinner started."

"Can we stay?" he asks as he follows her into the kitchen.

"What type of question is that? Why wouldn't you be allowed?"

"I don't know. You may slip up and give me the lustful eye." Manny teases. He has loved testing the waters with Bree. His advances have been rolling lately.

"You're toeing the line. I need you to take a couple steps back Sir!" Bree warns him.

"I have been instructed not to cross, toeing is very acceptable. And fun might I add," He smiles

"You are a piece of work. I do not have lustful eyes for you. I thought we had deaded this conversation long ago. You're so jealous. I just don't understand why." Bree says in a playful manner.

"You know why?" he snaps back in a serious tone.

"Honestly, I don't. But you keep on insisting that I do. Why don't you just tell me?"

"That would be crossing the line," he winks and walks back into the family room.

This time Bree is the one doing the following and continuing the conversation. "Glenn come here." She demands as she stopped dead in her tracks to make him walk back to her. She realizes that chasing after him is not a good look.

Manny complies and has returned to stand almost chest to chest with her. "Given our situation, what do you want to hear from me Brianna Monique?" He asks looking directly into her eyes.

Bree lowers her head because she knows that it's best to let this conversation float away for the millionth time, but this time it needs to be for good. "Nothing I suppose."

"Great! Now let's get out of the danger zone before your fiancé shows up." He suggests in a snarky tone.

Against his wishes Bree stays put. "So it's the title," she asks for clarification as she now sees his angle.

"No," he says and tries to walk away but Bree grabs his arm.

"What is it?" she asks confusingly.

"I'm not sure if you want me to say it to feed your ego or if you just don't get it. But I'm going to say it to please whatever it is just for you." He says gently, shaking her chin. "After I do, you don't get to ask follow-up questions. You deal with my response and we move on. Got it?" He asks as he looks at her for a silent agreement. "No woman that walks this earth will be able to say that they share a part of me. And for that you will always be number one in my book. I can no longer say the same."

Bree drops her eyes to the floor to break their gaze. She is speechless. Never in a million years has she looked at their three cord family in such a way. As Manny walks away, she is reminded that all the questions and concerns she has regarding this matter are left in the universe. She always thought that Manny not only knew, but accepted that she wanted to be married someday; possibly growing her family some day. She doesn't know how to process or what to do with this news. She cannot turn back the hands of time and do things differently. Manny knows why they cannot be together. Bree agreeing to have a baby with him seemed like the next best thing in her opinion. But the next best thing isn't the first best thing she rationalizes. She slowly walks over to him not knowing exactly what she wants to say. Even though according to him, there isn't anything for neither of them to say.

She reaches out for his hands to make him stand. "I'm sorry," she offers as she begins to wrap him in her embrace. Bree gets the vibe that he's not feeling the contact.

"It's quite alright," he says breaking their awkward moment. "It was contractual." He says as he sits back down onto the couch.

Bree stands stunned for a minute. Then she heads back into the kitchen to get dinner started.

# CHAPTER 42

"There's my smile," Reggie announces as he sits across the table from Bree. They just left the doctor's office.

"It's a girl!" Bree says gleefully.

"I know," he smiles. "Are you feeling better now?"

"I wasn't feeling bad."

"Something's been bothering you for the last couple of days. I've been letting you have your space. But I'm always here to talk baby."

"I'm okay."

"Talk to me."

"It's reflection, that's all. My life is changing with the baby; the marriage. These are all permanent decisions."

"Very permanent," he interrupts.

"And in that, I've been living in my head. It seems surreal sometimes."

"Are you backing out?" Reggie asks getting straight to the point.

"How can I back out of this?" Bree playfully asks as she grabs her belly.

It gives Reggie a chuckle. That was a silly way to ask the question. "Are you trying to find a way to not marry me?" He clarifies his question.

"Never! I didn't say that Baby. Don't jump off the cliff on me," she reels him back in. "Just thinking about my life that's all." She defends.

"And I hope that when you do, that you only see how wonderful it's going to be."

"The majority of the time, I do. But if I'm going to be honest, when I come to the fork in the road sometimes I drift down the arrow that is labeled disaster."

"And what would be a disaster?"

"Me raising two kids alone."

"Let me address this before I pound on the main concern. You will never be alone. For one, Manny takes care of his son and you should know that I would do the same with our daughter. However, I know that is far from the concern you have. Don't think that I haven't taken into consideration that you will now have two children with two different fathers. But reality is, whether it was me or someone else, this would still be the case."

"True," she chimes in.

"Baby, rest your mind. I'm not going anywhere. Do you think that I would ask you to be my wife if I didn't plan on spending the rest of my life with you?"

"Plans and reality are two different things."

"Agreed. Well the reality is that you're going to have to leave me if we ever cross that bridge. And if you do, then I better be afforded the same respect that you showed Manny when you are looking for a potential mate."

"While I know this conversation is really not worth having, it's funny that your bottom line comes to such a trivial issue." She chuckles. "Good thing we are not going to have to deal with either."

"There ya go. Get your head off the swivel and get focused again."

The waiter comes to drop off their lunch and Reggie continues to focus on the life ahead of them.

"Names?"

"Raileigh, that's it! I've thought about it since the day I found out I was pregnant."

"No say for me?"

"Sure, what do you suggest?"

"Nothing now that you declared her name. Spelling?"

"R-A-I-L-E-I-G-H"

"Interesting."

"I can't read you right now."

"Why are you trying?"

"Because I want to know how you feel."

"Ask."

"How do you feel?"

"I'm good with it. Seriously, I am." He says with confidence. "It's cute."

Bree sits in silence.

"I know that my body language and words are not aligning. I'm not upset at the name. I really do like it Bree. I'm uneasy more or so about the process or  lack thereof of getting to that conclusion. It would have been nice if you even tried to consider any of my suggestions."

"I'm sorry. You're right. You have just as much input and I. It's just that I have been secretly praying for a girl and in that I ran through so many scenarios in my mind of how things would be when she arrives. In my imagination I was forced to give her a name and that's what I chose."

"I wish I was a part of those wonderful thoughts."

"You can be. I thought that you were having a moment. You haven't been yourself lately. I guess that's why I have been a frequent visitor on a disastrous road lately."

"Explain."

"You've pulled away a little."

"I haven't noticed. What am I not doing or what am I doing that is making you feel this way?"

"Our love making…" Bree starts to try to explain herself.

"Hold up." He interrupts because he has to get this off his chest. "Let me stop you right there, you have a whole human being growing inside of you and you expect me to still bang it up?" He asks jokingly but is serious about the inquiry.

"No," she replies, letting out a chuckle because of his choice of words. "I do not expect for you to bang it up," she repeats. "I expect for you to still be present with me and give yourself to me."

"Ouch!"

"I'm sorry."

"No, don't apologize for how you feel." He dismisses the gesture. "It stung a little though." He admits.

"I need and want you here with me. Is there something that I'm doing wrong?"

"Not at all. Like I said I haven't noticed. Maybe I have been being distant because you were. And it seems that you have been being distant because of me. We have to communicate more. This silent communication can kill us."

"I agree. I have to ask because it would be a lie if I said that it hasn't crossed my mind. Is there another woman?"

"Absolutely not," he replies appallingly as he gets up to go and share her side of the booth. "I love you. There is not another woman in my life. There is not another woman I would want to have in my life." He confesses going a step further. "Baby, tell me how do we fix this? I cannot afford to have you walking around with these types of thoughts in your mind."

"Our emotional connection is very important to me." She sighs. "I am about to go out on a vulnerable limb here, so please be gentle with me." She cautions.

"Always," he agrees as he caresses her back and listens attentively.

"While I know it's not reasonable or ideal for me to depend on you for validation. I do. When we are emotionally connected it reassures my feelings and our love for each other. I have no idea why I need it but I do. I know that I should be confident in what we have, and for the most part I am. Sometimes, it's just something that I cannot put my finger on that lets my mind wander to a dark space. And it's not your fault. And I'm sorry that I'm putting this on you," she takes a deep breath, "I know I sound like a confused mess." She concludes.

"No you don't. I get it. I knew when I first met you that there is a lot of emotional ground that I had to reconstruct, build and sustain once built. I have dropped the ball in reassuring you that our love, my love is true and genuine. Although you may not feel like it's not my responsibility, I take on the challenge and will make a conscious effort to make sure that we are connecting in the way that you need to feel confident in us."

"Thank you." She nudges him with a smile.

"You're welcome." He returns the nudge. "So, are we off the limb because I have a question?"

'Yes, yes, go back over there," she sends him away to go back on his side of the table. "Shoot!" she says once he settles.

"Is love a choice or a feeling?" he asks.

"A choice," she laughs. She cannot believe that he remembers that conversation. And regardless of how she feels right now, she still stands by her words.

"You just described feeling our love."

"I did," she admits. "But even though I don't feel those feelings right now, I still love you. I chose to still love you in spite of," she winks. "And despite my emotional state, when it would be easier for you to walk away, you choose love."

He closes his eyes and lets out a laugh through his nose, "Point made."

# CHAPTER 43

Bree is about ready to drop this load. She has about four more weeks until the big day. She and Reggie successfully wed and had a mini honeymoon in December. Bree was sad because no one was a part of a moment that was so special to her. The fact that Reggie can't wear his ring just yet bothers her, as well as the fact that she isn't wearing her wedding band. But it's all in the name of love and sanity, so she's rolling with it.

"How is the little Princess," Latrice asks, rubbing Bree's belly.

"Oh she's just fine, I'm the uncomfortable one." Bree squirms. Her stomach didn't get very big so her baby girl is hitting every organ she can when making any movements.

"She'll be here soon," Latrice smiles

"I can't wait."

"Reggie is going to have her so spoiled. Don't get jealous," she cautions.

"Why does everyone say that?"

"Because it's a thing you know. Daddy's girl; Momma's boy."

"They can have at it. It will leave me more time to myself." Bree shrugs. "Trice I think I want to head out. I have a headache and just want to lie down."

"A headache? That's not good, let me check your pressure."

"Trice," Bree looks unenthused.

"I'll let you go if I can do a checkup first. You know headaches especially this late are not a good thing."

"Alright, let's go. But I'm fine. Just tired," Bree looks back as she walks towards the room.

Bree knows that she is fine because she doesn't have a headache. She milks this pregnancy every chance she gets. Manny is picking up Junior today and she wants to rest up before Reggie makes it home. Maybe they can go out or at least to Nia's house to hang. Charles and Nia were able to work out their differences, mainly because the baby is not his and even more importantly he didn't cheat with Lisa.

Manny is parked in the driveway as she pulls up to the house, so she parks on the street and heads to the front door to give him a piece of her mind. She knows that she is early and he may have every intention to move before she gets off work, but he shouldn't park in the driveway at all or at least block Reggie, he's home later than Bree. As Bree approaches the door she gets a warm sensation over her body. Her stomach suddenly feels queasy and she begins to run through the things she ate starting with breakfast. Her morning sickness has long subsided. However, some foods and smells still get her feeling ill. Once she opens up the door, she realizes that the feeling has absolutely nothing to do with her and everything to do with the energy inside the house. For no reason other than instinct she leaves the door open and begins to walk upstairs. It's all odd and confusing because normally Manny would be in the guest room if he's not in the living room or more likely raiding the refrigerator. As she walks slow and quietly towards her bedroom she hears something but can't make out what it is. Her heart is pounding with every step and the thumping sound of it is muffling all noise in the house.. She will lose her shit if he has someone in her home, in her bedroom. Bree walks to look inside the room and cannot believe her eyes. She stands immobile. She wants to cry but is too furious. She wants to scream but no sound is coming from her mouth. An uncontrollable gagging begins.

Manny finally turns to her, "Bree," he says like he's seen a ghost.

The sound of his voice releases her from the cement her feet feels stuck in and she immediately rushes downstairs.

Manny instantly came chasing after her. "Bree, please, please, please. Let me explain."

Bree is silent. She doesn't know what to do or to say. She doesn't know what reaction she should have. She walks into the kitchen then turns back out once she sees the knives. She might be tempted to do something that will ruin her life; as if it isn't already ruined enough.

"Bree, come here," Manny says, still following behind her.

Once Bree makes it back into the living room, Reggie is walking down the steps slowly. He isn't looking her way. Bree stops suddenly and Manny runs into the back of her because he isn't expecting the abrupt halt.

"I'm sorry," he says referencing the slight blow she just received to her back.

Bree turns around and faces Manny, "Let's go and get Junior and take him for ice cream. Then you can figure out what you will do until your flight leaves," she says calmly as she walks towards the door.

Reggie stops midway down and sits on the stairs. Manny looks at him and hangs his head, but continues to follow Bree out the door.

"Don't say anything to me right now," Bree screams at Manny once he shuts his car door. In a more calming voice she says, "Let's just go and get this over with."

Manny takes her advice, starts the engine and heads to Junior's school.

When they pull up to the school, Bree breaks her silence because she needs answers, "How long has this been going on?"

"Bree I promise you nothing is going on. Today is the first time anything has happened. It was just the kiss, I swear."

"Who initiated," she begins but catches herself. "You know what that doesn't matter because it shouldn't even have happened." She rationalizes to herself.

"Brianna I'm so sorry. I don't know what else to say," he says softly.

"You really don't have to say anything Glenn, it's expected from you. You're the community dick," she states.

"I wasn't trying to hurt you." He begins.

"Not trying to hurt me as my heart is shattered into a million pieces right now are you serious? What did you think I would do, be happy and join in?"

"It all happened so fast. I didn't even know he was there. You know me Bree. I go in, eat and then crash."

"And you're telling me this because?" she asks like any of that matters. "Obviously you went in, went into my bedroom and started kissing my husband."

"Your husband?" Manny shouts. "When the fuck did that happen?"

"Does it matter? Would knowing that have stopped you? No, because this is how you do." She answers the question herself.

"Yeah this is how I do," he says in an angry tone. "Yet you're mad at me because your *husband* likes men." He says with a faint chuckle.

"I'm not mad at you for that. Don't deflect. I'm talking to you right now. I'll deal with him when it's time. I'm mad at you because I thought you were my friend and regardless if he likes men, I should not have found out that information through the two of you lip locking in my bedroom. That was foul Manny and you know it," she says for him to take his blame.

"I fucked up. I know that Bree. I'm sorry." He says apologetically.

"I'll be back," she says, exiting the car cutting their conversation short.

Bree's mind is racing because she knows that she has to put on a fake smile for her son. Then she has to go home and deal with Reggie. She's not even sure she wants to go home. But how long can she avoid the situation?

# CHAPTER 44

Going out with Junior makes Bree relax a little. The three of them together is always a great time. And despite what happened she isn't going to direct any of her anger towards her son. Manny has eased his way back into her good graces. Not that it takes much for him to do so. He and Bree share something special that they both try to suppress. While they were eating their ice cream she had the chance to think, she's not going to let this break her nor define her. She's going to do what she needs to do and move on. It will be difficult but worth it.

As they pull up to the house Bree asks Junior if she wants to say goodbye to Reggie. She asks for numerous reasons, first to make everything appear normal, second because she needs them both to see the ripple effect this is going to have and lastly because she knows she's going to ask Manny to keep Junior until she feels that she's ready for him to come home. There's so much that she and Reggie needs to work through and Junior does not need to witness it.

"Reggie," Bree calls for him as she walks into the house

Reggie comes walking downstairs and forces a smile on his face when he sees Junior. "Hey squirt, you're getting ready to leave us?"

"Yes, take care of mom. I'll be back," Junior instructs like he's an adult. He has been helping so much since finding out Bree is pregnant. He's on his best behavior, tries to bring her breakfast in bed on the weekends and reads to his little sister nightly.

"You know I will," Reggie smiles, "Hey go and grab the books that I need to read. You know just what your sister likes," he directs Junior towards the steps.

As Junior runs up the stairs, Reggie stares trying to find something to say but Bree turns her back to him and begins to talk to Manny. "Make sure he doesn't get any more ice cream tonight, he's one spoonful away from a sugar high."

"I'm not. He did go all in didn't he? I'm surprised he didn't get a brain freeze and more surprised you let him keep going."

"Hey he's going with you. I'm going to sleep easy." She smiles

Junior comes down the steps with books in hand and gives them to Reggie.

"If you want her to move around and kick, then read this one. And if mom doesn't want to be bothered, then read this one. But this is the book that she loves," he says to Reggie like he doesn't already know. But it feels good for Bree to know that Junior's aware.

Reggie pulls him in for a hug, he knows that this is all going to end badly. "I'm going to miss you. I love you okay."

"I love you too. Ready Dad?" he asks excitedly heading to the door.

Bree and Manny follow him out. Reggie is a few steps behind but stops short of going outside.

At the car, Bree makes her request, "Well you know this is about to get ugly. And I have a lot to figure out. Do you mind keeping Junior, you know until this all blows over?"

"You know I don't mind but what am I supposed to tell him?"

"Junior," Bree calls him from out of the car. She stoops to his level, "How would you feel about staying with Dad for like a month?" she asks enthusiastically trying to make it sound fun. "Your sister will be here shortly and we have a lot of things to take care of. And I'm sure it will be no fun for you. But when you come back, she should be here."

"So I don't have to go to school," he jumps.

"You will still do your work online when the tutor comes just like any other time with Dad. But I'm sure you'll still have more fun than being here."

"Okay, make sure you call me mom." He says getting in the car.

"We'll video chat every night as usual. I love you."

"I love you too."

Manny goes in for a hug and Bree lets him. "I'm sorry. Let me know if you need anything," he offers.

"I'll keep that in mind." She replies. While Bree is upset with Manny, he is not the one that she has an issue with. All of her internal anger is for Reggie.

Reggie opens the glass door as Bree approaches. Bree walks through without a word.

"Bree can we at least talk,"

"I don't feel like talking," she brushes him off.

"But you can laugh and giggle with your best friend huh?" he asks because he's jealous that Manny is getting different treatment. They both shared the kiss and they both are wrong.

"Yeah I can," she says walking up the steps. She plans on gathering some items  for her to sleep in the guest room.

"I'm your husband," he uses his card.

"Are you now?" Bree looks at him with a shocking look on her face.

"How do you think I feel seeing that you're not mad at him?"

"Not as bad as I felt watching you kiss him. I know that for sure."

"So that's what this is, you're trying to hurt me?"

"No, I have no interest in that," she speaks as if she's removed from the situation. "Besides I've known that Manny is bisexual since I met him when we were fourteen. You on the other hand," she stops to let her words linger.

Reggie just stands there, he has nothing to say.

"Well," she grabs the bag she packed. "You can stay in this tainted room and I'll be downstairs."

With that she walks away. Reggie wants to stop her but he can't. All sorts of things are running through his mind. He wonders if Manny set him up to get caught. Reggie is willing to bet he's jealous. Manny wasn't too happy with the proposal and the pregnancy irritated him. He's going to get to the bottom of it, but first he has to deal with Bree.

# CHAPTER 45

Bree had no trouble sleeping or putting the incident out of her mind. She woke up refreshed and ready for the day. As she is whipping up some breakfast, more like brunch, she questions if she really loves her husband. Why hasn't she cried? Why doesn't she long for him? Why is she not trying to get to the bottom of this? Plenty questions and not one answer. "I love my husband," she says aloud to quiet the voices in her head. They seem to have a mind of their own. Did she settle because she was desperate? Did she miss the signs rushing to build a family? Is their relationship built on love or convenience? Bree once again reassures herself that she loves her husband and their rushed marriage wasn't out of desperation. She honestly thought they were on the same page. Giving her childhood, she knows that she can easily emotionally detach from anything. Out of sight, out of mind. As long as Reggie isn't around to give her any bad energy, she can pretend it never happened. When she goes back into the guest room she notices that she has a missed call from his sister and is instantly reminded that they are to be at his mother's house for dinner tonight. Her birthday was this past Wednesday and everyone is getting together to celebrate. Before calling her back she goes to ask Reggie if they are still going first.

"Hey," she says walking into their bedroom.

Reggie immediately jumps up from his lying position. "Hey!"

"Are we still heading to your mother's house? If so, then we need to start to get ready." She advises. Dinner isn't until six, but it's usually an all day affair at his mother's house.

"I wasn't sure if you still wanted to go." He expresses.

"Why not?"

"You don't even want to talk to me."

"I'm up for going out and pretending that we're a happy couple. That's what you've been doing all this time." She shrugs unbothered.

Reggie takes a deep breath and ignores her smart remark. "Yes, I want to go."

"Ok, I'm going to go and get ready."

About an hour later Reggie comes down to get Bree. "Are you ready?"

"Almost," she says touching up her make-up in the mirror. "Don't get too happy while we're there. I know there's a level of physical contact we need to make for us to look, for a lack of better word, normal. Don't overdo it. Hugs, belly rubs, maybe your chin on my head are all good." Then she turns to look at him, "Please don't put your lips on me." She turns back to the mirror for her last layer of lipstick. "Ready," she says, giving herself a last glance over.

Reggie speaks no words. He follows her out the door.

The ride to his parent's house is silent until his sister calls.

"Hey Tasha,"

"Bree why didn't you call me back,"

"I did call you back, what's up?"

"Oh I didn't see it. I was calling to see if you could whip up something."

"Damn, we're already on the road. Want us to pick up something?"

"No it's cool. I'll see ya'll when ya'll get here."

"What did she want?" Reggie asks, trying to get some conversation from Bree.

"Me to bake something,"

"She could have called me when you didn't answer."

Bree doesn't say anything else.

When they get out of the car, Bree grabs Reggie to stop him before going in. She stands face to face with him and grabs both of his hands. They are staring into each other's eyes. Her heart melts looking at him. She doesn't understand why this happened to her. In this moment right here all her emotions come rushing. She wants to ask so many questions but now is not the time.

"I don't want you to think that I don't love you because I don't want to talk to you." she says fighting back tears. "I'm just trying to process all of this and I don't need you in my ear with excuses." She pauses. "When we go inside I'm sure it's going to feel like everything is okay. Don't forget that it's not." She says with a deep sigh to gather herself back together. "I'm ready," she says, but she is convincing herself.

"Hey ya'll," Bree says with the brightest smile when she walks through the door.

"Come here so I can rub that belly for some good luck. I played some numbers this morning," his dad says.

"Now don't go blaming my baby if you don't win," Bree laughs as she abides by his request.

"You're so tiny Bree. How much have you gained?" Tasha asked.

"Eight pounds, but I have time, trust me. The ninth month brings on everything." She says before directing her attention to his mother. "Ms. Lynn, you're looking like you're trying to go out and catch a date. You better get her Mr. Harold."

"Have to look good for my big day," she spins around.

"Beautiful," Bree says going in for a hug.

"How's my grandbaby,"

"About to catch these hands if she doesn't get off my bladder," Bree jokes.

"I exist." Reggie says with a light chuckle.

"Awe my baby needs some attention," Bree says. She walks over into Reggie arms and rubs his chest.

"Ask Reg how much he's gained Tasha," she says ending with her hand on his belly.

"I didn't want to say anything, but he is looking kind of chunky lately," she laughs.

"It's muscle," he defends. It's true he's bulked up. It's because he gained so much weight. He's been hitting the gym extra hard. He hasn't lost any of the weight just gained more muscle as he tries to prevent it from turning into fat.

"It is muscle," Bree says, feeling his biceps.

"You're saying that because you love him," Tasha says rolling her eyes.

Bree has had enough of Reggie for the moment so she goes into the kitchen to see what she can eat.

"The food is almost ready Bree, but I'm sure you can find something to snack on," Mrs. Lynn advises.

"Where's Junior?" Tasha asks.

"It's the golden week,' Bree smiles before biting into an apple.

"They come around quickly."

"Tell me about it."

As Bree, Mrs. Lynn and Tasha sit and make small talk, Reggie is talking to his Dad. This is one of those times that he wishes he could ask for advice; however, his family doesn't know about his attraction to men. In fact, no one knows. He keeps that part of his life a total secret. When Toya was almost on his heels about it, he made it his business to leave her. Her distrust and insecurities would be too much to deal with along with trying to hide this secret. With Bree he doesn't have to worry about her checking his phone, following him around town or popping up at his workplace unannounced. All these things and more Toya did frequently. Although he must admit that Toya has aided him in covering his tracks much better which is why Bree had never had a suspicion.

As Reggie looks at Bree he cannot believe that he's hurt her. He can't believe that she even found out and the way she did. He vowed to himself long ago that when he found the woman he wanted to marry he would put the lifestyle away and focus on his family. After all it was always a dream of his to get married and have a family with a woman. He was just having fun experiencing exciting things with men or so he thought. The first few months of their relationship he was successful at keeping his urges at bay, but the feelings are something that he can't fully suppress. He's attracted to men and women and that's something that he needs to accept for himself. He should have come clean to Bree to avoid this very situation, but he knew if he did, that he would lose her. It seems as if he's losing her now anyway.

"I love you," he mouths to her as she finally brings her gaze his way.

"No, I love you," she says then turns back around.

Reggie gets up to go and be close to her. He knows his boundaries and he plans on meeting her right at the line. He walks up behind her and wraps his arms around her belly. Bree immediately falls back into his chest for support as the bar stool offers none. He puts his cheek on her hair refraining from placing a kiss on her neck as he often does.

"Are you okay?" Bree asks while rubbing the side of his face. As she sinks into his embrace, her heart melts, butterflies enter her stomach and she is aroused by the touch of him. She knows that all of these senses are heightened because she doesn't want them to be. Without thought, she tilts his head just enough for her to place a kiss on his lips. She knows she said she didn't want his lips on her but she can't resist. "Smile," she suggests as she shows her pearly whites.

He brings his lips to her ears and whispers, "I can't do this. We need to go."

Bree gets up from the stool in a concerned manner and addresses Reggie. "Are you sure, you can't stick it out? If not, then I can drive if it's that bad."

"What's wrong?" Mrs. Lynn asks.

Bree takes over because she knows that Reggie won't do well in this situation. "He's not feeling too well. He wasn't feeling that well before we left the house, but he wanted to make it for you."

"Reggie you didn't have to get out of bed if you didn't feel well. I would have understood. Go home and get some rest. Hopefully, it's not anything you can pass on to Bree and make her sick."

"Unfortunately, I think it's something that I may have passed on to him. I had a little bug the other day. Something turned my stomach." Bree truthfully admits. "I'll get him home and take care of him. Maybe we'll take you out to dinner one day next week."

"That would be nice," Mrs. Lynn smiles. "Feel better Reggie," she says.

"Son are we still on for painting tomorrow or do you want to wait?"

"We can paint. I should be better after I get some meds and rest."

"Thank you," Reggie says once inside the car.

"To think I still care about your feelings," Bree sighs. "You're welcome."

"Bree please talk to me."

"Reggie, I don't want to talk about it right now. I just want to ride out these last couple of weeks free of stress. Is my health and the health of our baby not a concern?"

"Of course it is. Why would you ask me something like that?"

"Well I didn't think I had to ask if you were attracted to men, but look at this conundrum."

Reggie let out a heavy sigh, because he has no leg to stand on in the matter.

"Look," Bree continues. "If we talk, then I'll make a hasty decision. I haven't even thought about it long enough to make a sound decision. I'm trying to remain calm so that my blood pressure doesn't rise, so that I don't commit an act of violence and so that I don't say things that I can't take back. So please, please, please, for my sanity, just leave it alone."

"I understand." Is all Reggie replies. The remainder of the ride is silent. There's no point in starting a conversation as it will always lead back to his attraction to men.

# CHAPTER 46

Bree walks into the house and makes her way to her new quarters.

"Brianna, come here please." Reggie pleads

"WHAT! REGGIE WHAT!" she yells. She's unraveling to her wits end faster than she anticipated.

"Nevermind," he lowers his head.

"No, you want to talk? Let's go." She walks into his face. "What do you want me to do? Don't answer with how you want me to treat you. Answer honestly, if you caught me cheating on you, what would you do?"

"I don't know, probably leave."

"So, you're rushing your departure?" she gives him the glare like that's exactly her answer to all of this.

"I'm trying to avoid that Brianna."

She walks over to sit on the couch. "Obviously you have no fucks to give to my mental or physical health, so let's hash this out."

Reggie follows reluctantly and sits on the love seat across from her.

"Talk," she encourages with an attitude. "It seems you have so much you want to say," Bree says after there is a moment of silence.

"Brianna, I know you don't want to hear apologies, there's not much for me to offer at this point. I just want to know what I need to do to make this right?"

"You're asking me this now? I don't know Reggie, the damage is done. How am I supposed to compete with you being attracted to men?"

"I'm not asking you to compete."

"Well what are you asking me?"

"Not to leave me."

"And deal with you cheating on me with men?"

"NO!"

"How can I be so sure? What's the longest you've suppressed the feeling?"

Reggie hangs his head low. He doesn't want to answer but knows that he can't hide from the truth anymore. "The longest was probably about five months," he says wiping his hands down his face to refrain from having to make eye contact with her.

"So, our whole relationship has been a lie?"

"Not a lie Brianna, I love you. I wanted to marry you. I'm happy we're growing our family."

"Are you being truthful?"

"Yes, I promise you."

"Well answer this...did you hide my birth control to get me pregnant?"

Dead silence fills the air. Brianna's heart sinks to an all time low. She knew it. She knew he was trying to trap her into being with him. Why didn't she trust her instants when he got upset at Disney World?

"I don't know how to begin to justify my actions."

"Are you fucking serious," Brianna asks in a rage. Now the tears are starting to stream down her face. "I guess the marriage was a part of it too?" she asks but doesn't wait for an answer. "You knew I would agree to marry you if I was pregnant. And to think that you came up with the plan so easily, let's do it December fourteenth," she mocks. "You know what Reggie, FUCK YOU!"

Bree gets up to go to lock herself in the room and deal with the new found news. Reggie quickly jumps up from behind her yelling.

"I'm tired of you acting like you run this show. I've let you go on long enough, giving demands and telling me what you will or will not do." He yells while he's on her heels.

"Who are you talking to?" Bree turns around calmly to get a good look at him. As soon as she does a 180 he's standing right there.

"You're not leaving me." He scolds confidently.

"Whatever," she turns to continue into the room. She doesn't want to escalate the situation. It's not just her she has to think about, it's her child's well being as well.

"Brianna," he begins while trying to grab her arm.

"Don't fucking touch me," she yells as she pulls her arm away and continues to walk into the bedroom. He is on her heels again so she is unable to shut the door behind her. In that moment, she feels that she has made a big mistake. The last thing she wants is to get in a heated argument in this confined space. Too many things can happen.

She stands in front of the mirror taking off her jewelry starting with the meaningless ring on her left hand. She feels Reggie staring at her and out of her peripheral vision can see that he's not himself. This is the first time Bree has felt uneasy in his presence to the point where she feels that she would need to defend herself. To make this next interaction run smoothly she figures that she would readjust her sights, but stick to the target.

"Reggie I'm hurt," she turns to look at him. "I'm confused, I'm lost, I'm angry," she continues. "I just need some time and space. That's all I'm asking."

"I fear the space," he quickly replies and that's the most sincere thing that Bree has heard him say since yesterday. "I don't want to lose you."

"You played your card and you knew the risk. I don't understand how you are faulting me."

"It's not your fault. I take full responsibility." He speaks as he makes his way closer to her. "I have to fix this."

"What if I tell you don't waste your time because this is beyond repair?"

"I won't accept it. I'm not choosing that. As long as we're both breathing it can be worked on."

"And why do you feel like you have a choice? I don't recall you giving me a choice. You put me in a situation blindly and you are now telling me to deal with it. At least I'm being courteous and honest in letting you know up front."

"So that's it? No fighting for our love, our marriage, our family?"

"Honestly I don't know what I want to do and you are not affording me the space and time to

let me think. I'm not equipped to go into this fight. I don't even want to go into this fight. And I don't think that it's fair for you to ask me to right now."

Reggie bypasses her pleas of support and begins to tug at her heart. It's the only way. "I'm still me. I'm still the man that you fell in love with. I'm here with you, love me Brianna." He says as he wraps her in his arms. He feels her sinking into his words. "I need you. Don't leave me. I love you," he says as he raises her chin for her to look him into his eyes.

"I love you too, but," and before she can finish he has begun kissing her passionately. The intense moment of anticipated pleasure has taken over the both of them. As he backs Bree up towards the bed he makes his request, "Let's give ourselves to each other so you can feel how real our love is," he suggests as he places kisses on her neck. When he lays Bree on the bed to begin to take off her clothes, he notices the tears running down her face.

"Are you okay," he pauses. "You don't want to do this?"

"I do."

"What's wrong?"

"It's just disappointing to know that after you cheated on me, you would stoop so low as to play on my emotions, insecurities and vulnerabilities to get what you want. None of this feels like real love."

"It doesn't have to. Choose to love me." Reggie pulls Bree words out to let her chew on them.

Bree sits for a moment to eat her words; rightfully so. Because according to her logic, she can still choose to love him. The problem lies in that she doesn't know if she should.

As she gets up from the bed she makes her last statement, "That's the thing Reggie, I'm leaning towards choosing not to. You can go now." She says and walks towards the bathroom.

"Brianna," he cries.

"Just go, please!" she says just before closing the bathroom door.

# CHAPTER 47

Bree was hoping that telling Reggie he could go would mean that he actually leaves the house. However, when she didn't hear the door open and his car started she couldn't say that she was surprised. Reggie is going to squeeze this teat until it produces some milk. He is not going to give up their marriage. This concerns Bree because she doesn't know at what cost. She acknowledges the sounds of her stomach and makes her way to the kitchen to get her something to eat. On the way, she grabs her phone to call Junior.

"Hi Manny, may I speak to Junior please," she asks when he answers the phone. While they ended their face to face interaction on a good note, she's back in that dark space she was in when she saw the two of them kissing.

"Hey Bree, hold on." Manny responds quickly and gives the phone to Junior. He can hear in Bree's voice that she isn't feeling herself, so he is avoiding small talk.

"Hi Mom, is she here?"

"No, not yet. Calm down she still has a couple of more weeks. What are you doing?"

"We are about to go to the park."

"Sounds fun."

"Where's Daddy?"

"He's upstairs. I'm about to make something to eat."

"Can I talk to him?"

"I think he's sleeping. When he wakes up I will have him call you." Bree says as she shifts her eyes to Reggie. He must have heard her in the kitchen and decided to join.

"Ok love you. We'll just talk on video when I get back from the park. Here's Dad."

"I love you too,"

"Hey you, how are you holding up? Is everything okay your way?" Manny inquires against his earlier objections.

"I'm good and yes."

Before Bree could end the conversation Manny keeps the lines of communication active, "Why don't you come here with us and get away for awhile." He suggests.

"I don't think that's such a good idea."

"And why not? You have a couple weeks before she's due and if she does come while you're here, I'll be sure to get you the best care."

"I appreciate that, but again, I don't think that's a good idea."

"Still talking," Reggie asks in a hateful tone. He has made his way in her personal space.

Bree ignores the remark.

"He's still there?" Manny questions.

Bree just takes a deep sigh.

"Are you okay?" Manny asks again this time wanting an answer. He thought Reggie would have been kicked out of the house.

"I'm okay."

"Are ya'll talking about Junior?" Reggie asks chiming in again.

"So you can't talk to me now?" Manny asks confusingly.

"I can," Bree begins as she heads to the bedroom to get some privacy. As she walks away Reggie comes behind her, grabs her phone and hangs it up.

"What the fuck!" Bree yells

"If you don't talk to me, then you don't talk to him. What type of fucked up shit is that. He is just as responsible for all of this."

"I hold the two of you to different standards," she clarifies while bringing her tone down because she doesn't want to have a shouting match every time they interact. "And unless you've been fucking him since I've known you, I'm sure this all on you." She scolds.

"No I haven't fucked him but he wants me to though," Reggie says with a conniving smirk on his face.

"I'm glad someone is finding humor in this fucked up situation," And before Bree can continue, her phone rings.

"Don't answer it," Reggie warns.

"Fuck you," Bree grabs her phone knowing that it's Manny calling back. She really doesn't want to answer because as much as she hates to admit it, she's sure that Reggie is correct in saying that Manny wants Reggie to fuck him. But she can't resist the opportunity to make Reggie hot.

"Hello," Bree answers as she looks directly at Reggie.

"Did he hang up on me?"

"Yup!" Bree says as she turns to walk into the bedroom. Reggie stays put.

"Is everything okay over there, do I need to head back to Texas?"

"No you don't. He's upset that I talk to you that's all. I get, I guess."

"Yeah, I don't know why you talk to me either honestly. I'm not complaining though," he rushes to clarify. "I know that I also betrayed your trust and I am so sorry Bree."

"I heard you the first time." She says sadly.

"Are you okay," he asks once more because he doesn't know what else to say.

"Yes," she says, more upbeat. "I'm going to go and eat my food and get a nap in. Have Junior call when you guys get back."

"Will do."

"Bye," she hangs up before receiving a response.

She goes into the kitchen to get her food from the microwave and also to face the music as she knows that Reggie is awaiting her return.

"Why do you insist on being disrespectful?" he asks, jumping right in. "I asked you not to answer the phone."

Disrespectful? He has a nerve. Bree ignores his outburst and continues to do what she set out to do.

"You're going to talk to me Brianna, especially since you've made it a point to against my request and talked to him."

"It sounded more like a demand and I don't take well to those. Excuse me," she says as she walks around him with her plate to go and sit at the table.

"Says the person who makes a demand every time we talk."

"You're point?" she says looking directly at him. "I have every right to make demands, you fucked up remember?"

"I'm getting tired of your mouth," he says angrily.

"Great! Maybe you'll stop talking to me," she shrugs.

"Bree stop. I don't want to get upset."

"And honestly," she interrupts and there is a slight pause as she stuffs her face with her leftover pasta. "I have been trying to avoid that, but you keep talking to me."

"Why do you talk to him?"

"He has our son." She swiftly answers.

"But you weren't talking about Junior, he was inquiring about you."

"I'm the mother of his child. My well being is a concern for him."

"What about me?"

"What about you?"

"You're the mother of my child."

"And you're not concerned about her or me right now. You're concerned about yourself."

"Don't sit up here and say that I don't care about my child. What the fuck is wrong with you?" he yells.

"I can ask the same, but since you always want to talk, go on." She dismisses his outburst in a

calm tone.

"Don't ever question my love for my child. This situation does not warrant that accusation."

"You're right the situation doesn't. Treating me like shit does not warrant me to conclude that you will treat her like shit. But that's not where I draw my conclusion, the fact that if I don't eat, she doesn't eat does lead me to that conclusion. You ruin my fucking appetite." Bree says as she pushes the plate away and gets up to head back into the bedroom.

"Brianna come here," he demands as he follows her.

Bree stops and turns to face him, "You're making me fucking sick. Conclusion point number two." She says before she turns back around to continue on her journey to bed.

Reggie turns Bree back around and wraps his hand around her neck tightly. It all happens so fast but her heart doesn't even skip a beat. She's been waiting for this moment since she's talked to Toya. He squeezes until he gets a nice grip and elevates her feet from the floor. Bree can't breathe but she continues to look him in the eyes. "I will kill you if you try to leave me." He says as a blank stare has come down like a veil over his face. His eyes are dark and cold. Bree has finally met the monster that he so desperately tries to hide.

Bree doesn't make a sound. She doesn't resist the hold he has on her. She can feel her face begin to feel puffy and warm. As she looks in Reggie's eyes she sees they start to soften. He looks down at his shoulder following his arm pass his elbow, then to his wrist until he reaches his grip around her neck. He has a look of shock as if he had no control over his limbs. Once he realizes what is going on he immediately releases her.

Bree stands there looking at him for a moment. She stands her ground against the beast. She doesn't shed a tear nor display any fear. "I'm not afraid of you," she says before she walks away to lock herself in the bedroom. And just before she shuts the door she turns to look at him.

"While technically giving her age she probably could, I'm going to use this opportunity to drive my point home. If I don't breathe, then she doesn't breathe. Conclusion point number three." She says before slamming the door.

Bree has not been to sleep. Even if she wanted to forgive Reggie and hopefully try to work it out somehow, how can she be with him now? He's digging a deeper hole for himself every time they speak. She has been giving him a pass with not wanting to talk about it because she knew it would lead to this. Out of all the things she doesn't know, what she does know is that she's going to teach him a lesson behind this. Just in case he thinks he will ever put his hands on her again.

Bree goes into the kitchen for a midnight snack and to prepare her plan. He clearly doesn't know who he's messing with. She tiptoes upstairs to see if he's asleep and quickly realizes he is when she hears his faint snoring once she reaches the top of the stairs. She goes back downstairs to get the saran wrap she's prepared. Once she's in the bedroom she stands over him trying to find the best approach. She was hoping he was on his side, but he's on his back. She doesn't know why she prefers his side, she just knows that she has to get the saran wrap to cover his face and seal it behind his head. Her only hope is that he jumps upon contact so she can seal it quickly. Bree takes a deep breath. If this doesn't work, then it will turn into a disaster. She leans in with the saran wrap extended fully from left to right and covers his face. "Reggie!" she whispers. As soon as he jumps up she crosses her hand behind his head and jumps back. He immediately inhales and begins to panic once he realizes that he can't take anymore air in. That long inhale made the saran wrap snug on his face. He jumps up off the bed trying to grab at the saran wrap to no avail because it's covered in Vaseline. He tries to take in another breath and panics further. He grabs at his chest trying to find a way to get a breath. Bree stands and watches him. He reaches out to her as if his mind is screaming HELP! She stands and watches not making a move. He's swinging his arms trying to find a way to get himself some air. He's failing at every chance. Then he relaxes as if he's trying to think of a plan. He bends and sits on his knees. His fingers are slipping all over the saran wrap as he is trying to find a way to peel it away. To add to the situation when he hands hit the hard floor they slip causing him to not have a stable position. He constantly tries to get the saran wrap off his face while sliding on the floor. When that doesn't work he returns to panic mode. He's fighting for his life and Bree is calmly watching. When she thinks he's about to give up, he does. He puts his weight on his knees in distress. His hands have found a stable place on the floor. She takes the knife that she brought along and makes a slit between his lips. As soon as he's able to get a pinch of air he sticks his finger through the opening and rips the saran wrap off of his head. He's still on his knees breathing heavily trying to process what just happened as his life flashed before his eyes, he finally raises his head to look at Bree.

She slowly walks over and stoops down to his level, "Don't you ever put your hands on me again unless you plan on killing me. Next time, I'll watch you die!" with that she turns and leaves the room to go and get herself a good night's rest. She feels much better.

Bree rolls over to look at the clock, "Shit," she lets out in an exhaustive manner. It's after eight o'clock. She was hoping to get up early and get out of the house before Mr. Harold shows up. Bree decides that it's best to get out of this house. One of them will not survive if they both stay here with their levels of anger and frustration. After a quick shower, she heads upstairs to pack her suitcase.

When Bree walks into the room, Reggie is sitting on the bed watching TV. His eyes are bloodshot red.

"How'd you sleep?" she asks with a light chuckle knowing he's probably scared to close his eyes around her and rightfully so. "Don't worry, I'll be out of your hair in a few." She makes it known as she begins to pack her bag. Reggie has yet to utter a word. She doesn't know how to take this Reggie. She can take the attitude. She knows how to deal with that. She can take the anger. She can control it to a point or at least knows what to expect. But this silence; creeps her out. She doesn't say anything else to avoid poking the beast and heads downstairs to gather the rest of her belongings that she's taking. When she gets inside the guest bedroom the doorbell rings. Great! She thinks. Just the path she doesn't want to take. She doesn't go to answer the door because she thinks Reggie will come and get it knowing that it's his father. Moments later the doorbell rings again. Bree grabs her items, puts on her jacket and answers the door.

"Good morning," she says to Mr. Harold and surprisingly Mrs. Lynn.

"Good morning, Bree where are you heading to?" Mrs. Lynn asks. She doesn't wait for a response before continuing, "I thought we could get breakfast while the guys paint."

"I wish I would have known you were coming because I'm heading out,"

And before she can finish with the excuses, Reggie comes down the stairs and interrupts. "Where are you going? No, let's not make this about you. Where are you taking my baby?" he asks firmly and directly. Bree sees he's still hanging onto that macho attitude.

Bree closes her eyes and takes a deep breath. Is he really going to start with his parents here?

"Excuse me Mrs. Lynn," Bree says as they are all currently standing in the doorway. "I need to go."

"What's going on?" his dad asks.

"Bree please, come and talk to us. Is everything okay?" Mrs. Lynn pleads.

"It's not something that I want to talk about right now." Bree informs the both of them.

"Brianna please don't leave," Reggie begs as he softens his voice. The games he plays.

"Brianna, come here," Mrs. Lynn grabs her hand and pulls her towards the couch. Mr. Harold shuts the door and follows them to the sitting area. Bree doesn't want to sit next to anyone so she opts for the chair.

"Talk to me," Mrs. Lynn says, sitting across from her with all her attention directed towards Bree. Reggie comes off the steps and sits next to his father.

"Mr. Harold, Mrs. Lynn," she nods at the both of them. "I love you. You both have taken me in and treated me like a daughter since the first time we've met. You have also welcomed my son with open arms. I appreciate that. I also appreciate your concern and offering to help sort our mess out. However, you're still his parents and your loyalty lies with him."

"Brianna," Mrs. Lynn says, "My loyalty lies in the truth and what's right. I don't bend in that regard."

"Fair enough. However, this situation is difficult and has many layers. I will allow Reggie to speak for himself. To disclose what he wants and how much he wants. At this point, I just want to leave."

"I know how it is when you just want to run away. I've been there," Mrs. Lynn offers, "You and Reggie are engaged to be married. In a marriage it's difficult to just up and leave. You stay and work it out. You can't run at the first signs of trouble."

Bree knows that she is only speaking from her perspective. Yesterday, she and Reggie looked so happy and in love. What could have happened in less than twenty-four hours that'll make Bree up and leave?

"I understand what you're saying Mrs. Lynn and I agree with you. It's just that I've tried that approach to no avail. Granted I'm not trying to work it out at this time, but I've asked that he give me space. That task seems impossible for him. I don't need any arguing. I'm trying to ride out the last few weeks of this pregnancy in a healthy state. It's best for me to get out of this environment and relax." Bree continues to talk as if Reggie doesn't even exist.

"I don't want you to leave. If you don't want me to talk to you, then I won't." Reggie joins in on their conversation.

Bree just sits there and looks at him. They both know that is a lie.

"I know you've asked me to refrain from talking to you before and I failed at the request." He sighs. "But you know damn well yesterday had an effect on me. You can't show me affection outside and when we come into the house you don't say one word to me." He expresses angrily. "I'm just trying to figure out where we go from here?"

Everyone is sitting around waiting for the next person to talk but no one says a word.

"Bree say something." Reggie encourages.

"Like I said, you can tell your own story. I'm not here to talk. I don't want to talk. I don't understand why you don't understand that. And after last night, I would think you would have glued your mouth shut, yet here we are." she says uninterested.

His parents are just sitting silently because they have no information to go on to offer anything of value to the conversation.

"If I want you to stay here, then what do I need to do?" he asks, surrendering.

"Leave." Bree gives a scoff. "I don't want to be around you. But seeing as though I have a room reserved and a massage appointment, I'll head out. You can stay here." She says getting up to continue on with her journey.

"Bree wait," Mr. Harold finally speaks. "What is going on here? Someone needs to start talking." He says leaving the floor open for whoever will speak.

Bree retreats back into her seat not wanting to be disrespectful and storming out. "The floor is yours," she looks to Reggie.

All eyes are on Reggie as he prepares what he wants to say. "I have hurt Bree and I don't know how to fix it," he says, giving the sweet version. "I was not as forthcoming and honest as I should have been..."

"I'm sorry," Bree interrupts, "But I can't sit here for this sideshow. If you can deduce all that we've experienced to my hurt is caused by you not being honest and forthcoming, then its worse than I thought."

"That's not what I'm trying to do." He says quickly. "I have been cheating, are you happy?" he asks knowing that's what she wants to hear.

"No, that's the thing. I'm not happy about it. But go on, own what you've done." She says waving his way in a shoo-ing manner while turning her head in disgust.

"Bree, you know that's not how I meant it," he sighs. "I don't know what you want me to say."

"I have been saying that you don't have to say anything, yet you insist on running your mouth continuously and nothing of substance comes out."

"I'm trying to fix it,"

"Fix what?" she snaps.

"Our relationship, we can move on from this."

An uncontrollable chuckle leaves Bree's mouth at his positive outlook. "Reggie when we first met and talked about being in love, you said that love is deceiving. I ignored the signs you gave because you are the Master of Deception. I feel bamboozled and trapped. The more I try to maneuver from out of this tangled web, the more you weave trying to keep me close. But it's not going to work anymore. Not today. Instead of you objecting to me wanting to leave; wanting to

take care of myself for the health of not only myself but our child. Maybe you should use this time to do some self inventory because your character is weak. Take this time to present to me a better man because the man that sits in front of me, I. DON'T. WANT. HIM. I have been having pains for the last two days but you're so angry and self centered that every time you open your mouth it's about you. You and this failing relationship are the last things on my mind right now. So, please give me some space and let me take care of myself." With that Bree proceeds to get up for the last time because she's leaving out the door.

"Can you at least tell me where you're going?" Reggie asks sadly.

"For you to show up there, do you want to drive me crazy?"

"No! So I can know that you and our baby are okay."

"I'll be in the city and if anything happens you'll be the first person I call."

"Bree just tell me," he asks annoyingly

"Reggie, my character, love or trust is not in question here. Don't hold me hostage in your mind as if I've done anything wrong. I've never lied to you, so why should I start? You'll be the first I call." She says as she looks at him. "I'll talk to you soon," she says to Mrs. Lynn as she gives her a hug.

Bree walks out of the door and for once she feels free. She knows this is the best decision for her. She can think clearly and evaluate the situation.

# CHAPTER 48

Going to work is no longer an option, it is necessary. If she and Reggie do not work out, then she must get her mind back into work mode. She will not be able to afford to sit at home for the year that they agreed upon. Every time Bree thinks about the future that she and Reggie were supposed to create, she finds all the hidden gems of entrapment. And each one of them, she naively agreed to with a pure heart. She has to give it to him though. He has successfully managed to manipulate her. If he hadn't got caught with Manny, then who knows if Bree would have ever found out about his secret life.

"Good morning my beautiful people," Bree sings as she walks onto her floor.

"Well good morning," Latrice is the first to speak. "Someone looks refreshed and rejuvenated." She notices.

"I am," Bree smiles. Yesterday was so relaxing. She powered off her phone and swam in her thoughts. Not in a negative way. She was finally able to do some soul searching, self-reflection and damage control to her self-esteem. The masseuse assisted by massaging all the negative tension right out of her body. She feels completely renewed.

"Oh Bree," John says as he reaches under the table. "Before I forget, this is for our little princess." He says as he hands a bag to Bree.

"Oh geez. John don't start with this," Bree warns.

"It's just a little something that I saw. I couldn't resist. Go on, open it," he encourages.

Bree opens the bag and pulls out a two piece bathing suit. "Where did you find a bathing suit in January?" Bree laughs. "You know her Dad is not going for this right?" she continues.

"Tell him don't be such a stick in the mud. She will be shown stopping at the beach," he says in a sassy voice.

"Ok Bree," Latrice adds her two cents. "I know we parent like this," she says rubbing the dark side of her hand, "And not like this," she says as she rubs the palm of her hand, "But I have to admit this is too cute," she smiles.

"Not you too, Trice," Bree smiles. "I'll see. If her Dad doesn't burn it first." She pauses. Lately her level of pain has been consistent. It isn't like before where it would come every now and then at various levels.

"Are you okay," Latrice asks

"Yes. I have been having pains. Nothing of concern," Bree assures them. "I'm not in labor."

"She's ready to enter the world," John announces happily.

"Let's check on her," Latrice suggests.

"It's alright! I'm good. I promise. I just need to get to work."

Latrice gives Bree the side-eye but complies with her request and they all get to work. Bree is caught up in her thoughts as usual. She has to figure out what she's going to do. While she would love to, she cannot stay in the hotel forever. She has to go home. When she gets there, she has to have the answer to whether Reggie is staying or leaving. She makes a mental list of the pros and cons of their relationship. The pros list is pretty substantial compared to the con list. However, the con list has some major violations that'll outweigh the pros list, bar none. The two main questions Bree refuses to address with herself are: how will life be if she stays, and how will life be if she leaves? She knows that she needs to explore both avenues to come to a concrete resolution, but she fears the truth of each avenue.

"Bree," John breaks her daydream. "Reggie's here to see you," he sings.

"I'll be right there," Bree manages a smile as John is filled with glee. She takes a moment to gather herself. She has to put on the mask of happiness.

Walking into his space she sees that Reggie has made it easy for her to dawn the mask. His handsome face and authentic smile brings joy within Bree. She wants to fight the feeling because she doesn't want to get sucked into his vacuum, but the force is too strong. Her smile shines bright without warning.

"There she is," he says as he hands her the flowers and places a kiss on her lips.

"Hi Baby. Thank you, they're beautiful," Bree expresses looking at the flowers. "It's not lunchtime." She continues. She wants to let him know that he's out of line with this pop up visit.

"I know, I just wanted to see this beautiful face."

"Hey Reggie," Latrice greets him as she comes from around the corner. "What a nice surprise."

"Right!" John jumps in. "Here Bree, let me put those in some water for you."

"Hi Latrice. I'm leaving," he surrenders.

"Don't make me out to be the bad guy. I didn't say anything."

"Trice, do you mind if I walk him out?" Bree looks apologetically.

"Got you," Trice confirms.

Reggie takes advantage of the moment and slips his hand into Bree's as they walk to the elevator. Bree is debating on how much conversation she is willing to have with him. Once they are in a semi-private area outside, Reggie breaks the silence.

"You don't have to say anything," he begins letting Bree know that replies are not needed. "First let me apologize for putting my hands on you. I was wrong and I promise you that it will NEVER happen again." He pauses and Bree stays silent. "I've thought about all that has happened and everything you've said to me. I did a thorough review of our relationship." He pauses to take in a deep breath. "You're right! I'm very selfish, deceiving, manipulating, I can go on, I'll spare myself. But Bree please don't forget that that's not all that I am." He pleads. "I'm going to take your advice and do some self inventory and work on me. I wanted to come and tell you face to face, that I love you very much. However, I am going to give you the time and space that you need to do what it is that you need to do. Don't take me not calling and trying to make contact as an indication that I don't care. That is far from the truth. I don't know how much weight my word holds with you anymore, but I promise you that I will not be in contact with anyone. I've thought about leaving the house, but honestly, I think that's the last place that you want to be which is why you left. I put money into your account to cover the hotel expenses since you'll be there for a while. If I'm wrong, then let me know and I'll leave." He says as he places his hand on her arm. Bree doesn't speak. He's right! She'd rather stay in the hotel. "Are you okay?" he asks, sensing the confusion on Bree's face.

"Yes, I'm okay," Bree manages to say although she feels heartbroken. It feels like he's breaking up with her. And she's confused by the feeling because if this is the case, then why does she care?

"The ball is in your court. I'm working on your time. Call me when you're ready. Okay." He says while his hand is on the back of her head looking directly into her eyes.

"Okay. Thank you," she says sadly as she walks away from him. The last thing she wants him to see is the tears that are forming in her eyes. Bree immediately goes into the bathroom to release the emotions and to get herself together before going back to her workstation.

She feels a sense of relief when she steps off the elevator and Latrice and John are nowhere in sight. She takes this moment to check her account to see how much money he deposited. "Three thousand dollars. Well shit how long is he expecting me to stay?" she questions herself quietly. She closes the tab on her phone, sticks it in her pocket and goes back to her room to finish cleaning.

"Lady Bug," Trices scares Bree out of her thoughts. "Why are you hiding? Let's go, I'm taking you to lunch."

"I don't really feel," Bree starts to whine.

"Let's go," Latrice demands, ignoring her resistance.

"Talk to me," is how Trice starts the conversation once they are seated in the cafeteria.

"'Bout what?" Bree plays stupid

"Why is Reggie in the doghouse? It's so obvious. To me anyway," she clarifies.

"Because he's stupid and gets on my nerves. It's dumb shit." Bree dismisses.

"Is it dumb shit like I'm in my third trimester ready to drop this load so even him breathing is annoying? Or, dumb shit that will still be lingering about once she arrives?"

"The latter."

"Want to talk about it?" she offers sincerely.

"Not really," Bree sighs.

"Just tell me that you're okay." Latrice begins but catches herself. "Don't say you're okay if you're not, but," she fumbles over her words. "Are you in danger?" She asks the important question knowing she's been in a bad place before and no one offered her an opportunity to say what she was going through.

"I'm not in danger Trice and I'm okay. Really." Bree assures her.

Silence fills the air as they have so much of the lunch hour left and at this point there is nothing to talk about. They each live in their thoughts.

"Brianna," Latrice breaks the silence. "I'm not going to pressure you into talking to me, but I just want you to know that this is a judgment free no gossiping zone. And while I do not know what is going on, I am going to offer my general unsolicited advice," she smiles. "Is that okay?"

"It's okay," Bree smiles.

"Whatever decision is it that you have to make, ensure that the foundation of your relationship is intact before moving forward. You don't want to rush things and build on sinking sand." She cautions. "And in doing that please do not compromise yourself away. Do you understand?" Latrice asks in her motherly voice.

Bree sits for a moment and takes in the powerful advice that was just given to her. Against her cries of keeping her mouth shut, she engages in the conversation because she needs answers.

"How will I know if I'm compromising myself away?"

"The moment you make excuses for someone who has turned your hard no's into soft yes's. The moment when you begin lying to yourself; the moment when you look in the mirror and you don't recognize the reflection; the moment when you become ashamed; the moment when you are no longer genuinely happy; when you realize that faking it until you make it only consists of faking it because you never make it are signs." She says with such conviction. "You know what you deserve. Demand it!"

"Thank you, Trice. I appreciate that more than you know."

# CHAPTER 49

It's been over a week and Bree hasn't had any contact with Reggie since he showed up at her place of employment. She knows she needs to call him because her contractions have been really bad lately. She just doesn't know how this will play out. Sadly, she misses him. She wants him near. They were supposed to be enjoying this time together; the special moments leading up to their baby girl's birth. The only upside from this separation is that Bree had plenty of time to think. She knows what she wants to do. For once, she's not going to worry about what anyone has to say about her or the way she lives her life. She's been so stuck on trying to look like the rest, being what the world wants her to be. Following the rules of love and putting her all into it regardless of her level of happiness. She's going to cast everyone's feelings aside and make herself happy.

"Hello," Reggie answers.

"I think it's time. Can you come and pick me up from the Four Seasons?"

"I'll be there as fast as traffic allows."

Bree is in so much pain. She wants to try for a natural birth but this pain is making her want to change her mind.

"May I rub your back?" Reggie asks Bree as she's bent over the bed trying her breathing techniques.

"Please," she moans.

Reggie goes near and begins to rub Bree's back and breathes in her ear to help her keep control.

"Hey," Mrs. Lynn taps on the door and she quickly takes a seat when she sees Bree is in distress.

The contraction finally passes and Bree can have a moment. "Hey, thank you for coming." She greets Harold and Lynn.

"How are you feeling, considering?" Lynn inquires.

"I think I'm going to get the epidural soon. I'm trying to hold out but I don't remember this much pain. It's too much."

"Do you want me to get the anesthesiologist?" Reggie asks

"Let me wait a little longer. I have some time to think about it."

"How many centimeters are you dilated?" Lynn continues with her questions.

"Six the last time they checked about an hour ago." Bree says pacing the room.

"How far apart are the contractions?" Harold asks

"Eight to ten minutes."

"How are you Reggie," his mom asks.

"I'm okay."

"It's good to see you."

"Same here." Reggie says. After Bree left the house, he asked his parents to leave and have been sulking in his feelings ever since. Eight days is way too long to not have any contact with Bree. He missed her like crazy. He's hoping that the baby brings about a change of heart. Hopefully she sees their daughter and wants to have a family.

"Mmmmhmmm," Bree begins to moan as she stops dead in her tracks. Reggie goes over to be of support. Bree grabs on to both of his arms and holds her head down trying to breathe. "Kiss me," she stands to be face to face with him.

When Reggie places his lips on hers the sparks reignite between the two of them. Bree grabs his face as his hands are around her waist and she kisses him again. "I've missed you." She whispers.

"I've missed you more Baby," Reggie replies.

Bree lays her head on his chest and braces herself for the pain. Reggie wraps her in his embrace and rocks her gently. Once the episode passes, he asks again, "Do you want me to get the doctor. There's no need for you to be in this pain if you don't have to be."

"I'm okay. I'll let you know when it's unbearable."

"Have you called Junior Bree? I know he's excited."

"No, not yet. I'm going to wait until she's here. Honestly, I may wait a few weeks. When Manny picked him up we decided that he will stay with him until I get things situated."

"It's awesome that you have that help. Gives the two of you time to bond without Junior feeling jealous."

"I know. I'm thinking maybe after my six weeks checkup he'll come home. I'll be more mobile and she'll be at an age where he can hold her and try to help as much as he wants."

"Mrs. Clarkson, may we come in?" The nurse asks as she taps on the door.

"Yes," Both Bree and Mrs. Lynn answered.

"Oh," the nurse looked surprised at the guest that wasn't there before. "I'm talking to the pregnant one," she smiles as she points to Bree.

"Brianna," Doctor Page says excitedly. "How are you doing? Do you mind lying down so I can check on how things are going?"

Bree lies on the bed and situates herself to get checked.

The doctor sits on the edge of the bed and inserts his hands up her vagina. "Doing good. Dilated to eight centimeters. How's your pain level?"

"Getting a bit uncomfortable."

"If you're going to say when, then say it now. It'll go pretty fast from here."

"OK, you can call for anesthesia." Bree instructs.

"Great! I hope you guys are ready, there will be a baby soon." He says as he gets up and leaves the room with the nurse.

Silence fills the air as an elephant has entered the room when the door opens. Bree lies on her side and lowers the head of the bed. She starts rocking knowing that contractions are coming again. Dr. Page aggravated her little one going in there fumbling about.

"Do you want to get up," Reggie asks.

"No, I can't get up. Oooooohhhhh." Bree lets out a sound of anguish.

Reggie is looking in her face helplessly. She's in so much pain and there is nothing he can do but watch. He slips his hand into hers and hopes it's enough.

"Aaaaahhhhhh," Bree releases as the pain is getting more severe by the minute. "Help me up," she looks to Reggie.

He takes her into his embrace and she grabs his face and kisses him. As they rock and kiss, the pains begins to subside. Reggie feels Bree's tense body relaxing. "Feeling better?" he asks.

Bree sits on the edge of the bed, "Yes. But that doctor better hurry."

"What does the kissing do?" Mr. Harold asks

"I've been wondering that myself," Reggie cosigns the question

"Supposedly kissing helps produce the hormone oxytocin, which helps to relax the body. I don't know about all of that, but it's a distraction at least."

"Interesting," Mrs. Lynn says. "I wish I would have known that when I was in labor."

"No, no. Kissing wasn't going to help you," Mr. Harold laughs. "You were not this calm. Bree isn't screaming thatshe hates Reggie and that she's not having any more kids. She's not telling the doctor's to take out her whole reproductive system."

"Ok, ok...that's enough," Mrs. Lynn laughs

Bree is enjoying the light chuckle. She hasn't laughed in days.

"There is my smile," Reggie whispers as he stands in front of her.

# CHAPTER 50

The epidural is finally kicking in and Bree is able to lie down and relax. She's munching on some ice chips waiting on the doctor to give her the green light to get this show on the road. She's looking at the machine but is not feeling any of the contractions that it's displaying that she's having; wondering why she didn't do this a long time ago.

"I'm sorry to pry, but Mrs. Clarkson," Mrs. Lynn finally breaks the silence on the matter. "Was there a wedding we weren't invited to?"

Bree looks at Reggie because this is not a conversation for her to have.

"We got married in December." He confirms.

"December," his mom says appallingly.

"When Bree found out she was pregnant she wanted to postpone the wedding because she didn't want to be pregnant walking down the aisle. I suggest that we get married last year to secure the date and wait a year to have the wedding." He informs, admitting but not admitting to his actions.

"So you talked her into marrying you, knowing that you were cheating?" he mother asks confusingly.

"Bingo!" Bree interjects. "But let's stand clear of that road because I'm actually in a good headspace right now." She requests.

Mrs. Lynn looks at Reggie with disappointment in her eyes.

"Hey Remi," Nia comes busting into the room.

"Hey Nia,"

"Hello," she says to Reggie's parents. "Hey Reggie Reg, taking care of my girl?"

"Of course," he smiles going in for a hug. "Where's my buddy?"

"Charles is probably out getting in trouble somewhere. I have to go and pick up the kids but I wanted to stop by and see if she's here yet." Nia and Charles' relationship has survived the infidelity and the aftermath. Nia is giving him one last chance to get things right.

"Nope, not yet." Bree says.

"Well keep me posted. I'll be back to see her."

"Damn, that's how it is, throwing me to the curb already."

"Yeah," Nia laughs like that is a stupid question.

"Cold," Bree says, giving her a hug. "I'll see you later."

"Do you need me to get Junior?"

"Nah, he's with Manny until..." Bree left the words hanging

"That's awesome! Well let me know if you need anything."

"Food when you come back to see her."

"Gotcha Rem. Bye!" Nia says before disappearing out the door.

# CHAPTER 51

Bree wasn't bringing her daughter back to a hotel, so the house it is. She's sure that Raileigh will keep them occupied enough to not have many deep conversations. To add further assurance, Bree plans to sleep when she sleeps so there is no alone time between her and Reggie.

"If you're breastfeeding, then when will I get a chance to feed her?" Reggie asks as he sits on the side of the bed watching Bree feed Raileigh.

"When I start pumping."

"And when will that be?"

"It's important for the baby to get the supply going in the first few weeks. I'll start pumping once I get comfortable with my milk supply."

"Can't you pump now?"

"I can but her suction is much stronger. I prefer to wait." Bree makes known. There's no rush so she intends on taking her time. "Before we switch you can burp her." She extends an offer.

Reggie is nervous as Bree hands Raileigh to him. Bree places the burp cloth on his shoulder and positions her so that Reggie can easily take over.

"You have to pat her a little harder than that." She instructs.

"I don't want to hurt her."

"You won't. She's stronger than you think." Bree informs him.

"Gosh! She's so tiny. I'm afraid I'm going to drop her."

"Now that we don't want.." Bree says bluntly. "Secure a firm hold. She's not going to break."

Once Raileigh lets out a nice burp Reggie grabs the back of her head and lowers her to face him so he can get a good look at her. "She's so beautiful Bree." He says and places a kiss on her forehead.

"Is she looking at you?" Bree leans up to see her face.

"Yes,"

"Talk to her."

"What do I say?"

"Whatever you want. She just needs to hear your voice." Bree lets him know. "And make eye contact." She adds.

"Hey beautiful," Reggie smiles at her. As soon as he finishes his words Raileigh begins to make a face as if she wants to cry. "Here, she doesn't even like me," he hands her over to Bree.

"Yes, she does. She's still hungry that's all. Come here pretty girl," Bree says as she takes her from Reggie. "Don't be mean to Daddy he's trying his best." Bree gets comfortable as she lets her latch on to continue with her feeding.

"Does that hurt?"

"It does if she doesn't latch on correctly. But this little greedy nugget has it all figured out. Don't you?" she asks looking at Raileigh brushing her hair out of her face.

After a few moments Reggie speaks, "I know that you don't want to talk about our situation and you don't know what you want to do right now. I'm not looking for answers in that regard. I am not trying to talk about anything that you don't want to. Okay?"

"Ok. What's up?" she asks knowing that he wants to get some conversation going between the two of them.

"I know that our future is hanging in the balance and there are many things you are uncertain of. I want to reassure you that taking off work for at least six months is still on the table. I still prefer a year, but will understand if you don't want to. I am committed to taking care of you and the kids financially as planned."

"Thank you. I appreciate that. It has been on my mind." Bree admits.

"Are you thinking of going back to work?" Reggie asks just to keep the conversation going. He's hoping it leads into something he wants to talk about.

"Yeah I am. But I really want to stay home and enjoy the moments. I missed everything with Junior, so I was looking forward to it."

"Are you going to sleep once she goes?"

"That is the plan," Bree smiles.

"I wanted to know if you wanted to talk to me." He says shyly. "Not to discuss anything, just to enjoy each other's company. I miss you Brianna," he confesses.

She ignores his advance and prepares Raileigh to get burped. Reggie sits in silence. Bree tends to the baby getting her comfortable and putting her in her bassinet. As Bree walks back to the bed she stops in front of Reggie. It's hard for her to resist him. She loves him. She wants him. If she could, then she would make love to him right now. Instead, she hugs him. He wraps his arms around her waist and lays his head on her chest. After a few moments Bree lifts his chin the way that he always does to her and says, "I love you. No matter how hard I try not to, I can't stop loving you." she seals her words with a passionate kiss. "I'm not sure if I want to talk. But I would love for you to lay with me."

Reggie climbs into the bed and extends his arms for Bree to come and lie in them.

"We haven't slept in this bed together in ages." He chuckles. Although Bree went home, she still hasn't gone into their bedroom.

"I know right. It brings back memories." She laughs. "Us sneaking around being nasty." She reminisces .

"You, trying to refrain from screaming my name," he smiles. "Fun times," he jokes.

"Yeah, yeah, yeah." She dismisses. "This pillow holds it all," she says as she pats the pillow they are lying on.

"There's my smile I miss so much." He says placing a kiss on her lips. "Please don't give up on us Bree," he says softly after he releases her lips.

"I'm horny," she changes the subject.

"Don't start. You have a long time for that," he smiles picking up where she's going and leaving his topic to disappear.

"I have to get my toy game back popping, since you were being jealous and all. All the good stuff is gone."

"You were enjoying them too much,"

"Well they are for entertainment."

"I got your entertainment," he says grabbing his crotch.

"I need something with lasting battery life," she jokes.

"Ouch! Okay, you got me," he says surrendering. He doesn't want to linger too long in this zone and she says something he doesn't want to hear.

"Are you going to buy me some?" she asks while rubbing his face.

"Of course, I will." He says sincerely. "But nothing too realistic or bigger than me."

"You are such a loser."

"I know," he winks.

Bree decides to leave well enough alone because she feels herself falling for Reggie all over again. The incident is long gone from her mind and she just wants to move forward and be a happy family.

Reggie senses Bree's mood change, "Come," he lies back and pats his chest. "Get some rest."

# CHAPTER 52

Over the last six weeks, Bree and Reggie have developed a new safe place where they reside in their relationship. Bree knows where she wants to take things and Reggie is hopeful that he will still remain in her life as her husband.

"Raileigh, your brother is coming to meet you today. Are you ready," Bree stops in front of her chair and asks while she is preparing dinner. "And your Grandma is coming and your Aunt and cousins. You are going to have lots of visitors today," she smiles.

Reggie comes in and places a kiss on Bree's cheek. "Smells good in here. Do you need any help?"

"No, I'm good. Just listen out for her if she gets cranky in that chair."

When Bree hears the door open she smiles at Raileigh, "He's here."

Junior comes running into the kitchen, "Where is she? Where is my sister?" he asks excitedly.

"She's right here. But first go and wash your hands."

"Hey Bree," Manny acknowledges with a kiss on her cheek.

"Reggie," he extends his hand for a shake.

It surprises Bree that she feels nothing. She thought the image and the feelings would come rushing back when she saw the two of them together. This just confirms that what she wants to do may actually work.

"All clean," Junior comes back into the kitchen and immediately kneels by the glider that Raileigh sits in.

"This is Raileigh Marie Clarkson. Raileigh this is your big brother Glenn Maurice Hicks,"

"Can I touch her?"

"Of course, do you want to hold her?" Bree suggests.

"I can hold her?" he asks shockingly.

"Yes, go and sit on the couch," Bree says as she's taking Raileigh out of the chair. She goes in and place Raileigh in his arms. "Reggie, I think your parents are pulling up," she yells.

Reggie and Manny both emerge from the kitchen and as Reggie proceeds to get the door. He blows Bree a kiss in passing.

"You two seem to be in a better place," Manny whispers in her ear.

"We'll talk," she assures him.

"Can I see the pretty Princess," Manny asks Junior.

"Yes, Dad come and sit next to me and be careful," he instructs.

"Hey, everyone," Mr. Harold bellows once he steps into the house. "Where's my grandbaby."

"I got her Papa Harold. Go and wash your hands." Junior demands

"Look at you, being an awesome big brother."

Everyone exchanges their hellos and swarms around Raileigh. Bree is happy that there are other people around. Gives her time to get the courage up to face the two of them and lay down what her plan is moving forward. The evening is turning out pretty well. Raileigh slept through dinner, giving Bree a chance to enjoy her food. Once Raileigh woke up, got changed and ate she was on her best behavior letting everyone pass her around like a doll baby. The kids went back to running through the halls. Everyone is enjoying themselves. Bree leaves the center of the happenings to go and clean up the kitchen.

"How's everything going Bree?" Mrs. Lynn separates herself from the pack and corners Bree in the kitchen.

"It's going."

"How are you and Reggie doing? Haven't seen you two since leaving the hospital."

"We're okay for now. Still haven't addressed any issues, just trying to adjust to Raileigh being here."

"You can't stay in limbo forever," she cautions.

"I know," Bree interrupts. "I plan on talking to him this evening."

"May I ask why you waited until now? I would have thought you would have tried to have this figured out before Junior came home."

"Well Manny is a part of this family and he has to be in on what changes will take place. This affected all of us unfortunately. Junior's feelings have to be considered."

"I understand. Do you know what you want to do?"

"I do. I don't know if Reggie will subscribe to it. I have some stipulations."

"As you should, he has to earn your trust back. But I am happy that you are willing to work it out. Bree, Reggie loves you. When you came along I've seen noticeable changes in him all for the better."

"I have too," Bree smiles.

"Mom, can I go and stay at Aunt Tasha's house please?" Junior interrupts with his pleas.

"Junior you just got home don't you want to spend time with your sister?" Mrs. Lynn asks.

"She can't play with me," he pouts.

"If Aunt Tasha says yes, then you can go." Bree says.

"She already said yes,"

"Well ask Dad to help you pack a bag."

Moments later Manny comes into the kitchen, "You're letting him leave?"

"He wants to go. It's fine." Bree says.

"Let me go and snatch Raleigh," Mrs. Lynn excuses herself.

"When are you leaving? I was hoping we could talk tonight." Bree asks Manny.

"I'm available. I have something I want to talk about also."

"Like?" Bree questions.

"What's going on with my career."

"Want to talk now or save it for later."

"Later."

After Bree finishes cleaning, she says her goodbyes to everyone. She's ready to get this talk going so she can know what her future looks like.

"Thank you guys so much for coming and making this a special evening for Junior."

"No problem. Thanks for having us. We're happy we finally got to come and see Raleigh," Tasha laughs. "You had my niece on lock down."

"It wouldn't have been fair to Junior for everyone to get their love on before him. But I guess he didn't care about it."

"Not at all," Tasha confirms as they watch the kids run to the car.

"Goodnight, I'll see ya'll tomorrow."

# CHAPTER 53

Bree walks back into the house and Reggie and Manny are in the kitchen sitting at the table.

"Let's talk." Manny starts the conversation as she walks in.

"Do you want to talk about your career first? I have a feeling my conversation is going to take a while."

"No! Wherever this goes it may lead me to change my mind," he says honestly.

Bree lays Raileigh on her chest to put her to sleep. All the stimulus activity has worn her out.

"I'm trying to find a good place to begin." She pauses. "I have no interest in asking either one of you to deny who you are. Manny you know that. I have known you for half my life and I accept who you are. Reggie now that I know this is who you are, I'm forced to make a decision. I have two options to deal with it or to leave." She pauses again. "I'm not looking for any apologies or excuses. I don't care how it happened and who started it, because it doesn't change the fact that it happened." She pauses again. "I haven't talked to either one of you about this. So, I don't want either of you to think that anyone is conspiring against the other." She makes clear. "I have thought long and hard and I'm not in the best situation. But I don't think it's the worst situation. I have taking a lot of factors into consideration and I have tried to consider everyone's feelings objectively as I can. I have a proposal in which we all have to agree to. At this point, it's all or nothing for me. So," she pauses to take a deep breath, "I propose that WE stay together as a family."

Both Manny and Reggie go to speak at the same time asking for clarification.

"Reggie I know that it's impossible for you to suppress your urges." Bree begins to silence them. "You said so yourself. If Manny agrees, then I will feel comfortable with you dealing with him and only him. Manny I'm asking you to be with us." She attempts to clarify

"Wait, am I understanding you correctly that you want us to have a threesome?" Manny asks.

"NO! I don't want to have a threesome or want to watch the two of you engaged in sexual activity. What I am proposing is that you join us and be a part of our family. Be a part of our relationship. Like brother/husband's I guess." She says unsure of herself now. "With a twist." She adds. "I am willing to try a polyandrous relationship."

"So we all will engage in sexual activity with each other, just not at the same time?" Reggie asks.

"Yes," she confirms. They both look at Bree like she's crazy. "Let me explain my thought process. I feel like everyone wins in this situation. Reggie, you and I stay together. Manny, you and I get to be together. And you both get to handle the urges that neither of you can shake."

"And how do you win?" Reggie asks.

"I feel like I get the best of both worlds." She says. "Reggie, you being an alpha male, you take charge and lead our family. I love this about you. No nonsense, get it done, very masculine, assertive and allow my femininity to shine through. Manny you being a beta male,"

"I'm not a beta male," he interrupts.

"Cocky, but you're still a beta male. It's understandable as your mom wears the pants in their relationship. But we're not here to debate this topic. I love that you take my feelings into consideration and we can talk about anything. When I can't talk to Reggie about a bad day, because he doesn't understand why I just can't suck it up, you make me feel that my feelings are valid. I can move forward if I have the both of you."

Silence fills the air as everyone is digesting what has been laid on the table.

"How will this work?" Reggie asks.

"Honestly, I don't know." Bree admits. "That's why we're here. First to see if you both agree, then to set boundaries that work for us."

"And I can't date anyone else?" Manny asks.

"Why would you want to?" Bree answers his question with a question.

"Is that a yes or a no?" he asks again for clarification.

"NO!" Bree says and looks at him like he's crazy.

"We still get married?" Reggie asks.

"Yes," Bree confirms.

"I know ya'll are already married. Let's cut the bull." Manny makes known. "I'm failing to see what I am getting out of the deal besides a nut." Manny speaks frankly getting back to his dilemma.

"A relationship. We're all going to be together. Do you not understand that part?" Bree asks.

"Are we living together? Sleeping in the same bed? Announcing this to the world? Let me know because I'm still confused. I don't understand how the two of you get to be married and I'm the third wheel."

"So, it's a no for you?" Bree asks bypassing the fluff.

"I'm not saying no. I'm trying to understand my role in all of this besides a sex toy." Manny clarifies.

"Like you have a problem with that," Bree spits in a playful tone. "What do you propose?" Bree asks. "We are here trying to see if this will work."

"If the two of you stay married, then I want my other baby."

"Other baby?" Reggie asks shockingly.

"Yes, the plan was when Junior turned five if neither of us weren't in a serious relationship, then we would have baby number two. Then all of a sudden she gets engaged shy of his fifth birthday and months later turns up pregnant. So, I want our baby."

Reggie now sees why Manny was so upset with the pregnancy and proposal. He imposed on the plans that they had.

"Hell no!" Reggie rejects the notion. "I'm not going for that."

"Okay, so it's not going to work." Bree sighs. "That's fine." She says getting up. It's no use running in circles if they're not going to agree with it.

"Where are you going?" Reggie asks not wanting to be done with the conversation. He likes the idea but doesn't want to give in on certain things.

"To lay her down, I'll be back."

When Bree returns they are both sitting there not uttering a word.

"So, what's the verdict?" She asks, wanting to get this over with. She wants them to think about it; on the other hand, she wants an answer. Tonight!

"There's just so much to discuss," Manny says.

"I like the idea," Reggie throws out there. "But I agree. There are a lot of issues to discuss."

"I'm not saying we are going to figure out everything now." Bree says. "I know there are boundaries that need to be discussed. My main point of bringing it up is to give the two of you something to think about. I honestly think it could work, IF, the two of you compromise with me. We all have to understand that there will be some uncomfortable moments until we all get used to this."

"My issue is that I'm going to get pushed to the back burner." Manny starts to speak, "The two of you will present to the world this happy couple and I'm in the background. I can't date anyone so I have to wait around on one of you to want me." He speaks honestly.

"Here's the thing. I've thought about this and I don't care if the world knows what we have going on. This is our life and we live it the way we want and the way that will make us happy. I am under the impression that the two of you had images you wanted to maintain and in that sense, yes I guess you will be on the back burner." Bree admits.

"I don't know Bree," Reggie says and that's all that he has to add.

"I'm failing to realize how this is not a good idea," Bree puffs. When the idea randomly popped in her head, she thought for sure at least Manny would be on board without hesitation.

"On the surface, it sounds awesome." Manny agrees. "But when you start peeling back the onion you see the difficulty. Your presentation makes it so that someone always ends up being alone. If we're not having sex together, someone will be alone. If we're not sleeping in the same house in the same room, then someone will be alone. The danger in that is jealousy. That can ignite in either one of us when we're alone." He reiterates.

"You're right. I guess I didn't think about that." Bree agrees. "Reggie say something." Bree encourages.

"I'm still stuck on him wanting another baby from you. I'm at a loss with that. Like I said, I like the idea. BUT, we stay married and he doesn't get another baby. That's non-negotiable. Anything else, I'll consider."

"We stay married and neither one of you gets another baby." Bree proposes. "I don't want another one anyway."

"Okay. Ya'll stay married, no more kids and no wedding." Manny states his limit. "I don't want to deal with that shit."

"Okay," Reggie agrees.

"Fine with me," Bree cosigns.

And like that the ball is rolling and Bree fills with excitement. She thought that Reggie wouldn't go for this arrangement.

"Sleeping arrangements," Reggie brings up. "Bree sleeps with me."

"For now," Bree adds.

"What do you mean for now?" Reggie asks with a puzzling look.

"Eventually, we'll all sleep together." She says thinking back to Manny's earlier objection.

"How is that going to work? What is Junior going to think?" Reggie asks.

"What is Junior going to think?" Manny echo's like the thought never crossed his mind.

"That we're a family which we are." Bree says confidently. "Just no PDA from the two of you in front of him."

"You and I?" Manny asks.

"I don't see why not. We kiss and hug now, just not on the lips and passionately so it wouldn't be too strange."

"I have to watch the two of you exchange lustful moments?" Reggie voices his uncertainty.

"Is that a no-go for you?" Bree asks seriously because she doesn't see the problem.

"I don't think I can go for that right now. Maybe once you and I are back in a great space intimately, I'll be able to deal with that."

"Fair enough," Bree agrees.

"How long will that take?" Manny asks.

"Shouldn't be too long, I can start having sex again." She offers the information freely. "And that brings me to birth control." She quickly changes subjects because Reggie is uncomfortable. "You are not to be trusted," she looks at Reggie. "I say, ya'll get vasectomies."

"Nope!" They both said in unison.

"Well how in the hell are we going to be sure that I don't get pregnant?"

"Birth control." Manny suggests.

"Well Mr. Reggie hid my birth control and now Raileigh is here."

"So he was trying to trap you?" Manny asked shockingly. "To think I was on your side telling Bree you weren't." he looks at Reggie.

"Ya'll talked about that?" Reggie looks with perplexity.

"Yes," Bree answers. "We talk about everything. Which takes me back to my earlier point that he's here for me emotionally."

"Get your tubes tied," Reggie suggests.

"Too many complications." Bree shakes her head no. "How about ya'll get vasectomies and we freeze sperm. That way if and that's a big IF we decided in the future to have more kids then we will have the option."

"I don't know Bree," Reggie says. "I have to think about that."

"That's cool. Take your time. Well this concludes all the time I'm spending on this today." Bree says as she slaps the table while dismissing the two of them because she doesn't want to talk anymore. "Oh your career," She looks at Manny and sits back down for him to share his news.

"Well I'm taking a break from the big screen and doing a sitcom. With that, I'm moving back here to the city. There's no need for me to stay in California." He gives the short version.

"Guess that worked out," she smiles. "Are you heading out?"

"Yeah, I'll be back tomorrow though," Manny says as he goes in for a hug. "I can't wait to feel your skin on mine." He whispers.

"Can we go and sleep in our bed tonight," Reggie asks Bree once Manny is gone.

"I'd love that." She smiles.

Bree has to settle Raileigh back down when they get upstairs. "I knew I shouldn't have moved her," she looks at Reggie while pacing the room.

"Talk to me Baby," he pulls her near when she gets into the bed. "Where are you going with all of this?"

"Trying to be happy."

"And this will make you happy?"

"I believe so. I mean to have the two men who adore me most in this world. Jackpot!" She jokes.

"Bree if this doesn't work, then you don't walk away with him. If you do, then we will have a big problem," he threatens.

"If this doesn't work, then I'm walking away from the both of you." She assures him. "Look Reggie, you have to leave the jealous feelings at bay and enjoy our life. I know that Manny and I's relationship will appear to be much better than ours. That is only because we have so much history and a genuine friendship. Don't make yourself an outcast, include yourself in our circle. And most importantly don't forget that I love you."

"Okay," he sighs.

"Tell me how you really feel about all of this."

"Bree you are an amazing woman to propose this. But I have mixed emotions from this arrangement."

"Are you mad at me?"

"No. No I'm not. I don't understand how you accept me and I don't even accept myself at times."

"That's something that I can't help you work on in the sense of self acceptance." She admits. "But I'm trying to let you be who you are."

"And I thank you for that. Are you going to be okay to know what the two of us will be doing?"

"Yes, because strangely in my mind it's just Manny. And I guess that's the reason that I wasn't too upset with him, because I expect this type of behavior from him. With you I felt deceived. The hurtful part was that you were unable to talk to me and you were going behind my back. I thought that we were better than that."

"I agree. I should have been better than that. Sexuality is a tough conversation to have when it goes against the norm," he offers his excuse. "Do you understand why I didn't want to tell you though?"

"I do. You feared me leaving you."

"I did."

"But did I?"

"Ultimately no. But it was touch and go there for a while."

"No it wasn't. You took a long time to give me the space I asked for and that caused our tension. If sleeping with a man is the only thing I have to worry about, then I figured I'll provide you a man to sleep with. Let's hope nothing else surfaces with you."

"What are you thinking?" he asks knowing there is something else on her mind.

"The issue with your hands," she says sadly.

"Brianna, I am so sorry. I never wanted you to meet that side of me. When we first met I vowed to myself that I would be a better man for and to you. I am confident that it will not happen again."

"How can you be sure, you were not in control of that monster," she admits because she knows he was not himself.

"I agree he has a mind of his own at times. But Bree, baby, understand that monster, as you call it, was the gatekeeper of my secret. That was me trying to control every aspect of you to avoid my secret being found out. Trying to instill fear in you in hopes that you would turn a blind eye to my secret, that side of me is laid to rest because the secret is out." He speaks honestly.

"Are you now completely honest and open?"

"Yes." He assures her

"Well let's move on. Are you going to be okay with me sleeping with Manny?"

"It'll grow on me."

"Well here," she says as she straddles him on the bed. "Let me have something else grow on you."

# CHAPTER 54

"I'm making crab cakes and salad for lunch," Bree tells Reggie as he walks into the kitchen.

"Hey beautiful," he says, giving Raileigh a kiss. "You are such a big girl, you didn't even interrupt us last night," he laughs.

"Whatever!" Bree laughs. "I said I am sorry, give me a break."

Last night after Bree had Reggie all hot and ready, she reneged and went to bed.

"I was trying to break you off," he admits and he grabs her from behind placing kisses her neck.

"I'm going to get there. Soon," she promises as she spins around to give him a kiss.

"Don't get me started," he warns as he begins to walk away.

"No, don't leave," she whines, pulling him back. "At least hug on me."

Reggie comes back and wraps Bree in his embrace as she continues preparing lunch.

"Good morning," Manny greets as he walks in. "Smells good."

"Good afternoon," Bree corrects as Manny places a kiss on her cheek.

"Hey," she stops him in his tracks. "Kiss me," she encourages. She would be lying to herself if she said that she doesn't miss Manny. While they have kept their desires in check for the sake of Bree finding love, they no longer have to suppress their feelings. And against Reggie's objection, Bree can't wait until they are in a better space intimately.

Without hesitation, Manny steps back and kisses Bree. As their lips lock she feels Reggie gripping her hip. Bree places her hand on his to give him some attention.

"So," she stops Manny in his tracks again. "Where's his kiss?" she nods.

"You said," Manny begins to explain hesitantly.

"I said not in front of Junior." She clarifies.

In this moment Bree thought that she would feel awkward or at least they would not want to engage so quickly. She doesn't and they did. She continues slicing tomatoes until they are finished.

"Manny, someone is excited," she announces as she rubs her ass on Reggie as his manhood jumps when he and Manny's tongues tangoed.

"Be quiet," Reggie suggests as he slaps Bree's ass and leans on the counter.

Manny picks up Raileigh on his way to the barstool.

"How was your night?" Bree asks Manny. "You could have stayed here."

"It was good and I was trying to give ya'll some space since you can have sex and all," he mocks.

"I don't know why." Reggie butts in, "Baby, I'm scared I can't do it right now," he mimics Bree's demeanor from the night before.

"Ha. Ha. Ha." she points the knife in her hand at Reggie. "Can we let that go?"

"Okay, okay," he surrenders.

"You want a plate?" she turns to Manny.

"Yeah, can I get one?" he asks, eyeing the tomatoes.

She feeds him a cherry tomato and then she begins to make their plates.

"She's so alert," Manny speaks to no one in particular. "I don't remember Junior eyes and ears being so open," he chuckles. "That nosey woman gene is already present."

"I'm sure she's thinking, who the hell is this and why is he in my face," Bree says sarcastically. "Put her down while she's quiet so I can enjoy my lunch."

"When is Junior coming home?" Manny starts the conversation.

"One of us has to go and pick him up. You know he's not ready now though," Bree answers.

"I'll go and get him," Reggie volunteers. "Since we all have to make joint decisions now Manny, Bree and I have been discussing her not going back to work for a while. Are you okay with that?" Reggie asks, making his attempt to make this unit cohesive.

"Of course. Bree works because she wants to. I told her to quit when she had Junior."

"Ugh! Finances," Bree moans.

"It's not so bad." Manny says as usual, not making a big deal out of anything money related. "You don't worry about it. Reggie and I will discuss it." He assures Bree.

"Great," she smiles, "Just factor in me getting a bigger vehicle."

"Like we'll go into debt over it," Manny laughs.

There is no secret that Manny holds the bank, although Reggie is above average in comparison to his peers. Bree isn't going to touch that subject with a ten foot pole. She hopes that Reggie is able to accept the fact that he is no longer the breadwinner.

"Yeah, yeah, yeah," Bree dismisses his smart remark. "Manny, Reggie brought up a great point last night, so I want to clear the air. If for any reason this doesn't work out, then we all walk away single. Right?" she gives a look of uncertainty.

"I'm cool with it," Manny answers swiftly.

"Right," Reggie answers reluctantly.

"I'm just saying," she says lightly. "If ya'll think ya'll are going to leave me and be together, then ya'll must want Crazy Bree to wake from her hibernation," she laughs.

"Crazy Bree is not a laughing matter. I don't want you waking me up suffocating me," Manny makes known.

"She told you," Reggie asks, taking back.

"Yes," Bree and Manny says in unison.

"I forgot, ya'll talk about everything." Reggie retreats.

Manny hesitates then speaks, "While we're on the subject, we all are going to keep our hostile hands to ourselves." He says inclusively but looking at Reggie. "There will be no threats made either. If you want to leave, then leave. There is absolutely no reason to put our hands on each other; other than in a loving way." He finishes. He knows Bree might be mad at him because she didn't want him to confront Reggie about it, but he has to say his peace. And in his defense this is extremely mild compared to the way he initially wanted to step to Reggie.

Reggie just nods in approval. Bree has never seen him cower before and she must admit she feels a little sorry for him. But it serves him right for choking her.

"It's been real, but it's time for Rai and I to take a nap. You got this?" She looks at Reggie but refers to the kitchen.

"Got it!" he replies knowing exactly what she is talking about.

Bree gets up and kisses Reggie, picks up Raleigh and goes to kiss Manny. "Pull your weight," she says to Manny.

"What?" he asks, confusingly wondering if he's to help with the kitchen.

"He's horny." She makes known and disappears to leave them to their own discretions.

# CHAPTER 55

"Hello," Bree softly answers her ringing phone.

"Hey Baby. Are you still sleeping?"

"Yes. What time is it?"

"Six o'clock."

"Dammit! Have you taken anything out for dinner?"

"No. Don't worry about it. I'll pick something up."

"Where are you?"

"At Tasha's picking up Junior. Is Raileigh still sleep?"

"Yes. We're both going to be up all night." Bree accepts. "Is Junior giving you a hard time?"

"He was."

"Let me talk to him."

"No. You didn't even let me finish. I gave him his fifteen minute warning."

"He's going to talk you into another fifteen minutes. Let me talk to him."

"No because you're going to yell at him and he's going to get mad. Please let me handle this. "We'll see you shortly. I love you." Bree says giving up. She'll let him try it his way.

"Ok. Love you too."

Bree decides to use this free time to go and gather her things from the guest room. As she makes her way down the steps she sees Manny on the couch.

"Oh hey, I didn't know you were still here."

"Yeah, I'm waiting to see Junior before I head out."

When Bree makes it around the couch she sees the look on Manny's face. "Looking a little satisfied there partner." She jokes.

"Are you comfortable with this conversation?"

"With you? Yeah," Bree confirms as she plops on the couch next to him. She's use to listening to Manny's bedroom stories.

"But it's your husband," he mocks.

"And he's your boyfriend," she laughs.

"You've been handling that." He gives Bree her props.

"I try. I still stumble here and there."

"I can't blame you. He definitely has enough for the both of us." He says leaving it at that sparing her the details. "Come here beautiful," he grabs Bree to come and straddle him.

As soon as she sits down they go to town. Bree is half naked before she stops Manny. She stops him for two reasons, one because they are in the living room and Reggie and Junior should be here soon. And two, deep down she wants to have sex with Reggie first. She feels she owes it to him. "Wait," she whispers. "There is not enough time for me to do what I want to do to you," she says in a sultry voice.

"I've missed you," he says, placing kisses on her breast.

"I've missed you, too!" she confirms. Although Bree and Manny have only had sex to conceive Junior, the months they had together were great.

"I know you want to sleep with him first. Just so you know. It's cool." Manny outs Bree as she is fixing her clothes.

"Do you need the 'don't get jealous talk' that I gave Reggie last night?"

"I handle my jealousy well. You know that."

"Meh," she partly agrees because he has had his moments.

"I don't know how you pulled this off, but I'm here for the ride. I'm not going to mess this up." He stands to place a soft kiss on her lips. "I love you Bree."

"I love you too," she smiles before walking away.

She hears Raileigh begin to cry. She goes upstairs to go and get her and it is perfect timing because Reggie comes through the door as she's changing Rai's diaper.

Bree latches Rai on and heads downstairs.

"Hey Champ, did you have fun over Aunt's Tasha house."

"Yes. Can I go back next weekend?"

"No, Junior." She snaps. Gosh! She knows he likes the company but she doesn't want him to wear out his welcome. "Maybe we'll have Frankie come over here." She suggests once she sees his face.

"Ewww,"

"What?"

"That's nasty," he says as he points to Raileigh eating under the blanket but knowing what she is doing.

"No it's not nasty Junior. It's natural. This is how she eats. My body produces milk for your sister to have something to eat."

"She's drinking milk?"

"Yes!"

"Like the baby goats at the petting zoo?"

"Yes."

"Oh!" he says like a light bulb went off. "So why do some babies drink from a bottle?" he pries with a confused face.

"Some moms don't produce milk, some moms don't want to use the milk they produce and some moms pump milk from their breast into a bottle." She educates him on the options.

"Are you going to pump so I can feed her?"

"Yes, I have to go and buy one. And I will soon."

"I can't wait," Reggie says walking up into their conversation in the living room. He's been asking for weeks for Bree to start pumping. "Ready to eat?"

"Sure," Bree says making her way to the kitchen. "Pizza? I know who chose tonight's dinner." She smiles at Junior.

They are all sitting at the table and for once Bree feels uncomfortable. This is how their life will be from now on. The thoughts of Junior dealing with this are creeping into her mind, because she doesn't know how she will explain any of this to him. With him not being home it was easy for her to picture their relationship. And honestly it's because her picture is a sexual one. But they will be walking a fine line in reality. This is what Reggie was concerned about.

"Hey Junior, did Dad tell you the good news?" Bree asks and as soon as the question leaves her mouth, she knows it is going to be taken out of context and giving the looks on Reggie's and Manny's face, it is.

"No,"

"He's moving back here to Texas!" Bree exclaims.

"Are you Dad?" Junior asks as he jumps into his arms.

"Yes,"

"Are you going to live with us?"

Bree's face brightens because this is the opening they need. "We've talked about it. How would you feel if Dad lived with us?"

"Happy. Because Raileigh will have her Dad and I will have my Dad."

"I see. You know it's not going to happen for a couple of months. Dad has to sell his house in California and we have to find a bigger house for all of us." Bree discloses.

"Are we going to get a big house like Dad's?"

"Yes," Manny answers quickly.

"We have to discuss that," Bree looks at Manny. The last thing she needs is a huge house to maintain.

"Well I want a big house." Junior makes known. "With a pool," he adds.

"I'll see what I can do Champ," Manny smiles.

"What does all of us together look like Junior?" Reggie asks the important question being the mature one.

"A big house with a lot of rooms, so when Dad finds another girlfriend there will be room for her."

Reggie looks to Bree then to Manny. "That sounds good." he smiles. He knows that he wants to have Bree for himself, so he's okay with the idea of Manny getting a girlfriend.

"Are you ready to go back to school?" Bree asks, changing the subject. She doesn't want to entertain the idea of Manny having a girlfriend.

"Yes, I miss Mrs. Walker."

"I'm sure she misses you too. It's almost time to get ready for a bath."

"Whyyyy," he starts to whine.

"Junior go and take a bath," Manny intervenes, not giving him any transition time.

As soon as Junior is out of ear shot, Reggie seizes the moment, "It looks like you have to get a girlfriend." He states happily.

"No," Bree objects.

"And why not?" Reggie needs to know.

"Because that was not the agreement."

"Manny, how do you feel about it?" Reggie redirects his attention before he gets angry.

"For image, I think that I should," he looks at Bree. "It'll be better all around." He continues

"So we're going from polyandry to polyamory?" Bree asks.

"I don't even know what either of those mean. But if it means that I get to have a girlfriend then, yes!" Manny says.

"Are you going to find someone to subscribe to what we have going on? Someone who also understands that I have no interest in sleeping with a woman?"

"I'm sure I can. I'm Glenn Hicks," he says in his cocky I'm somebody voice.

"So, I can sleep with her too?" Reggie inquires.

"NO," Bree looks at Reggie like he's crazy.

"And how is that fair?" he asks. If Manny can sleep with Bree, then he should be able to sleep with his significant other.

"Okay, if ya'll both get a vasectomy, then I'll agree to it. She's not going to come in here and leave with a baby from neither one of you."

"I'm in," Manny says without hesitation.

"Reggie," she looks at him.

"I'll do it." He says.

# CHAPTER 56

The past few months have been a blur for all of them. With Manny making his big move, Reggie getting promoted at work and Bree trying to settle into the stay at home mom life, they are moving off fumes. The only thing that isn't lacking between them is their sex life. Bree is enjoying going back and forth between the two feeling total satisfaction. And she's sure they feel the same as there are no complaints. The jealous train has left the station as Manny has his girlfriend Keisha. She is coming to visit and stay a few days with her son Kennan.

"Okay. Wait a minute. Let me get this alcohol in my system so it'll help me understand." Nia says before she sips her drink.

"Well maybe if you are sober, it'll make more sense." Bree offers.

"No, no shit like this needs an altering substance. So, is Keisha moving in? I mean I don't understand how you even got Manny and Reggie to agree to live under the same roof. This is too much," she says before taking another sip.

"Eventually, that's the plan. Pending we all get along. For now, she's just coming to meet us and introduce us to her son."

"Remi, are you cool with this? What if she starts liking Reggie and they hit it off or something. I don't think I would be able to risk that."

"I'm pretty solid in my marriage. That thought is non-existent." Bree lies. She wants to tell Nia the set up so bad, but doesn't want to risk her telling Charles which would in turn out Reggie. "Reggie has too much to lose. She wouldn't want him after I take his ass to the cleaners. In fact, no one will." Bree smiles.

"You are on a whole other level of confidence. But if you like it," she stops to sip again. "How old is her son?"

"I want to say nine or ten. Not too far ahead of Junior."

"About Junior. How is he handling ya'll under the same roof?"

"He loves it. It was actually his idea when Manny announced he was moving back to Texas."

"I'm speechless, Bree. I don't know what to say or think."

"You don't have to say or think anything. I'm so happy Nia. I know it looks weird from the outside, but we are a well oiled machine. And the addition of Keisha will make things run much more smoothly. Sometimes it feels as if Manny is a third wheel. Having her around will make the plain even."

"Well I'm happy that you're happy." She shrugs. "Be honest. Have you and Manny ever messed around?"

"Nope!"

"Seriously," she asks surprisingly.

"Why would we? We haven't all these years."

"True. I guess I figured since ya'll are in the same house and Reggie be travelling that ya'll will sneak a taste."

"Had I not already tasted the meal, then I probably would. But that's an old stale entrée."

"I'm going to stop trying to understand because clearly we are cut from a different cloth. I would be lighting Manny's ass up," she laughs. "He's so damn sexy Bree." She admits as she takes another sip.

"Please don't feed his over inflated ego," Bree rolls her eyes to play the part as she gets wet at the image of Manny. "Give me this," Bree take the paper napkin out of Raileigh's hand.

"She's a busy body."

"That she is. Thanks for meeting us for lunch. I'm trying to keep her up in hopes that she goes to sleep tonight. I don't want to have to deal with her while talking at dinner."

"Do you want to bring her to the house?"

"No thank you. Keisha needs a realistic picture of what she's walking into."

"Well call me first thing in the morning, because I want to hear all the details," Nia laughs.

"You know I am." Bree smiles. "Thank you," she grabs the check from the waitress. "Let's let Manny pay for this." She says aloud before she immediately hands the check back to the waitress.

"You got that man's card?" Nia asks

"I told you I'm happy over here." Bree winks.

"What does Reggie say?"

"Nothing."

"Bullshit!"

"Seriously, he doesn't mind. They have to intertwine finances to pay the bills."

"I need to know what the hell you're doing to pull this mess off. This is unbelievable."

"Well believe it. It's been real but I have to go to the grocery store."

"CALL ME!" Nia speaks firmly.

"I WILL," Bree says mimicking her tone.

# CHAPTER 57

"Hey," Bree acknowledges Manny, Keisha and Kennan as they walk into the kitchen. Manny walks over to greet her with a kiss. She gives him her cheek for the sake of Keisha, but he grabs her face and places the kiss on her lips.

"Hey Sweetie, how was your day?" he asks.

"Good. Ya'll travels."

"A commute," he tells her. "Brianna, this is Keisha and Kennan. This is Brianna."

"Keisha," Bree says, extending her hand towards Keisha.

"Hey it's nice to finally meet you," she smiles.

"Same here," Bree says as she checks her out. She's very pretty, short hair, mocha complexion, medium build, maybe about 5"6 because she has a little height on Bree.

"And how was your day cutie pie?" Bree asks Kennan, stooping to his level. "Junior isn't home yet but he should be home soon."

"Good." He says shyly, dropping his head.

"Do you want me to show you where the toys are?" Manny asks.

"Yes," his face brightens as he replies.

"This is Raileigh," Bree says to Keisha. "Here have a seat," she continues as she pulls out the stool.

"Gosh, she's so pretty," Keisha expresses.

"Thank you. She is a handful. Do you want anything to drink or snack on? Dinner is almost done. Reggie and Junior should be here in a few."

"No I'm good. Thank you."

"Double R," Manny says coming back into the kitchen without a care in the world. "Please tell me you talked to your mom."

"I did. I wasn't ignoring her I promise. I was out all day and I missed her call, but I did call her back." She makes known. Since Manny has been around Bree has been talking to her mother and sister lately. It is actually going better than Bree could have imagined.

"Are you okay?"

"Yeah. I think I'm going to go home this weekend to see my grandmother. The last time I saw her Junior was two."

"Are you taking the kids?"

"That's the plan. Again Junior was two when she last saw him and of course she hasn't met Rai."

"Do you want me to go or is Reggie going with you?"

"I haven't talked to him yet, but keep your offer on the table. I'd prefer you come with," she confirms.

"You don't want Reggie to see OKC Bree," he laughs.

"Hell no! I'm going to have my hands full making sure that my grandmother's care plan is in order, so I don't need the whispers. I might have to deliver a beat down." She laughs.

"Hey Princess," Manny finally acknowledges Raileigh. "I didn't see you hiding over here, you're being quiet for once."

As soon as she see's Manny her face lights up and she extends her arms for him to pick her up.

"You know why she wants you to pick her up right?" Bree questions looking over her shoulder.

"She's tired?"

"Yup!"

"Can she go to sleep?"

"Yeah you can put her down. I was trying to keep her up as long as possible so she can sleep through dinner."

"I got you," Manny says, pulling her out the chair.

"Wipe her down first please."

"Okay," he says walking towards the nursery.

"Are you okay?" Bree asks Keisha because she's as quiet as a mouse.

"I'm just soaking this all in." she chuckles.

"We create our own normal, so insert yourself when you want," Bree offers. "So how long have you and Manny known each other?"

"Years…gosh! Maybe about three or so. We met when he came through my agency."

"Oh okay. Ya'll are finally getting around to dating?" Bree shifts her eyes to look up at her.

"No. We've dated when we first meet. He was with Samantha," she says rolling her eyes. "He wasn't in a position to get rid of her because of his schedule and her doing so much for Junior, so I was playing the side role for a little bit." She admits. "That ended when she found out and told me he doesn't like me because he likes men."

"WOW! Sam said that? Whew, she was cool with it for years. But maybe that was just a front for me though."

"Well with that I took off. I didn't want to deal with him. I could not fathom being with a man that also likes men." She speaks honestly.

"So how did ya'll end up here?"

"We've always kept in touch. I love Glenn. I really do. It was hard for me to just give him up despite the circumstances. We started getting back heavy around six months ago. As time moved on he presented the living situation and asked would I agree to be a part of it. At first I thought he was lying. But when I found it was true, we talked about it."

"And here you are," Bree finishes her sentence.

"Yup!"

"Hi Mom, who is that in the playroom?"

"Hey Champ that is Kennan and this is Ms. Keisha."

"Oh I remember you," Junior says. "I saw you at Mr. Stan's house. I forgot your name," he smiles.

"I just said Ms. Keisha." Bree repeats.

"Ms. Keisha. Is that your son?"

"Yes," she answers and looks towards Reggie as he enters the kitchen.

"Go and introduce yourself and play. Dinner is almost ready," Bree nudges him. "Hey handsome," she steps to Reggie and goes in for a kiss.

"Beautiful," he smiles after their lips separate.

"This is Keisha. Keisha, this is my husband Reggie."

"Hi nice to meet you," Keisha stands to greet him.

Bree knows she likes what she sees because she has that same twinkle in her eyes that Bree had when she first met Reggie.

"Same here." He says and directs his attention towards Bree. "Where's Rai?"

"Probably sleep. Manny went to put her down about fifteen minutes ago. How was your day?"

"Not too bad other than the fact that I have to head out to Chicago on Thursday."

"That's cool. My mom called and said my grandmother is in the hospital, so I was thinking of taking the kids to OKC this weekend."

"Is she going to be okay? Do you want me to come with you?" he asks as he leans on the counter.

"We're hoping. And it's okay Baby, Manny offered. You can go handle business."

"Are you sure?"

"Positive!" She looks at him. "I actually prefer it. I have some loose ends to tie up and you don't need to meet Brianna," she nudges him.

"Oh I've met her." He says with a snarky tone recalling his sleep being interrupted.

"Nah, that was just a cliff note, far from a detailed bio," Bree laughs.

"Wow! Yeah I'll stand clear then," he raises his hands in a surrendering motion. "Is dinner about ready, I'm going to go and change."

"Yes," Bree walks to stand face to face. She unbuttons his blazer, unloosens his tie and unbutton his shirt. "There," she places a kiss on his lips while patting his chest.

"Thank you my love," he says before walking away.

"Can I get a high-five," Keisha raises her hand to Bree once Reggie is down the hall. "Girl you are in here handling shit."

"Are you joining me," Bree smiles. For some reason she feels comfortable around Keisha. She seems pretty cool.

"I'm here." She pauses. "Is it appropriate for me to say that your husband is FINE?" she inquires.

"Once ya'll get to know each other, he'll be your boyfriend, so sure," Bree shrugs welcoming the compliment.

"How did you pull this off? I need to know," she scoots up towards the island as if she's leaning into a secret.

"Opportunity presented itself and I jumped."

"Obviously but how did you get them to agree to this?"

"Short version is they are attracted to each other. I tried to fit society norms and have a monogamous relationship that produces a nuclear family, it didn't work. Now I'm doing my own thing and I love it." Bree smiles.

"So did you know that your husband is bi-sexual?"

"Not until I caught those two knuckles heads kissing. That's when I proposed my plan. I knew I wanted to keep my family. I love my husband unconditionally. I've always known about Manny since we were fourteen. I just figured if Reggie has an itch Manny can scratch it. At least I don't have to worry about diseases or about people exposing his lifestyle choices out of spite."

"Makes perfect sense."

"Let me round them up for dinner." Bree says as she makes her way out of the conversation. She doesn't mind having the talk, but she would rather do it when they are all together. That way everyone gets to tell their own story.

# CHAPTER 58

When the boys finally leave the table it gives the adults a chance to address the main concerns of their arrangement.

"Keisha, we'll let you have the floor to ask any questions and address any concerns. We have all been in this space for a while and if you choose to stay I want to be sure that you are comfortable coming in." Bree says starting their conversation off.

"I don't know where to begin," she says readjusting herself in her chair. Manny places his hand on her back for comfort. "I have watched how you guys have been operating and it seems like a very loving and understanding situation to be in. For me though, I have never willingly participated in an open relationship. Now I've been in plenty of compromising situations," she chuckles. "But I don't know how I'm going to feel, you know? I hope you understand."

"Completely," Reggie says, bringing the focus on him. "It was quite an adjustment for all of us in the beginning. As Bree said, we've been in this space for a while. However, we understand your apprehension. Just let us know how we can make this go a little more smoothly for you."

"Baby, you know I wouldn't put you in an unstable situation. We both know that the only reason that we weren't together was because of my sexuality. This fixes that." Manny speaks giving his go to spill.

For once, the feeling of jealousy shoots through Bree's veins. Manny has never expressed this amount of love for anyone in Bree's presence. She also had no idea that Keisha nor this level of feeling for her existed.

"I know," Keisha says as she looks to him and places a soft kiss on his lips. "I'm here because I like the setup. I know that it's something that I want to be a part of, especially with you," she says, still looking at Manny. "I just need to know how okay you are with the terms of this agreement?" she pauses. She then directs her attention back to the table to let everyone know that she's addressing the group with this next concern. "It is my understanding that you and I can sleep together," she shifts her eyes to Reggie. "And I know that the two of you do what ya'll do." She slowly looks to Bree. "How okay are you with this? With me giving myself to him? With you being so close to Bree?" she turns to Manny.

"I am one hundred percent okay with it. I would not have asked you if I wasn't. What is your concern?"

"This is Brianna," she says like that's enough to answer his question yet she continues, "The woman that you protect, that no one can say a bad thing about, that can get you to drop any and everything to tend to her needs."

Reggie squirms in his seat because he is uneasy about what is being disclosed.

"Just like you," Manny says, throwing on the charm.

"Did you know about me," she asks, looking at Bree. Then she immediately dismisses her question, "No don't answer that. I'm sorry. I don't want to bring you into this. Did she know about me," she asks, directing her question to Manny.

"Yes,"

"Liar." She calls him out. "Glenn, I'm talking about before this whole talk of adding me to this blended family came about, did she know anything about me?"

"No!" he answers honestly.

"And why not?"

"Because I was with Samantha," he says like that's the legit reason.

"I still call bullshit," she huffs.

"I hope that I'm not overstepping my boundaries here," Bree jumps in to relax everyone's mind. She sees Reggie is not taking a liking to how Manny feels about her. "I know that there is a reason as to why you feel that way Keisha. Please don't think that I'm taking up for Manny or trying to diminish your feelings with what I'm about to say. His reason for not telling me about you is purely situational and not related to feelings. He knows how I feel about various women around our son, me knowing or at least thinking it was only Sam kept me sane. As a woman and a parent I hope you understand that."

"I do," she says, softening her stance.

Bree takes the opportunity to embrace Reggie to make him feel a little better about the situation.

"I apologize if that made you feel hesitant about our relationship," Manny says to Keisha.

"I get it." She says, "But if we're all being open and honest here, then I have to say that I will always feel like I am number two."

"Not the case," Manny swiftly moves in for the save to keep her from running on about his and Bree's relationship. Keisha knows more than Reggie and he tends to keep it that way. "Number one," he seals with a kiss.

"Keisha, Reggie and I are married. Legally." Bree discloses to get her to see how childish she sounds to compare their level of love from Manny.

"Oh so, he's really your husband and you're not just saying that? I thought it was a label for the outside world." She expresses.

"Well it is," Bree confirms. "But it's accurate."

"Feel better?" Reggie asks.

"Much better," she confirms. "Continuing to ride the honesty train," she pauses. "I would appreciate it if the two of your hold out on intimacy for a bit, just until I can wrap my head around everything."

Bree makes a face that reads fair request and she checks Manny's way to see if his reaction is the same.

"Can you be more specific? When communicating we have to ensure that we are being as distinctive as possible to avoid any misunderstandings."

"No sex, no hugs, no kissing, pretty much no physical contact."

"That's a fair request." Reggie says siding with Keisha.

"I agree," Bree says, hopping on the bandwagon.

"Granted." Manny says.

***

After dinner, everyone retreats to their bedrooms. The remainder of the conversation went well and everyone is on board with Keisha moving in. The next few trial days will be to see if this is actually something she can live in and with, and not just in theory.

"So how are you feeling?" Bree asks Reggie as they get into bed. "She's very pretty and well rounded."

"I agree. She seems to fit right in. Where is Kennan's dad?"

"According to Manny, not in the picture. I am not quite sure what that means. I guess once Keisha gets comfortable we'll find out. Bottom line is, I don't think we have to worry about him."

"Great! How do you feel? I know initially this is not what you had in mind." Reggie inquires.

"I'm cool with it. What about you?"

"I'm a little excited. Have a few things I wouldn't mind doing?"

"Like?" Bree questions because she is unsure of what he feels she cannot do.

"A few things that I don't want my wife or the mother of my child doing," he confirms. "Are you sure you're not going to get jealous?"

"Of course I'm sure, why would you think that?" Bree backs down because she has an idea of the less than appealing things that he wants to do.

"Because you're about to play a different position, I just want to make sure you're ready."

"I'm ready because I know that she can't have you. She can have this," Bree says as she grabs in between his legs. "But she'll never be able to touch this," she places her hand on his chest above his heart. "Love wins in a war with lust." She says confidently.

"I couldn't agree more. I love you,"

"I love you more."

"Honestly, I am a bit nervous," he restarts the conversation after their kiss.

"Nervous about what?" she catches herself from answering with an attitude. She wants to move on from this subject.

"You and Manny," he lets slide off his tongue. "The way she spoke of the two of you made me cringe a little.

"Love wins in the war with lust, I just said that." She refreshes his memory.

"That's the thing it's not lust with the two of you,"

"And it's not lust with the two of us," she halts his negative thoughts because she doesn't want to get into this subject either.

"Compared to our love ya'll love is,"

"It's..." Bree attempts to interrupt and reassure.

"It's deeper," he continues.

"It's different." Bree speaks truthfully continuing on with her thoughts. "I honestly do not know what type of love Manny and I have. It's not familial; it's deeper than a friendship, but not quite romantic." She says sifting through her thoughts aloud.

"Was that supposed to make me feel better?"

"I didn't know that I am responsible for your feelings at this moment. I'm being honest." She slightly jabs.

"I appreciate your honesty, but that didn't make me feel any better about this situation. I mean if that was the goal of having this conversation." He delivers a jab back.

"How I feel about you compares to no one." She addresses because he's right, she has to give him a leg to stand on. "Even though I've opened our marriage, our relationship, our life up and allowed others to come in, never forget that you are in a league of your own with me."

"So I'm putting my all and trust in a feeling of love that you said holds no significance?"

Reggie asks as he falls back on the same conversation that they have had over and over again.

"I don't recall saying that the feeling of love holds no significance. My point was and still is that love is a choice. And while yes, at the moment I am singling you out based on my feelings that I have for you, my commitment and dedication to you is absolutely a choice. If I relied solely on feelings, then we would not be here. I chose and will continue to choose love with you."

Reggie takes her words in and lets them marinate. He decides that he is going to attempt to exceed the boundaries that are in place to put his mind at ease. "Baby," he says smoothly as he looks directly into her eyes, "Don't think that I'm trying to devise a plan or anything, I just need an answer to put my heart and mind at ease. If this arrangement somehow takes a turn for the worst, then will you still choose love with me?"

"Yes," Bree answers without hesitation. She wanted to stand clear of making such a distinct line that can potentially ruin what they have put in place. However, she knows that in this moment this is something that Reggie needs. He needs to hear that at the end of the day that she will choose her vows over any situation that may arise. Now she just hopes that he doesn't start any shit to dismantle the structure that they are trying to build.

"Thank you so much! You don't understand how much that means to me and how much better it has made me feel."

"You're mine and I'm yours and they're fun!" she winks.

"I love the way you think," he smiles as he brings her closer.

# CHAPTER 59

Keisha has some business to finish up in California, so she headed out to go there. Bree and Manny have talked her into letting Kennan stay at the house. It is best to get him enrolled in school and for him to start establishing his little life here.

"How did Kennan do when you dropped him off?" Manny asks when Bree returns to the house. "Where's Rai," he continues when he notices that Bree is empty handed.

"He did well. And I dropped her off at the center for a couple of hours. I didn't want to take her up to the school, but surprisingly the process wasn't too bad."

"Bree come here," Manny calls because as she is talking, she is walking away.

"What?" she stops in her tracks but doesn't go back to him.

"What's wrong with you?"

"Nothing"

"It is something. I've felt it since we had our talk at the table."

"You put on quite the show, or were you being truthful?" she glares at him.

He walks closely and tries to wrap her in his arms.

"Aht, aht, aht, no physical contact," she says maneuvering her way out of his embrace.

"So that's it? You agreed to it also if I remember correctly; first actually."

"Second and I was being a team player. And no, that's not it! No one told you to confess that she's number one." Bree says shockingly and at herself because she didn't mean to say that. She was going to try to bury her jealous feelings deep down.

"You know she's not and she knows she's not. Thanks for the save by the way." He dismisses her concern as invalid

"I hate that you've let it come from your mouth. That is all." Bree dismisses like that's all she needs to hear.

"I had to do something Bree."

"I get it!"

"Do you?"

"Yes,"

"Besides you and Reggie are married legally." He spits in a playful tone.

"We are."

"And I hate that you married him."

"I had to do something Glenn," she says, mocking his tone.

"As much as I would love to believe that, we both know it isn't true. You love him and I'm okay with that. I love Keisha and I need you to be okay with that."

"I'm okay with that!" she says unsure.

"Are you going to be okay once she gets back?"

"Yup!"

"Not convinced."

"I don't know what you want me to say or do. I'll adapt."

"I don't understand how you are allowed to be jealous and I'm not." Manny states baffled at Bree's thought process.

"Because you are also fucking my husband. Did you forget about the perks you receive? I get nothing from Keisha, but her dictating our relationship and her fucking my husband once they get around to it."

"You have a point there!"

"And the one thing that I thought couldn't be taken away from me, was stripped from my grasp instantly." She shares sadly as she snaps her fingers.

"She cannot take that away. But I understand how you feel that she did. I will reestablish your position with her."

"If you say so,"

"Bree she knows that it will always be you. I had to stop her from going there in front of Reggie because he would be the only one with hurt feelings had I let her go on. Give me some credit for that."

"You're right. Thank you." She caves. "I know that, which is why I stepped in to quickly agree. It just hurt a little that's all. Keisha is the only one that has a revolving door around here and she needs to know that she can't get cocky." Bree asserts her dominance in their relationship. She really does like Keisha but she needs to find her lane and stay there.

"The jealous Bree is cute," he begins to butter her up to take her mind off of the one thing that everyone knows.

"The loving Bree is better," she says rolling her eyes.

"I agree, but I've never fucked jealous Bree, maybe I'll like it!" he says to make his advances. And Bree lets him. This is the main reason why she left Rai at the center. Now, she and Manny have all day to make up.

# CHAPTER 60

Upon Keisha's return, Bree notices that Manny must have laid some sort of ground rules because he picked back up with the pet names, kissing and loving on her like before. Bree must admit that she's happy. She didn't know how long she would have been able to keep up not being physical with Manny when Keisha is around.

"Hey Baby," Reggie approaches Bree with a kiss on the lips. Bree, Keisha and the kids are in the playroom hanging out.

"Keisha," he leans to kiss her on the cheek.

Bree does a double take at their body language. But continues on, "My love, Keisha is going to keep the kids so we can go out tonight. Nia called and asked if we can meet them for dinner."

"Great! Come with me, so we can get ready."

"You're good?" Bree looks to Keisha.

"Yeah go ahead girl."

"Daddy," Junior jumps up to give Reggie a hug.

"Hey Champ, hey Keen. What do you two have going on in here?"

"We are trying to make a comic strip, do you want to see?" Kennan speaks in his shy voice. He has yet to come fully out of his shell.

"Yes, let me take a look at it." Reggie says as he sits next to the table to see what they have going on. "You both are some mighty fine artist. I'm impressed. Are you guys just handling the graphics right now?"

"Yes," Junior answers. "We were hoping that we could use your computer to type the other stuff. Mom says it has auto something to help us with the spelling." He says shaking his head from his brain fart.

"Auto-correct and it does, but that's no way to learn how to spell. How about this, once you guys have everything written down, we go and shop for a laptop specifically for your comics," he smiles.

For once, Kennan has a genuine smile on his face. "That would be awesome!"

"Baby girl," Reggie looks to Raileigh pulling at his pants. "Where did you come from?" he asks because he didn't see her when he came in, he thought she was asleep. Rai has been making progress with being mobile slithering across the floor.

"She was hiding in the tent," Keisha answers. "She loves this little thing."

"Oh Keisha the food," Bree panics as she finally puts a scent to the weird smell.

"Dammit! I told you I'm no good at this stuff," she says as she gets up and runs out of the room.

Reggie and Bree make it to the kitchen with Rai in hand.

"Girl bye," Keisha says as she throws the burnt lasagna on the counter. "We're getting pizza," she laughs.

"What the hell girl. What did you have the oven on?" She asked. Bree returned home from picking up the kids to Keisha attempting to make dinner.

"I don't know," she says as she turns to look at the temperature. "450."

"No Keisha that is entirely too high. 400 max." Bree says. "Well it's a good thing we're going out huh Baby."

"Great thing!" he agrees.

"Bree you handle this kitchen shit. It's not my thing. I tried."

"You did and thank you. Yes, I will resume my duties because girl this is a tragedy." Bree laughs.

"The boys will be happy with pizza," Keisha reassures herself.

"Extremely," Bree agrees.

"Want me to take Rai while you two get ready?" Keisha says walking towards Reggie with her arms extended.

"No," Reggie says, giving Rai a kiss. "She's coming with us." He says and turns to head to the room. "Thanks though," he expresses as he walks away.

"Are you all going out or staying in?" Bree asks. "Because Rai can go with Brittany."

"No, she can come with us. She's really not a bother." Keisha says.

"I know it's not her directly, just the things we have to do for her that slows us down. The car seat, the attention, the feeding," Bree exhales.

"I'm fine. I like it. I love the baby phase and she's so sweet. I can dump these boys though. Is that an option," she snickers.

"They are a handful. And so damn active. Thanks again Keisha and throw the whole damn pan away, let's not try to salvage it." Bree says walking away.

"Five steps ahead of you," she concurs.

Instead of sitting down at a fancy restaurant, Reggie and Bree meet Charles and Nia at the sports bar. The guys want to catch the game. Charles and Reggie immediately walked into some friends. Bree and Nia go to get situated at the booth.

"Guess we can count them out," Bree says as she and Nia look at how comfortable they have gotten at the bar.

"Who cares? How have you been?" Nia expresses

"Good and you?"

"Pregnant!"

"Shut up! Congratulations Nia," Bree says excitedly.

"Girl I'm too old for this shit. What am I going to do with four damn kids?"

"Raise them. You'll be fine." Bree consoles her thoughts. "How far along are you?"

"I don't know. Rem I'm not excited about this shit. I can't have a drink. My partying days are O-V-E-R."

"Nia you don't have to be excited, but you do have to take care of yourself. Have you been to the doctor's?"

"My appointment next week. Now let's address the real issue, my life is over."

"No it's not. A new life it about to begin," Bree smiles

"How is your new life? Keisha moved in right? How is that going?"

"Great! She's the babysitter tonight," Bree boasted. "It's going good. No complaints."

"Still haven't fucked Manny?"

"NO! And why are you stuck on that?"

"Because I don't believe you. Rem, bring me over there I'll fuck him. Good too!"

Bree burst out laughing because she knows that Nia is dead serious. She has the biggest crush on Manny, which is why she doesn't and hasn't brought Nia around much. She knows that Nia will dangle and Manny will pounce.

"For one, you're pregnant."

"Don't remind me," Nia quickly interjects.

"And secondly, I'm sure that Keisha is taking care of him. Don't ruin either of ya'll happy homes."

"I would still be happy if I got a taste. I don't know about anyone else. I mean Manny will be happy too!" she jokes.

"Is Charles happy with the new addition?" Bree changes the subject

"Girl yes! It was his bright idea. I swear he did something."

"Birds of a feather, I wouldn't put it past him."

"What do you mean?"

"With my pregnancy I later found out that Reggie hid by birth control pills. He had me going crazy thinking that I'd lost them."

"That's fucked up and you're probably right. Mysteriously, my appointment for my shot disappeared from my calendar and suddenly reappeared after. He had to go through great lengths though because I get text reminders to confirm appointments. I didn't see one which is why I didn't know I missed the appointment."

"What the hell is wrong with them? They already got us!" Bree says knowing what Reggie's reasoning and now is side-eyeing Charles.

"Digging themselves in a hole. Well Charles is putting himself in a deeper hole. He won't have a dime to his name if we split." Nia laughs.

"No splitting going on around here," Bree makes known and sets her eyes on Reggie and just in time to see him checking his phone. He notices her unhappy gaze and makes his way to the table.

"Hey Baby, did you order?" He asks as he sits his phone face up on the table.

"No, we are waiting for the two of you," she says in a snide tone with her eyes locked with his phone screen.

"Let me go and get him," he suggests while leaving his phone there.

"Damn Remi, you got him shook."

"What are you talking about?"

"You made that man leave his conversation to bring you his phone."

"I did not. He did that on his own."

"If your eyes had a trigger, then he'd be dead. You gave him a deathly stare when he checked his phone."

"Did I?" Bree had to question. She knew that she felt some type of way but didn't know that she displayed it on her face. And it's only because she thinks that Keisha and Reggie have crossed the line. She felt it when he gave her a kiss earlier and Bree can't shake the feeling.

"You did! And at least he complies. Are you going to check it?" Nia pries.

"No, why?"

"Because you did all of that. See who it is." She encourages me.

"No, that's not how we operate."

"I screen all Charles's shit. No more passes from me after the shit I've been through."

"That's no way to live, Nia."

"No way for you to live." She corrects. "I can say the same about your home life."

"Touche" Bree exits the conversation. If she's going to be honest with herself she wants to check. Just not here.

"Finally," Nia huffs as they make their way over.

"Just Reggie, Nia is eating for two," Bree smiles.

"I heard. Congratulations. Ya'll about to have a basketball team up over there."

"I'm working on it," Charles says, pulling Nia close. And although she tries to play tough she cuddles into his arms and smiles. "When is the next one coming along." Charles inquires.

"Naw man, we're done. I don't know how you do it. It's not enough time in the day for me. Kids need a lot of attention. Bree and I have to carve too much time out for each other as is." Reggie gives his spill although if it was up to him, he would have more.

"I hear ya. It does get tiring but I love them." Charles smiles.

A night with friends is just what the doctor ordered for Bree and Reggie. It was so invigorating. Takes Bree go back to the early days in her and Reggie's relationship.

"I really enjoyed myself tonight, Baby," Bree says as she looks to Reggie while he's driving.

"I really did too," he smiles. "It felt different. Difficult to describe."

"I hear you. I know exactly what you mean. I don't think it's difficult to describe, I just think that we don't want what we say or how we say it to be taken incorrectly."

"Yes, then you know exactly what I mean." He confirms.

"Let me just say, that I love this type of reconnecting and we need to do it more often."

"Agreed."

As they walk into the house, they can tell that everyone has turned in for the night. At least they thought they did. Manny and Keisha are in the family room watching a movie.

"Hey," Bree says as she bends down to greet them. Manny grabs her face and gives her a kiss. "Keisha," Bree says.

"Hey," she says pausing the movie. "The kids are asleep. Raileigh is in the nursery. I was going to put her in your room but decided against it."

"Thank you so much. Let's see how long she lasts."

"Reggie," Keisha says. Bree assumes she's looking for a kiss that she doesn't receive.

"Hey, I'm about to turn it in. I'm beat. Let's go Baby," he says tapping Bree on the ass.

"Goodnight ya'll," Bree begins her departure.

Reggie bends down and gives Keisha a kiss and Bree isn't sure if it's on the lips or the cheek.

"Goodnight!" he says as he walks away.

Manny and Reggie halted their PDA early on. The first consensual kiss that Bree witnessed was the last kiss Bree witnessed. It's a mystery on when they do what they do and Bree actually likes it this way.

"Ya'll fucking?" Bree dives in head first as soon as she hears the door latch.

"We fucked. –ED. One time," he answers. "That was the plan right? We all knew this train was pulling into the station right? Am I wrong?" Reggie responds immediately on the defense.

"No,"

"But," he encourages her to keep going.

"I just felt the vibe that's all and I wanted to confirm my gut feeling."

"That's all?"

"May I check your phone?" she asks with her handout.

Reggie takes his phone from his pocket and hands it to Bree. "Thanks for asking," he applauds as he hands it over as if Bree is the sneaky one.

Bree opens the phone and goes straight to the messages and what do you know, a text from Keisha.

*Keisha: She misses you.*

*Reggie: Oh really*

*Keisha: You don't sound excited. Didn't like it?*

*Reggie: I did. I'm just out with my wife and now is not the time*

*Keisha: Got it!*

"Are you okay,"

"Sort of,"

"Next issue." He continues.

"Why did you kiss her when I turned my back and did you kiss her on the lips?"

"This is an issue as you have tongued down Manny on many occasions in my face?"

"Can you answer the questions?"

"Yes it was on the lips. And I sent you away because I knew you wouldn't want to see it. Bree I have to make Keisha feel comfortable with what's going on and me not being engaging and inviting will not help her progress. I also know that this is new for you and will take you some time to get used to despite how you keep saying that you're okay. I know what I'm doing. Had you not turned back around, everything would have gone smoothly. When I send you along, GO!" he demands.

"Fine,"

"Nope, come back here." He stops her from storming off and shutting down. "I would like it if you said yes, for once and listened to me."

"Yes Sir," she says rolling her eyes as he's holding her arms so that she stays put.

"You said you were okay with playing this position. I thought we went over this."

"We did, but that was before I had to actually deal with it. Plans vs Reality." She says

"Are you jealous?"

"A little." She admits

"Why? What's our motto? You're mine, I'm yours, they're fun! Isn't that what you said?"

"I did and I don't want you to have too much fun," she speaks in a serious tone. This is not how Bree envisioned this plan playing out. She wanted to be on the pedestal as Manny and Reggie catered to her. Now she has to share the spotlight.

"You're cute, jealous, you know that?" he switches gears.

"It makes you feel good?" she asks with an attitude.

"It makes me feel great! Now you can understand my position. I know that I can be extreme at times," he defends his less than mild jealous nature. "But the doubt of love in that moment is very real. You've reassured me in my time of need and now I must do the same. My heart is all yours forever and always."

"Thank you and thank you for the message you sent. I feel good knowing that she knows where she stands."

"She will always know with me, understand?"

"Yes," she replied and made sure to leave it at that.

# CHAPTER 61

Their home life receives a lot of questions from everyone, especially Reggie's parents. However, given that Bree and Reggie are maneuvering as a couple as well as Manny and Keisha, and the family is healthy and thriving they've backed off a little. Manny's parents, well his mother, just thinks that it's something he's going along with for Bree and for once she's right, but Bree will never tell her.

"Are you nervous? You have been avoiding my mother like the plague," Reggie asks as they are finally heading to his parents house to confront the issue.

"I haven't really been avoiding her, our schedules just haven't lined up. Besides, I thought you would have talked to her by now." Bree side eyes Reggie. While yes, it's true that she's made sure to keep her schedule packed to avoid this conversation, she wishes that Reggie would have stepped up and said his peace to lay this all to rest.

"I don't know what to say," he admits.

"For starters that you are happy and that this was a mutual decision. I get the feeling that she thinks that it was all my bright idea. And it was, but I didn't come up with this for no reason." She reminds him.

"You're right. And I'm sorry that I placed this burden on you. Bree, this is your strong suit. You handle things like this very well. You know exactly what to say and how to play the hand that you're dealt, even when a trump card is thrown. I love this about it. I depend on you in this area if I'm being honest."

"If we're ever in a similar situation where you are to depend on me, then be honest with me to let me prepare better. I feel like I'm being thrown under the bus. I got it though."

"I know you do," he says as he throws the car in park.

"Hey, hey, hey," Reggie greets as they walk into the house.

"Look what the wind blew in," Harold speaks first. "How have ya'll been? And you," he grabs Rai from Bree's arms. "I've missed you Pumpkin."

"We are doing great!" Bree answers.

"Where's Junior?" Lynn inquires.

"With his Dad, it's Keisha's birthday so they took her on vacation."

"I need a vacation," she discloses.

"We should all take one together?" Bree throws out there. "Where's Tasha?"

"They left not too long ago. I was hoping that we could talk alone." Lynn speaks honestly.

"I figured as much," Bree acknowledges. "Rai should be going down for a nap soon, then we can get this show on the road." She says before taking a deep breath. The main reason for coming here was to have "The Talk" so there's no need to beat around the bush.

"Give me my grandbaby," Lynn takes Rai from Harold. "You see she's trying to get over here."

Harold complies and hands Rai over. "Reggie come take a look at this," he says as he walks towards the garage.

"She is getting big Bree. I heard she's crawling already. Is she moving out the way?"

"Oh no! I'm not doing that again. She is not a pro yet, but she's getting there. She moves just enough to get to where she needs to go."

"That's the goal." She smiles. "Oh my! When did she get her ears pierced?"

"About a month or so ago. She was a straight trooper too. Reggie was more nervous than me and was about to cry and Rai was taking it like a champ." Bree laughs.

"She's going to have Reggie wrapped around her finger."

"She already does and it's sickening," Bree informs her. "Do you know that he still has trouble with letting her sleep in the nursery? They both take up the whole bed."

"Reggie needs to stop. He's creating a monster. That's a difficult habit to break." She warns.

"Tell him about it because I've said all that I can say."

"About what," Reggie asks, coming in on the tail end of the conversation.

"Rai sleeping with us."

"I don't want to hear it," he says walking away.

"Told you. And this is why I'm not having any more kids. Not like I can anyway. Here let me feed her so she can go to sleep," Bree says reaching for Rai.

"Bree do you want to lay her down?" Lynn asks once Bree finally gets her to sleep.

"Reggie is getting the pack and play out of the car."

Bree has killed all the time she can to prolong this talk. Rai is now comfy and there is no reason why they shouldn't begin.

"So," Lynn says getting right to it. She wants to know what's going on.

"Before you begin," Bree interrupts. "I would just like to say that I have been avoiding this moment. And it's not because I'm ashamed or don't want to talk about it, it's because I had to rearrange my thought process. Had I come in here prior to today, I would have been on the defense. I want a respectable level headed conversation. I want to be able to answer your questions and address your concerns with tact and maturity and not feel offended. At the end of this, you still may not understand our living arrangements. And I have come to peace with that is okay. We just need your support with our decision that we have made for our life."

"Fair enough." Lynn says taking back a little. "Thank you for your honesty. Let me be clear, you don't owe me an explanation because like you said it's ultimately ya'll decision on how you live your life, but Reggie is my son. And as a mother I still worry about him regardless of his age. From the outside looking in, the set-up looks sketchy. And if I'm being honest, I remember you saying that you had stipulations for Reggie and I am just wondering if this is something he had to agree to in order for you to remain with him?"

"You both had a conversation about us?" Reggie asks with confusion on his face. He didn't know that Bree and his mother spoke of their issues privately.

"I wouldn't say it was a conversation about us." Bree looks at him. "When it was time for me to make my decision, your mother asked me if I knew what I wanted to do and I said yes, with stipulations. And that was the end of that." She clears the air. "Mrs. Lynn to answer your question, this was not a part of my trust package. The timing was purely coincidental. When Reggie and I went through our rough patch,

Manny was taking a break from the big screen and doing a sitcom. In that, he stated he was moving back to Texas. Our son was extremely excited and wanted his Dad to move in with him. Manny and I have not lived together with Junior. And in trying to foster a healthy life and relationship with our son, we thought it was best if we lived together. If only for a short while. I am fortunate that Reggie understands the vision and has agreed to help us be the best parents that we can be."

"Manny's girlfriend moved in?" Harold asks with skepticism.

"Yes, Keisha. And you both should come and meet her sometime. I hate that we are not as close as we used to be. It's okay to come to the house and hang out with us and the kids. Maybe if you did, then you would see that we're fine and feel a little bit more comfortable about our family dynamics."

"I'm old school Bree," Lynn picks back up. "And this is just not how it's supposed to be. You two are married. You don't open up your marriage like this. There's too much temptation walking around."

"In order to be tempted there needs to be a desire." Bree replies. "Our living arrangement is not temptation island, it's no different than if we were living with Tasha and the kids; or a family member of mine. It's a support system. It's a system that is working for us."

"How are the kids handling it?" Harold asks.

"They love it!" Reggie finally chimes in.

"Again, if you came to the house you would see that." Bree reiterates. "Our house is like two little houses in one. We share the common areas but have our own space."

There is a moment of silence.

"Mrs. Lynn," Bree breaks the silence to offer her last words to this conversation. And she hopes it's enough. "I completely understand your reservations. Knowing what Reggie and I have been through and how our trust was broken has aided in your concern. You feel like there's temptation because you are coming from the perspective that our trust is still in limbo. However, I am here to tell you that Reggie and I are better than before. As a mother, I can also understand your concerns for your child. There is nothing like a mother's love. But I promise you that every day, I strive to reach your level of love for Reggie. I strive to love him unconditionally, without judgment, and always offering a safe space for him to reside. He is the sun in my world and I want to be the moon in his. I love him too much to put our love in jeopardy. I would not ask him to do something that he is uncomfortable doing. We are happy with our living situation. It may not be this way next week, next month, next year, but it's this way right now and we are both happy with it. I ask that you support our decision and try to be a part of our family. He misses you. I miss you. The kids miss you." Bree let her unfeigned confession roll off her tongue.

"Baby, you are such a phenomenal woman," Reggie confesses before anyone else can get a word in. "You are my moon and my stars. If I never expressed my appreciation for you, then let it be known that I appreciate you so much. You love me beyond measure and you have shown that in so many ways. Your love is my safe space. Your love allows me to love myself. You motivate me, support me and never throw my flaws in my face. I love you so much for that. I am happy to be on this journey with you. I agreed to this arrangement and I don't want you to feel bad about it or let anyone else make you feel bad about it. I stand fast on our love, your love because it's genuine and pure." Reggie continues his heartfelt confession looking Bree in the eyes. He seals it with a kiss. For that moment his parents disappeared from the room. It is him and Bree against the world. It is at this moment that he knows that he has to get her back to himself again.

"I can see the love between you too," Harold speaks breaking their trance. "It will take me some time to get used to, I won't lie to you. But you have my support."

"Thanks, Dad!" Reggie smiles.

"I guess we'll be over to meet Keisha," Lynn smiles.

"Thanks, Mom!"

"I knew you would handle it well," Reggie admires. "Thank you," he expresses rubbing her knee with his eyes on the road.

"It was easy. It's always easy when you speak from the heart."

# CHAPTER 62

Bree and Manny have fallen into the role of the stay at home parents when Manny isn't away for filming for weeks at a time. Reggie and Keisha are the workhorses of the family, leaving the house every day; weekends included for Keisha at times. Business trips are sprinkled here and there for both Keisha and Reggie. Bree seems to be the only one without a life and when she started to show some signs of being over the whole stay at home mom gig, Keisha asked if she could help with her business. Bree fell into the personal assistant role pretty quickly and when it came time to travel, Bree started taking trips with Keisha without hesitation. Enrollment in daycare and a nanny on standby was all that was needed for Bree to get back into a flexible part-time work life. In the beginning, Reggie was against the idea of Bree going back to work, especially, before her year's time. But he caved after hearing Bree's argument that staying home caring for three adults, three kids and a house with over ten thousand square feet wasn't the plan at first.

The very first time Bree went to the Big Apple on a business trip with Keisha, she knew immediately that she wanted to move there. She has never been anywhere to live other than Oklahoma and Texas, the east coast is so intriguing and lively. She knows it won't be hard to sell because it will help Keisha's career as she visits there often, it really doesn't matter where Manny is and Reggie is due for a bigger step in his career. She just needs to plan out her approach to get everyone on board together.

"There's my crush," Bree smiles as she walks into the kitchen where Manny is sitting at the table.

"What do you want?" he acknowledges with an over it voice.

"Why do I have to want something to love on you?" Bree asks as she wraps her arms around his neck from behind and places a kiss on his cheek.

"Because I know you," he continues with his accusation.

"What are you doing?" she asks, finally facing him while making him scoot his chair back from his empty plate.

"Reading this script my agent sent."

Bree grabs it from his hand. "Manipulating Love," she reads aloud. "Don't we know all about it?" She smiles as she straddles him. "Kiss me." She demands.

Manny complies with the request. "And this is not our type of love as it ends with a tragic death." He lets her know while tossing the script onto the table. "Come, take a ride with me," he suggested, patting both of her hips.

"Will it be quick? I have to get Rai and get to the grocery store before I pick up the boys."

"You'll have plenty of time." He confirms. "Let me go and get my keys."

"Oh you want to take a car ride," she laughs. "I thought," she begins. "Nevermind let me go and get my purse."

They meet in the car and Bree plans to use this as an opportunity to explore the New York move. She needs an ally and Manny is her first pick. Keisha will be the second in line. Reggie will be the, everyone else already agrees so get on board last resort.

"I need my best friend," Bree looks at Manny. As of late, it's been more a relationship with them. Not that she opposes, it's just that they don't frequent the friend zone much these days.

"I thought you had a new best friend," he questions.

"We went over this when I first meet Reggie,"

"No, Keisha," he interrupts.

"Are you jealous?" she shoots him a playful glare. "I'm trying to make her feel comfortable and her being cool makes it easier."

"I know and I appreciate it." He comes down after he sees how ridiculous he appears.

"But you're still jealous," Bree laughs.

"Whatever, what do you want? Trouble in paradise?" he asks diving in.

"No! I'm happy. I just want to run something by you to get your honest opinion."

"You want to move to New York?"

"How do you know?"

"Keesh expresses your excitement to me every time the two of you visit. I know you Bree. The next wave is coming in and you want to ride it into shore." He speaks matter of fact. "And we both know that the only one is who is going to have a problem with the move is Reggie," he continues and then looks at her when he stops at the red light. "To be honest, I talked Keisha out of a New York move to come here with us. So, she's ready when I say when."

"Excuse me, Mr. I know everything,"

"Are you going to talk to him?" he halts her rant.

"I was thinking we both could tag team." She speaks candidly.

"I was thinking Keisha and I could go regardless." He throws in his plans.

"What the fuck! NO! NO!," Bree interrupts shaking her head dismissing the idiotic thought.

"Temporarily, damn let me finish." Manny tries to lower her temperature. "If I accept this role, then I have to go and film this movie." He attempts to give his spill.

"You're trying to leave me?" she interrupts again.

"No,"

"Then why do you want to move?"

"Can you just listen?"

"I don't want to talk about it," she huffs and turns her back to him as much as she can being confined by the seat belt.

"I thought I was talking to my best friend?" he reminds her.

Bree ignores his smart remark and remains quiet. Manny handles his business at the drive-thru bank and takes them for a ride to the airport, so they can watch planes take off and talk.

"Baby," he turns to grab her face once they are parked. "I am not," he gives her a kiss, "Trying," he places another kiss, "To leave you," he seals with his final kiss.

"That's what it sounds like." She speaks with an attitude.

"Can you just listen, please?" he begs.

"I'm listening, but I can tell you now that I'm not going to like it and my answer is NO!" she says as she pushes his hands from her face.

"Stop being a spoiled brat,"

"Stop trying to leave me,"

Manny lets out a sigh and continues on with the spill he was trying to give earlier. "If I accept this role, then I have to go and film this movie. Keisha will still be travelling and you will have Kennan, Junior and Rai. I was thinking that Keisha, Kennan and I would move to New York temporarily. This way, Kennan is out of your hair, I can do my job and I can get Keisha's mind together. She loves the set-up but hates Texas. I think a break from here and our living arrangement will do her some good."

Bree sifts through his excuses and she has to admit that it makes sense. Yet, her feelings are still uncertain of their emotional relationship. "What about us?"

"I can come back when I can and your business with Keisha can bring you that way. We're all still in this together Brianna. It's just temporary."

"And how long is temporary?"

"About nine months" he cringes.

"Fine!" she says in her I'm not really agreeing, just do what you want to do voice.

"Bree don't make this difficult. If we are going to try to continue this lifestyle forever, then we have to make moves like this to give us some space to regroup. There are no changes in our arrangements or love life. We'll just be away on business for an extended amount of time."

"Regroup? You haven't even lived here for nine months." She scolds.

"Brianna Monique,"

"Glenn Maurice,"

"What do you suggest I do?"

"Marry Keisha," she says dead serious. Him leaving to New York with Keisha is just as serious of a commitment in Bree's eyes.

Manny's laughter gives her no choice but to join in because he is really beside himself. Everyone knows marrying Keisha is off the table.

"Stop it!" he says through his laughter. "It's just temporary, we'll be back," he assures her as he calms down.

"And if she doesn't?"

"Then I will," he speaks from the heart.

That's all that Bree needs to hear. She needs to know that no matter the side of the coin this toss lands on, that she wins.

Later that evening Bree resurfaces the topic of moving with Reggie just to see where his head is at with a move. She decides to bypass Keisha because honestly, she may not be around for as long as Bree anticipated.

"Manny and I talked today," Bree jumps right in as Reggie is getting out of his work clothes.

"About what?" He asks, walking into the bathroom to the laundry basket.

"They may be moving to New York. He got a part for a movie that he's thinking about accepting. And if he does, then it's best he's there for filming."

"When?" Reggie tries to ask uninterested to cover his excitement. This is the exit that he's been looking for to get him and Bree back in a 'normal' marriage.

"I don't know, but most likely soon."

"How do you feel?"

"Sad,"

"Why?"

"This is not going the way I thought," she answers honestly.

"And what did you think?" Reggie asks as he sits beside her. He can admit that he knew that Bree was in fairytale land when she proposed this arrangement.

"I don't know,"

"Bree did you honestly think that we would be like this forever? That we would grow old together? All of us? Living in the same house? I thought you knew better than that. It was fun while it lasted but please don't tell me you didn't think this was temporary. It was always going to come to an end. And I am happy that it will be peaceful instead of blowing up in our face. This is a good exit and I think we should roll with it." He speaks his peace trying to isolate their relationship.

"I can't have this conversation with you," she expresses getting up to leave the conversation and the room

"And why not?" he asks as he's chasing her to the door. He shuts the door to continue with the conversation.

"Because I don't want to, can I go?"

"Talk to me."

"About what?"

"You told me that it's me and you always, if he's going to leave then let him. We move on with our lives like none of this ever happened." Reggie gives his advice.

"You're right, that would be best. I can do that!" Bree speaks half heartedly.

"You love him and you don't want him to leave." He says starting to piece her unspoken words together. "What the fuck Brianna? Why are you holding on to this?"

Bree stands emotionless with her eyes darting across the floor trying to find the words to say.

"Bree answer me,"

"I need time to think."

"What is there to think about? Our love? Our marriage? You don't want it?"

"I want to be able to be able to process my thoughts in a peaceful place."

"What is there to think about?" he asks again.

"How life is going to look now." She yells because he's starting to get on her nerves.

"Like it did before all of this went down."

"Easier said than done," Bree complains.

"It's not. Where are you going?" he asks because she is making her way to the door again.

"To clear my head." She snaps.

"To go and talk to your best friend," he says in a condescending tone.

"Why, yes. Yes I am. I'll get some empathy and a hug at least." She rolls her eyes.

"I'm trying to understand and talk to you Bree," He caves, not wanting to chase her into Manny's arms.

"No you're not. You're being accusatory and childish. I have to talk to Junior and Kennan, what am I to tell them? I have to find my feelings and confront them. I have to think about you and what you will be doing now that Manny's gone. I am knee deep in helping Keisha with her business. I mean yes, I love you and I want our marriage, BUT it's more to it than that. It's more than you and about you. You always go on a jealous kick when you feel vulnerable. All you can think about are my feelings for Manny, nothing else." She throws a good lashing of her tongue. "Now can I get some time to think, please?"

Reggie doesn't utter another word. He steps out of her way to let her continue on her venture to find some comfort.

# CHAPTER 63

"Thank you for coming over," Bree smiles as she greets Reggie's family. As soon as they are warming up to their living arrangements it's all about to come to a halt. But it feels good for Bree to know that they were at least willing to try to support them.

"Bree, this house is beautiful," Tasha says as she takes in the scenery.

"Thank you. I wish ya'll would have helped me decorate."

"Auntie Bree, I have my bathing suit."

"And we have a pool," she smiles while pinching Tabby's cheeks. "Did you guys bring swimwear?"

"I did. I want Brandon to get in the water and lord knows Frankie can't go in there alone." Tasha answers first.

"No water for me," Lynn confirms.

"Papa Harold is going to teach me to swim," Tabby reveals.

"Is that right," Bree gives him a playful side-eye.

"Yeah, yeah I was an instructor back in my day." He boosts.

"Well teach Junior too because I can only save myself," Bree laughs. "C'mon let's go in the backyard. That's where everyone is."

"Brandon," Tasha lunges to get him before he grabs the vase on the table. "Don't go breaking anything in here, you will be given as collateral."

"He's fine. B you can break that ugly vase. That wasn't my idea," Bree smirks.

"Frankie," Junior yells as soon as he sees him walk through the sliding door. "Are you getting in the pool?"

"Mom can I?" he looks at Tasha.

"I don't care."

Reggie comes over to greet his family and introduce them to Keisha and her son.

"Goodness, he is such an eye catcher and has a wonderful personality," Keisha says looking at Brandon as he is warming up to everyone. "Have you ever thought about getting him in print or commercials?" she asks Tasha.

"Family time," Bree interrupts.

"Baby, no work!" Manny piggybacks.

"Alright, alright," she caves. "But don't leave without my card," she says to Tasha.

Everyone is having fun and getting along very well. Keisha has won the heart of Lynn and the kids are playing like they've known each other all their lives. Bree feels herself going into a sad state as all of this is about to come to an end. She can't help but think that once Manny leaves it's going to be all over for them. Reggie prefers that he doesn't return and Manny is in no rush to. They have talked to the kids about the move and they are okay with it. Bree is not surprised as kids adapt pretty well and fairly quickly. Junior is excited that he will be able to go to New York and see another part of the country. And the plan is to have Kennan come back to Texas to visit. Bree will continue to help Keisha with her business with the possible travel to New York every so often. This is the only thing keeping Bree on the positive side. At least she will still get to see Manny and spend time with him. She just hopes that she doesn't get placed in the backseat since technically she'll be imposing on their arrangements.

Bree and Reggie hashed out their feelings and where they each were coming from. Reggie pledged to be open and honest about his urges, if he has them, and they will discuss how he will handle those, with the options of him and Manny paying each other a visit. After their discussion, Bree has become accepting of her feelings. While she is very sad that she and Manny won't be able to have the sexual relationship that they had, she cannot deny that she would love for her and Reggie to just be again. And in being honest with herself, she knows it's because Keisha is in the mix. It would not be fair for her to ask Manny to be alone. But if she had her way, then it would just be her, Manny and Reggie.

"Are you okay?" Manny walks up behind her as she stands by the edge of the pool.

"Yeah I'm good."

"Well smile you look like you're in deep thought over here. What are you thinking?"

"You're leaving me." She lets come out with ease. Kicking herself because this is not the place and now is definitely not the time.

Manny steps up next to her and turns to gaze at the kids in the pool to make it seem as they are having a relaxing whimsical conversation. "Stop saying it like that. I'm not leaving you. We're still together. I hope you don't take this as me breaking the agreement that we have. If you think I'm leaving, then you have to leave Reggie because none of us stays together, remember?"

Bree bursts into laughter and pushes Manny in the pool. "You're right!" she yells. "I remember," she confirms. "And don't push me in again because I quit!" she adds.

"Don't bring that mess over here," Reggie warns once Bree makes it to the table.

"I'm not, Junior dared me," she laughs.

"Bree, Keisha told us that they're moving to New York." Lynn says excitedly.

"Oh yes, I forgot to tell you guys. Manny is filming and New York is just the place for Keisha and her career. They'll always have a place to stay here, so ya'll better come and visit us." Bree says, looking Keisha's way.

"You know we will and you guys will always be welcomed there." Keisha smiles. "Bree is amazing," Keisha says to Lynn and Tasha. "She has welcomed me and my son with open arms and has created such a loving environment. I almost don't want to take him," she says turning to look at Kennan in the pool. "Bree has him focused on a schedule, he's doing well in school, it's so stable here. When we get to New York we'll be back to Nannies and tutors." She says sadly.

"Bree has told us that this is a very supportive arrangement." Lynn discloses.

"It is. Gosh! My business has flourished thanks to Bree not only helping out directly but indirectly. With her taking care of the home it allowed me to dive in head first. I was tiptoeing around because my son comes first, always. But Bree had him and I was at ease knowing that. Thank you," she gets up to give Bree a hug.

"You're welcome. Don't make me mushy because I'm going to miss ya'll." Bree says pushing her away after their friendly embrace.

"We're coming back," Keisha says confidently, "Or ya'll can move to New York." She ends with excitement.

"Come back because we're not moving," Reggie throws in his two cents.

"Damn, Baby. You didn't even give me a chance to get excited for a second." Bree says with disappointment.

"Nope! Don't even think about it," he laughs.

# CHAPTER 64

Bree finds the driver that Manny has sent for her and is excited that she is back in the Big Apple. She's more excited that she gets to see Manny. She is in a state of euphoria. She could definitely see herself living here with Reggie and the kids. There's so much to see and do; so much culture. She has been chipping away at Reggie trying to wear him down to at least consider moving. He hasn't even let her give her reasons why it would be beneficial for their family. Bree has a whole PowerPoint presentation ready for when he gives the green light. She knows that it's not the city that he's avoiding, it's falling back into the arrangement with Manny and Keisha. If she's being honest, then she has to admit that their life is actually very good right now. But she knows that this is a temporary state because they've been here before. She's going to enjoy the moments while they are genuine and when the next opportunity arises, meet it full on. She knows exactly what she wants to say and how she's going to get Reggie on board.

Bree walks in and straight into the shower because she knows what she came here for. Yes, she is to attend this casting call with Keisha, but that's not necessarily her number one priority. The feelings are mutual because she doesn't even have to wait, her shower is graciously interrupted.

"Can I join you?"

"Anytime," she smiles.

And those are the last words that they uttered from either of their lips.

As she lays sexually satisfied, Bree thinks about her life. She is brought back to the days when this was everyday routine. Now she has to wait months before she's touched in the ways that she loves.

"I love you,"

"I love you, too," Bree replies, sealing hers with a kiss.

"Have you talked to Reggie about moving here?"

"No, he's not feeling it. But I haven't given up hope. I want to be here. Let's give him some time." She pleads.

"Remind me again why we can't leave this arrangement and be together?"

"Because we agreed that if one person wants out, then no one stays together, remember?" Bree recalls the agreement.

"But I wasn't there to agree to that," Keisha replies.